KT-487-563

WITHDRAWN
FOR SALE

05079758

THE ICE CHILD

Also by Camilla Lackberg

The Ice Princess
The Preacher
The Stonecutter
The Stranger (previously titled *The Gallows Bird*)
The Hidden Child
The Drowning
The Lost Boy
Buried Angels

Short stories

The Scent of Almonds & Other Stories

CAMILLA LACKBERG

The Ice Child

Translated from the Swedish by Tiina Nunnally

HarperCollins*Publishers*

HarperCollins*Publishers*
1 London Bridge Street
London SE1 9GF

www.harpercollins.co.uk

Published by HarperCollins*Publishers* 2016
1

Originally published in 2014 by
Bokförlaget Forum, Sweden, as *Lejontämjaren*

A catalogue record for this book
is available from the British Library

ISBN: 978-0-00-751833-3

Set in Meridien by Palimpsest Book Production Ltd,
Falkirk, Stirlingshire

Printed and bound in Great Britain by
Clays Ltd, St Ives plc

For Simon

The horse could smell the fear even before the girl emerged from the woods. The rider urged the horse on, digging her heels into the animal's flanks, though it wasn't really necessary. They were so in tune that her mount sensed her wishes almost before she did.

The muted, rhythmic sound of the horse's hooves broke the silence. During the night a thin layer of snow had fallen, and the stallion now ploughed new tracks, making the powdery snow spray up around his hooves.

The girl didn't run. She moved unsteadily, in an irregular pattern with her arms wrapped tightly around her torso.

The rider shouted. A loud cry, and the horse understood that something wasn't right. The girl didn't reply, merely staggered onward.

As they approached her, the horse picked up the pace. The strong, rank smell of fear was mixed with something else, something indefinable and so terrifying that he pressed his ears back. He wanted to stop, turn around, and gallop back to the secure confines of his stall. This was not a safe place to be.

The road was between them. Deserted now, with new snow blowing across the asphalt like a silent mist.

The girl continued towards them. Her feet were bare,

and the pink of her naked arms and legs contrasted sharply with all the white surrounding her, with the snow-covered spruces forming a white backdrop. They were close now, on either side of the road, and the horse heard the rider shout again. Her voice was so familiar, yet it had a strange ring to it.

Suddenly the girl stopped. She stood in the middle of the road with snow whirling about her feet. There was something odd about her eyes. They were like black holes in her white face.

The car seemed to come out of nowhere. The sound of squealing brakes sliced through the stillness, followed by the thump of a body landing on the ground. The rider yanked so hard on the reins that the bit cut into the stallion's mouth. He obeyed and stopped abruptly. She was him, and he was her. That was what he'd been taught.

On the ground the girl lay motionless. With those peculiar eyes of hers staring up at the sky.

Erica Falck paused in front of the prison and for the first time studied it closely. On her previous visits she had been so busy thinking about who she was going to meet that she hadn't given the building or its setting more than a cursory glance. But she would need to give readers a sense of the place when she wrote her book about Laila Kowalski, the woman who had so brutally murdered her husband Vladek many years ago.

She pondered how to convey the atmosphere that pervaded the bunker-like building, how she could capture the air of confinement and hopelessness. The prison was located about a thirty-minute drive from Fjällbacka, in a remote and isolated spot surrounded by fences and barbed wire, though it had none of those towers manned by armed guards that always featured in American films. It had been constructed with only one purpose in mind, and that was to keep people inside.

From the outside the prison looked unoccupied, but she knew the reverse was true. Funding cuts and a tight budget meant that as many people as possible were crowded into every space. No local politician was about to risk losing votes by proposing that money should be invested in a new prison. The county would just have to make do with the present structure.

The cold had begun to seep through Erica's clothes, so she headed towards the entrance. When she entered the reception area, the guard listlessly glanced at her ID and nodded without raising his eyes. He stood up, and she followed him down a corridor as she thought about how hectic her morning had been. Every morning was a trial these days. To say that the twins had entered an obstinate stage was an understatement. For the life of her she couldn't recall Maja ever being so difficult when she was two, or at any age. Noel was the worst. He had always been the more energetic one, but Anton was all too happy to follow his lead. If Noel screamed, he screamed too. It was a miracle that her eardrums – and Patrik's, for that matter – were still intact, given the decibel level at home.

And what a pain it was to get them into their winter clothes. She gave her armpit a discreet sniff. She smelled faintly of sweat. It had taken her so long to wrestle the twins into their clothes so she could take them and Maja to the day-care centre, she hadn't had time to change. Oh well. She wasn't exactly going to a social gathering.

The guard's key ring clanked as he unlocked the door and showed Erica into the visitor's room. It seemed so old-fashioned that they still made use of keys in this place. But of course it would be easier to get hold of the combination to a coded lock than to steal a key. Maybe it wasn't so strange that old measures often prevailed over more modern solutions.

Laila was sitting at the only table in the room. Her face was turned towards the window, and the winter sun streaming through the pane formed a halo around her blond hair. The bars on the window made squares of light on the floor, and dust motes floated in the air, revealing that the room hadn't been cleaned as thoroughly as it should have been.

'Hi,' said Erica as she sat down.

She wondered why Laila had agreed to see her again. This was their third meeting, and Erica had made no progress at all. Initially Laila had refused to meet with her, no matter how many imploring letters Erica had sent or how many phone calls she'd made. Then a few months ago Laila had suddenly acquiesced. Perhaps the visits were a welcome break from the monotony of prison life. Erica planned to keep visiting if Laila continued to agree to see her. It had been a long time since she'd felt such a strong urge to tell a story, and she couldn't do it without Laila's help.

'Hi, Erica.' Laila turned and fixed her unusual blue eyes on her visitor. At their first meeting, Erica had been reminded of those dogs they used to pull sleds. Huskies. Laila had eyes like a Siberian husky.

'Why do you want to see me if you don't want to talk about the case?' asked Erica, getting right to the point. She immediately regretted her choice of words. For Laila, what had happened was not a 'case'. It was a tragedy and something that still tormented her.

Laila shrugged.

'I don't get any other visitors,' she said, confirming Erica's suspicions.

Erica opened her bag and took out a folder containing newspaper articles, photos, and notes.

'Well, I'm not giving up,' she said, tapping on the folder.

'I suppose that's the price I have to pay if I want company,' said Laila, revealing the unexpected sense of humour that Erica had occasionally glimpsed. She had seen pictures of Laila before it all happened. She hadn't been conventionally beautiful, but she was attractive in a different and compelling way. Back then her blond hair had been long, and in most of the photos she wore it loose and straight. Now it was cropped short, and cut the same length all over. Not exactly what you would call a hairstyle. Just cut in a way that showed it had been a long time since Laila had cared about her appearance. And why should she? She hadn't been out in the real world for years. Who would she put on make-up for in here? The nonexistent visitors? The other prisoners? The guards?

'You look tired today.' Laila studied Erica's face. 'Was it a rough morning?'

'Rough morning, rough night, and presumably just as rough this afternoon. But that's the way it is when you have young children.' Erica sighed heavily and tried to relax. She noticed how tense she was after the stress of the morning.

'Peter was always so sweet,' said Laila as a veil lowered over those blue eyes of hers. 'Not even a trace of stubbornness that I remember.'

'You told me the first time we met that he was a very quiet child.'

'Yes. In the beginning we thought there was something wrong with him. He didn't make a sound until he was three. I wanted to take him to a specialist, but Vladek refused.' She shivered and her hands abruptly curled into fists as they lay on the table, though she didn't seem aware of it.

'What happened when Peter was three?'

'One day he just started talking. In complete sentences.

With a huge vocabulary. He lisped a bit, but otherwise it was as if he had always talked. As if those years of silence had never existed.'

'And you were never given any explanation?'

'No. Who would have explained it to us? Vladek didn't want to ask anyone for help. He always said that strangers shouldn't get mixed up in family matters.'

'Why do you think Peter was silent for so long?'

Laila turned to look out of the window, and the sun once again formed a halo around her cropped blond hair. The furrows that the years had etched into her face were mercilessly evident in the light. As if forming a map of all the suffering she had endured.

'He probably realized it was best to make himself as invisible as possible. Not to draw attention to himself. Peter was a clever boy.'

'What about Louise? How old was she when she started to talk?' Erica held her breath. So far Laila had pretended not to hear any of the questions that pertained to her daughter.

It was no different today.

'Peter loved arranging things. He wanted everything to be nice and orderly. When he was a baby he would stack up blocks in perfect, even towers, and he was always so sad when . . .' Laila stopped abruptly.

Erica noticed how Laila had clenched her jaws shut, and she tried to use sheer willpower to coax Laila to go on, to let out what she had so carefully locked up inside. But the moment had passed. The same thing had happened during Erica's previous visits. Sometimes it felt as though Laila were standing on the edge of an abyss, wishing deep in her heart that she could throw herself into the chasm. As if she wanted to pitch forward but was stopped by stronger forces, which made her once again retreat into the safety of shadows.

It was no accident that Erica was thinking about shadows. The first time they'd met, she had a feeling that Laila was living a shadow existence. A life running parallel to the life she should have had, the life that had vanished into a bottomless pit on that day so many years ago.

'Do you ever feel like you're going to lose patience with your sons? That you're about to cross that invisible boundary?' Laila sounded genuinely interested, but her voice also had a pleading undertone.

It was not an easy question to answer. All parents have probably felt a moment when they approached that borderline between what is permitted and what isn't, standing there and silently counting to ten as they think about what they could do to put an end to the commotion and upheaval exploding in their heads. But there was a big difference between acknowledging that feeling and acting on it. So Erica shook her head.

'I could never do anything to hurt them.'

At first Laila didn't answer as she continued to stare at Erica with those bright blue eyes of hers. But when the guard knocked on the door to say that visiting time was over, Laila said quietly, her gaze still fixed on Erica:

'That's what you think.'

Erica recalled the photographs in the folder and shuddered.

Tyra was grooming Fanta with steady strokes of the brush. She always felt better when she was around the horses. She would have much preferred to be grooming Scirocco, but Molly wouldn't let anyone else take care of him. It was so unfair. Just because Molly's parents owned the stable, she was allowed to do anything she wanted.

Tyra loved Scirocco. She had loved him from the first moment she saw him. And the horse had looked at her as if he understood her. It was a wordless form of communication that she'd never experienced with any other animal. Or even with any person. Not with her mother. And not with Lasse. The mere thought of Lasse made her brush Fanta harder, but the big white mare didn't seem to mind. In fact, she seemed to be enjoying the strokes of the brush, snorting and moving her head up and down as if bowing. For a moment Tyra thought it looked like the mare were inviting her to dance. She smiled and stroked Fanta's grey muzzle.

'You're great too,' she said, as if the horse had been able to hear her thoughts about Scirocco.

Then she felt a pang of guilt. She looked at her hand on Fanta's muzzle and realized how trivial her jealousy was.

'You miss Victoria, don't you?' she whispered, leaning her head against the horse's neck.

Victoria, who had been Fanta's groom. Victoria, who had been missing for several months. Victoria, who had been – who was – Tyra's best friend.

'I miss her too.' Tyra felt the mare nudging her cheek, but it didn't comfort her as much as she'd hoped.

She should have been in maths class right now, but on this particular morning she hadn't felt able to put on a cheerful face and fend off her worry. She had gone over to the school bus stop but instead sought solace in the stable, the only place where she could find any respite. The grown-ups didn't understand. They saw only their own anxiety, their own sorrow.

Victoria was more than a best friend. She was like a sister. They had been friends from the first day of school and had remained inseparable ever since. There was nothing they hadn't shared. Or was there? Tyra no longer knew for sure. During those last months before Victoria disappeared, something had changed. It felt like a wall had popped up between them. Tyra hadn't wanted to nag.

She thought that when the time was right, Victoria would tell her what was going on. But time had run out, and Victoria was gone.

'I'm sure she'll come back,' she now told Fanta, but deep inside she had her doubts. Though no one would admit it, they all knew that something bad must have happened. Victoria was not the kind of girl to disappear voluntarily, if such a person existed. She was too content with her life, and she didn't have an adventurous nature. She preferred to stay home or in the stable; she didn't even want to go into Strömstad on the weekends. And her family was nothing like Tyra's. They were super nice, even Victoria's older brother. He had often given his sister a lift to the stable early in the morning. Tyra used to love visiting their home. She'd felt like one of the family. Sometimes she'd even wished that Victoria's family was hers. An ordinary, normal family.

Fanta gave her a gentle nudge. A few tears landed on the mare's muzzle, and Tyra quickly wiped her eyes with her hand.

Suddenly she heard a sound outside the stable. Fanta heard it too. The mare pushed her ears forward and raised her head so swiftly that she rammed into Tyra's chin. The sharp taste of blood filled the girl's mouth. She swore, pressed her hand to her lips, and went outside to see what was going on.

When she opened the stable door she was dazzled by the sun, but her eyes quickly adjusted to the light and she saw Valiant coming across the forecourt at full gallop with Marta on his back. Marta pulled up so abruptly that the stallion almost reared. She was shouting something. At first Tyra didn't understand what she was saying, but Marta kept on yelling. And finally the words made sense:

'Victoria! We've found Victoria!'

* * *

Patrik Hedström was sitting at his desk in the Tanumshede police station, enjoying the peace and quiet. He'd come to work early, so he'd missed having to get the kids dressed and take them to the day-care centre. Lately that whole process had become a form of torture, thanks to the twins' transformation from sweet babies into mini versions of Damien in the film *Omen*. He couldn't comprehend how two such tiny people could require so much energy. Nowadays his favourite time with them was when he sat next to their beds in the evening and watched them sleep. At those moments he was able to enjoy the immense, pure love he felt for his sons without any trace of the tremendous frustration he felt when they howled: 'NO, I WON'T!'

Everything was so much easier with Maja. In fact, sometimes he felt guilty that, with all the attention he and Erica devoted to her little brothers, Maja often ended up neglected. She was so good at keeping herself busy that they simply assumed she was happy. And as young as she was, she seemed to possess a magical ability to calm her brothers down even during their worst outbursts. But it wasn't fair, and Patrik decided that tonight he and Maja would spend time together, just the two of them, snuggling and reading a story.

At that moment the phone rang. He picked it up distractedly, still thinking about Maja. But the caller quickly grabbed his attention, and he sat up straight in his chair.

'Could you repeat that?' He listened. 'Okay, we'll be right there.'

He threw on his jacket and shouted into the corridor, 'Gösta! Mellberg! Martin!'

'What is it? Where's the fire?' grunted Bertil Mellberg, who unexpectedly showed up first. But he was soon followed by Martin Molin, Gösta Flygare, and the station secretary, Annika, who had been at her desk in the reception area, which was the furthest away from Patrik's office.

'Somebody found Victoria Hallberg. She was hit by a car near the eastern entrance to Fjällbacka, and she's been taken by ambulance to Uddevalla. That's where you and I are headed, Gösta.'

'Oh, shit,' said Gösta, and he dashed back to his office to grab his jacket. No one dared venture outdoors without the proper warm clothing this winter, no matter how big an emergency it was.

'Martin, you and Bertil need to go out to the accident site and talk to the driver,' Patrik went on. 'Call the tech team and ask them to meet you there.'

'You're in a bossy mood today,' muttered Mellberg. 'As the chief of this station, of course I'm the one who should go out to the scene of the accident. The right man in the right place.'

Patrik sighed to himself but didn't comment. With Gösta in tow, he hurried outside, jumped into one of the two police vehicles and turned on the ignition.

Bloody awful road, he thought as the car skidded into the first curve. He didn't dare drive as fast as usual. It had started snowing again, and he didn't want to risk sliding off the road. Impatiently he slammed his fist on the steering wheel. It was only January and, given how long Swedish winters lasted, they could expect at least two more months of this misery.

'Take it easy,' said Gösta, clutching the strap hanging from the ceiling. 'What did they say on the phone?' He gasped as the car skidded again.

'Not much. Just that there had been a traffic accident and the girl who'd been struck was Victoria. Unfortunately, it sounds as though she's in bad shape, and apparently she has other injuries, which have nothing to do with being hit by a car.'

'What kind of injuries?'

'I don't know. We'll find out when we get there.'

Less than an hour later they arrived at Uddevalla hospital and parked at the front entrance. They hurried to the ER and accosted a doctor named Strandberg, according to his name badge.

'I'm glad you're here. The girl is just going into surgery, but it's not certain she'll make it. We heard from the police that she has been missing and, in the circumstances, we thought it best if you were the ones to notify her family. I assume you've already had a great deal of contact with them. Am I right?'

Gösta nodded. 'I'll phone them.'

'Do you have any information about what happened?' asked Patrik.

'Only that she was hit by a car. She has severe internal bleeding, as well as a head injury, though we don't yet know the extent of that injury. We'll keep her sedated for a while after the operation in order to minimize any brain damage. If she survives, that is.'

'We heard that she had suffered some sort of injuries prior to the accident.'

'Yes,' said Strandberg, hesitating. 'We don't know exactly which injuries are the result of the accident and which occurred previously. But . . .' He seemed to be struggling for the right words. 'Both of her eyes are gone. And her tongue.'

'Gone?' Patrik looked at the doctor in disbelief. Out of the corner of his eye he saw Gösta's equally astonished expression.

'Yes. Her tongue has been severed, and her eyes have somehow been . . . removed.'

Gösta covered his mouth with his hand. His face had taken on a slightly greenish tinge.

Patrik swallowed hard. For a moment he wondered

whether he was having a nightmare, and hoped he would soon wake up. Then he would be relieved to find it was all a dream and could turn over and go back to sleep. But this was real. Disgustingly real.

'How long do you think the surgery will take?'

Strandberg shook his head. 'It's hard to say. As I mentioned, she has massive internal bleeding. Maybe two or three hours. At the least. You can wait here.' He gestured towards the large waiting room.

'I'll go and ring the family,' said Gösta, moving away down the corridor.

Patrik didn't envy him the task. The Hallberg family's initial joy and relief at hearing that Victoria had been found would swiftly be replaced with the same despair and dread they'd been living with for the past four months.

He sat down on one of the hard chairs. Images of Victoria's injuries whirled through his mind. But his thoughts were interrupted when a frantic nurse stuck her head in the door and shouted for Strandberg. Patrik hardly had time to react before the doctor dashed from the waiting room. Out in the corridor Patrik could hear Gösta talking on the phone with one of Victoria's relations. The question was, what news would they hear next?

Ricky tensely studied his mother's face as she talked on the phone. He strained to read every expression, hear every word. His heart was pounding so hard in his chest that he could hardly breathe. His father sat next to him, and Ricky sensed that his heart was hammering just as hard. It felt like time was standing still, as if it had stopped at that exact moment. All his senses were somehow heightened. Even as he focused his full attention on the phone conversation, he could clearly hear every other sound. He could also feel the wax tablecloth under his clenched fists, the wisp of hair that was tickling the back of his neck under his collar, and the linoleum floor under his feet.

The police had found Victoria. That was the first thing they heard. His mother had recognized the number and grabbed the phone. Ricky and his father had instantly stopped eating their food when they heard her say, 'What's happened?'

No courteous greeting, no 'hello', no mention of anyone's name, which was his mother's usual way of answering the phone. Lately all such things – common courtesies, social rules, what one should or should not do – had ceased to matter. Those sorts of things belonged to their life before Victoria disappeared.

Neighbours and friends had arrived in a steady stream, bringing food and awkwardly offering well-intentioned words. But they never stayed long. Ricky's parents couldn't bear all the questions or the kindness, concern, and sympathy in everyone's eyes. Or the relief, always the same hint of relief that they were not the ones in this situation. Their children were all at home, safe and sound.

'We'll leave right now.'

His mother ended the conversation and slowly placed her mobile on the worktop, which was the old-fashioned kind, made of steel. For years she had nagged his father to replace it with something more modern, but he had grumbled that there was no need to replace anything that was clean and in one piece and still fully functional. And his mother had never insisted. She simply brought up the topic on occasion, in the hope that her husband would suddenly change his mind.

Ricky didn't think his mother cared any longer about what sort of kitchen worktop they had. It was strange how things like that quickly lost all importance. All that mattered was finding Victoria.

'What did they say?' asked Ricky's father. He had stood

up, but Ricky was still sitting at the table, staring down at his clenched fists. His mother's expression told them they wouldn't want to hear what she had to say.

'They've found her. But she's seriously injured and in hospital in Uddevalla. Gösta said we need to get there fast. That's all I know.'

She burst into tears and then sank down as if her legs could no longer support her. Her husband just managed to catch her. He stroked her hair and hushed her, but tears were running down his face too.

'We need to get going, sweetheart. Put on your jacket, and we'll leave right away. Ricky, help your mother. I'll go out and start the car.'

Ricky nodded and went over to his mother. Gently he put his arm around her shoulders and got her to move towards the front hall. There he grabbed her red down coat and helped her to put it on, the way a parent would help a child. One arm in, then the other, and he carefully zipped up the coat.

'All right,' he said, placing her boots in front of her. He squatted down and helped her to put them on too. Then he quickly put on his own jacket and opened the door. He could hear that his father had the car running. He was scraping off the windows so frantically that he'd created a cloud of frost, mixed with the vapour from his breath.

'Bloody winter!' he cried, scraping so hard that he was probably scratching the windscreen. 'What a damn, sodding, bloody winter!'

'Get in the car, Pappa,' said Ricky. 'I'll do that.' He took the scraper away from his father, after first settling his mother in the back seat. His father complied, offering no resistance. They had always let him believe that he was the one in charge in the family. The three of them – Ricky, his mother, and Victoria – had a secret agreement to allow

Markus Hallberg to think that he ruled with an iron fist, even though they knew he was too nice to rule even with one finger. It had always been Helena Hallberg who had ensured that everything was done as it should be done – until Victoria disappeared. She had deflated so swiftly that Ricky sometimes wondered whether his mother had always been this shrivelled and dispirited person who was now sitting on the back seat, staring blankly into space, whether she had ever possessed a sense of purpose. Yet for the first time in months he saw something else in her eyes, a mixture of eagerness and panic prompted by the phone conversation with the police.

Ricky got in behind the wheel. It was strange how a gap in the family was filled, how instinctively he had stepped up to take his mother's place. As if he possessed a strength he'd never known he had.

Victoria used to tell him that he was like Ferdinand the bull. Lazy and foolishly nice on the outside, but in moments of crisis he would always come through. He'd give her a playful nudge and pretend to be offended, but secretly he was happy to be compared to Ferdinand the bull. Although lately he no longer had time to sit and smell the flowers. He wouldn't be able to do that again until Victoria came back.

Tears began running down his cheeks and he wiped them off on the sleeve of his jacket. He hadn't allowed himself to think that she might never come home. If he'd done that, he would have fallen apart.

And now Victoria had been found. Though they didn't yet know what awaited them at the hospital. He had a feeling they might not want to know.

Helga Persson peered out of the kitchen window. A short while ago she'd seen Marta come riding into the yard at full gallop, but now everything was quiet. She had lived here a long time, and the view was very familiar, even though it had changed a bit over the years. The old barn was still there, but the cowshed, where they'd kept the cows she'd taken care of, had been torn down. In its place was the stable Jonas and Marta had built for their riding school.

She had been happy that her son had decided to settle so close by, that they were neighbours. Their houses stood only a hundred metres apart, and since he ran his veterinary clinic at home, he frequently stopped in to see her. Every visit made her day a little brighter, which was what she needed.

'Helga! Helgaaaa!'

She closed her eyes as she stood next to the worktop. Einar's voice filled every nook and cranny of the house, enveloping her and making her clench her fists. But she no longer had the will to flee. He had beat it out of her years ago. Even though he was now helpless and completely dependent on her, she was incapable of leaving him. That wasn't something she considered any more. Because where would she go?

'HELGAAAA!'

His voice was the only thing left that still retained its former strength. The illnesses and then the amputation of both legs as a result of neglecting his diabetes had robbed him of his physical strength. But his voice was as commanding as ever. It continued to force her into submission just as effectively as his fists used to do. The memories of all those blows, the cracked ribs and throbbing bruises, were still so vivid that the mere sound of his voice could provoke terror and the fear that this time she might not survive.

She straightened up, took a deep breath, and called out:

'I'm coming!'

Briskly she climbed the stairs. Einar didn't like to be kept waiting, he never had, but she didn't understand why there was always such a hurry. He had nothing else to do but sit and grumble, his complaints ranging from the weather to the government.

'It's leaking,' he said when she came into the room.

She didn't reply. Simply rolled up her sleeves and went over to him to find out how great the damage might be. She knew he enjoyed this sort of situation. He could no longer use force to hold her captive. Instead he relied on his need for care and attention, which she should have bestowed on the children she'd never had, the ones he had beaten out of her body. Only one had lived, and there were times when she thought it might have been best if that child had also been expelled in a rush of blood between her legs. Yet she didn't know what she would have done if she hadn't had him. Jonas was her life, her everything.

Einar was right. The colostomy bag was leaking. And not just a little bit. Half his shirt was soaked through.

'Why didn't you get here faster?' he said. 'Didn't you hear me calling? I suppose you had something more important to do.' He glared at her with his watery eyes.

'I was in the bathroom. I came as quick as I could,' she said, unbuttoning his shirt. Carefully she pulled his arms out of the sleeves, not wanting to get even more of his body wet.

'I'm freezing.'

'I'll get you a clean shirt. I just need to wash you off first,' she said with all the patience she could muster.

'I'm going to catch pneumonia.'

'I'll be fast. I don't think you'll catch cold.'

'Oh, so now you're a nurse too, huh? I suppose you even know better than the doctors.'

She said nothing. He was just trying to throw her off

balance. He liked it best when she cried, when she begged and pleaded with him to stop. Then he was filled with a great sense of calm and satisfaction that made his eyes shine. But today she wasn't going to give him that pleasure. These days she usually managed to avoid such scenes. Most of her tears had been shed years ago.

Helga went into the bathroom to fill a basin with water. The whole procedure had become routine: fill the basin with water and soap, wet the rag, wipe off his soiled body, put him into a clean shirt. She suspected that Einar purposely made the bag leak. According to his doctor, it was impossible for it to leak so frequently. Yet the bags kept on leaking. And she kept on cleaning up her husband.

'The water's too cold.' Einar flinched as the rag rubbed at his stomach.

'I'll make it warmer.' Helga stood up, went back to the bathroom, put the basin under the tap and turned on the hot water. Then she returned to the bedroom.

'Ow! It's scalding! Are you trying to burn me, you bitch?' Einar shouted so loud that she jumped. But she didn't say a word, just picked up the basin, carried it out, and filled it with cold water, this time making sure that it was only slightly warmer than body temperature. Then she carried it back to the bedroom. This time he didn't comment when the rag touched his skin.

'When is Jonas coming?' he asked as she wrung out the rag, turning the water brown.

'I don't know. He's working. He went over to the Andersson place. One of their cows is about to calve, but the calf is in the wrong position.'

'Send him up here when he arrives,' said Einar, closing his eyes.

'Okay,' said Helga quietly, as she wrung out the rag again.

* * *

Gösta saw them coming down the hospital corridor. They were hurrying towards him, and he had to fight his impulse to flee in the opposite direction. He knew that what he was about to tell them was written all over his face, and he was right. As soon as Helena met his eye, she fumbled to grab Markus's arm and then sank to the floor. Her scream echoed through the corridor, silencing all other sounds.

Ricky stood there as if frozen in place. His face white, he had stopped behind his mother while Markus carried on walking. Gösta swallowed hard and went to meet them. But Markus passed him with unseeing eyes, as if he hadn't seen the same bad news in Gösta's expression that his wife had seen. He kept on walking along the corridor with no apparent goal in mind.

Gösta didn't move to stop him. Instead, he went over to Helena and gently lifted her to her feet. Then he put his arms around her. That was not something he usually did. He had let only two people into his life: his wife, and the little girl who had lived with them for a brief time and who now, through the inexplicable workings of fate, had come into his life again. So it didn't feel particularly natural for him to be standing there, embracing a woman whom he'd known for such a short time. But ever since Victoria disappeared, Helena had rung him every day, alternating between hope and despair, anger and grief, to ask about her daughter. Yet he'd been able to give her only more questions and more worry. And now he had finally extinguished all hope. Holding her in his arms and allowing her to weep on his chest was the least he could do.

Gösta looked over Helena's head to meet Ricky's eye. There was something odd about the boy. For the past few months he had been the family's mainstay, keeping them going. But now he stood there in front of Gösta, his face white and his eyes empty, looking like the young boy he actually was. And Gösta knew that Ricky had lost for ever the innocence granted only to children, the belief that everything would be okay.

'Can we see her?' asked Ricky, his voice husky. Gösta felt Helena stiffen. She pulled away, wiped her tears on the sleeve of her coat and gave him a pleading look.

Gösta fixed his gaze on a distant point. How could he tell them that they wouldn't want to see Victoria? And why.

Her entire study was cluttered with papers: typed notes, Post-it notes, newspaper articles, and copies of photographs. It looked like total chaos, but Erica thrived in this sort of working environment. When she was writing a book, she wanted to be surrounded by all the information she'd gathered, all her thoughts on the case.

This time, however, it felt as if she might be in over her head. She had accumulated plenty of background details and facts, but it had all been obtained from second-hand sources. The quality of her books and her ability to describe a murder case and answer all the questions readers might have relied on her ability to secure first-hand accounts. Thus far she had always been successful. Sometimes it had been easy to persuade those involved to talk to her. Some had even been eager to talk, happy for the media attention and a moment in the spotlight. But occasionally it had taken time and she'd been forced to cajole the person, explaining why she wanted to dredge up the past and how she intended to tell the story. In the end she had always won out. Until now. She was getting nowhere with Laila. During her visits to the prison she had struggled to get Laila to talk about what happened, but in vain. Laila was happy to talk to her, just not about the murder.

Frustrated, Erica propped her feet up on the desk and let her thoughts wander. Maybe she should ring her sister. Anna had often been a source of good ideas and new angles in the past, but she was not herself these days. She had gone through so much over the past few years, and the misfortunes never seemed to stop. Part of her suffering had been self-imposed of course, yet Erica had no intention of judging her younger sister. She understood why certain things had happened. The question was whether Anna's husband could understand and forgive her. Erica had to admit that she had her doubts. She had known Dan all her life. When they were teenagers they'd dated for a while, and she knew how stubborn he could be. In this instance, the obstinacy and pride that were such a feature of his personality had proved self-destructive. And the result was that everyone was unhappy. Anna, Dan, the children, even Erica. She wished that her sister would finally have some happiness in her life after the hell she had endured with Lucas, her children's father.

It was so unfair, the way their lives had turned out so differently. She had a strong and loving marriage, three healthy children, and a writing career that was on the upswing. Anna, on the other hand, had encountered one setback after another, and Erica had no idea how to help her. That had always been her role as the big sister: to protect and support and offer assistance. Anna had been the wild one, with such a zest for life. But all that vitality had been beaten out of her until what remained was only a subdued and lost shell. Erica missed the old Anna.

I'll phone her tonight, she resolved as she picked up a stack of newspaper articles and began leafing through them. It was gloriously quiet in the house, and she was grateful that her job made it possible for her to work at home. She had never felt any need for co-workers or an office setting. She worked best on her own.

The absurd thing was that she was already longing for the hour when she would leave to fetch Maja and the twins. How was it possible for a parent to have such contradictory emotions about the daily routines? The constant alternating between highs and lows was exhausting. One moment she'd be sticking her hands in her pockets and clenching her fists, the next she'd be hugging and kissing the children so much that they begged to be let go. She knew that Patrik felt the same way.

For some reason thinking about Patrik and the kids led her back to the conversation with Laila. It was so incomprehensible. How could anyone cross that invisible yet clearly demarcated boundary between what was permitted and what was not? Wasn't the fundamental essence of a human being the ability to restrain his or her most primitive urges and do what was right and socially acceptable? To obey the laws and regulations which made it possible for society to function?

Erica continued glancing through the articles. What she had said to Laila today was true. She would never be capable of doing anything to harm her children. Not even in her darkest hours, when she was suffering from postnatal depression after Maja was born, or caught up in the chaos following the twins' arrival, or during the many sleepless nights, or when the tantrums seemed to go on for hours, or when the kids repeated the word 'No!' as often as they drew breath. She had never come close to doing anything like that. But in the stack of papers resting on her lap, in the pictures lying on her desk, and in her notes, there was proof that the boundary could indeed be crossed.

In Fjällbacka the house in the photographs had become known as the House of Horrors. Not a particularly original name, but definitely appropriate. After the tragedy, no one had wanted to buy the place, and it had gradually fallen into disrepair. Erica reached for a picture of the house as it had looked back then. Nothing hinted at what had gone on inside. It looked like a completely normal house: white with grey trim, standing alone on a hill with a few trees nearby. She wondered what it looked like now, how run-down it must be.

She sat up abruptly and placed the photo back on her desk. Why not drive out there and have a look? While researching her previous books she'd always visited the crime scene, but she hadn't done that this time. Something had been holding her back. It wasn't that she'd made a conscious decision not to go out there; more that she had simply stayed away.

It would have to wait until tomorrow though. Right now it was time to go and fetch her little wildcats. Her stomach knotted with a mixture of longing and fatigue.

The cow was struggling valiantly. Jonas was soaked with sweat after spending several hours trying to turn the calf around. The big animal kept resisting, unaware that they were trying to help her.

'Bella is our best cow,' said Britt Andersson. She and her husband Otto ran the farm which was only a couple of kilometres from the property owned by Jonas and Marta. It was a small but robust farm, and the cows were their main source of income. Britt was an energetic woman who supplemented the money they made from milk sales to Arla by selling cheese from a little shop on their property. She was looking worried as she stood next to the cow.

'She's a good cow, Bella is,' said Otto, rubbing the back of his head anxiously. This was her fourth calf. The previous three births had all gone fine. But this calf was in the wrong position and refused to come out, and Bella was obviously exhausted.

Jonas wiped the sweat from his brow and prepared to make yet another attempt to turn the calf so it could finally slide out and land in the straw, sticky and wobbly. He was not about to give up, because then both the cow and the calf would die. Gently he stroked Bella's soft flank. She was taking, short, shallow breaths, and her eyes were open wide.

'All right now, girl, let's see if we can get this calf out,' he said as he again pulled on a pair of long rubber gloves. Slowly but surely he inserted his hand into the narrow canal until he could touch the calf. He needed to get a firm grip on a leg so he could pull on it and turn the calf, but he had to do it cautiously.

'I've got hold of a hoof,' he said. Out of the corner of his eye he saw Britt and Otto craning their necks to get a better look. 'Nice and calm now, girl.'

He spoke in a low voice as he began to tug at the leg. Nothing happened. He pulled a little harder but still couldn't budge the calf.

'How's it going? Is it turning?' asked Otto. He kept scratching his head so often that Jonas thought he would end up with a bald spot.

'Not yet,' said Jonas through clenched teeth. Sweat poured off him, and a strand of hair from his blond fringe had fallen in his eyes so he kept having to blink. But right now the only thought in his mind was getting the calf out. Bella's breathing was getting shallower, and her head kept sinking into the straw, as if she were ready to give up.

'I'm afraid of breaking something,' he said, pulling as hard as he dared. And something moved! He pulled a bit harder, holding his breath and hoping not to hear the sound of anything breaking. Suddenly he felt the calf shift position. A few more cautious tugs, and the calf was lying on the ground, feeble but alive. Britt rushed forward and began rubbing the newborn with straw. With firm, loving strokes she wiped off its body and massaged its limbs.

In the meantime Bella lay on her side, motionless. She didn't react to the birth of the calf, this life that had been growing inside of her for close to nine months. Jonas went over to sit near her head, plucking away a few pieces of straw close to her eye.

'It's over now. You were amazing, girl.'

He stroked her smooth black hide and kept on talking, just as he'd done throughout the birth process. At first the cow didn't respond. Then she wearily raised her head to peer at the calf.

'You have a beautiful little girl. Look, Bella,' said Jonas as he continued to pat her. He felt his racing pulse gradually subside. The calf would live, and Bella would too. He stood up and finally pushed the irritating strand of hair out of his eyes as he nodded to Britt and Otto.

'Looks like a fine calf.'

'Thank you, Jonas,' said Britt, coming over to give him a hug.

Otto awkwardly grasped Jonas's hand in his big fist. 'Thank you, thank you. Good work,' he said, pumping Jonas's hand up and down.

'Just doing my job,' said Jonas with a big smile. It was always satisfying when something worked out as it should. He didn't like it when he wasn't able to resolve things, either on the job or in his personal life.

Happy with the final results, he took his mobile phone out of his jacket pocket. For a few seconds he stared at the display. Then he dashed for his car.

FJÄLLBACKA 1964

The sounds, the smells, the colours. Everything so bedazzling, radiating excitement. Laila was holding her sister's hand. They were too old for that sort of thing, but instinctively she and Agneta would reach for each other's hand when anything unusual happened. And a circus in Fjällbacka was undeniably something out of the ordinary.

They had hardly ever been away from the small fishing village. Two day-trips to Göteborg. That was the furthest they'd gone. The circus brought with it the promise of the big wide world.

'What language are they speaking?' Agneta whispered, even though they could have shouted without anyone hearing because of the buzz of voices all around them.

'Aunt Edla said the circus came from Poland,' she whispered back, squeezing her sister's sweaty hand.

The summer had consisted of an endless string of sunny days, but this had to be the hottest day so far. Laila had been allowed to take a day off from her job selling sewing accessories. She looked forward to every minute she didn't have to spend inside that stuffy little shop.

'Look! An elephant!' Agneta pointed excitedly at the big grey beast ambling past them, accompanied by a man who looked to be in his thirties. The sisters stopped to watch the elephant, which was so impressively beautiful and so completely out of

place in the field outside of Fjällbacka, where the circus was setting up.

'Come on, let's go look at the other animals. I heard they have lions and zebras too.' Agneta tugged at her sister's hand, and Laila followed, out of breath. She could feel the sweat running down her back and making damp patches on her thin summer dress with the floral pattern.

They ran between the wagons parked around the big tent which was being raised. Strong men in white undershirts were working hard to get everything ready for the next day when Cirkus Gigantus would have its first performance. Many of the locals hadn't been able to wait until then and had come over to gawp at the spectacle. Now they were staring wide-eyed in wonder, never having seen the like before. Except for the two or three bustling summer months when tourists arrived to spend time on the beach, daily life in Fjällbacka was anything but exciting. One day followed the other with nothing in particular happening. The news that a circus was coming to town for the first time had spread like wildfire.

Agneta kept on tugging at Laila, drawing her over to the wagons where a striped head was sticking out of a hatchway.

'Oh, look how beautiful it is!'

Laila had to agree. The zebra was so sweet, with his big eyes and long lashes. She had to restrain herself from going over to pet him. She assumed that touching the animals was not allowed, but it was hard to resist.

'Don't touch,' growled a voice in English behind them, making them jump.

Laila turned around. She had never seen such a big man. Tall and muscular, he towered over them. The sun was at his back, so the sisters had to shade their eyes to see anything, and when Laila met his glance, it felt like an electric current surged through her body. She had never experienced such a sensation before. She felt confused and dizzy; her whole face burned. She told herself that it must be the heat.

'No . . . We . . . no touch.' Laila searched for the right words. Even though she had studied English in school and had learned a good deal from watching American films, she had never needed to actually speak the foreign language.

'My name is Vladek.' The man held out a calloused fist, and after a few seconds of hesitation, she responded, watching her own hand disappear in his grasp.

'Laila. My name is Laila.' Sweat was now coursing down her back.

He shook her hand as he repeated her name, though he made it sound so different and strange. When her name issued from his lips it sounded almost exotic and not like an ordinary, boring name.

'This . . .' She frantically searched her memory and then ventured: 'This is my sister.'

She pointed at Agneta, and the big man greeted her as well. Laila was a bit ashamed of her stammered English, but her curiosity won out over her embarrassment.

'What . . . what do you do? Here. In the circus.'

His face lit up. 'Come, I show you!' He motioned for them to follow and then set off without waiting for them to reply. They had to trot to keep up with him, and Laila felt her blood racing. He strode past the wagons and the circus tent that was still being raised, heading for a wagon that stood apart from the others. It was more like a cage, with iron bars instead of walls. Inside two lions were pacing back and forth.

'This is what I do. This is my babies, my lions. I am . . . I am a lion tamer!'

Laila stared at the wild beasts. Inside of her something entirely new began to stir, something frightening but wondrous. And without thinking about what she was doing, she reached for Vladek's hand.

It was early morning at the station. The yellow-painted walls of the kitchen looked grey in the winter haze that hovered over Tanumshede. No one said a word. None of them had slept much, and weariness covered their faces like a mask. The doctors had fought heroically to save Victoria's life, but without success. At 11.14 yesterday morning, she had been pronounced dead.

Martin had filled everyone's coffee cup, and Patrik now cast a glance at his colleague. Since his wife's death, he rarely smiled, and all their attempts to bring back the old Martin had failed. Pia had clearly taken part of Martin with her when she died. The doctors had thought she would live one more year, but things had progressed much faster than anyone anticipated. Only three months after her diagnosis, she was gone, and Martin was left alone with their young daughter. Fucking cancer, thought Patrik as he stood up to begin the briefing.

'As you know, Victoria Hallberg has died from the injuries she sustained when she was struck by a car. The driver of the vehicle has not been charged with any crime.'

'That's right,' Martin interjected. 'I spoke with him yesterday. David Jansson. According to him, Victoria suddenly appeared in the road, and he had no time to brake. He tried to veer around her, but the road was slippery and he lost control of the car.'

Patrik nodded. 'There's a witness to the accident: Marta Persson. She was out riding when she saw someone come out of the woods and then get hit by a car. She was also the one who called the police and ambulance. And she recognized Victoria. From what I understand, she was suffering from shock yesterday, so we'll need to talk to her today. Can you handle that, Martin?'

'Sure. I'll take care of it.'

'In addition, we urgently need to make some progress in our investigation of Victoria's disappearance. That means finding the individual or individuals who kidnapped her and subjected her to such horrific treatment.'

Patrik rubbed his face. The images of Victoria as she lay on the gurney had been etched into his mind. He had driven straight from the hospital to the police station and then spent several hours going through the material they had collected so far. He had studied the interviews they'd conducted with family members, as well as the girl's classmates and friends at the stable. He was trying to map out Victoria's inner circle of family and friends and determine what she had been doing in the hours before she disappeared on her way home from the Persson riding school. He had also reviewed the information they had about the other girls who had disappeared over the past two years. Of course the police couldn't be sure, but it seemed unlikely to be a coincidence that five girls, all about the same age and similar in appearance, had disappeared from a relatively small area. Yesterday Patrik had also sent out new information to the other police districts and asked them to respond in kind if they had anything more to add. It was always possible that something had been overlooked.

'We're going to continue to cooperate with the other

districts involved and combine efforts as best we can while investigating this case. Victoria is the first of the girls to be found, and maybe this tragic event can at least lead us to the others. And then we can put a stop to the kidnappings. Someone who is capable of the kind of sadistic treatment Victoria was subjected to . . . well, someone like that can't be allowed to go free.'

'Sick bastard,' muttered Mellberg, causing his dog Ernst to raise his head uneasily. As usual, he'd been sleeping under the table with his head resting on his master's feet, and he was sensitive to the slightest change in Mellberg's tone of voice.

'What can we glean from her injuries?' Martin leaned forward. 'Why would the perpetrator do something like that?'

'If only we knew. I've been wondering whether we should bring in a profiler to assist us. So far we don't have a lot to go on, but maybe there's a pattern that might prove interesting, a connection that we haven't seen.'

'A profiler? You mean one of those psychology guys? A so-called expert who has never had contact with any real criminals? You want someone like that to tell us how to do our job?' Mellberg shook his head so hard that his comb-over tumbled down over one ear. With a practised hand he pushed it back in place.

'It's worth a try,' said Patrik. He was all too familiar with Mellberg's resistance to any form of innovation or modern methods when it came to police work. In theory, Bertil Mellberg was chief of the Tanumshede police station, but everyone knew that Patrik was the one who did all the work, and it was thanks to him that any crime ever got solved in their district.

'Well, it'll be on your head if the top brass start whining about unnecessary expenses. I wash my hands of the whole business.' Mellberg leaned back and clasped his hands over his stomach.

'I'll find out who's available,' said Annika. 'And maybe we should check with the other districts in case they've already gone down this route and forgotten to tell us. We don't need to duplicate their efforts. That would be a waste of time and resources.'

'Good idea. Thanks.' Patrik turned to the whiteboard where he'd already taped up a photograph of Victoria and jotted down the basic facts about her.

From the corridor they could hear the sound of a radio playing pop music. The upbeat melody and lyrics were a sharp contrast to the gloomy mood in the kitchen. The station had a conference room but it was cold and impersonal, so they preferred to hold meetings in the more pleasant surroundings of the kitchen, which also had the advantage of placing them closer to the coffeemaker. They would be drinking many litres of hot coffee before they were done.

Patrik paused to think and stretch his back before doling out the work assignments.

'Annika, I'd like you to pull together all the materials we have relating to Victoria's case, along with any information we've obtained from the other districts. We'll need to send as much information as possible to the profiler, when we find one. And please see to it that the file is kept updated with any information we discover from now on.'

'Of course. I'm taking notes,' said Annika, who was sitting at the kitchen table with paper and pen. Patrik had tried to get her to start using a laptop or tablet instead, but she refused. And if Annika didn't want to do something, there was no budging her.

'Fine. Also, schedule a press conference for four o'clock this afternoon. Otherwise we'll have the reporters breathing down our necks.' Out of the corner of his eye, Patrik noticed that Mellberg was smoothing down his hair with a pleased expression. Obviously there would be no keeping him away from the press conference.

'Gösta, find out from Pedersen when the autopsy report will be ready. We need all the facts ASAP. And please have another talk with the family. See if they've thought of something that might be important to the investigation.'

'We've already talked to them so many times. Don't you think they should be left in peace on a day like this?' Gösta was looking dejected. He'd had the difficult task of speaking to Victoria's parents and brother at the hospital, and Patrik could see that the experience had taken its toll on him.

'Yes, but I'm sure they're anxious for us to find out who did this. Just be as tactful as you can. We're going to have to talk to a lot of people that we've already interviewed – her family members, friends, and anyone at the stable who may have seen something when she disappeared. Now that Victoria is dead, they might decide to tell us something they previously didn't want to reveal. For instance, we ought to talk to Tyra Hansson again. She was Victoria's best friend. Could you do that, Martin?'

Martin murmured his acquiescence.

Mellberg cleared his throat, reminding Patrik that, as usual, he needed to come up with some trivial task for Bertil. Something that would make him feel important without putting him in a position to do any significant damage. Patrik thought for a moment. Sometimes it was wisest to have Mellberg close by so he could keep an eye on him.

'I talked to Torbjörn last night,' Patrik went on. 'And the forensic examination of the crime scene produced no results. It wasn't an easy job, because it was snowing.

They found no trace of where Victoria might have come from. Now they've run out of manpower, so I was thinking of summoning volunteers to help by searching a wider area. She might have been held prisoner in some old cabin or summer cottage in the woods. When she reappeared, it wasn't too far from where she was last seen, so it's possible she was somewhere in the vicinity the whole time.'

'That's what I was thinking too,' said Martin. 'Wouldn't that indicate that the perpetrator is from Fjällbacka?'

'Perhaps,' said Patrik. 'But not necessarily. Not if Victoria's case is connected to the other disappearances. We haven't found any clear link between the other towns and Fjällbacka.'

Mellberg again cleared his throat, and Patrik turned to look at him.

'I thought you could help me with this, Bertil. We'll go out to the woods, and with a little luck, we may be able to find the place where she was being held.'

'That sounds good,' replied Mellberg. 'But it's not going to be much fun in this cold.'

Patrik didn't answer. Right now the weather was the least of his worries.

Anna was listlessly gathering up the laundry. She was unbelievably tired. She had been on sick leave ever since the car accident. By now the physical scars on her body had begun to fade, but emotionally her injuries had not yet healed. She was struggling not only with the grief of losing the baby but also with a hurt for which she alone was to blame.

Feelings of guilt churned inside her like a never-ending nausea. Every night she lay awake, going over and over what had happened and re-examining her motives. But even when she tried to give herself the benefit of the doubt, she still couldn't work out what had made her sleep with another man. She loved Dan, and yet she had kissed someone else and allowed that man to touch her body.

Was her self-esteem so weak and her need for acknowledgement so great that she had thought another man's hands and lips would give her something that Dan could not? She didn't understand it, so how could she expect Dan to understand? He was loyalty and security personified. People said it was impossible to know everything about a person, but she knew that Dan would never even think of being unfaithful to her. He would never have touched another woman. The only thing he wanted was to love her.

After the initial outbursts of anger, the harsh words had been replaced by something much worse: silence. A heavy, suffocating silence. They tiptoed around each other like two wounded animals, while Emma, Adrian, and Dan's daughters were like hostages in their own home.

Anna's dreams of running her own home-decorating business had died the moment Dan's hurt gaze met hers. That was the last time he had looked her in the eye. Now, whenever he was forced to speak to her directly – about something concerning the kids or even something as banal as asking her to pass the salt – he would mumble the words with his eyes lowered. And that made her want to scream. She wanted to shake him, force him to look at her, but she didn't dare. So she too kept her eyes lowered, not because she felt hurt, but out of shame.

Naturally the children had no idea what was going on. They didn't understand, but they were suffering from the effects. They went around in silence, trying to pretend that everything was normal. But it had been a long time since Anna had heard any of them laugh.

Her heart was so filled with remorse that she thought

it might burst. Anna leaned forward, buried her face in the laundry, and wept.

This was where it all happened. Erica cautiously entered the house, which looked as if it might come crashing down at any moment. Abandoned and neglected, battered by the weather, it had stood here all these years until there was hardly anything left to remind people of the family that had once lived in this place.

Erica ducked under a board hanging down from the ceiling. Pieces of glass crunched under the soles of her winter boots. Not a single windowpane remained intact. The floor and walls bore clear signs of random occupants, with scrawled names and words that meant something only to whoever had written them. Four-letter words and insults, many of them misspelled. Those who chose to spray-paint epithets in empty buildings seldom exhibited any great literary talent. Discarded beer cans lay scattered about, and a condom wrapper had been tossed next to a blanket that was so filthy it made Erica feel sick. Snow had blown inside, piling up in nooks and crannies.

The whole house gave off an air of misery and loneliness. Erica pulled from her bag the folder of photographs she'd brought along to help her visualize the scene. They showed a different house, a furnished home where people had lived. Yet she couldn't help shuddering because she thought she could see traces of what had happened in this place. She took a good look around. And then she saw it: dried blood, still visible on the wooden floor. And four marks where the sofa had once stood. Erica again glanced at the photos, trying to orient herself. She was starting to picture the room as it had looked back then. She saw the sofa, the coffee table, the easy chair in the corner, the TV on its stand, the floor lamp to the left of the easy chair. The whole room seemed to materialize before her eyes.

She could also see Vladek's corpse. His big, muscular body semi-reclining on the sofa. The gaping red gash in his throat, the stab wounds on his torso, his eyes staring up at the ceiling. And the blood gathering in a pool on the floor.

In the photographs the police had taken of Laila after the murder, her eyes looked completely blank. The front of her jumper was soaked with blood, and there were streaks of blood on her face. Her long blond hair hung loose. She looked so young. Nothing like the woman who was now serving a life sentence in prison.

It had been an open-and-shut case. It seemed to have a certain logic to it that everyone simply accepted. Yet Erica had a strong feeling that something wasn't right, and six months ago she had decided to write a book about the crime. She'd first heard about the case when she was a child, listening to people talk about the murder of Vladek and the family's terrible secret. The events that took place in the House of Horrors had grown into a legend as the years passed. The house became a place where children could test their mettle, a haunted house they used to scare their friends, where they could show off their bravery and defy their fear of the evil within those walls.

Erica turned away from the family's old living room. It was time to go upstairs. The chill inside the house was making her joints stiff, so she jumped up and down a few times to get warm before heading for the stairs. She carefully tested each step before proceeding upwards. She hadn't told anyone that she was coming here, so she didn't want to crash through a rotting step and end up lying here with her back broken.

The stairs held, but she was equally cautious about deciding to cross the floor on the second level. The floorboards creaked loudly, but they seemed able to bear her weight, so she continued on with greater confidence as she looked about. It was a small house, so there were only three rooms upstairs along with a short hallway. Directly across from the stairway was the larger bedroom that had belonged to Vladek and Laila. The furniture had been removed or stolen, so all that remained were the tattered and dirty curtains. Here too Erica found discarded beer cans. An old mattress indicated that someone had either slept in the empty house or used it for amorous activities far away from watchful parental eyes.

She squinted, trying to visualize the room based on the photographs she'd seen. An orange rug on the floor, a double bed with a pine bedstead and duvet covers with big green flowers. The room screamed the 1970s, and judging by the pictures the police took after the murder, it had been immaculate. Erica was surprised the first time she looked at the photos. Based on what she knew, she had expected to see a home in shambles, dirty and messy and neglected.

She left the parents' bedroom and entered the next one, which was a little smaller. It had once been Peter's. Erica found the relevant photo from the file. His room was also nice and tidy, though the bed was unmade. It was traditionally furnished, with blue wallpaper decorated with tiny circus figures. Happy clowns, elephants with plumed headdresses, a seal balancing a red ball on its nose. Lovely wallpaper for a child's room, and Erica could understand why they had chosen that particular pattern. She raised her eyes from the photograph to study the room. Bits and pieces of the wallpaper were still there, but most of it had flaked off or been covered with graffiti. There was no trace of the thick wall-to-wall carpet except for a few patches of glue on the dirty wooden floor. The bookcase that had held toys and books was gone, as were the two small chairs and the table that were just the right size for a child to sit there and draw pictures. The bed that had stood in the corner to the left of the window was also long gone. Erica shivered. Here too the windowpanes were broken and snow had blown in to whirl across the floor.

She had purposely left the one remaining upstairs room for last. Louise's bedroom. It was next to Peter's, and when she took out the photo, she had to steel herself for what she knew she would see. The contrast was so bizarre. While Peter's room had been so nice, Louise's room looked like a prison cell, and it had essentially been just that. Erica ran her finger over the big bolt that was still on the door, although it hung loose from several screws. A bolt that had been installed to keep the door securely locked from the outside. To keep the child in.

Erica held up the photo as she stepped inside. She felt the hairs on the back of her neck stand on end. The room had an eerie air about it, but she knew this had to be her imagination. Rooms and houses possessed no memory, no capacity for recalling the past. No doubt it was the knowledge of what had happened in this house that was making her feel so uneasy in Louise's room.

The room had been virtually empty. The only thing inside was a mattress on the floor. No toys, not even a proper bed. Erica went over to the window. Boards had been nailed across it, and if she hadn't known better, she would have guessed this had been done after the house was abandoned. She glanced at the photograph. The same boards were evident back then. Here a child had been locked inside her own room. Tragically, that was not the worst thing the police had discovered when they came to the house after being notified of Vladek's murder. Erica shuddered. It felt as if a cold wind was sweeping over her, but this time it wasn't because of a broken window. The chill seemed to be coming from the room itself.

She forced herself to stay there a while longer, refusing to succumb to the strange mood. But she couldn't help breathing a sigh of relief when she emerged into the hall. Cautiously she made her way down the stairs. There was only one more place to see. She went into the kitchen where she found the cupboards empty and gaping, all the doors having been removed. The cooker and fridge were gone, and the mouse droppings in the spaces where they had once stood showed that rodents had been roaming freely, both inside the house and out.

Erica's fingers trembled as she pressed down the handle on the cellar door to open it, encountering the same strange chill she'd noticed in Louise's room. She cursed as she peered into the intense darkness, realizing that she hadn't thought to bring along a torch. She might have to wait until another time to explore the cellar. But she fumbled her hand over the wall and finally located an old-fashioned switch. When she turned the knob, by some miracle, the cellar light came on. It was impossible for a light bulb from the seventies to be still functioning, so someone must have replaced it.

Her heart was pounding as she went down the stairs. She had to duck to avoid cobwebs, and she tried to ignore the creepy feeling on her skin as she imagined spiders slipping under her clothes.

When she reached the cement floor, she took a few deep breaths to calm her nerves. This was just an empty cellar inside an abandoned house. Nothing more. And it did look like an ordinary basement. A few shelves remained, and an old work bench that had belonged to Vladek, but no tools. Next to it stood an empty oil can, and several crumpled old newspapers had been tossed in a corner. Nothing startling to look at. Except for one small detail: the chain, about three metres in length, which had been fastened with screws to the wall.

Erica's hands shook badly as she searched for the right photograph. The chain was the same as back then, merely rustier. But the shackles were missing. The police had taken them. And in the police report, she'd read that they had been forced to saw them off, because they couldn't find the key. She squatted down and picked up the chain, weighing it in her hand. It was heavy and solid, clearly sturdy enough to have restrained a much larger person than a thin and undernourished seven-year-old girl. How could anyone do that to a child?

Erica felt a wave of nausea rise to her throat. She was going to have to take a break from visiting Laila. She didn't know how she could face her again after coming here and seeing with her own eyes these traces of the woman's wickedness. Photographs were one thing, but as she held the cold, heavy chain in her hands, she had a much clearer idea of what the police must have found on that day in March 1975. She felt the same horror they must have felt when they came down to the cellar and discovered a child chained to the wall.

A rustling in the corner made Erica stand up abruptly. Her pulse again began racing. Then the light went out and she screamed. Panic seized hold of her and she started taking short, shallow breaths. Close to tears, she fumbled her way towards the stairs. Odd little sounds were coming from all directions, and when something brushed against her face, she screamed again. She flailed her arms about until she realized that it was just another cobweb. Feeling sick to her stomach, she threw herself in the direction where the stairs ought to be and then had the breath knocked out of her when she ran right into the railing. The light flickered and then came back on, but she was so filled with terror that she grabbed hold of the railing and dashed up the stairs. She missed one of the steps and hit her shin, but then managed to stumble the rest of the way up to the kitchen.

Gratefully she fell to her knees after slamming the cellar door closed behind her. Her leg and midriff were bruised, but she ignored the pain, focusing all her attention on breathing calmly. She felt a bit ridiculous as she sat there, but her childhood fear of the dark never seemed to go away, and in the cellar sheer terror had surged through her whole body. For a few minutes she had experienced a little of what Louise must have felt down there in the basement. The big difference was that she had been able to rush upstairs to the light and freedom, while Louise had been chained down there, in the dark.

For the first time a real awareness of the girl's fate struck her with full force, and Erica bowed her head and wept. She was crying for Louise.

Martin studied Marta as she switched on the coffeemaker. He had never met her before, but like everybody else in the Fjällbacka area, he knew of the veterinarian and his wife. She was as beautiful as everyone had said, but it was an inaccessible type of beauty, and the slightly cold impression that she gave was further enhanced by the fact that she was remarkably pale.

'Maybe you should talk to someone,' he now said.

'You mean a pastor? Or a psychologist?' Marta shook her head. 'I'm not the one who's in a bad way. I'm just a bit . . . upset.'

She looked down at the floor but then raised her head to fix her gaze on him.

'I can't stop thinking about Victoria's family. They finally got her back, only to lose her again. Such a young and talented girl . . .' Marta fell silent.

'I know. It's awful,' said Martin. He looked around at the kitchen. It wasn't exactly ugly, but he could tell that the people who lived here didn't care much about home decor. Everything seemed to have been put together haphazardly, and even though the room appeared to be clean, there was still a faint odour of horse.

'Do you have any idea who could have done this to her? Are other girls in danger?' asked Marta. She poured the coffee and sat down across from him.

'That's not a question we can answer.' He wished he had a better reply, and his stomach clenched when he thought about how worried all the parents of young girls must be right now. He cleared his throat. It would do no good to get caught up in those kinds of thoughts. He needed to focus on doing his job and find out what happened to Victoria. That was the only way he could help them.

'Tell me about yesterday,' he said, taking a sip of coffee.

Marta took a few minutes to formulate her response. In a low voice she then told him how she'd gone out riding and how she'd seen the girl come out of the woods. She hesitated a couple of times, but Martin didn't try to rush her. He let her tell the story at her own pace. He couldn't begin to imagine how awful a sight the girl must have been.

'When I realized it was Victoria, I called to her several times. I tried to warn her about the oncoming car, but she didn't react. She just kept walking forward, like a robot.'

'Did you see any other vehicle nearby? Or anyone in the woods?'

Marta shook her head.

'No. I've tried again and again to recall the details, but that's all I saw, both before and after the accident. The driver and I were the only ones around. Everything happened so fast, and I had all my attention focused on Victoria.'

'Were you and Victoria close?'

'That depends what you mean by that,' replied Marta,

running her finger along the rim of her coffee cup. 'I try to establish a close relationship with all the girls at the stable, and Victoria had been coming to the riding school for years. We're like a family here, even though it can be a dysfunctional one at times. And Victoria was part of the family.'

As she looked away, Martin saw tears welling up in her eyes. He reached for a paper napkin on the table and handed it to her. She took it and dabbed at her eyes.

'Do you remember anything suspicious happening around the stable, anyone who seemed to be spying on the girls? Have you had anyone working here that we should take a closer look at? I know we've asked you these questions before, but they're even more relevant now that Victoria was found so close by.'

Marta nodded. 'I understand. But I can only repeat what I've already said. We haven't had any problems like that, and we don't have any employees. The riding school is in such a remote location that we would notice if anyone started hanging about. Whoever did this must have seen Victoria somewhere else. She was a lovely girl.'

'Yes, she was,' said Martin. 'And she seems to have been a nice girl too. What did the other girls think of her?'

Marta took a deep breath. 'Victoria was well-liked at the stable. She had no enemies that I know of. She was a completely ordinary teenager from a good family. I can only think that she was unlucky enough to fall into the hands of an extremely sick individual.'

'You're probably right,' said Martin. 'Although the word "unlucky" doesn't seem adequate, given the circumstances.'

He stood up, signalling that the conversation was over.

'That's true.' Marta made no sign of getting up to accompany him to the door. '"Unlucky" can't begin to describe what happened.'

* * *

The hardest thing to get used to back when she started her prison time was that the days were all the same. But gradually the routines had become Laila's lifeline. She took comfort in knowing that each day would be exactly like the previous day. It was a way of fending off her fear of staying alive. That had been the reason for her suicide attempts during those first few years. The fear of seeing life stretching out endlessly before her as the weight of the past pulled her down into darkness. Because of the routines, she had been able to cope. But the weight was ever-present.

Now everything had changed, and it was too big a burden for her to bear alone.

With trembling hands she turned the pages of the evening papers, which could be read only in the common room. The other inmates wanted to read them too, and they were growing impatient because she was taking so long. So far the journalists didn't seem to know much, but they were making the most of the few details they had. The sensational tone of the reports disturbed her. She knew what it was like to be on the other side of the big headlines. Behind every such article was someone's life, and real suffering.

'Are you done yet?' asked Marianne, coming over to her.

'Almost,' Laila murmured without looking up.

'You've had the papers for ever. Finish reading them so we can have a turn.'

'All right,' she said as she continued to study the same pages that she'd spread open on the table quite a while ago.

Marianne sighed and went over to a table near the window to sit down and wait.

Laila couldn't take her eyes off the photo on the left-hand page. The girl looked so happy and innocent, so unaware of the evil that existed in the world. But Laila could have told her all about it. How evil could live right next to what was good, in a community where people wore blinkers and refused to see what was right in front of their noses. Once you saw evil up close, you could never close your eyes to it again. That was her curse, and her responsibility.

She closed the newspaper, got up, and set it down in front of Marianne.

'I'd like to have it back when all of you are done with it,' she said.

'Sure,' muttered Marianne, already engrossed in the entertainment section.

Laila stood there for a moment, looking at Marianne as she bent over an article about the latest Hollywood celebrity divorce. How nice it must be to go through life wearing blinkers, she thought.

What bloody awful weather. Mellberg couldn't understand how his partner Rita, who was originally from Chile, had been able to get used to living in a country with such a terrible climate. Personally, he wouldn't mind emigrating. Maybe he should have taken the time to go home and change into warmer clothes, but he hadn't expected to be sent into the woods. As police chief, he was the one who was supposed to tell people what to do. His plan had been to brief the people who had turned up to help with the search, telling them in which direction to go while he stayed in the car with a thermos of hot coffee.

But that wasn't what happened. Of course Hedström had insisted that the two of them should help with the search. What foolishness! Aside from being a waste of his supervisory skills, he'd probably end up getting sick after plodding around in the freezing cold, and then how would the station function? The whole place would fall apart within hours. It was a mystery to him why Hedström didn't realize that.

'Damn it!' His thin shoes slipped on the icy ground and he instinctively reached out to grab a tree branch in order to stay upright. The manoeuvre shook the tree, causing snow to come tumbling down and over him like a cold blanket, seeping under his collar and down his back.

'How's it going?' asked Patrik. He didn't seem to notice the cold, no doubt because he had on a fur hat, heavy boots, and an enviably thick winter jacket.

Mellberg angrily brushed off the snow. 'Don't you think I should head back to the station to get things ready for the press conference?'

'Annika is taking care of all that. And it's not until four this afternoon. We've got plenty of time.'

'But this is a total waste of time. The snow that fell yesterday wiped out her tracks, and even the dogs can't find a scent in this cold.' He motioned towards a gap in the trees where they could see a handler with one of the two police dogs that Patrik had managed to call in. The dogs had been given a head start so as not to confuse them with new tracks and smells.

'So tell me again, what exactly should we be looking for?' asked Mats, one of the volunteers. He'd come from the local sports club after hearing the appeal for help with the search. Everyone in the community wanted to contribute in whatever way they could.

'Anything that Victoria might have left behind. Footprints, bloodstains, broken branches . . . Anything that catches your attention,' Mellberg told him, repeating word for word what Patrik had said when he spoke to the volunteers before they began the search.

'We're also hoping to find the place where she was being held,' added Patrik, pulling his fur hat further down over his ears.

'She couldn't have walked far. Not in the condition she was in,' Mellberg muttered, his teeth chattering.

'No, not if she was on foot,' said Patrik, slowly continuing onward as his eyes swept the ground and the surrounding area. 'But she could have escaped from a car. If the perpetrator was in the process of moving her, for example. Or she could have been dropped off here on purpose.'

'Would the perp really have let her go free? Why would he do that? That would be a very risky thing for him to do.'

'Why?' Patrik stopped. 'She couldn't speak, she couldn't see, and she was probably seriously traumatized. Presumably we're dealing with a perpetrator who is starting to feel extremely confident, given that he's been at large for two years and the police haven't found so much as a trace of the girls who disappeared. Maybe he wants to taunt us by releasing one of his victims and showing us what he's done. As long as we don't know anything, we can't assume anything. We don't know for sure that she was being held in the vicinity, but it's possible she was.'

'Okay, okay. You don't need to talk to me like I'm some amateur,' said Mellberg. 'I'm just asking the questions that the general public will be asking us.'

Patrik didn't reply. He had bent down to focus his attention on the ground again. Mellberg shrugged. Junior officers could be so touchy. He crossed his arms to hug his chest while he tried to stop his teeth from chattering. Another half hour and then he planned to supervise the search from his car. There had to be a limit to such a waste of resources. He just hoped that the coffee in the thermos would still be hot.

Martin didn't envy Patrik and Mellberg wandering about in the snow. He felt as if he'd drawn the winning lottery ticket when he was assigned to interview Marta and Tyra. In truth, he didn't think it was making optimal use of

Patrik's time for him to be out combing the woods, but over the years they'd worked together enough for Martin to understand why his colleague was doing this. For Patrik it was important to get close to the victim, physically to be on-site, aware of the same smells, listening to the same sounds, in order to have a sense of what happened. That instinct and ability had always been Patrik's strong suit. The fact that it would also allow him to keep Mellberg occupied was a positive side effect.

Martin was hoping that Patrik's instinct would lead him in the right direction, because thus far their investigation had failed to come up with any explanation for Victoria's disappearance. They desperately needed to uncover some clue out there in the woods that would tell them where she'd been all these months. If they didn't, and if the autopsy produced no concrete results, then it was going to be difficult to find any new leads.

While Victoria was missing they had talked to everyone with whom she might have come into contact. They had gone over her room with a fine-tooth comb and searched through her computer, looking for chat contacts, emails, and text messages, but without result. Patrik had cooperated with the other police districts, and they had devoted a good deal of time to looking for common denominators between Victoria and the other missing girls. But they hadn't found any connection. The girls didn't seem to share common interests or like the same music; they had never been in contact with each other, or been members of the same Internet forums, etc. No one in Victoria's family or circle of friends recognized the name of any of the other girls.

Martin got up and went into the kitchen to pour himself a cup of coffee. He was drinking too much coffee these days, but with so many sleepless nights, he needed caffeine in order to function. After Pia died, his doctor had prescribed sleeping pills and antidepressants, which he'd tried for a week. But the pills wrapped him in a shroud of indifference, which scared him. So on the day of Pia's funeral, he tossed them in the bin. He no longer remembered what it felt like to sleep through a whole night. In the daytime things were gradually getting better. As long as he kept busy – worked hard, fetched Tuva from daycare, cooked dinner, cleaned the house, played with his daughter, read her stories, put her to bed – he managed to hold on. But at night he was overwhelmed by grief, and thoughts kept whirling through his head. Hour after hour he would lie in bed and stare up at the ceiling as memories came rushing in and he was filled with an unbearable longing for a life that would never return.

'How's it going?' Annika placed her hand on his shoulder, and he realized he was standing in the middle of the room holding the coffee pot in his hand.

'I'm still not sleeping well,' he said, filling his cup. 'Would you like some?'

'Sure. Thanks,' she said, reaching for a cup.

Ernst came ambling in from Mellberg's office, no doubt hoping that a coffee break in the kitchen meant there would be some treat for him too. When Martin and Annika sat down at the table, he lay down underneath and placed his head on his paws, keeping an eye on their every move.

'Don't give him anything,' said Annika. 'He's starting to get fat, and that's not good for his health. Rita does what she can to make sure he gets exercise, but she can't keep up with the pace that would be needed to balance out what he eats.'

'Are you talking about Bertil or Ernst?'

'I suppose it would apply to both of them.' Annika smiled, but then her expression turned serious. 'So how are you really doing?'

'I'm okay.' He noticed Annika's sceptical look. 'It's true. I'm just not sleeping much.'

'Is anyone helping out with Tuva? You need a chance to rest and get caught up with things.'

'Pia's parents have been fantastic, and my parents too. So you don't have to worry, but . . . I miss her. And no one can help me with that. I'm grateful for the wonderful memories of our life together, but at the same time I wish I could rip them out of my head, because they're what hurts the most. And I don't want to feel like this any more!' He stifled a sob. He didn't want to cry at work. This was his free zone, and he refused to allow his grief to invade here too. Then he would have no place left to flee from the pain.

Annika gave him a sympathetic look. 'I wish I had lots of wise and comforting things to say. But I have no clue how it must feel. Just the thought of losing Lennart almost makes me fall apart. The only thing I can tell you is that it's going to take time, and I'm here for you, if that helps at all. You know that, don't you?'

Martin nodded.

'And try to get some sleep. You're starting to look like a wrung-out dishrag. I know you don't want to take sleeping pills, but go to the health-food shop and see if they might have some sort of supplement that could help you.'

'All right. I'll do that,' he said, deciding that it might actually be worth a try. He wouldn't be able to keep going if he didn't get at least a couple of hours of uninterrupted sleep at night.

Annika got up to refill their cups. Ernst raised his head from his paws, but lowered it again, disappointed to see that no pastries were being offered to him.

'What did the other districts say about the idea of bringing in a profiler?' asked Martin, deliberately changing the subject. Annika's concern warmed his heart, but it was too draining to talk about his grief for Pia.

'They seemed to think it was a good idea. None of them

has tried it yet, and any new suggestions would be welcome. Everyone is really shaken by what happened. And they're all thinking the same thing: Have their missing girls been subjected to the same treatment as Victoria? They're also worried about how the families will react when they hear the details. We can only hope that won't happen for a while.'

'Unfortunately, I don't think it will take long. People seem to have a sick tendency to blab to the press. And given the number of medical personnel who saw the girl's injuries, I'm afraid the news will leak out soon – if it hasn't already.'

Annika nodded. 'We'll find out at the press conference, in that case.'

'Is everything ready?'

'Yes. It's just a matter of finding some way to keep Mellberg out of there. That would make me feel a lot less nervous about things.'

Martin raised his eyebrows, and Annika held up her hands. 'I know,' she said. 'Nothing would keep him away. Not even death. He would rise out of his grave like Lazarus just to attend a press conference.'

'A very apt analogy.'

Martin set his cup in the dishwasher. As he was about to leave the kitchen he stopped and gave Annika a hug.

'Thank you,' he said. 'Now I have to be off to interview Tyra Hansson. She should be home from school by this hour.'

With a gloomy expression Ernst followed him out of the room. As far as he was concerned, the coffee break had been a big disappointment.

FJÄLLBACKA 1967

Life was wonderful. Amazing and totally unreal, yet so natural all the same. Everything had changed on that hot summer day. When the circus left Fjällbacka, Vladek did not go with it. He and Laila had agreed to meet on the evening of the last performance, and it was tacitly understood that he would then pack up his belongings and go back to her flat. He left everything behind for her. His mother and brothers. His life and his culture. His whole world.

Since then they had been happier than she could ever have imagined. Every night they fell asleep in each other's arms, snuggled together in her bed, which was much too small, and yet there was space enough for the two of them and their love. The entire flat was actually too small. It was only a bedsit with a tiny kitchen in one corner, but oddly enough Vladek was content. They made do with the space they had, and day by day their love for one another grew.

And now they would need space for one more. She placed her hand on her stomach. The slight swelling was still hardly visible, but she couldn't resist running her hand over it now and then. She had an urge to pinch herself to make sure this was real. That she and Vladek were actually going to be parents.

She saw Vladek come walking across the courtyard outside the block of flats, at exactly the same time he always did after a day's work. She still felt as if an electric current passed through her every time she saw him. He seemed to sense her gaze, because he raised his head to look up at their window. With a big smile, filled with love, he waved to her. She waved back as she again caressed her stomach.

'How is Pappa today?' asked Jonas. He kissed his mother on the cheek and sat down at the kitchen table, trying to muster a smile.

Helga didn't seem to hear him.

'It's so awful what happened to that stable girl,' she said instead, setting in front of him a plate with several big slices of freshly baked sponge cake. 'It must be terribly hard for all of you.'

Jonas picked up the piece on top and took a big bite. 'You spoil me, Mamma. It almost feels like you're trying to fatten me up.'

'I know. But you were always such a skinny little boy. So thin we could count your ribs.'

'Uh-huh. I've heard you say that a thousand times, how tiny I was when I was born. But now I'm almost six foot two, and there's certainly no problem with my appetite.'

'It's good for you to eat, considering how busy you are. All that running about. That can't be healthy.'

'Right. Exercise is known to be a real health hazard. Didn't you ever do any vigorous exercising? Not even when you were young?' Jonas reached for another piece of cake.

'When I was young? You make it sound like I'm ancient.' Helga spoke sternly, but she could feel a smile tugging at the corner of her mouth. Jonas could always make her smile.

'No, not ancient. I think "antique" is the word I was going for.'

'Stop that now,' she said, giving him a swat on the shoulder. 'If you don't watch out, there won't be any more sponge cake, or any home-cooked meals either. Then you'll have to make do with whatever Marta puts on the table.'

'Good Lord, then Molly and I would starve to death.' He took the last piece of cake from the plate.

'It must be hard for the girls in the stable to hear that one of their friends suffered such a horrible end,' Helga went on, wiping some invisible crumbs from the table.

The kitchen was always kept in perfect order. Jonas couldn't recall ever seeing it messy, and his mother never stopped moving as she cleaned, baked, cooked, and took care of his father. Jonas looked about. His parents weren't keen on modernizing anything, so the room had looked exactly the same all these years. The wallpaper, cupboards, linoleum, and furniture – everything was just as he remembered from his childhood. The refrigerator and worktop were the only things they had reluctantly replaced. But he liked the fact that so little had changed. It gave his life a sense of continuity.

'It was quite a shock, of course. Marta and I are going to have a talk with the girls this afternoon,' he said. 'But don't worry about it, Mamma.'

'No. No, I won't.' She picked up the plate, which now held only a few crumbs. 'How did it go with the cow yesterday?'

'Good. It was rather complicated, but—'

'JOOONAS!' His father's voice thundered from upstairs. 'Arc you there?'

His displeasure ricocheted off the walls, and Jonas noticed how his mother instantly clenched her jaw.

'Best if you go up,' she said as she began wiping the table with a wet rag. 'He's cross because you didn't come to see him yesterday.'

Jonas nodded. As he climbed the stairs he could feel his mother's gaze following him.

Erica was still feeling a bit shaky when she arrived at the day-care centre. It was only two o'clock, and she usually didn't fetch the children until four. But after her experience in the cellar of the abandoned house she was longing to see them so much that she decided to drive straight to the centre. She needed to see her kids, give them a hug, and hear their bubbly voices, which could make her forget everything else.

'Mamma!' Anton came running towards her with his arms outstretched. He was dirty from head to toe, with one ear sticking out from under his cap. He looked so sweet that Erica thought her heart would burst. She squatted down and held out her arms to draw him close. Her clothes were going to get dirty too, but that didn't matter.

'Mamma!' She heard another little voice calling from the playground, and Noel also came running. He had on red overalls instead of the blue ones that Anton wore, but his cap was crooked, just like his brother's. They were so alike, and yet so different.

Erica set Noel on her lap too, hugging another dirty child who burrowed his face against her neck. Noel's nose was ice cold, and she shivered as she laughed.

'Hey, you little ice cube, are you trying to warm up that nose of yours on my neck?'

She pinched his nose, making him laugh. Then he lifted up her jumper and pressed his cold and grubby mittened hands against her stomach, evoking a shrill scream from Erica. Both boys howled with laughter.

'What a couple of rowdy boys you are! Hot baths for the pair of you as soon as we get home.' She set them down, stood up, and straightened her jumper. 'Come on, kids, let's go and fetch your sister,' she said, pointing towards Maja's part of the school. The twins loved to go over there because it gave them a chance to roughhouse with the older children in Maja's group. And Maja was always delighted to see them. Even though her little brothers could be such pests, she always showered them with love.

When they arrived home, the cleaning-up process began. Usually this was a task that Erica hated, but today she didn't care how much dirt and debris got scattered over the floor. And she didn't let it bother her when Noel immediately lay down and began screaming about something only he understood. None of this was of any importance after she'd spent time in the cellar of the Kowalski house and realized the horror that Louise must have experienced as she sat there, chained to the wall in the dark.

Her own children lived in the light. Her children were the light. Noel's shrieks, which usually made her cringe, had no effect today. She merely reached down to stroke his hair, which surprised him so much that he stopped crying.

'Come on, let's go put you in the bathtub. Then we'll thaw out a whole bunch of Grandma's cinnamon buns and eat them with hot chocolate while we watch TV. Doesn't that sound like a good idea?' Erica smiled at her children as they sat on the wet floor in the front hall. 'And let's forget about making dinner tonight. We'll just eat all the rest of the ice cream in the freezer instead. And you can stay up as long as you want.'

Not a sound came from the children. Maja gave her mother a worried look and then went over to touch her forehead.

'Are you sick, Mamma?'

Erica couldn't help laughing.

'No, sweetheart,' she said, and then drew all three kids close. 'Mamma isn't sick or crazy. I just love you so much.'

She gave them a big hug, wanting to hold them even tighter. But in her mind she saw a different child. A little girl who was sitting all alone in the dark.

Ricky had hidden her secret deep inside, in a special corner of his heart. Ever since Victoria had gone missing, he had turned that secret over and over, studying it from all angles and trying to work out whether it might have had anything to do with her disappearance. He didn't think so, but there was still a slight doubt in his mind. *Think it over again.* That phrase kept whirling through his head, especially at night when he lay in bed and stared up at the ceiling. *Think it over again.* The question was whether he'd done the wrong thing, whether it had been a terrible mistake to keep quiet. It would be so easy to let the secret remain hidden, buried for ever, just as Victoria was now going to be buried in the cemetery.

'Ricky?'

Gösta's voice made him flinch as he sat there on the sofa. He had almost forgotten about the police officer and all his questions.

'Have you thought of something else that might be relevant to the investigation? Now that it turns out Victoria may have been held captive somewhere nearby?'

Gösta's voice sounded gentle and sorrowful, and Ricky could see how tired he was. He had grown fond of this older policeman who had been their family liaison officer during the past few months. And he knew that Gösta liked him too. Ricky had always got on well with grown-ups. Ever since he was a child, he'd been told that his was an old soul. Maybe that was true. Regardless, he felt as if he'd aged a thousand years since yesterday. All joy and anticipation about the life that lay ahead of him had vanished the moment Victoria died.

He shook his head.

'No, I've already told you everything I know. Victoria was an ordinary girl, with ordinary friends and ordinary interests. And we're just an ordinary family. Perfectly normal . . .' He smiled and glanced at his mother, but she didn't return his smile. The sense of humour that had always united the family had also died with Victoria.

'I heard from a neighbour that you've asked the public for help in searching the woods,' said his father. 'Do you think that will produce any results?' Markus's face was ashen with exhaustion, but there was a spark of hope in his eyes as he looked at Gösta.

'We hope so. Lots of people have volunteered to help, so with luck we might find something. She must have been held somewhere.'

'What about the other girls? The ones we read about in the newspapers?' Helena reached for her coffee cup. Her hand was shaking, and Ricky's heart ached to see how thin his mother had become. She had always been slender and petite, but now she had lost so much weight that her bones were clearly visible under her skin.

'We're continuing to work with the other police districts. Everyone is determined to solve this case, and we're helping each other by exchanging information. We're going to put all our resources into finding whoever kidnapped Victoria and presumably the other girls too.'

'I mean . . .' Helena hesitated. 'Do you think the same

thing . . .' She couldn't bear to finish the sentence, but Gösta knew what she was asking.

'We don't know. But it's certainly possible that . . .' He too couldn't bring himself to say it out loud.

Ricky swallowed hard. He didn't want to think about what Victoria had gone through. But the images from the photographs kept creeping into his mind, and he felt nausea rise into his throat. Her beautiful blue eyes, which had always held such warmth. That was how he wanted to remember them. He couldn't stand to think about the horror of what had happened to his sister.

'We're going to hold a press conference this afternoon,' said Gösta after a moment. 'And I'm afraid the reporters will probably show up here too. The disappearance of the girls has been national news for a while, and this will only . . . Well, I just want you to be prepared.'

'They've already been here and rung the bell a few times. And we've stopped answering the phone,' said Markus.

'I can't understand why they won't leave us in peace.' Helena shook her head. Her dark hair, cut in a page-boy style, swayed around her face. 'Don't they realize . . .'

'No, unfortunately they don't,' said Gösta, standing up. 'I need to go back to the station now. But don't hesitate to call. You can reach me anytime, day or night. And I promise to keep you informed.'

He turned to Ricky and placed his hand on the boy's arm. 'Take care of your mother and father.'

'I'll do my best.' He felt the weight of responsibility settle on his shoulders. But Gösta was right. As things stood, he was stronger than either of his parents. He was the one who would have to keep everything together.

Molly felt the sting of tears in her eyes. Disappointment filled her body, and she stomped her foot so hard on the stable floor that a cloud of dust rose up.

'You're a sodding idiot!'

'Watch your language, please.' Marta's voice was ice cold, and Molly shrank back. But her anger was so great that she couldn't stop herself.

'But I want to go! I'm going to talk to Jonas about it too.'

'I know you want to go,' said her mother, crossing her arms. 'But in the circumstances, it's not a good idea. And your father will agree with me.'

'What do you mean, "in the circumstances"? It's not my fault that such awful things happened to Victoria. Why should I have to suffer?'

Tears were now running down Molly's face, and she wiped them off on the sleeve of her jacket. She peered up at Marta from under her fringe to see if her tears would have any effect, though it seemed unlikely. Her mother merely stared at her with that guarded expression of hers, which Molly hated. Sometimes she wished that Marta would get furious instead, that she would scream and swear and show some emotion. But she never lost her composure. She never gave any sign of yielding.

Molly's tears poured out, her nose was running, and her jacket sleeve was now soaked.

'But it's the first competition of the season! I don't understand why I can't participate, just because of what happened to Victoria. I'm not the one who killed her!'

Slap! Marta's hand struck her cheek before she even saw it coming. Molly touched her face in disbelief. It was the first time her mother had hit her. The first time anyone had ever hit her. Her tears stopped abruptly as she stared at Marta, who was again utterly calm. She stood there motionless, her arms crossed over the green quilted riding vest she wore.

'That's enough now,' she said. 'You can stop begging like some spoiled brat and behave decently.' Marta's words cut just as deep as the slap. Molly had never been called a spoiled brat. Well, the other girls in the stable might have called her that behind her back, but that was only because they were jealous.

Still holding her hand to her cheek, Molly kept on staring at Marta. Then she turned on her heel and ran out of the stable. The other girls began whispering to each other when they saw her crying as she ran across the yard, but she didn't care. They probably thought she was crying about Victoria, like everyone else had been doing since yesterday.

Molly ran for home, going around back to the door to her father's veterinary clinic, but it was locked. There were no lights on, and Jonas wasn't there. Molly wondered where he could be as she stood in the snow for a moment, stomping her feet to stay warm. Then she took off running again.

She tore open the door to her grandparents' house.

'Grandma!'

'Good Lord, where's the fire?' Helga came out to the front hall, drying her hands on a dish towel.

'Is Jonas here? I need to talk to him.'

'Calm down. You're crying so hard I can barely understand you. Is this about the girl that Marta found yesterday?'

Molly shook her head. Helga led her into the kitchen and got her to sit down at the table.

'I . . . I . . .' Molly stammered, but then she had to stop and take several deep breaths. Just being in her grandmother's kitchen helped her to calm down. In this house, time stood still. Nothing ever changed in here while outside the world continued to rush onward.

'I need to talk to Jonas. Marta says I can't take part in the competition on the weekend.' She hiccupped and then fell silent so her grandmother had time to take in how unfair the situation was.

Helga sat down. 'Well, Marta likes to make the decisions. You'll have to wait and see what your father says. Is it an important competition?'

'Yes, it is. But Marta says it wouldn't be appropriate to compete after what happened to Victoria. And of course I think it's sad, but I don't see why that's any reason for me to miss the competition. That cow Linda Bergvall is bound to win if I'm not there, and then she'll be so annoying, even though she knows I could have beat her. I'll die if I'm not allowed to go!' With a dramatic expression, she leaned over the kitchen table, rested her face on her arms, and began to sob.

Helga patted her gently on the shoulder. 'Now, now, it's not the end of the world, and your parents are the ones who make the decisions. They'd do anything for you, but if they think you shouldn't compete . . . well, then there's not much to be done about it.'

'But don't you think Jonas would understand?' said Molly, giving Helga a pleading look.

'I've known your father since he was this big,' said Helga, holding her thumb and index finger only a centimetre apart. 'And I've known your mother for a long time too. Believe me when I say that it's impossible to make them change their minds, once they've made a decision. So if I were you, I'd stop complaining and look forward to the next competition instead.'

Molly dried her face on the paper napkin that Helga handed her.

She blew her nose and then got up to toss the napkin in the bin. The worst thing was that her grandmother was right. It was hopeless to try and talk to her parents once they'd decided. But she was still planning to try. Maybe Jonas would take her side, in spite of everything.

It had taken Patrik a whole hour to thaw out, and it was going to take Mellberg even longer. It had been sheer madness to go out in the woods when the temperature was minus seventeen degrees Celsius and he was wearing thin shoes and only a windproof jacket instead of a proper winter coat. Mellberg's lips were blue as he stood in a corner of the conference room.

'How's it going, Bertil? Are you still cold?' asked Patrik.

'Bloody hell,' said Mellberg, slapping his arms against his body. 'I could use a stiff whisky. That might warm me up from the inside.'

Patrik shuddered at the thought of an intoxicated Bertil Mellberg at the press conference. Although that might actually be an improvement over the sober version.

'So what approach do you think we should take?' Patrik asked.

'I thought I'd take charge, and you can back me up. The reporters like to see a strong leader, someone they can turn to in situations like this.' Mellberg tried to sound as authoritative as he could with his teeth chattering.

'Of course,' said Patrik, sighing to himself so heavily that he thought Mellberg might hear. Always the same story. Getting Mellberg to do anything useful in an investigation was about as easy as trying to catch flies with a pair of chopsticks. But the minute he had the chance to step into the spotlight, or claim credit for work done by the rest of the team, no one could keep Bertil away.

'How about letting in the hyenas?' said Mellberg, turning to Annika, who got up and went over to the door. She had made all the arrangements while they were out in the woods. She'd given Mellberg a quick rundown of the most important points and also printed out key words on a piece of paper for him. Now they could only cross their fingers and hope that he didn't embarrass them any more than necessary.

The journalists shambled into the room, and Patrik greeted several that he knew – some from the local media and some who worked at the national level, reporters that he'd run into on various occasions. As usual there were also a few new faces. The newspapers seemed to have a high turnover rate where journalists were concerned.

They all sat down, exchanging a few murmured remarks, while the photographers good-naturedly jostled for the best positions. Patrik hoped that Mellberg's lips wouldn't look quite so blue in the photos; at the moment he looked as though he belonged in the morgue.

'Everybody here?' said Mellberg, shivering. The reporters had already started waving their hands in the air, but he motioned for them to stop. 'We'll take questions in a moment, but first I want to turn over the floor to Patrik Hedström, who will give you a brief report on what has happened.'

Patrik gave his boss a surprised look. Maybe Mellberg realized after all that he didn't have a grasp of the big picture, which was what this crowd of reporters needed to hear.

'Thank you. All right then,' Patrik replied. He cleared his throat and came over to stand next to Mellberg. He paused to gather his thoughts, trying to work out what he should tell them and what he should withhold. An unguarded word to the media could destroy so much, and yet the journalists were their link to one of the greatest assets any investigation could have: the public. He needed to give the press enough information to trigger a ripple effect that would start tips coming in from ordinary people. There was always someone who had seen or heard something that might turn out to be relevant even though that person might not think so. But handing out the wrong information, or revealing too many details, could give the perpetrator an advantage. If he or she knew what sort of leads the police were following, it would be easier to hide their tracks or simply refrain from making the same mistake next time. And that was everyone's greatest fear right now, that this horrific crime would be repeated. A serial criminal rarely stopped of his own accord. Most likely not in this instance, at any rate. Patrik had a bad feeling about this one.

'Yesterday Victoria Hallberg was found near a wooded area east of Fjällbacka. She was then struck by a car, and we are convinced it was an accident. She was taken to Uddevalla hospital, where all possible efforts were made to save her life. Unfortunately, her injuries were too severe and at 11.14 she was pronounced dead.' He paused and reached for a glass of water that Annika had placed on the table. 'We have searched the area where she was found, and I'd like to thank all the volunteers from Fjällbacka who turned up to help. There is little more I can tell you. We are continuing to cooperate with other police districts investigating similar cases. We need to find the girls who have gone missing, and we need to catch the person who kidnapped them.' Patrik took a sip of water. 'Any questions?'

Everyone instantly stuck their hand in the air, and several reporters began speaking at once. The photographers in the front of the room had started snapping pictures as Patrik spoke, and he had to restrain an urge to smooth down his hair. It was always a strange feeling to see big pictures of his own face printed in the evening papers.

'Kjell?' He pointed to Kjell Ringholm from *Bohusläningen*, which was the local paper with the most subscribers. Kjell had offered the police valuable assistance on previous cases, so Patrik tended to give him preferential treatment.

'You mentioned that Victoria had suffered severe injuries. What type of injuries? Were they the result of being struck by the car, or was she injured prior to the accident?'

'I can't comment on that,' replied Patrik. 'I can only say that she was struck by a car and she died from her injuries.'

'We have information that she had been subjected to some sort of torture,' Kjell went on.

Patrik swallowed hard, picturing in his mind Victoria's empty eye sockets and her mouth, with a stump where her tongue had been. But those were details they didn't want to release. He cursed whoever hadn't been able to resist talking to the press. Was it really necessary to divulge such information?

'Given the ongoing police investigation, we can't comment on any details or the extent of Victoria's injuries.'

Kjell was about to say something else, but Patrik held up his hand to stop him, and then called on Sven Niklasson, a reporter for *Expressen*. He had also dealt with this journalist before, and he knew that Niklasson was always sharp. He did his homework and never wrote anything that might damage an investigation.

'Was there any indication that she had been sexually abused? And have you found any link to the disappearance of the other girls?'

'We don't know yet. The autopsy is scheduled for tomorrow. As far as the other missing girls are concerned, at this time I can't divulge what we know about any possible links. As I said, we are continuing to work with the other police districts, and I'm convinced that this cooperative effort will lead to the arrest of the perpetrator.'

'Are you sure that we're talking about only one perpetrator?' The reporter from *Aftonbladet* took the floor without being called on. 'Couldn't it be several individuals, or even a gang? Have you looked into possible connections with trafficking?'

'At the present time we are not ruling out anything, and that also applies to the number of perpetrators involved. Of course we've discussed the possibility of a link to human trafficking, but Victoria's case does not seem consistent with that theory.'

'Why's that?' persisted the reporter from *Aftonbladet*.

'Due to the nature of her injuries, it seems unlikely that she was going to be sold,' Kjell interjected, as he scrutinized Patrik's expression.

Patrik didn't comment. Kjell's conclusion was correct and revealed more than the police wanted to say, but as long as he refused to confirm anything, the newspapers could only print speculations.

'As I said, we are investigating all possible leads. We are not ruling out anything.'

He allowed the reporters to ask questions for another fifteen minutes, but he was unable to answer most of them, either because he didn't know the answer or because he didn't want to release more details. Unfortunately, the more questions thrown at him, the clearer it became just how little the police actually knew. It had been four months since Victoria disappeared, and even longer since the girls in the other districts had gone missing. Yet there was so little to go on. Frustrated, Patrik decided the time had come to stop taking questions.

'Bertil, is there anything you'd like to say in conclusion?' Patrik adroitly moved aside to make Mellberg feel that he was the one who had been conducting the press conference.

'Yes, I'd like to take this opportunity to say it was a blessing in disguise that it was in our district that the first of the missing girls was found, given the unique expertise available at our station. Under my leadership, we have solved a number of high-profile murder cases, and my list of previous successes shows that . . .'

Patrik interrupted him by placing a hand on his shoulder.

'I wholeheartedly agree. We'd like to thank all of you for your questions, and we'll stay in touch.'

Mellberg glared at him, angry at missing an opportunity for a little self-promotion, but Patrik steered him out of the room while the journalists and photographers gathered up their things. 'Sorry about cutting in like that, but I was afraid they would miss their deadline if we kept them here any longer. After that great presentation you gave, we want to be certain they'll file their reports in time for the morning editions.'

Patrik was ashamed of the drivel he was spouting, but it seemed to work because Mellberg's face lit up.

'Of course. Good thinking, Hedström. You do have your useful moments.'

'Thanks,' said Patrik wearily. Handling Mellberg took as much effort as running the investigation. If not more.

'Why are you still unwilling to talk about what happened? It was so many years ago.' Ulla, the prison therapist, peered at Laila over the rims of her red-framed glasses.

'Why do you keep asking me about it? After so many years?' replied Laila.

Back when she started serving her sentence she'd felt pressured by all the demands to describe everything, to open her soul and reveal the details from that day as well as the preceding period. Now it no longer bothered her. No one expected her to answer those questions; they were both just going through the motions. Laila knew that Ulla had to continue to ask about that time, and Ulla knew that Laila would continue to refuse to answer. For ten years

Ulla had been the prison therapist. Her predecessors had stayed for varying lengths of time, depending on their ambitions. Tending to the psychological well-being of prisoners wasn't particularly rewarding monetarily or in terms of career development or satisfaction at receiving good results. Most of the prisoners were beyond saving, and everybody knew it. Yet someone still had to do the job, and Ulla seemed to be the therapist who felt most content with her role. And that in turn made Laila feel calmer about being with her, even though she knew the conversation would never lead anywhere.

'You seem to look forward to Erica Falck's visits,' said Ulla now, startling Laila. This was a new topic. Not one of the usual, familiar subjects that they danced around. She felt her hands start to shake as they lay on her lap. She didn't like new questions. Ulla was aware of this and she fell silent, waiting for a reply.

Aware that her usual replies, which she could rattle off in her sleep, wouldn't suffice, Laila couldn't decide whether to respond or keep quiet.

'It's something different,' she said at last, hoping that would be enough. But Ulla seemed unusually persistent today. Like a dog refusing to let go of a bone.

'In what way? Do you mean it's a break from the daily routines here? Or something else?'

Laila clasped her hands to keep them still. She found the questions confusing. She hadn't a clue what she was hoping to achieve by meeting with Erica. She could have gone on declining Erica's repeated requests to visit her. She could have gone on living in her own world while the years slowly passed and the only thing that changed was her face in the mirror. But how could she do that now that evil had forced its way in? Now that she realized it wasn't simply a matter of taking new victims. Now that it was happening so close.

'I like Erica,' said Laila. 'And of course her visits are a break from all the dreariness.'

'I think there's more to it than that,' said Ulla, pressing her chin to her chest as she studied Laila. 'You know what she wants. She wants to hear about what we've tried to talk about so many times. What you don't want to discuss.'

'That's her problem. No one is forcing her to come here.'

'True,' said Ulla. 'But I can't help wondering whether deep down you'd like to tell Erica everything and in that way lighten the burden. She seems to have somehow reached you, while the rest of us have failed, in spite of all our attempts.'

Laila didn't answer. They had tried so often, but she wasn't sure she could have told them even if she had wanted to. It was too overwhelming. And besides, where should she begin? With their first meeting, with the evil that grew, with that last day when it happened? What sort of starting point could she possibly choose so that someone else would understand what even she found inexplicable?

'Is it possible that you've fallen into a pattern with us, that you've kept everything inside for so long that you just can't let it out?' asked Ulla, tilting her head to one side. Laila wondered whether psychologists were taught to adopt that pose. Every therapist she'd ever met did the same thing.

'What does it matter now? It was all so long ago.'

'Yes, but you're still here. And I think in part that's your own doing. You don't seem to have any desire to lead a normal life outside these prison walls.'

If Ulla only knew how right she was. Laila did not want to live outside of the prison; she had no idea how she would manage that. But that wasn't the whole truth.

She didn't dare. She didn't dare live in the same world as the evil she had seen close-up. The prison was the only place where she felt safe. Perhaps it wasn't much of a life, but it was hers, and the only one she knew.

'I don't want to talk any more,' said Laila, standing up.

Ulla's gaze didn't waver, seeming to go right through her. Laila hoped not. There were certain things she hoped no one would ever see.

Normally it was Dan who took the girls to the stable, but today he was busy at work, so Anna had driven them there instead. She felt a childish joy that Dan had asked her to step in, that he had asked her anything at all. But she wished she could have avoided the stable. She had a deep-seated dislike of horses. The big animals frightened her. It was a fear stemming from her childhood when she had been forced to take riding lessons. Her mother Elsy had decided that she and Erica should learn to ride, leading to two years' torment for both sisters. It had been a mystery to Anna why the other girls at the stable were so obsessed with horses. Personally she found them totally unreliable, and her pulse would still race at the memory of how it felt to cling to a rearing animal. No doubt the horses could sense her fear from far away, but that made no difference. Right now she was thinking of simply dropping off Emma and Lisen and then retreating to a safe distance.

'Tyra!' Emma jumped out of the car and rushed over to a girl walking across the yard. She threw herself at Tyra, who gathered her up and swung her around.

'You've grown tall since the last time I saw you! Soon you'll be taller than me,' said Tyra with a smile. Emma's face lit up with joy. Tyra was her favourite of the girls who were always hanging about the riding school. She was devoted to her.

Anna went over to them. Lisen had run straight into the stable as soon as she got out of the car. She wouldn't reappear until it was time to go home.

'How are you feeling today?' she asked, patting Tyra on the shoulder.

'Awful,' said Tyra. Her eyes were red-rimmed, and she looked as though she hadn't slept.

From the other side of the yard someone approached in the fading afternoon light, and Anna saw that it was Marta Persson.

'Hi,' she said as Marta came closer. 'How's it going?'

She had always found Marta to be incredibly attractive, with her sharp features, high cheekbones, and dark hair, but today she looked tired and worn out.

'Things are a bit chaotic,' replied Marta curtly. 'Where's Dan? You don't usually come here voluntarily.'

'He had to work overtime. They're having teacher evaluations this week.'

Dan was at heart a fisherman, but since fishing could not provide him with a living in Fjällbacka, he had taken a teaching job in Tanumshede years ago to supplement his income. The fishing had gradually become a sideline, but he struggled to earn enough so he could at least hold on to his boat.

'Isn't it time for the girls' lesson?' asked Anna, glancing at her watch. It was almost five.

'It's going to be a shorter lesson today. Jonas and I feel it's important to tell the girls about Victoria. You're welcome to stay if you like. It might be nice for Emma to have you here.'

Marta headed indoors. They followed her into the conference room and sat down along with the other girls. Lisen was already there, and she gave Anna a sombre look.

Marta and Jonas stood next to each other, waiting for the buzz of voices to die down.

'I'm sure you've all heard about what happened,' Marta began. Everyone nodded.

'Victoria is dead,' said Tyra quietly. Big tears ran down her cheeks, and she wiped them on her shirt sleeve.

Marta didn't seem to know what else to say, but then she took a deep breath and went on.

'Yes, that's right. Victoria died in hospital yesterday. We know that you've all been very worried about her, that you've missed Victoria. The fact that it should end like this . . . well, it's terrible.'

Anna saw Marta turn to her husband for support. Jonas nodded and then spoke.

'It's terribly difficult for any of us to understand how something like this could happen. I suggest that we hold a minute's silence to honour Victoria and her family. It's worse for them than for anyone else right now, and I want them to know that we're thinking of them.' He fell silent and bowed his head.

Everyone followed his example. The clock in the conference room ticked quietly, and when the minute was up, Anna opened her eyes. All the girls were looking scared and anxious.

Marta took the floor again. 'We don't know any more than you do about what happened to Victoria. But the police will probably come here to talk with us again. Then we'll find out more. And I want everyone to be available to answer the officers' questions.'

'But we don't know anything. We've already talked to them several times, and nobody knows a thing,' said Tindra, a tall blonde that Anna had spoken to on one occasion.

'I know it may seem like that, but maybe there's something you don't realize might help. Just answer the questions the police ask.' Jonas fixed his eyes on the girls, one after the other.

'Okay,' they murmured.

'Good. We all need to do whatever we can to help,' said Marta. 'So now it's time for the riding lesson. We're all still feeling the shock, but maybe it would be good to think about something else for a while. So let's get going.'

Anna took Emma and Lisen by the hand and headed for the stable. The two girls seemed surprisingly calm. With a lump in her throat, Anna watched as they got the horses ready. Then the girls led them into the riding hall and mounted them. She didn't feel nearly as composed. Even though her son had lived only a week, she knew how desperately painful it was to lose a child.

She went over to sit on a bench. Suddenly she heard someone weeping quietly behind her. When she turned around, she saw Tyra sitting further up, with Tindra beside her.

'What do you think happened to her?' asked Tyra between sobs.

'I heard that her eyes were gouged out,' whispered Tindra.

'What?' Tyra practically shrieked. 'Who told you that? When I talked with the policeman, he didn't say anything about that.'

'My uncle was one of the medics in the ambulance that picked her up yesterday. He said both her eyes were gone.'

'Oh, no,' moaned Tyra, bending forward. It looked like she was going to vomit.

'Do you think it's someone we know?' said Tindra with ill-concealed excitement.

'Are you crazy?' said Tyra, and Anna realized that she needed to put an end to this conversation.

'That's enough,' she said as she went up to the girls and put her arm around Tyra. 'It's no good speculating. Can't you see that Tyra is upset?'

Tindra stood up. 'Well, I think it has to be the same madman who murdered those other girls.'

'We don't know that they're dead,' replied Anna.

'Of course they're dead,' said Tindra boldly. 'And I bet their eyes were gouged out too.'

Anna shuddered with revulsion as she hugged Tyra's trembling body even closer.

Patrik stepped inside the warmth of the front hall. He was bone tired. It had been a long work day, but the fatigue he felt had more to do with the responsibility that weighed him down on an investigation of this nature. Sometimes he wished he had an ordinary nine-to-five job in an office or a factory, and not a profession where someone's fate depended on how well he did his job. He felt a great responsibility for so many people. Especially for the family members who placed their trust in the police to deliver the answers they needed if they were ever to come to terms with what had happened. Then there was the victim, who seemed to plead with him to find the person who had prematurely put an end to her life. But his greatest responsibility was to the missing girls who might still be alive, and for those who might be at risk from the kidnapper. As long as the perpetrator was on the loose and unidentified, more girls might disappear. Girls who lived, breathed, and laughed, unaware that their days were numbered because of some sadistic murderer.

'Pappa!' A little human projectile threw himself at Patrik, followed instantly by two more, which meant that they all ended up in a heap on the floor. The melted snow on the doormat was seeping into his trousers, but he didn't care. It was good to have his children so near. For a few seconds everything was perfect, but then the bickering started.

'Hey!' Anton screamed. 'Noel pinched me!'

'No!' cried Noel. And as if to show that he hadn't, he gave his brother a pinch. Anton howled and flailed his arms about.

'All right now . . .' Patrik separated the boys and tried to look stern. Maja stood off to one side, imitating his expression.

'No pinching!' she said, wagging her finger at her brothers. 'If you keep fighting, you'll get a dime-out.' Patrik had to stop himself from laughing. When she was much younger, Maja had misunderstood the expression 'time-out', and it had been impossible to get her to say it correctly.

'Thanks, sweetheart. I'll handle this,' he said, getting up and holding the twins by the hand.

'Mamma, the twins are fighting,' called Maja as she ran to Erica in the kitchen. Patrik followed with his sons.

'Really?' said Erica, her eyes wide. 'They're fighting? Never!' She smiled and kissed Patrik on the cheek. 'Dinner is ready, so let's stop all the fuss. Maybe pancakes will improve everyone's mood.'

That did the trick. After the children had finished eating and settled in front of the TV to watch *Bolibompa*, Erica and Patrik were able to enjoy a rare moment of peace and quiet at the kitchen table.

'How's it going?' asked Erica, sipping her tea.

'We've hardly begun.' Patrik reached for the sugar bowl and dumped five teaspoonfuls into his cup. Right now he didn't want to think about any diet rules. Erica had been watching his food intake like a hawk ever since he'd developed heart problems at the same time the twins were born. But tonight she didn't say a word. He closed his eyes, savouring the first taste of the piping hot and very sweet tea.

'Half the town was out in the woods today helping us,

but we didn't find anything. And then there was the press conference this afternoon. Have you already seen the news about it online?'

Erica nodded. She hesitated as if debating her next move, then got up and took the last of Kristina's home-made buns out of the freezer. She put them on a plate and stuck it in the microwave. A minute later the delicious fragrance of butter and cinnamon filled the kitchen.

'Isn't there a risk of destroying evidence with half of Fjällbacka tramping through the woods?'

'Sure. Of course. But we have no idea how far she walked or where she came from, and by this morning the snow had already obliterated any footprints. I thought it was worth the risk.'

'So how did the press conference go?' Erica took the plate out of the microwave and set it on the table.

'There's not much we can tell the press. Mostly it was reporters asking questions that we couldn't answer.' Patrik reached for a bun but swore and quickly dropped it back on the plate.

'Let them cool off a bit.'

'Thanks for telling me.' He blew on his fingers.

'Was it because of the ongoing investigation that you couldn't answer?'

'I wish that was the reason. But the fact is we haven't got a clue. When Victoria disappeared it was like she went up in smoke. Not a trace left behind. No one saw anything, no one heard anything, and there were no links to the other missing girls. Then all of a sudden she just reappeared.'

Neither of them spoke as Patrik touched the buns again and decided they had cooled off enough to eat.

'I heard something about her injuries,' said Erica cautiously.

Patrik paused before saying anything. He wasn't

supposed to discuss the girl's injuries, but obviously word had already spread, and he needed to talk to someone. Erica was not only his wife, she was also his best friend. Besides, she had a much keener mind than he did.

'It's all true. Although I don't know what you heard.' He was buying himself a little time by chewing on a cinnamon bun, but suddenly he lost his appetite, and it didn't taste as good as it should.

'I heard she had no eyes.'

'Yes, her eyes were . . . gone. We don't know how it was done. Pedersen is doing the autopsy early tomorrow morning.' He hesitated again. 'And her tongue had been cut out.'

'Good Lord,' said Erica. Now she lost her appetite too. She set a half-eaten bun back on the plate.

'How long ago did it happen?'

'What do you mean?'

'Were the injuries new or had they healed?'

'Good question. But I don't know. I hope to get all the details from Pedersen tomorrow.'

'Could it be some religious thing? Eye for an eye, tooth for a tooth? Or some horrible expression of hatred for women? She wasn't supposed to look at him, and she was supposed to keep quiet.'

Erica waved her hands about as she talked, and as always Patrik was impressed with the shrewdness of his wife's mind. Such thoughts hadn't occurred to him when he was trying to speculate about a possible motive.

'What about her ears?' Erica went on.

'What about her ears?' He leaned forward, getting crumbs on his hands.

'Well, I was just wondering about something . . . What if the person who did this, the one who took away her ability to see and speak, also damaged her hearing? If so, she would have been in a sort of bubble, without any means to communicate. Think about what power that would give the perpetrator.'

Patrik stared at her. He tried to imagine what Erica had just described, but the mere idea made his blood run cold. What a horrifying fate. If that was true, then it might have been a blessing that Victoria hadn't survived, even though it seemed cold-hearted to think such a thing.

'Mamma, they're fighting again.' Maja stood in the kitchen doorway. Patrik glanced at the clock on the wall.

'Oh, it's time for bed.' He got up. 'Shall we do rock, paper, scissors?'

Erica shook her head and got up to kiss him on the cheek.

'If you put Maja to bed, I'll take care of the boys tonight.'

'Thanks,' he said and took his daughter by the hand. They headed for the stairs as Maja chattered about what she had done during the day. But Patrik wasn't listening. His thoughts were on the girl inside the bubble.

Jonas slammed the front door so hard that Marta came rushing out of the kitchen, then stood leaning against the doorjamb with her arms folded. He could tell that she'd been expecting this conversation, and her calm demeanour made him even angrier.

'I just talked to Molly. What the hell were you thinking? Shouldn't we be making decisions like this together?'

'Yes, we should. But sometimes you don't seem to understand what has to be done.'

He forced himself to take a deep breath. Marta knew that a disagreement about Molly was the only thing that could make him lose his temper.

Jonas lowered his voice. 'She's been looking forward to this competition. It's the first one of the season.'

Marta turned around and went back into the kitchen.

'I'm making dinner. You'll have to come in here if you want to argue.'

He hung up his jacket, took off his boots, and swore as he set his feet on the floor. His socks were instantly soaked from the snow he'd tracked in. It was never a good thing when Marta decided to cook. The smell coming from the kitchen did not bode well.

'I'm sorry for yelling.' He went over to stand behind his wife, placing his hands on her shoulders. She was stirring something in a pot, and he looked down to see what it was. He couldn't tell what was simmering inside, but whatever it was, it didn't look appetizing.

'Sausage stroganoff,' she said in reply to his unspoken question.

'Could you just explain to me why?' he said gently as he continued to massage her shoulders. He knew her so well, knew that it would do no good to shout and scream. So he was trying a different tactic. He had promised Molly that he would at least try. She had been inconsolable when she told him about Marta's decision, and the front of his shirt was still wet from her tears.

'It would look insensitive if we went to the competition right now. Molly needs to learn that the world does not revolve around her.'

'I don't think anybody would object if she . . .' he ventured.

Marta turned around and looked up at him. He had always found it endearing that she was so much shorter than he was. It made him feel strong, like he was her protector. But in his heart he knew that was not the case. She was stronger than him and always had been.

'But don't you understand? You know how people talk. It's obvious we can't allow Molly to compete after what happened yesterday. The riding school is barely breaking even, and our reputation is our most important asset. We can't risk it. So we'll just have to let Molly sulk. You should have heard the way she spoke to me today. It's not acceptable. You let her get away with far too much.'

Jonas reluctantly had to admit that she was right. But that was not the whole truth, and she knew it. Jonas pulled her close, feeling her body against his own and the current that passed between them, as always. He would always feel it. Nothing was stronger. Not even his love for Molly.

'I'll talk to her,' he said with his lips pressed against Marta's hair. He inhaled her scent, so familiar yet still so exotic. He felt himself responding, and Marta did too. She moved her hand down to his crotch and began stroking him through his trousers. He groaned and leaned down to kiss her.

The stroganoff on the stove was burning, but they didn't care.

UDDEVALLA 1967

Everything had fallen into place so nicely for them that Laila could hardly believe it. Vladek was not only an excellent lion tamer, he also possessed a talent that was more practical for everyday use. He was an expert at fixing things. It hadn't taken long before word of his skill had spread through town, and people began coming to Vladek to get help with everything from faulty dishwashers to broken-down old bangers.

In all honesty, he'd probably attracted a large number of such jobs because of the interest his presence had stirred. Plenty of people wanted to have a look at someone as remarkable as a genuine circus performer. But after the initial curiosity had faded, they retained a solid respect for his handyman skills. Everyone soon grew so accustomed to him that it was as if he had always been part of the community.

His self-confidence grew, and when he saw an advert for a workshop in Uddevalla, it seemed only natural that they should seize the opportunity and make the move, although Laila was sad not to be closer to Agneta and her mother. Yet Vladek was finally going to turn his dream into reality and start his own business.

Here in Uddevalla they had found their dream house. They fell in love with it on first sight. It was quite plain and a bit run-down, but for a modest sum they were able to do some renovations and make changes so that it was now their paradise.

Life was good, and they were counting the days until they could hold their child in their arms. They would soon become a real family. Laila, Vladek, and the baby.

Mellberg awoke to find a little person jumping on him. The only person who was allowed to wake him. Or jump on him, for that matter.

'Get up, Grandpa. Up!' Leo urged him, bouncing up and down on Mellberg's big stomach. So Mellberg did as expected and grabbed the boy, tickling him so he howled with laughter.

'Good Lord, what a noise you two are making!' shouted Rita from the kitchen. That was also part of the routine, but he knew that she loved to hear their rowdy playtime in the morning.

'Hush,' said Mellberg, holding his finger to his lips and opening his eyes wide. Leo did the same. 'There's a wicked witch out in the kitchen. She eats little children, and she has probably already eaten both of your mothers. But there's one way we can defeat her. Do you know what it is?'

Even though Leo knew full well what Mellberg was going to say, he shook his head.

'We have to sneak in there and tickle her to death! But witches have extra sharp ears, which means we have to do our best to move quietly so she won't hear us, or else . . . or else we're done for!' And Mellberg made a motion as if slashing his throat. Again Leo copied him. Then they tiptoed out of the bedroom and into the kitchen, where Rita was waiting for them.

'ATTACK!' yelled Mellberg, and he and Leo ran over to Rita to tickle her.

'EEEK!' cried Rita, laughing. 'This is what I get for my sins!' The two dogs, Ernst and Señorita, rushed out from under the table and began dashing back and forth, barking happily.

'Wow, what a ruckus,' said Paula. 'It's a miracle you haven't been evicted long ago.'

Everyone fell silent. They hadn't heard the front door of the flat open.

'Hi, Leo. Did you sleep well?' said Paula. 'I was thinking of coming up here to have breakfast with all of you before going to the day-care centre.'

'Is Johanna coming too?' asked Rita.

'No, she already left for work.'

Slowly Paula went over to the kitchen table and sat down. In her arms she held Lisa, who for once was sound asleep. Leo ran over to give her a hug, studying his little sister a bit anxiously. Ever since Lisa's birth, Leo had been sleeping at 'Granny and Grandpa Bertil's place'. Partly to escape the baby's colicky crying, but also because he slept so well curled up in Mellberg's arms. The two of them had been inseparable from the beginning, since Mellberg had been present at Leo's birth. Now that the boy had a sister and his mothers were so busy with her, he often sought out his grandfather, who conveniently lived in the flat upstairs.

'Is there any coffee?' asked Paula. Rita filled a big cup, added a dash of milk, and set the coffee on the table in front of her. Then she kissed both Paula and Lisa on the top of the head.

'You look upset, love. This must be so hard for you. Why doesn't the doctor do something?'

'There's not much he can do. It will pass in time. Or so he hopes.' Paula took a big gulp of coffee.

'But have you been getting any sleep at all?'

'Not much. But I suppose it's my turn now. Johanna can't exactly show up for work after going night after night without any sleep,' she said, sighing heavily. Then she turned to Mellberg. 'So, how did it go yesterday?'

Mellberg was holding Leo on his lap and was totally focused on spreading jam on slices of Skogaholm rye bread. When Paula saw what her son was about to have for breakfast, she opened her mouth to say something, but then refrained.

'That might not be the best for him,' said Rita when she saw that Paula didn't have the energy to protest.

'There's nothing wrong with Skogaholm rye bread,' said Mellberg, defiantly taking a big bite. 'I grew up eating this bread. And jam? It's just berries. And berries have vitamins. Vitamins and oxidants. All good things for a growing boy.'

'Anti-oxidants,' Paula corrected him.

But Mellberg wasn't listening. What nonsense. Nobody needed to tell him anything about nutrition.

'Okay, but how did it go yesterday?' she repeated her question, realizing it was a losing battle to argue about breakfast food.

'Excellent. I ran the press conference in my usual authoritative and intelligent manner. We need to buy copies of the newspapers today.' He reached for yet another piece of bread. The first three were just for starters.

'I'm sure you were amazing. I wouldn't expect anything less.'

Mellberg cast a suspicious glance at Paula to see if there was any hint of sarcasm, but her face remained impassive.

'Aside from that, have you made any progress on

the case? Are there any leads? Do you know where she came from? Where she was being held captive?'

'No, nothing yet.'

Lisa started squirming, and Paula's expression showed how exhausted and frustrated she felt. Mellberg knew she hated to be left out of an investigation. It didn't come easy to her, being away from work on maternity leave, and this initial period hadn't exactly been tinged with maternal joy. He placed his hand on her knee and noticed through her pyjamas how thin she'd grown. She'd been practically living in pyjamas for weeks now.

'I promise to keep you updated. But at the moment we don't know much, and—' He was interrupted by a shrill shriek from Lisa. It was astounding that a tiny body could produce such a piercing scream.

'Okay, thanks,' said Paula, getting up. Moving like a sleepwalker, she began pacing the kitchen as she hummed softly to Lisa.

'Poor little thing,' said Mellberg, taking another slice of bread. 'It must be awful to have a tummy ache all the time. I'm lucky I was born with an iron stomach.'

Patrik was standing in front of the whiteboard in the station's kitchen. Next to it on the wall he'd tacked up a map of Sweden, and he had inserted pins to mark the places where the girls had disappeared. He suddenly had a flashback to a case from several years earlier, when they'd also stuck pins in a map of Sweden. Back then they'd successfully solved the case. He hoped they'd be able to do the same this time.

The investigative materials that Annika had collected from the other districts were now sorted into four piles on the table, one for each missing girl.

'It's impossible for us to proceed as if Victoria's death

is an isolated case. We need to make sure we stay updated regarding the other disappearances.'

Martin and Gösta nodded. Mellberg had arrived at the station but had almost immediately gone back out to take Ernst for a walk, which usually meant that he would be stopping at the local bakery. He'd most likely be gone for at least an hour. It was no coincidence that Patrik had chosen this particular moment to review the case with his other colleagues.

'Have you heard anything from Pedersen?' asked Gösta.

'No, but he said he'd phone as soon as he finished the autopsy,' replied Patrik. He picked up the first stack of documents. 'I know we've gone through everything before, but I want to go over the information about the other girls again, in chronological order. Maybe some new idea will turn up.'

He leafed through the papers and then turned to write the key points on the whiteboard.

'Sandra Andersson. Fourteen years old, about to turn fifteen when she disappeared two years ago. Lived in Strömsholm with her mother, father, and younger sister. The parents own a clothing shop. No sign of any family problems. According to everyone interviewed, Sandra was a conscientious teenager who received excellent marks in school. She was planning to become a doctor.'

Patrik held up the first photograph. Sandra was a brunette. Pretty in a quiet sort of way, with intelligent eyes and a serious expression.

'What were her other interests?' asked Martin. He took a sip of his coffee but grimaced at the taste and set the cup back on the table.

'Nothing special. She seemed to be totally focused on her studies.'

'And nothing suspicious that occurred before she disappeared?' asked Gösta. 'No anonymous phone calls?

Nobody sneaking about in the bushes? No letters arriving in the post?'

'Letters?' said Patrik. 'For someone like Sandra, it would be more likely that she'd get emails or text messages. Kids her age hardly know what a letter or a postcard is any more.'

Gösta snorted. 'I know that. I'm not that old and decrepit. But who's to say that the perpetrator is so up on things? Whoever did this might belong to the snail-mail generation. You didn't think of that, did you?' With a triumphant smile Gösta leaned back and crossed his legs.

Patrik reluctantly agreed that his colleague had a point. 'Nothing like that was reported,' he said. 'And the police in Strömsholm have been just as thorough in their investigation as we have. They've talked to her friends and classmates, searched her room and her computer, and looked into any other contacts she may have had. But they haven't found anything out of the ordinary.'

'That in itself seems fishy. A teenager who hasn't got into the slightest mischief?' muttered Gösta. 'Sounds unhealthy, if you ask me.'

'Personally, I think it sounds like a parent's dream,' said Patrik, thinking with dread about what might be awaiting him and Erica when Maja reached her teenage years. He'd seen too much in his line of work, and he felt his stomach clench at the thought of what lay ahead.

'Is that all?' Martin cast an anxious glance at the few words written on the whiteboard. 'Where did she disappear?'

'She was on her way home from visiting a friend. When she failed to return, her parents rang the police.'

Patrik didn't have to consult the papers. He'd already read them several times. He placed Sandra's stack of files aside and moved on to the next one.

'Jennifer Backlin. Fifteen years old. Disappeared from Falsterbo eighteen months ago. As in Sandra's case, there don't seem to have been any problems at home. She comes from a wealthy middle-class family; her father owns an investment firm, her mother is a housewife. One sister. Jennifer was an average student academically, but a promising athlete. She'd done well enough in gymnastics to win a place at a sports academy.' He showed the others a photo of a girl with brown hair, a nice smile, and big blue eyes.

'Did she have a boyfriend? Did Sandra?' said Gösta.

'Jennifer did have a boyfriend, but he's been cleared of any involvement. No boyfriend in Sandra's life.' Patrik reached for his glass of water and took a sip. 'The same situation in both cases: no one saw or heard anything. No conflicts in Jennifer's family or among her circle of friends. Nothing suspicious observed either before or after she disappeared, nothing online . . .'

Patrik began writing on the board, and the points were disturbingly similar to what he'd written about Sandra. Most striking of all was the lack of significant information or leads. Usually their enquiries would turn up someone who'd seen or heard something, but these girls seemed to have been swallowed up by the earth.

'Kim Nilsson. A little older than the other girls – sixteen. She disappeared from Västerås about a year ago. Her parents own an upmarket restaurant, and Kim sometimes helped out, along with her sister. No boyfriend. Good marks in school, no particular interests other than school. Like Sandra, she seemed focused on her studies. Her parents said that she dreamed of studying economics at university, and then wanted to run her own business.'

Yet another photo of a pretty girl with dark hair.

'Could we take a short break? I need to empty my bladder,' said Gösta. His joints creaked as he stood up, and Patrik was suddenly reminded that his colleague was fast approaching retirement age. To his surprise, he realized that he would miss Gösta. For years Patrik had been irritated by his colleague's tendency to opt for the course of least resistance and do only what was absolutely necessary. But he had also seen other sides of him, times when the older man demonstrated what a good police officer he really was. And under that gruff exterior of his, Gösta had a big heart.

Patrik turned to Martin. 'Okay, while we're waiting for Gösta, why don't you tell me about your interview with Marta. Did you find out anything?'

'No, not a thing.' Martin sighed. 'She didn't see anyone and no vehicles passed that way before Victoria came out of the woods. And there were none afterwards, other than the car that struck the girl. Marta and the driver both stayed with Victoria while they waited for the ambulance to arrive. I didn't learn anything new about her disappearance either. Apparently there have been no developments at the stable since the last time we talked to Marta.'

'What about Tyra?'

'Exactly the same as last time. But I did have a feeling that there was something she didn't want to share. As if she might have a suspicion, but she didn't dare tell me about it.'

'Huh,' said Patrik, frowning as he studied the notes he'd jotted down on the whiteboard, printed in bold letters. 'If that's true, let's hope she changes her mind soon. Do you think we ought to lean on her a bit?'

'I'm back,' Gösta announced as he sat down again. 'This damned prostate of mine has me running to the loo every fifteen minutes.'

Patrik held up his hand. 'Okay, thanks, but that's more than I want to know.'

'Are we done with Kim?' asked Martin.

'Yes. The information is pretty much the same as in the two other cases. Not a trace left behind. Nothing suspicious. Nothing at all. But it's a little different when we get to the fourth girl. It's the only instance when an eye witness reported seeing a suspicious individual.'

'Minna Wahlberg,' said Martin.

Patrik nodded, wrote down the name, and picked up a photo of a girl with blue eyes. Her brown hair was gathered in a messy topknot. 'Yes. Minna Wahlberg. Fourteen years old, from Göteborg. Disappeared about seven months ago. Her background is different from the other girls. Raised by a single mother, with lots of reports of trouble at home while Minna was growing up. Her mother's boyfriends were usually to blame. Minna's name started appearing in social welfare records for things like shoplifting and smoking hash. Unfortunately, it's the classic story of a young girl gone astray. She was frequently absent from school.'

'Any siblings?' asked Gösta.

'No. She lived alone with her mother.'

'You haven't added any comment about how Jennifer and Kim disappeared,' Gösta pointed out. Patrik turned to look at the board and realized he was right.

'Jennifer disappeared on her way home from school, after gymnastics practice. Kim disappeared near her home. She had gone out for a walk and planned to meet a friend, but she never turned up. In both cases the police were notified early on that the girls were missing.'

'But that didn't happen in Minna's case, did it?' said Martin.

'No. You're right. Minna hadn't been seen at school or home for three days when her mother realized that something was wrong and phoned the police. Clearly she didn't keep a close eye on her daughter. Minna came and went as she pleased. She would stay with various girlfriends or guys she knew. So wc don't know exactly what day Minna disappeared.'

'What about the witness?' Martin took another sip of coffee, and Patrik had to smile at his frown when he tasted the bitter brew, which had been sitting in the pot for hours.

'Damn it, Martin. Why don't you make some fresh coffee?' said Gösta. 'I could use a cup, and I'm sure Patrik could too.'

'Why don't you make it yourself?' Martin replied.

'Never mind. It's not necessary.'

'I don't think I've ever met anyone as lazy as you,' said Martin. 'Maybe it's your age.'

'Hey, I'm not that old.' Gösta often joked and grumbled about his age, but he didn't like it when anyone else alluded to it.

Patrik wondered what an outsider would think about the banter that went on between them, even during the most harrowing investigations. But it was something they all needed. Sometimes the work left them so weighed down that they had to take a moment to relax, tease each other, and laugh. That was how they coped with all the sorrow, death, and despair.

'Shall we go on? Where were we?'

'The witness,' Martin reminded him.

'Right. Well, this is the only case with a witness – an eighty-year-old woman. The information she provided is a bit hazy, and she had difficulty remembering the exact time, but it appears to have happened the first day Minna didn't return home. The witness stated that she saw Minna get into a small white car outside the ICA supermarket on Hisingen.'

'But she wasn't able to identify the type of car?' said Gösta.

'No, she wasn't. The Göteborg police have tried everything they can think of to get more details from her about the car, but it was no use. All she could tell them was that it was an "older white car".'

'And the witness didn't see who was sitting inside?' asked Martin, even though he already knew the answer.

'No. She thought it might be a young man sitting behind the wheel, but she couldn't say for sure.'

'I can't believe this,' said Gösta. 'How the hell can five teenage girls just disappear? Somebody must have seen something.'

'Well, so far no one has come forward,' replied Patrik. 'And that's in spite of all the media coverage. After all the column space the papers have devoted to the missing girls, you'd think someone would have contacted the police if they'd seen anything.'

'Either the perpetrator is extraordinarily clever, or he's so obsessive that he never leaves any evidence behind.' Martin was thinking aloud.

Patrik shook his head. 'I think there must be a pattern. I can't say why I think so, but it's there somewhere, and once we discover it . . .' He threw out his hands. 'By the way, have you had any luck finding someone to put together a psychological profile of the perpetrator for us?'

'Turns out it's not that straightforward,' Martin said. 'There aren't many specialists in that field, and most of them are booked up. But Annika just told me that she's found an expert who does profiling. A man named Gerhard Struwer. He's a criminologist at Göteborg University, and he can meet with us at his office this afternoon. She emailed him all the information we have. It's rather strange that the Göteborg police haven't already talked to him.'

'I don't think it's so strange. We're the only ones stupid enough to believe in that sort of thing. Next we'll be bringing in a fortune teller,' muttered Gösta, who shared Mellberg's opinion on the matter.

Patrik ignored his remarks.

'He might not be able to put together a profile, but he could still give us some guidance. Maybe we should also drop by and meet Minna's mother, since we'll be in Göteborg anyway. If the perpetrator was the driver of the car, Minna might have had a personal relationship with him – or her. That would explain why she got into the vehicle voluntarily.'

'Don't you think the Göteborg police must have already interviewed her mother?' said Martin.

'Sure, but I'd like to talk to her myself and see if we can find out anything more—'

Patrik was interrupted by the ringing of his mobile. He picked it up, glanced at the display, and then looked at his colleagues.

'It's Pedersen.'

With a grunt, Einar pulled himself up into a sitting position in bed. His wheelchair stood nearby, but he stuffed a pillow behind his back and stayed where he was. There was nowhere for him to go. This room was his world now, and that was enough for him, because in here he was able to live in his memories.

He heard Helga pottering about downstairs, and the revulsion he felt brought a metallic taste to his mouth. He found it disgusting to be so dependent on someone as pitiful as his wife. The balance of power had shifted so that she was now the strong one who could control his life instead of the other way round.

Helga had been special, filled with such joy and with such a light in her eyes. It had given him tremendous satisfaction to slowly extinguish that light. It had been gone a long time now, but when his health had betrayed him and he was confined to this prison that was his own body, something had changed. She was still a broken woman, but lately he'd caught the occasional glimpse of rebellion in her eyes. Barely discernible, but enough to annoy him.

He cast a glance at the wedding photograph that Helga had hung on the wall above the chest of drawers. In the black-and-white picture she was looking at him with a radiant smile, blithely unaware how her life would turn out with the man in the suit standing beside her. Back then he had been a handsome young fellow. Tall and blond with broad shoulders and steady blue eyes. Helga was also fair-skinned. Now her hair was grey, but in her youth she'd had long blond hair, pinned up under the bridal veil and myrtle wreath. Of course he was aware how lovely she was, but in many ways he found her even more beautiful later on, after he'd shaped her in accordance with his wishes. A cracked vase was more beautiful than one that was whole, and the cracks had occurred without much effort on his part.

He reached for the remote control. His huge stomach was in the way, and he was filled with hatred for his body. It had been transformed into something that bore no resemblance whatsoever to the person he once was. But when he closed his eyes he always pictured himself as young. Everything was as clear to him now as it had been back then: the touch of the silky skin of all the women, the feel of their shiny long hair, their breath in his ear, the sound that had made him so hot and excited. The memories freed him from the prison of this bedroom, where the wallpaper had faded and the curtains had remained unchanged for decades. These four walls that now enclosed his worthless body.

Jonas sometimes came to help him, lifting Einar over to his wheelchair and carefully pushing it down the ramp on the stairs. Jonas was strong, just as strong as he had once been. But the brief excursions outdoors didn't give him much joy. It felt as if his memories became diminished and faded outside, as if the sun on his face made him forget. So he preferred to stay here in this room, where he was able to keep his memories alive.

The light in her study was dim even though it was still morning. Erica was sitting at her desk, staring straight ahead and getting nothing done. Her experience the previous day was still haunting her: the darkness in the cellar, the bedroom with the bolt on the door. And she couldn't stop thinking about what Patrik had said about Victoria. She had followed the course of the investigation as he and his colleagues had tried to find the missing girl, and now Patrik had told her about what had happened to Victoria. Erica's heart ached at the thought of what her death must mean for her family and friends. But what if she'd never been found? How could any parent live with something like that?

Four other girls were still missing, vanished without a trace. Maybe they were dead and would never be seen again. Their families were living with the loss round the clock, wondering and agonizing, still hoping, even though they knew there was no hope. Erica shivered. She suddenly felt chilled, so she got up from her desk chair and went into the bedroom to put on a pair of heavy socks. She decided to ignore the mess. The bed had not been made, and clothes were scattered about. On one bedside table was a glass containing Patrik's mouth guard, which was gathering bacteria. The table on her side of the bed was cluttered with bottles of decongestant spray. Ever since she was pregnant with the twins she'd become dependent on decongestant spray, and the right time to quit never seemed to present itself. She'd tried it before, so she knew quitting would involve three days of hell when she could hardly breathe. So it had been all too easy to go back to using the spray. She could understand why it must be a struggle to quit smoking once you were hooked, or for an addict to stop using drugs. She couldn't even wean herself from something as banal as an addiction to decongestants.

The very thought made her nose close up, so she went over to the nightstand and shook several of the little bottles until she found one that wasn't empty. Then she sprayed twice in each nostril. The sensation when her nasal passages cleared was almost like an orgasm. Patrik liked to joke that if she ever had to choose between Sinex and sex, he would have to get himself a mistress.

Erica smiled. The thought of Patrik with a lover seemed so ridiculous. First, because he would never dare. Second, because she knew how much he loved her, even though daily life all too often put a damper on romance. The burning passion from their first years together had long since faded, to be replaced by a more serene glow. They knew each other so well, and she loved the sense of security their marriage gave her.

Erica went back to her study. The thick socks were blissfully warm, and she tried once again to focus on what was on her computer screen. But today seemed to be one of those days when it was impossible to concentrate.

Listlessly she scrolled through the document she had opened on her computer. She was having a hard time making any progress with her book, which of course was largely due to Laila's unwillingness to cooperate. Without the assistance of the key players she couldn't write her true crime books – at least, not in the way she would like. Merely repeating what was recorded in the investigative reports and describing the police procedures wouldn't lend flesh-and-blood to her account. She was looking for emotions and thoughts, everything that had gone unsaid. And in this instance, Laila was the only one who could tell her what had actually happened. Louise was dead, Vladek was dead, and Peter had disappeared. In spite of persistent attempts, Erica had been unable to locate him, and it was doubtful that he'd be able to tell her much about that day. He'd been only four years old when his father was murdered.

Erica closed the document, annoyed. Her thoughts returned to the current police cases, to Victoria and the other missing girls. Maybe it wouldn't be such a bad idea to spend some more time thinking about them. She often found it energizing to put aside her own work and deal with something else for a while. And she wasn't tempted to use her free time doing the laundry.

She opened a desk drawer and took out a pad of Post-it notes. She had used them so many times before when she needed to bring some sort of order to her thoughts. After opening a web browser, she began searching for articles. The disappearance of the girls had been front-page news on a number of occasions, and it was easy to find the information she was looking for. She wrote their names on five different notes, using a different colour for each, in order to keep the cases separate. Then she used more Post-it notes to write down the rest of the basic information: hometown, age, names of parents and siblings, time and place of disappearance, interests. She stuck the notes on the wall, one column for each girl. She felt a pang in her stomach as she stared at them. Each column represented indescribable sorrow and grief. A parent's worst nightmare.

She sensed that something was missing. She wanted to put a face to each girl's name. So she printed out photos, which were also easy to find on the newspaper websites. She wondered how many extra copies of the papers they had sold when they reported on the disappearances, but quickly dismissed such a cynical thought. The newspapers were just doing their job, and she was in no position to criticize them, given that she made a living by writing about other people's tragedies – and her books offered a much more detailed and in-depth description than the newspapers ever could.

Finally she printed out a map of Sweden in several sections, which she then taped together. She hung it up beside the Post-it notes and used a red pen to mark the places where the girls had disappeared.

She got up and took a step back. She now had a basic structure, or skeleton. Years of research had taught her that answers could often be found by simply getting to know the victim. What was it about these girls that had made the perpetrator single them out? She didn't believe in coincidence. The girls shared something more than appearance and age, something about their personality or living situation. What was the common denominator?

She stared at the five faces in the photographs on the wall. So much hope, so much curiosity about what life had to offer. Her eyes settled on one of the photos and suddenly knew where she should begin.

Laila spread out the newspaper clippings and felt her heart start pounding wildly. It was a physical reaction to psychological anxiety. Faster and faster, a sense of powerlessness quickening her pulse until there seemed to be no oxygen left.

She tried to take several deep breaths, drawing in as much as she could of the stale air in the small room, forcing her heart to slow down. Over the years she had taught herself a great deal about handling fear, so she knew what to do when the panic attacks came, without seeking help from a therapist or drugs. In the beginning she had taken all the pills they gave her, downing anything that might allow her to disappear into the fog of forgetting, where she could no longer see the evil. But when nightmares began slipping inside the fog, she had stopped the medication. She handled the nightmares best when her mind was clear and alert. If she lost control, anything might happen. And all her secrets might then seep out.

The oldest newspaper clippings had started to yellow. They were creased and wrinkled from being folded up in the little box that she'd managed to hide under her bed. Whenever it was cleaning day, she would tuck it away in her clothes.

Her eyes scanned the words. It wasn't necessary for her to read them, since she knew these texts by heart. Only the more recent articles required closer attention because she hadn't yet read them often enough to commit the words to memory. She ran her hand over her cropped hair. It still felt strange. She'd had her long hair cut short during the first year in prison. She didn't know why. Maybe it was her way of creating a distance, signalling an end. Ulla would no doubt have some theory to explain it, but Laila hadn't asked her. There was no reason to go rooting around in anything concerning herself. For the most part she knew why things had turned out the way they had. She had all the answers in her possession.

Talking with Erica was like playing with fire. She would never have sought out someone to talk to, but Erica had made contact just as another clipping had been added to the collection in the box, so she was probably feeling especially vulnerable that day. Laila didn't remember the details. The only thing she recalled was that she had surprised even herself by agreeing to a visit.

Erica had arrived that very same day. And even though Laila didn't know at the time – and still didn't – whether she would ever respond to Erica's questions, she had met with her, talked to her, and listened to the queries, which hovered unanswered in the visitor's room. Sometimes the panic would return after Erica's visits. She was aware that it was becoming urgent, that she needed to tell someone about the evil, and that Erica might be the right person to hear her story. But it was so hard to open the door that had been closed for so long.

Yet she looked forward to the visits. Erica asked the same questions as everyone else, but she did so in a different way. Not with a ghoulish desire to hear all the scandalous details, but with genuine interest. Maybe that was why Laila continued to see her. Or maybe it was because she knew that eventually she had to tell someone what she knew. She was starting to fear what might happen if she didn't.

Tomorrow Erica would come to see her again. The staff had told Laila that she had requested another visit. Laila merely nodded at the news.

She placed the newspaper clippings back in the box, folding them up in precisely the same way so no new creases would appear. Then she closed the lid. Her heart was again beating calmly.

Patrik went over to the printer and with trembling hands picked up the sheet of paper. He was overcome with waves of nausea, and he had to pause for a moment before he walked down the narrow corridor to Mellberg's office. He knocked on the closed door.

'What is it?' called Mellberg, sounding annoyed. He had just come back from his purported walk, and Patrik surmised that he was now settling down to take a nap.

'It's Patrik. I have Pedersen's report, and I thought you'd want to see the results of the autopsy.' He resisted an impulse to yank open the door. He had done that once, only to find his boss snoring away, clad only in a pair of worn underpants. That was the sort of mistake he didn't want to repeat.

'Come in,' said Mellberg after a moment.

When Patrik entered the room he saw his boss sitting at his desk and making a show of going through some papers to indicate he was a busy man. Patrik sat down in the visitor's chair, and was immediately greeted by Ernst, who emerged from his usual place under the desk. The dog had been named after a former colleague who had now passed away. Patrik had never been one to speak ill of the dead, but he couldn't help thinking the dog was considerably more likeable than his namesake.

'Hi, fella,' he said, scratching Ernst's head.

'You're white as a sheet,' said Mellberg. It was unusual for him to be so observant.

'It's not very pleasant reading.' Patrik placed the printout in front of Mellberg. 'Do you want to read through it yourself, or should I summarize the main points?'

'Sure. Go ahead. Let's hear it,' said Mellberg, leaning back in his chair.

'I hardly know where to begin.' Patrik cleared his throat. 'She lost her eyes because someone poured acid on them. The wounds had healed; judging by the scar formation, Pedersen thinks it was done shortly after Victoria was kidnapped.'

'Bloody hell.' Mellberg leaned forward and propped his elbows on his desk.

'Her tongue was severed with a sharp tool of some description. Pedersen couldn't say exactly what was used, but he reckoned it could have been done with shears, a hacksaw, or something of that nature. Probably not a knife.' Patrik could hear how gruesome his words sounded, and Mellberg looked sick to his stomach.

'In addition, a sharp object had been inserted into both

ears, doing enough damage that Victoria had also lost her hearing.' He reminded himself to tell Erica about this. Her idea of a girl in a bubble had turned out to be accurate.

Mellberg stared at him. 'So you're saying that she couldn't see, hear, or speak?' he queried.

'That's right,' said Patrik.

For a moment neither of them said anything. They were trying to imagine what it must feel like to lose three such important senses, to be imprisoned in a silent and impenetrable darkness without the ability to communicate.

'Bloody hell,' Mellberg said again. Then the silence in the room continued. There were simply no words to express what they were thinking. Ernst gave a little yelp and gazed at them uneasily. He could sense the heavy mood that had descended over them, but he didn't know why.

'All of these injuries probably occurred right after she was captured. And she was mostly likely kept bound. Her wrists and ankles bore scars from a rope. Some were old, some were new. She also had bedsores.'

Now even Mellberg's face had gone pale.

'The toxicology report is also available,' Patrik added. 'There were traces of ketamine in her blood.'

'What's that?'

'Ketamine is a sedative. Classified as a narcotic.'

'Why would she have something like that in her blood?'

'Hard to say, but according to Pedersen, the effect can vary, depending on the dosage. With a higher dose the individual will be unconscious and feel no pain. A lower dose can provoke psychosis and hallucinations. Who knows what effect the perpetrator was intending. Maybe both.'

'And where would someone get hold of this narcotic?'

'Drug dealers sell it, just like any other narcotic, but

it's a speciality drug. You have to know how to use it and what dose to take. Kids who ingest it in nightclubs don't want to get knocked out for a whole night, which happens if they take too much. So it's often mixed with ecstasy. But generally it's used mostly in hospitals. And as an anaesthetic for animals. Especially horses.'

'Shit,' said Mellberg when he made the connection. 'Have we taken a close look at that veterinarian, Jonas?'

'Of course. Victoria disappeared after leaving their stable. But he has a solid alibi. At the time he was out on an emergency call. The owners of the sick horse confirmed that he arrived only fifteen minutes after Victoria was last seen at the stable, and he stayed for several hours. We didn't find any link between him and the other missing girls.'

'But in light of what we've just learned, don't you think we ought to put him under the microscope?'

'Definitely. When I told the others, Gösta recalled that there had been a break-in at Jonas's office some time ago. He's checking the incident report to see if ketamine is mentioned. But the question is whether Jonas might have reported the theft as a cover in case he was asked to account for the missing ketamine. No matter what, we need to have another talk with him.'

Patrik paused for a moment before continuing.

'There's one more thing. I thought Martin and I should take a little trip today.'

'Oh?' said Mellberg. He looked up sharply, on the alert at the prospect of additional expenses being incurred.

'I want to drive to Göteborg to have a talk with Minna Wahlberg's mother. And while we're there . . .'

'Yes?' Mellberg sounded suspicious.

'Well, since we'll be there already, we can take the opportunity to talk to a man who might be able to help us by analysing the perpetrator's behaviour.'

'You mean one of those psychology guys?' Mellberg's expression betrayed exactly what he thought of that particular profession.

'I know it's a long shot, but it won't entail any extra expense since we're going to Göteborg for another purpose.'

'Okay, okay. Just don't try and drag in some fortune teller too,' muttered Mellberg, which reminded Patrik how much he and Gösta had in common. 'And for God's sake don't step on any toes at the Göteborg police station. You know as well as I do how territorial they are. So be careful.'

'I'll handle them with kid gloves,' replied Patrik as he left the room, closing the door behind him. Before long Mellberg's loud snoring would be echoing down the corridor.

Erica knew full well that she could be impulsive. Occasionally too impulsive. At least, that was Patrik's opinion. According to him, she had a tendency to get mixed up in things that were none of her business. Yet she had frequently helped him with his investigations, so he really shouldn't complain.

This was one of those instances when he would probably say she shouldn't get involved. And for that reason, she wasn't planning to tell him in advance. Instead, she would wait and see if her expedition turned out to be productive. If not, she could just offer the same excuse she'd given to her mother-in-law, Kristina, who had been summoned on short notice to babysit for the kids. Erica had told her that she needed to meet with her agent in Göteborg to discuss a contract with a German publisher.

She put on her jacket, grimacing as she glanced around. It looked as if a bomb had exploded inside the house. Kristina would have a few things to say about the mess, and Erica would no doubt receive a long lecture about the importance of keeping her home neat and tidy. Strangely enough, Kristina never lectured her son on that topic. She seemed to think that he, as the man of the house, was above such chores. And Patrik seemed to have no objections to his mother's way of thinking.

No, now I'm being unfair, thought Erica. Patrik was amazing in so many ways. He did his share of the housework without complaint, and he took on an equal amount of responsibility for the children. Yet she still couldn't say that they were a hundred per cent equal. She was the one who acted as team leader, the one who noticed when the children had outgrown their clothes and needed new things. She was the one who knew when they were supposed to take a packed lunch to the day-care centre, and when it was time for them to have their vaccinations. And she kept track of thousands of other things. She noticed when the laundry detergent was nearly gone, and when it was time to buy more nappies. She knew which lotion worked best when the twins had a rash, and she always knew where Maja had left her current favourite stuffed animal. Such concerns came naturally to her, while Patrik found it impossible to keep track of such things. She wasn't sure he even tried. In the back of her mind Erica always had a suspicion that he was more than happy to leave everything to her, but she had chosen not to dwell on that thought. Instead, she had accepted the role of team leader, grateful that her husband was willing to take on whatever tasks she assigned to him. Many of her women friends were not as lucky.

When she opened the front door, the cold air almost made her step back. What a freezing winter they were having. She hoped the roads wouldn't be too slippery. She was not especially fond of driving, and she got behind the wheel only when it was absolutely necessary.

Erica turned to lock the door behind her. Kristina had a key, which was both good and bad, but she willingly gave a hand with the children if she was needed. Erica frowned as she walked to the car. Kristina had asked if it was all right to bring along a friend, since Erica had asked for help without giving her much notice. Her mother-in-law had a busy social life and many female friends who sometimes came with her to babysit, so her request wasn't all that strange. But there had been something odd about the way Kristina had said the word 'friend'. Was it possible that for the first time since her divorce from Patrik's father, Kristina had met a new man?

The thought amused Erica, and she smiled as she turned the key in the ignition. Patrik would go through the roof. He had no problem with the fact that his father had remarried long ago, but it was a different story when it came to his mother. Whenever Erica had teased him by saying she was going to sign up Kristina for an online dating service, Patrik looked worried. But it was time for him to accept that his mother had her own life. Erica giggled as she started driving towards Göteborg.

Jonas wore an exasperated expression as he briskly tidied the veterinary clinic. He was still annoyed that Marta had said no to the jump racing competition. Molly should have been allowed to compete. He knew how important it was to his daughter, and her disappointment cut him to the quick.

When she was younger, it had been extremely convenient to have his office in their home. He hadn't trusted Marta to take care of Molly properly, so when he was working he used to take a break between patients to check that his daughter was all right.

Unlike Marta, he had wanted a child, someone to carry on the family. He wanted to see himself in the child, and for that reason he'd always imagined having a son. But then Molly had arrived. Even right after her birth he was amazed by the emotions that had overwhelmed him. Emotions he didn't know were possible.

Marta, on the other hand, had placed the infant in his arms with an impassive expression. The hint of envy in her eyes had quickly disappeared. He had expected her to feel that way. Marta was his, and he was hers. But with time she would realize that the child wouldn't change anything; on the contrary, having a daughter would bring them closer.

The first time he saw Marta, he knew that she was perfect for him. She was his twin, his soul mate. Such words were used far too often, to the point of being clichés, but in their case the words were true. Their only difference of opinion was regarding Molly. Yet for his sake, Marta had tried her best. She had raised their daughter according to his wishes, and she had allowed Jonas and Molly to have their relationship in peace. She, in turn, devoted all her energy to her relationship with her husband.

He hoped that Marta realized how much he loved her, and how important she was to him. He was constantly trying to show her this. He was forbearing, and allowed her to take part in everything. On only one occasion had he harboured any doubts. For a moment he had sensed a chasm open up between them, a threat to the symbiosis that had marked their life together for so long. But that doubt was now gone.

Jonas smiled as he straightened a box containing latex gloves. He knew there were so many reasons he should be grateful. And he was.

When Mellberg attached the lead to Ernst's collar, the dog eagerly dashed for the front door of the police station.

Annika glanced up from her desk in the reception area, and Mellberg explained that he was going home to have lunch. Then with a great sense of relief he stepped outside. As soon as the door fell shut, he took in a deep breath. After what Hedström had told him, his office had suddenly felt cramped and stifling.

By the time he reached the building where he lived, he was feeling better. The fresh air had cleared his mind. He'd come round to thinking that this new case could turn out to be a positive development, offering him an opportunity to show off his detecting skills.

'Hello?' he called as he stepped inside the flat. Paula's shoes were in the hall, which meant she and Lisa were visiting.

'We're in the kitchen,' replied Rita. Mellberg removed the dog's lead so Ernst could run in and say hello to Señorita. Then he stomped the snow from his shoes, hung up his jacket, and followed the dog inside.

Rita was setting the kitchen table for lunch while Paula was rummaging through a cupboard. Lisa was snuggled in a baby carrier on her mother's stomach.

'We ran out of coffee downstairs,' Paula explained.

'In the back on the right,' Rita told her, pointing. 'I'll set a place for you too. You might as well have some lunch, now that you're here.'

'Thanks. That would be nice. So how's it going at the station?' said Paula, holding a packet of coffee in her hand as she turned to face Mellberg. The coffee was exactly where Rita had said it would be. Her kitchen was organized with military precision.

Mellberg wondered whether he should relay the autopsy results to a woman who was both exhausted and a nursing mother. But he knew that Paula would be furious if she later found out that he had withheld information. So he briefly told her what Patrik had reported.

Standing at the worktop, Rita froze for a moment but then continued to take cutlery from the drawer.

'My God, that's awful,' said Paula, sitting down at the kitchen table. She absentmindedly rubbed Lisa's back. 'Did you say her tongue had been cut off?'

Mellberg pricked up his ears. He had to admit that Paula had on occasion shown an aptitude for police work, and she also had a phenomenal memory.

'What are you thinking?' He sat down on a chair next to her with an eager expression.

Paula shook her head.

'I'm not sure. But it reminds me of something. Hmm . . . This damn brain of mine. All this nursing is making my mind fuzzy! It's driving me crazy!'

'It'll pass,' said Rita. She was putting together a big salad.

'I know, but it's so annoying,' said Paula. 'Anyway, there's something familiar about the fact that her tongue was cut off.'

'I'm sure it will come to you if you just let it go for a while,' Rita told her.

'Hmm, maybe,' replied Paula. Mellberg could see that she was wracking her brain. 'I wonder if it's something I read in an old police report. Is it okay if I drop by the station later on?'

'You can't be planning on taking Lisa over there when it's so cold outside!' Rita objected. 'Besides, you're not supposed to be working. Not when you're so tired.'

'I can just as well be tired over there as here,' said Paula. 'And do you think Lisa could stay here with you? I won't be gone long. I just want to have a look in the archives.'

Rita muttered something inaudible, but Mellberg knew she would be more than happy to babysit Lisa, even though there was a risk the baby might have one of her crying spells. He thought Paula was actually looking a bit more alert at the mere thought of going over to the station.

'I'd also like to have access to the autopsy report while I'm there,' she said. 'Hope that's okay, even though I'm officially on maternity leave.'

Mellberg snorted. It made no difference whether she was on leave or not. He had no idea what the rules were, but if he paid attention to all the rules and regulations regarding work places in general and the police force in particular, he'd never get anything done.

'Annika has the report, along with all the other case materials. Just ask her to show it to you.'

'Great. I think I'll take a shower before going over there, for my sake and for everyone else's.'

'But first you need to eat lunch,' said Rita.

'Sure, Mamma.'

Enticing aromas were filling the kitchen, making Mellberg's stomach growl. Rita was a phenomenal cook. Her only fault was that she rarely served dessert. In his mind's eye he pictured the pastry case in the local bakery. He'd already stopped by once today, but maybe he could nip in on his way back to the station. No meal was complete without something sweet to finish it off.

Gösta no longer expected much from life. His uncle always used to say that if you can keep your feet and head warm, then you should be content. These days Gösta was starting to understand what his uncle meant. It was important not to make too many demands. And ever since Ebba had come back into his life after the strange events of the past summer, he had been much more content. She had moved back to Göteborg, and for a while he'd worried that she might disappear again, reluctant to stay in contact with an old codger she'd known for a brief period when she was a child. But she got in touch with him every so often, and whenever she came to see her mother in Fjällbacka, she would always stop by to see him too. Of course Ebba was feeling fragile after what she'd been through, but each time he saw her, she seemed stronger. He sincerely hoped that her wounds would heal and that one day her faith in love would be restored. Maybe sometime in the future she would meet a new man and become a mother again. And maybe, with a little luck, he'd be a stand-in grandfather and once again have a chance to pamper a child. That was his greatest dream: to walk among the raspberry bushes in his garden at home, with a child at his side, a child who, with tottering steps and holding his hand, would help him pick the sweet berries.

But for now that had to remain a daydream. In the meantime he needed to concentrate on the investigation. He shivered at the thought of what Patrik had told him about Victoria's injuries, but forced himself to set aside his feelings of revulsion. He couldn't afford to let emotion cloud his judgement. He'd seen plenty of misery during his years as a police officer, and even though the ugliness of this case surpassed any other he'd encountered, the principle remained the same: he needed to do his job.

Gösta skimmed over the report, digesting the contents. Then he went next door to Patrik's office.

'Jonas reported the break-in only a few days before Victoria disappeared. And ketamine was one of the substances purportedly stolen. I'd like to drive over to have a talk with him while you and Martin go to Göteborg.'

He saw Patrik's look of surprise, and even though he felt rather insulted, he could understand it. He hadn't always been the most industrious member of the team, and to be honest he still wasn't. But he was a capable officer, and lately he'd had a renewed sense of determination. He wanted to make Ebba proud. Besides, he sympathized with the anguish of the Hallberg family after several months as their police liaison.

'It sounds as though there's a strong possibility the two events are connected. Good job,' said Patrik. 'But do you want to go there alone? If not, I could go with you tomorrow.'

Gösta waved a hand in dismissal. 'It's okay. I can handle it. It's no big deal, and I was the one who filed the original report. Good luck in Göteborg.' He gave Patrik a curt nod and left to go out to his car.

It took only five minutes to drive to the farm. He turned in to the yard and parked near the house belonging to Marta and Jonas.

'Knock, knock,' he said as he opened the door at the back of the house.

The veterinary clinic wasn't large. A minuscule waiting room, not much bigger than an entryway, in addition to a kitchenette and treatment room.

'No boa constrictors, spiders, or other creepy animals, I hope,' he joked when he caught sight of Jonas.

'Hi, Gösta. No, don't worry. There aren't many creatures like that in Fjällbacka, thank goodness.'

'Could I come in for a minute?' Gösta stepped inside, wiping his shoes on the mat.

'Of course. I don't have another patient for an hour. Doesn't look as though it's going to be one of my busier days. Take off your coat. Would you like some coffee?'

'That would be great. Thanks. Unless it's too much bother?'

Jonas shook his head and went to the kitchenette. Gösta could see an expensive-looking coffeemaker on the worktop.

'I invested in this luxury for the sake of my own sanity. Strong or weak? Milk? Sugar?'

'Strong, with milk and sugar. Thanks.' Gösta took off his jacket and sat down in one of the two visitor's chairs.

'Here you are.' Jonas handed Gösta a cup and sat down across from him. 'I assume this is about Victoria.'

'Not exactly. I wanted to ask you about the break-in you had here.'

Jonas raised his eyebrows. 'I thought you wrote up a report about that. I have to admit I've been a little disappointed that the police haven't made any progress with that matter, even though I realize that Victoria's case has to be your top priority. Can you tell me why you're suddenly so interested in the break-in?'

'I'm afraid not,' said Gösta. 'How did you discover that someone had broken in? I know we've already gone over this, but I'd like to hear it again, if you don't mind.' He waved his hand apologetically and almost knocked over his coffee cup. He caught it as it started to tip and then picked it up, just to be on the safe side.

'Well, as I already said, when I came over here in the morning, I found the door had been forced. That was about nine o'clock. That's my usual starting time, because people rarely want to come any earlier. At any rate, I could tell immediately that the place had been burgled.'

'And how did it look inside?'

'Not too bad, actually. Some things had been pulled out of the cupboards and were scattered over the floor, but that's about it. The worst part was that the cabinet where I keep substances classified as narcotics had been smashed open. And I'm always so careful to keep it locked. There's not much crime in Fjällbacka to worry about, but the few junkies who do exist probably know that I keep drugs in the clinic. I've never had any problems before though.'

'I know who you mean, and we had a talk with them right after the break-in. We didn't get anything out of them, and I don't think they would have been able to keep their mouths shut if they'd managed to get into the clinic. None of the fingerprints matched theirs.'

'In that case it must have been someone else.'

'So what exactly was missing? I realize it's in the report, but tell me again.'

Jonas frowned. 'I can't remember all the details, but the controlled substances included ethyl morphine, ketamine, and codeine. Plus a number of medical supplies, like gauze bandages, antiseptics, and . . . latex gloves, if I recall. Ordinary, cheap supplies that you could buy in any chemist's shop.'

'Unless you wanted to avoid attracting attention because you were buying large quantities of medical supplies,' said Gösta, thinking aloud.

'Sure. I suppose that's true.' Jonas drank the last of his coffee, then stood up to get some more. 'Would you like a refill?'

'No, thanks. I have plenty,' said Gösta, realizing that he had forgotten all about drinking his coffee. 'Tell me more about the controlled substances. Would any of them be of special interest to a drug addict?'

'Ketamine definitely would. I've heard it's starting to be popular among junkies. It's apparently known as Special K, as a party drug.'

'What do you use it for in your veterinary practice?'

'Vets and physicians both use it as an anaesthetic for surgical procedures. If you use ordinary anaesthetics, there's a risk of heart attack and respiration slows. But ketamine doesn't have that side effect.'

'What type of animals do you use it on?'

'Mostly dogs and horses. It's a way to sedate them safely and effectively.'

Gösta stretched out his legs. His joints were feeling more and more creaky and stiff for every winter that passed. 'How much ketamine was taken?'

'If I remember right, we're talking about four bottles that each contained a hundred millilitres.'

'Is that a lot? How much would you use for a horse, for example?'

'That depends on the weight of the horse,' said Jonas. 'But we usually estimate about two millilitres per hundred kilos.'

'What about for a human being?'

'I'm not sure. You'd have to ask a surgeon or anaesthesiologist, they'd be able to give you the precise dosage. I took a few courses in general medicine, but that was years ago. I know about animals, not people. Why are you so interested in ketamine?'

Gösta hesitated. He wasn't sure he ought to say anything that would give away the true purpose of his visit. At the same time, he was curious to see how Jonas would react. If it turned out, contrary to all expectations, that he was the one who had used the ketamine and reported it stolen simply to divert suspicion, then maybe his expression would give him away.

'We've received the autopsy report,' Gösta told him. 'Victoria had traces of ketamine in her body.'

Jonas looked startled. Gösta saw both surprise and horror in his eyes. 'Are you saying that you think the ketamine that was stolen from my clinic may have been used to kidnap her?'

'At this point we can't say for sure, but considering it was stolen only days before she disappeared, and close to where she was last seen, it certainly seems possible.'

Jonas shook his head. 'That's terrible.'

'So you have no idea who might have broken in? You didn't notice anything suspicious either before or afterwards?'

'No. I have no clue. As I said, this is the first time it's ever happened. I've always been very careful about locking things up.'

'And you don't think any of the girls would have . . .?' Gösta motioned towards the stable.

'No, absolutely not. They've probably tried out some home brew in secret a few times, and no doubt they've smoked a cigarette or two. But none of them is worldly wise enough to know that veterinarians keep controlled substances that could be used as party drugs. Talk to them, if you like, but I can promise you that none of them has ever heard of ketamine.'

'I'm sure you're right,' murmured Gösta. He tried to think of more questions to ask, and Jonas seemed to notice his hesitation.

'Is there anything else you want to know?' Jonas gave him a crooked smile. 'If not, maybe we can talk more some other time. I've got to see to my next patient. Nelly the mouse has eaten something that made her sick.'

'Oh.' Gösta wrinkled his nose in disgust. 'I can't understand why people want to keep creatures like that as pets.'

'I can think of worse things,' said Jonas, shaking his hand firmly as they said goodbye.

UDDEVALLA 1968

From the very beginning she realized that things were not as they should be. It was as if something essential was missing. Laila couldn't put her finger on it, and she seemed to be the only one who noticed. Time after time she tried to talk to Vladek about her concern, suggesting they should let a doctor examine the little girl. But he refused to listen. Their daughter was so sweet, so calm. There was nothing wrong with her.

Eventually the signs became more obvious. The girl's face was always so sombre, and Laila kept waiting for the first smile, but it never came. Then even Vladek began to sense that something wasn't right, but still no one took it seriously. At the child welfare office Laila was told it could be various things, that there was no set template, and each child developed differently. But she was certain that something would always be missing in their daughter.

The girl never cried. Sometimes Laila couldn't help pinching her, shaking her, anything that might provoke a reaction. When the child was awake, she would lie quietly and stare at the world with an expression so dark that it made Laila flinch. It was a primeval darkness, not only in her eyes but radiating from her whole body.

Becoming a mother was not what she had imagined it would be. The images she had conjured up, the emotions she had thought she would experience when the child lay in her arms – none of them matched reality. She sensed this was because of the child, but she was the girl's mother. And a mother's task was to protect her child, no matter what happened.

Riding in the car with Patrik was as terrifying as usual. Martin had a tight grip on the handle of the passenger door, and he offered up repeated prayers, even though he wasn't at all religious.

'The roads are in good condition today,' said Patrik.

They passed Kville church, and he slowed down a bit as they drove through the small community. But he soon accelerated again, and when they came to a sharp bend a couple of kilometres further on, Martin was flung so hard against the door that his cheek ended up pressed against the window.

'You can't take the curves so fast, Patrik! I don't care what your old driving instructor told you when you were learning to drive. That's not the way to do it.'

'I'm an excellent driver,' muttered Patrik, but he did ease up for a while. They'd had this conversation before, and no doubt they'd have it many more times in the future.

'How's Tuva?' he asked then, giving his colleague a nervous look.

Martin wished that people wouldn't be so timid around him. He didn't mind the questions. On the contrary. It showed that they cared about him and Tuva. And asking questions wouldn't make things any worse. The worst had already happened. Nor did the questions open new wounds. The same wounds were ripped open every evening when he put his daughter to bed and she asked for her mother. And again when he tried to sleep, lying on his side of the bed, next to the empty space that used to be Pia's. And every time he picked up the phone to call home to ask what groceries he should buy, and then realized that she would never be there to answer.

'Tuva seems to be doing fine. She asks for Pia, of course, but mostly she just wants me to talk about her mother. She seems to have accepted that Pia is gone. In that sense I think children are wiser than we are.' Then he fell silent.

'I can't even imagine what I'd do if Erica had died,' said Patrik quietly.

Martin knew that he was thinking about what had happened a couple of years earlier, when both Erica and the unborn twins had almost died in a car accident.

'I don't know if I would have been able to go on.' Patrik's voice quavered at the memory of that day when he'd nearly lost her.

'Yes, you would,' said Martin, staring at the snowy landscape they were passing. 'You have to. And there's always someone to live for. You would have had Maja. Tuva is everything to me now, and Pia lives on through her.'

'Do you think you'll ever meet someone else?'

Martin noticed that Patrik had hesitated before asking the question, as if it might be a forbidden topic.

'Right now I can't imagine anything like that, but it's also hard to picture myself spending the rest of my life alone. If it happens, it happens. At the moment I have my hands full trying to find some sort of balance in life for me and Tuva. We're doing our best to fill the emptiness that Pia left behind. Besides, it's not just a matter of me being ready for a new relationship; Tuva also has to be ready to let someone else into our family.'

'Sounds sensible,' said Patrik. Then he grinned. 'Besides, there aren't many girls left in Tanum. You ran through most of them before you met Pia. So you'll have to expand your search area unless you're interested in reruns.'

'Ha, ha. Very funny.' Martin could feel himself blushing. Patrik was exaggerating, but he did have a point. Martin had never been a hunk in the conventional sense, but his boyish charm combined with his red hair and freckles had ensured that the girls always found him attractive. But when he met Pia, he had put an end to his flirting. He'd never even glanced at another girl after that. He had loved her so much, and he missed her every second of every day.

Suddenly he couldn't bear to talk about his wife any more. The pain he felt was so fierce and merciless that he had to change the subject. Patrik got the message, and for the rest of the drive to Göteborg they talked about nothing but sport.

Erica hesitated for a moment before ringing the doorbell. It was always difficult to decide how to start up a conversation with a family member, but Minna's mother had sounded so calm and pleasant on the phone. She didn't have the sharp or sceptical tone of voice that so many did whenever Erica contacted family members with regard to a book she was writing. And this time she wanted to talk about an ongoing case and not one that had been solved long ago.

She pressed the bell. A few moments later she heard footsteps approaching, and then the door opened halfway.

'Hello?' Erica ventured. 'Are you Anette?'

'Yes. But call me Nettan,' replied the woman and then stood aside to let her in.

The word 'mournful' was what instantly came to mind when Erica stepped inside the front hall. Both the woman and the flat seemed mournful, and this was probably not due solely to Minna's disappearance. The woman standing in front of her seemed to have given up hope long ago, crushed by all the disappointments that life had presented.

'Come in,' said Nettan and led the way to the living room.

Things lay scattered about, as if they had landed there and then never moved. Nettan cast an anxious glance at a pile of clothes on the sofa and then simply shoved everything on to the floor.

'I was planning to do some cleaning . . .' she said vaguely.

Erica sat down on the edge of the sofa and surreptitiously studied Minna's mother. She knew that Nettan was almost ten years younger than she was, but it didn't show. Her face was grey, probably from years of smoking, and her hair was dull and dishevelled.

'I was just wondering if . . .' Nettan pulled her nubby cardigan closer as she seemed to be mustering her courage to ask Erica something. 'Sorry. I'm a little nervous. I don't often get a visit from such a famous person. Actually never, now that I think about it.'

She laughed, and for a moment Erica caught a glimpse of what Nettan must have looked like when she was younger. When she still had a zest for life.

'That's so embarrassing,' Erica said with a grimace. She hated it when people called her famous. She just couldn't relate to that.

'But you *are* famous. I've seen you on TV. Although you were wearing a little more make-up then.' From under her fringe Nettan peered at Erica's face, which today was completely devoid of make-up.

'I know. They shovel it on when you're going to appear

on TV. But I suppose if they didn't, those lights would make you look really ghastly. Normally I don't wear make-up at all.' She smiled and saw that Nettan was starting to relax.

'Me neither,' said Nettan, and there was something touching about her pointing out the obvious. 'What I wanted to ask you was . . . Well, why are you here? The police have already interviewed me several times.'

Erica paused before replying. She didn't have a good answer. Curiosity was closest to the truth, but she couldn't say that.

'I've assisted the local police with a number of cases in the past. So they trust me to help out when they're short on manpower. And after what happened to the girl who disappeared from Fjällbacka, they need help.'

'Oh, I see. I supposed that . . .' Nettan again left her thought unfinished, and Erica let it go. She wanted to ask her about Minna.

'Tell me about when your daughter disappeared.'

Nettan pulled her cardigan even tighter around her. She stared down at her lap, and when she began to speak, her voice was so low that Erica had to strain to hear what she was saying.

'At first I didn't realize she was missing. I mean, really missing. She's always come and gone as she pleases. I've never been able to control Minna. She's so strong-willed, and I suppose I haven't exactly . . .' Nettan raised her head to look out of the window. 'Sometimes she would stay with friends for a couple of days. Or with some boy.'

'Anyone special? Did she have a boyfriend?' asked Erica.

Nettan shook her head.

'Not that I know of, at any rate. There were several boys, but I don't think she had a steady boyfriend. Though she had seemed happier than usual, so I did wonder. But

I've asked some of her friends, and no one knew anything about a boyfriend. And they would have known, since it was the same group of kids that always hung out together.'

'So why do think she was happier?'

Nettan shrugged. 'I don't know. But I think about how I felt as a teenager. With sudden mood swings. Maybe it was because Johan had moved out.'

'Johan?'

'My boyfriend. He lived here for a while. But he and Minna never got along.'

'When did he move out?'

'I don't remember exactly. But it must have been about six months before Minna disappeared.'

'Did the police talk to him?'

Again Nettan shrugged.

'I think they talked to several of my ex-boyfriends. Some of them could get a little rough.'

'Were any of them ever threatening or abusive towards Minna?' Erica had to rein in the anger that surged inside of her. She'd had plenty of experience with how victims of abuse reacted. And after the way Lucas had treated Anna, she knew how fear could shatter a person's will. But how could anyone allow their child to be subjected to something like that? How could the maternal instinct become so weakened that a woman would let anyone harm her child, either psychologically or physically? She couldn't understand it. For a moment her thoughts turned to Louise, all alone and chained in the cellar of the Kowalski house. That was the same thing, only much worse.

'Sometimes. But Johan never hit her. They just screamed and yelled at each other all the time. So I think she was relieved when he moved out. One day he just packed up his things and left. And I never heard from him again.'

'When did you realize that Minna wasn't just staying with a friend?'

'She was never gone more than a day or two. So after three days passed and she still hadn't come home, and when she didn't answer her mobile, I tried calling her friends. No one had heard from her for the past three days, so then I . . .'

Erica clenched her teeth. How could anyone let a fourteen-year-old girl go missing for three whole days before reacting? She was thinking of keeping an iron grip on her own kids when they were teenagers. She would never let them go off without telling her where they were headed and who they planned to visit.

'At first the police didn't take me seriously,' Nettan went on. 'They had dealt with Minna before. She'd been involved in some . . . trouble, so they didn't even want to take a report.'

'When did they realize that something must have happened to her?'

'It took another day. Then they found that woman who had seen Minna getting into a car. Considering there were other girls who had disappeared, it shouldn't have taken them so long. My brother thinks I should sue them. He says if she was a rich girl, like some of the others, the police would have acted immediately. But they don't listen to people like us. And it's not right.' Nettan looked down and began nervously plucking at her cardigan.

Erica had to revise her previous opinion. She was interested to hear Nettan call the other girls rich. They were actually middle-class, but class differences were often relative. She herself had come here with a number of preconceived notions that had been confirmed the moment she entered the flat. Yet who was she to criticize Nettan? She had no clue about the circumstances that had shaped this woman's life.

'They should have listened to you,' said Erica, impulsively reaching out to touch her hand.

Nettan flinched as if she'd been burned, but she didn't pull her hand away. Tears began spilling down her cheeks.

'I've done so many stupid things. I . . . I don't . . . and now it might be too late.' Her voice broke as the tears poured down her cheeks.

It was as if someone had turned on a tap. Erica sensed that Nettan must have been holding back her tears for far too long. Now she wept not only for her missing daughter, who most likely would never return, but also for all the bad decisions she'd made, which had given Minna a life that was very different from the one Nettan had no doubt once dreamed for her.

'I wanted us so badly to be a real family. I wanted someone to take care of Minna and me. But nobody ever has.' Nettan was shaking as she sobbed, and Erica moved closer to put her arm around the woman, letting her cry on her shoulder. She stroked Nettan's hair and quietly murmured to her, just as she did with Maja and the twins whenever they needed consoling. She wondered if anyone had ever comforted Nettan this way before, or whether she had ever comforted Minna. It seemed as if the woman had suffered a long series of disappointments and her life had not turned out the way she had hoped.

'Would you like to see some pictures?' said Nettan suddenly, pulling away. She wiped her eyes on the sleeve of her cardigan and gave Erica an expectant look.

'Of course.'

Nettan got up to fetch several photo albums from a rickety IKEA bookshelf.

The first album covered Minna's early years. The pictures showed a young and smiling Nettan holding her daughter in her arms.

'You look so happy,' said Erica before she could stop herself.

'I know. That was a wonderful time. The best. I was only seventeen when I had her, but I was so happy.' Nettan ran her fingertip over one of the photos. 'My God, look at those clothes.' She laughed, and Erica had to smile too. Styles back in the 1980s were awful, but the 90s really weren't much better.

They leafed through the albums, seeing the years pass. Minna had been a sweet-looking child, but the older she got, the more closed her expression became, and the light in her eyes gradually faded. Erica could tell that Nettan had noticed the same thing.

'I thought I was doing my best,' she said quietly, 'but I wasn't. I shouldn't have . . .' She fixed her gaze on one of the men who appeared in the photographs. Erica saw that there were a lot of men. All those men who had come into Nettan's life, bringing more disappointment, and then vanished.

'This is Johan, by the way. Our last summer together.' She pointed to a picture obviously taken in the heat of summer. A tall, fair-haired man had posed with his arm around Nettan as they stood in an arbour. Behind them was a red-painted house with white trim, surrounded by greenery. The only dissonant element in the idyllic setting was a sullen-looking Minna who sat nearby, glaring at Johan and her mother.

Nettan abruptly closed the album.

'I just want her to come home. Everything will be different, I promise. Everything.'

Erica didn't reply. For a while they sat in silence, neither of them knowing what else to say. But the silence was soothing rather than uncomfortable. Suddenly the doorbell rang, and they both gave a start. Nettan got up to open the door.

When Erica saw who came in, she jumped up in surprise.

'Hi, Patrik,' she said, smiling sheepishly.

Paula went into the station's kitchen and found Gösta sitting there, just as she'd expected.

'Paula? Hi!' he exclaimed, giving her a big smile.

She smiled back. Annika had also been overjoyed to see her and had leapt up to give her a bear hug, asking a hundred questions about little Lisa.

Now Gösta got up to hug her, although a bit more cautiously than Annika. Then he held her at arm's length as he studied her face.

'You're as white as a sheet and look like you haven't slept in weeks.'

'Thanks, Gösta. You certainly know how to pay a compliment,' Paula teased him, but then she realized he wasn't joking. 'These past months have been rough,' she admitted. 'It's not all sunshine and happiness being a mother.'

'I've heard the baby has really been putting you through your paces. So I hope this is just a courtesy call, and you're not thinking of wearing yourself out by doing any work here.'

He took her arm to usher her over to the chair next to the window.

'Sit down. Have some coffee.' He poured her a cup and set it on the kitchen table. Then he filled his own cup and sat down across from her.

'Both work and pleasure, you might say,' she told him, sipping her coffee. 'It seems strange to be out on my own, but it's also great to feel like my old self, at least for a little while.'

Gösta frowned. 'We're doing okay holding down the fort here.'

'I know that. But Bertil was telling me about the case, and it made me remember something. Or rather, it made me think there was something I ought to remember.'

'What do you mean?'

'He was talking about the autopsy report. And the fact that the girl's tongue had been cut out. That sounded familiar, but I can't recall why, so I thought I'd take a look in the archives to see if that might spark my memory. My brain isn't what it used to be, unfortunately. It's no myth that a woman's brain turns to mush when she's nursing. These days I can hardly even figure out how to use the remote control.'

'God, yes. I know what you mean about hormones. I remember when Maj-Britt . . .' He turned away to look out of the window. Paula realized that he was thinking about the child he and his wife had had but then lost. And he knew that she knew. She let him sit in silence for a moment, remembering.

'So you have no idea what the autopsy results remind you of?' he asked at last, turning to face her again.

'I'm afraid not,' she said with a sigh. 'It would be a lot easier if only I knew where to begin looking. It could take quite a while to go through the archives.'

'It does sound like a big job to do a random search like that,' Gösta agreed.

She grimaced. 'I know. So I might as well get started.'

'Are you sure you shouldn't go home and rest instead? And take care of yourself and Lisa?' He was still looking at her with concern.

'Believe it or not, it's actually more restful here than at home. And it feels great to wear something besides pyjamas for a change. Thanks for the coffee.'

Paula stood up. Nowadays almost everything was archived digitally, but all of the older investigative materials were still stored on paper. If they'd had the resources, they could have scanned all the information on a single hard drive instead of filling an entire room in the basement. But they currently didn't have the funding, and it was possible they never would.

She went downstairs, opened the door, and paused for a moment on the threshold. Good Lord, what a lot of paper. Even more than she remembered. The investigations were filed by year, and in order to give her search some sort of strategy, she decided simply to start with the oldest and proceed from there. With an air of determination she lifted down the first file box and sat down on the floor.

An hour later she'd made it only halfway through the box, and she realized the search could turn out to be both time-consuming and fruitless. Not only was she unsure exactly what she was looking for, she didn't even know whether it could be found here in this room. But ever since she started work at the police station, she'd spent a good deal of time reading through old cases. Partly out of personal interest and partly because she wanted to know about the crime history of the area. So it did seem logical that she would find what she was looking for here in the archives.

A knock on the door interrupted her. Mellberg peeked in.

'How's it going? Rita rang to say that I should come down here and find out how you're doing. Plus she wanted me to tell you that everything is fine with Lisa.'

'Oh, good. And I'm doing great here. But I assume that's not the real reason you're here.'

'Er, well . . .'

'I'm afraid I haven't got very far, and I haven't found what I'm looking for. I'm starting to wonder whether my poor brain is just overtired and playing tricks on me.' Frustrated, Paula pulled her dark hair back into a loose ponytail, fastening it with an elastic band she had around her wrist.

'No, no. Don't start having doubts,' said Mellberg. 'You have a great intuition, and you need to trust your gut feeling.'

Paula looked at him in surprise. Encouraging words from Bertil? Maybe she ought to go out and buy a lottery ticket today.

'You're probably right,' she said, making a neat stack of the papers in front of her. 'I know it reminded me of something, so I'll just keep looking.'

'We need all the help we can get. Right now we have no leads at all. Patrik and Martin are in Göteborg talking to some guy who thinks he can work out who the perpetrator is by looking into a psychological crystal ball.' Mellberg put on a pompous expression and continued in an affected manner: 'I see the murderer is between twenty and seventy years old, either a man or a woman, who lives in a flat or perhaps a small house. The individual has taken one or more trips abroad, usually shops for groceries at ICA or Konsum, eats tacos on Fridays and always watches *Let's Dance* on TV. Plus *Allsång på Skansen* in the summertime.'

Paula couldn't help laughing at his play-acting. 'You're the very model of an open-minded person, Bertil. I have to say that I don't share your opinion. I think getting assistance from a profiler might be productive, especially given the special circumstances of this case.'

'Well, I suppose we'll eventually see who's right. Just keep searching. But don't wear yourself out, or Rita will kill me.'

'Don't worry, I won't,' said Paula with a smile. Then she turned back to the files and went on reading.

Patrik was boiling with fury. His surprise at finding his wife in the living room belonging to Minna's mother had swiftly changed to anger. Erica had an annoying tendency to get involved in things that were none of her business, and on several occasions it had led to dire consequences. But he couldn't allow his emotions to show in front of Nettan. Instead, he kept his expression impassive the whole time he conducted the interview while Erica sat nearby, listening wide-eyed and with a Mona Lisa smile on her lips.

As soon as they left the building and were out of Nettan's earshot, Patrik exploded.

'What the hell do you think you're doing?' It was rare for him to lose his temper, and he felt the onset of a headache as soon as the words were out of his mouth.

'I just thought that . . .' Erica began, trying to keep up with Patrik and Martin as they headed for the car park. Martin didn't say a word and looked as though he'd prefer to be somewhere else.

'No, you didn't! I can't imagine you were doing any thinking at all.' Patrik coughed. His outburst had made him draw in several hasty breaths of the cold winter air.

'You're so short on manpower that you can't do everything, so I just thought that . . .' Erica ventured again.

'Couldn't you have at least checked with me first? I would never have allowed you to talk to a family member about an ongoing investigation, and I suspect that's why you didn't ask me.'

Erica nodded. 'You're probably right. But I also needed to take a break from my book. I'm feeling stuck, and I thought that if I focused on something else for a while, then maybe . . .'

'As if this case was some sort of work therapy?' Patrik shouted so loudly that several birds perched on a nearby telephone wire flew off in fright. 'If you've got writer's block, you need to find a better solution than sticking your nose in a police investigation. Are you off your rocker?'

'Sounds like the slang from the forties is making a comeback,' said Erica in an attempt to lighten the mood, but it only made Patrik even angrier.

'This is ridiculous. Straight out of a bad English detective novel, with some nosy old woman running around interviewing everybody.'

'Okay, but when I write my books, I sort of do the same thing you do. I talk to people, gather the facts, fill in the holes in the investigation, check the statements from witnesses . . .'

'Right. And you're a great writer. But this is a police investigation, and by definition it's the police who should be doing the work.'

They had now reached the police car. Martin stood next to the passenger side, not sure what to do as he seemed directly in their line of fire.

'But I've helped you out in the past,' said Erica. 'You have to admit it.'

'Yes, you have,' said Patrik reluctantly. In fact, she had done more than help. She had actively contributed to solving several homicide cases, but he wasn't about to admit that.

'Are you driving back home now? It seems like a long way to come just to talk to Nettan.'

'You drove all the way here just to talk to her,' Patrik countered.

'Touché.' Erica smiled, and Patrik felt his fury starting to subside. He could never stay angry with his wife for long, and unfortunately, she knew it.

'But I don't have to worry about wasting police resources,' she went on. 'What else are you planning to do here?'

Patrik cursed silently. Sometimes she was a little too clever for her own good. He glanced at Martin for support, but his colleague merely shook his head. Coward, thought Patrik.

'There's someone else we need to talk to.'

'Like who?' asked Erica, making Patrik grit his teeth. He was well aware how stubborn she could be, and how curious. And that combination could be extremely annoying.

'We're going to consult an expert,' he replied. 'By the way, who's going to fetch the children? My mother?' He was trying to steer the conversation on to a different topic.

'Yes. Kristina and her new boyfriend,' said Erica, looking like a cat who'd swallowed a canary.

'Her what?' Patrik could feel a migraine coming on. This day was getting worse and worse.

'I'm sure he's very nice. So, what sort of expert are you going to see?'

Patrik slumped against the car. He gave up.

'We're going to talk to someone who does psychological profiling.'

'A profiler?' said Erica, her face lighting up. 'Okay, I'll go with you.' And she started towards her own car.

'Now, wait a minute . . .' Patrik called after her, but Martin stopped him.

'You might as well call it quits. You haven't got a chance. Let her come along. As she said, she's helped us out before, and if we're there, we can keep her in line. Three pairs of ears are probably better than two.'

'Oh, all right,' muttered Patrik, getting into the driver's seat. 'And after all this, we didn't find out anything useful from Minna's mother.'

'No, but if we're lucky, Erica did,' said Martin.

Patrik glared at him. Then he turned on the ignition, and they sped off.

'What clothes do you think we should bury her in?' His mother's question felt like the stab of a knife. Ricky hadn't imagined the pain could get any worse, but the thought of Victoria being lowered into eternal darkness was so horrible that he wanted to scream out loud.

'Let's choose something pretty,' said Markus. 'Maybe that red dress she always liked so much.'

'She was ten when she wore that dress,' said Ricky. In spite of his grief he couldn't help smiling at his father's faulty memory.

'Really? Was it that long ago?' Markus got up and started washing dishes but then abruptly stopped and went back to the table to sit down. It was like that for all of them. They tried to do ordinary things, routine tasks, only to discover they just didn't have the energy. They couldn't do anything. Yet now they had to make a lot of decisions about the funeral service and burial even though they were incapable of deciding what to have for breakfast.

'Choose the black one. From Filippa K,' said Ricky.

'Which one?' asked Helena.

'The one you and Pappa always thought was too short for her to wear in public. Victoria loved that dress. And it didn't make her look like a slut. Not at all. She looked terrific.'

'Do you really think so?' said Markus. 'A black dress? Isn't that a little depressing?'

'Choose that one,' Ricky insisted. 'She loved wearing that dress. Don't you remember? She saved her money for six months before she could afford to buy it.'

'You're right. Of course she should wear the black dress.' Helena gave her son a pleading look. 'What about music? What kind of music should we have? I have no idea what she liked.' And she burst into tears. Markus clumsily patted her arm.

'We should have "Some Die Young" by Laleh,' said Ricky. 'And then "Beneath Your Beautiful" by Labrinth. Those were two of her favourites. And they're appropriate.'

Having to make all the decisions was wearing him down, and he felt a sob lodge in his throat. He was always on the verge of tears.

'What about afterwards? What should we serve?' Yet another quandary. His mother's hands moved restlessly on the kitchen table. Her fingers were so pale and thin.

'*Smörgåstårta*. She loved that traditional savoury dish. Don't you remember it was her favourite?'

Ricky's voice broke, and he knew that he was being unfair. Of course they remembered. They remembered far more than he did, and their memories stretched back further than his own. But at the moment all the memories were so overwhelming that they couldn't sort them out. He needed to help them.

'And *julmust*. She could drink litres of that Christmas soda. We should still be able to find it in the shops. Don't you think so?' As he tried to recall if he'd seen any on the shelves lately, he was instantly seized with panic. It suddenly seemed like the most important thing in the world. They had to find *julmust* so they could serve it after the funeral.

'I'm positive we can still find some,' said his father soothingly, placing his hand on Ricky's. 'That's a great idea. Everything you've suggested is great. Including the black dress. I'm sure Mamma knows where it is, and she can iron it. And we'll ask Aunt Anneli to make several *smörgåstårtor* for the occasion. Victoria always loved the ones she made. We were planning to serve them at her graduation from school this summer, and . . .' For a moment he seemed to lose his train of thought. 'Anyway, I know we can still buy *julmust*. That'll be great, just great.'

No, it won't, Ricky wanted to bellow. They were sitting here talking about putting his sister in a coffin and burying her in the ground. Nothing was ever going to be good again.

Deep inside, the secret was still chafing. He thought for sure everyone would be able to see that he was hiding something, but his parents didn't seem to notice. They stared vacantly out of the window as they sat here in the small kitchen with the lingonberry-patterned curtains that Helena loved so much. The curtains that Ricky and Victoria had always tried to get her to replace.

Would everything change once they awoke from their trance? Would they then see and understand? Ricky knew that sooner or later he would be forced to speak to the police. But would his parents be able to bear the truth?

Sometimes Marta felt like the horrible orphanage supervisor in *Annie*. Girls, girls, everywhere nothing but girls.

'Liv was allowed to ride Blackie three times in a row!' cried Ida, her cheeks bright red as she came striding across the yard. 'It should be my turn now.'

Marta sighed. All these constant quarrels. There was a definite hierarchy in the stable, and she saw, heard, and understood more of the girls' arguments than they knew. But today she had no patience for such things.

'You'll have to settle this dispute yourselves. Don't come to me with such trivial matters.'

She saw Ida flinch. The girls were used to the fact that Marta was stern, but she seldom lashed out in anger.

'I'm sorry,' Ida hastened to say, though her apology didn't sound sincere. She was a spoiled girl who frequently whined, and she ought to learn better manners, but Marta had to be practical. They were dependent on the income from the riding school. They could never live solely on what Jonas earned as a veterinarian, and the girls – and by extension, their parents – were her customers. So she was forced to handle them with kid gloves.

'Forgive me, Ida,' she said now. 'I'm just upset because of what happened to Victoria. I hope you understand.'

She gritted her teeth and then smiled at the girl, who immediately relaxed.

'Of course I do. It's so awful. The fact that she's dead and all.'

'Okay, let's go and have a talk with Liv, and you can ride Blackie today. Unless you'd rather ride Scirocco?'

Ida's face lit up with joy. 'Can I really? Isn't Molly going to ride him?'

'Not today,' said Marta, her expression hardening at the thought of her daughter, who was in her room brooding over the cancelled competition.

'Then I'd rather ride Scirocco, and Liv can have Blackie,' said Ida generously.

'Perfect. So that's decided.' Marta put her arm around Ida and they headed into the stable. The smell of horse filled the air. This was one of the few places in the world where she felt at home, where she felt like a real person. The only one who had ever loved the smell as much as she did was Victoria. Every time she had stepped inside, a blissful look would come into her eyes, a look that Marta shared. She was surprised at how much she missed the girl. Victoria's death had struck her with a force that was unexpected and confusing. She paused in the middle of the stable aisle, only vaguely aware of Ida triumphantly calling to Liv, who was grooming Blackie in his stall.

'Go ahead and ride him today. Marta says I can ride Scirocco instead.' The spiteful glee in her voice was all too evident.

Marta closed her eyes and pictured Victoria. Her dark hair flying around her face as she raced across the stable yard. The way she was able, with gentle firmness, to get all the horses to obey her slightest command. Marta had the same inexplicable power over horses, but there was a big difference. Horses obeyed Marta because they respected her, but also because they feared her. They had obeyed Victoria because of her gentle handling combined with a strong will. And this contradiction had always fascinated Marta.

'Why does she get to ride Scirocco? Why can't I?'

Marta opened her eyes to find Liv standing in front of her, arms crossed.

'Because you don't seem especially willing to share Blackie. So you can ride him today, just as you wanted. And then everyone will be happy.' She could tell that she was about to lose her temper again. Her job would have been much easier if she'd only had the horses to worry about.

To make matters worse, she had her own little brat to deal with. Jonas hated it when she called Molly a brat, even though she pretended to do it in fun. She couldn't understand how he could be so blind. Molly was becoming insufferable, but Jonas refused to listen, and there was nothing Marta could do about it.

Ever since they first met, she had known that he was the puzzle piece that was missing in her life. After exchanging only a single glance, they realized they belonged together. She had seen her own soul reflected in his, and he had done the same. And they would always feel that way. The only friction between them was caused by Molly.

Jonas had threatened to leave Marta if she refused to have a child, so she had relented. In reality, she hadn't thought he was serious. He knew as well as she did that if they split up, they would never find anyone else who understood them in the same way. But she didn't dare take the risk. She had found her soul mate, and for the first time in her life she had submitted to another person's will.

When Molly was born, things had turned out just as she had feared. From that point on she'd been forced to share Jonas with someone else. A huge piece had been stolen from her by someone who initially possessed neither will nor identity. She couldn't understand it.

Jonas had loved Molly from the very first second. His love for the child was so natural and unconditional that Marta hardly recognized him. And from that moment a wedge had been driven between them.

Marta went over to help Ida with Scirocco. She knew that Molly would be furious when she heard that someone else was going to ride the horse, but after her daughter's sulky behaviour, the thought gave Marta a certain satisfaction. No doubt Jonas would be cross with her too, but she knew how to make him think of other things. The next equestrian competition was in a week's time, and by then he would be putty in her hands.

What Paula was attempting to do was no easy task, and Gösta couldn't help worrying about her. She had looked so pale.

Restlessly he leafed through the papers on his desk. It was frustrating that the investigation had stalled. None of the work they'd done since Victoria disappeared had produced any results, and now they were almost out of ideas. The interview with Jonas hadn't proved useful either. Gösta had insisted that he go over everything one more time, in the hope he might say something different from his first statement. But Jonas had recited exactly the same details as before, with no discrepancies. And when he heard that ketamine might have been used on Victoria, his reaction had seemed both genuine and entirely believable. Gösta sighed. He might as well spend some time on the other police reports that were gathering dust on his desk.

It was mostly petty crime: stolen bicycles, shoplifting, arguments between neighbours over stupid matters and exaggerated claims. But certain reports had been neglected too long, and he was a bit embarrassed about that.

He got out the file from the bottom of the stack, which meant that it was the oldest. A suspected break-in. Or was it? A woman by the name of Katarina Mattsson had discovered mysterious footprints in her garden, and one evening she saw someone standing on her property, staring into the dark. Annika was the one who had taken the report, and as far as Gösta knew, the woman hadn't been heard from again. So the matter had probably been resolved. But he should still follow up on it, and he decided to ring her later.

He was just about to put down the file when something caught his eye. He looked at the address of the woman, and thoughts began whirling through his head. It could be a coincidence, of course, but maybe not. He read through the report again, thinking hard. Then he made up his mind.

A short time later he was in his car, driving towards Fjällbacka. The address he was heading for was in a residential neighbourhood called Sumpan, though he had no idea why it had been given that name. He turned on to the quiet street where the gardens were small and the houses stood close together. He knew it was possible that she might not be home, but when he found the house he saw there were lights on in the windows. Tense with anticipation, he rang the bell. If he was right, he might have discovered something important. Gösta glanced at the house on the left but didn't see anyone. He hoped no one would choose this moment to look outside.

He heard footsteps approaching and then a woman opened the door and gave him a surprised look. Gösta quickly introduced himself and explained why he was there.

'Oh, that was a long time ago. I almost forgot about it. Come on in.'

She stepped aside to let him in. Two boys who looked to be about five years old peeked out from the next room, and Katarina nodded in their direction.

'My son Adam and his friend Julius.'

The boys' faces lit up when they saw Gösta standing there in his uniform. He waved awkwardly, and they rushed forward to look him up and down.

'Are you a real policeman? Do you have a gun? Have you ever shot anyone? Do you have handcuffs with you? Do you have a radio so you can talk to other policemen?'

Gösta laughed and held up his hands.

'Take it easy, boys. Yes, I'm a real policeman. Yes, I have a gun, but I didn't bring it with me. And I've never shot anyone. Now what else did you ask me? Oh, yes. I do have a radio so I can call for backup if the two of you get too rowdy. And here are my handcuffs. You can have a look at them later, if you like. But right now I need to talk to Adam's mother for a moment.'

'Really? We can look at them? Okay!' The boys jumped up and down with joy, and Katarina shook her head.

'You've really made their day. Actually, their whole year. But listen to me, boys, you heard what Gösta said. You can look at the handcuffs and radio later, but first he and I need to have a talk. So why don't you go back to the film you were watching, and we'll call you when we're done. Okay?'

'Okay,' said the boys as they went back to the TV, giving Gösta one last admiring glance.

'I'm sorry for the way they grilled you,' said Katarina, leading the way to the kitchen.

'It was fun,' said Gösta as he followed her. 'Besides, I should enjoy it while it lasts. In ten years they may be screaming "you dirty cop" at me instead.'

'Oh, don't say that. I'm already dreading those delightful teenage years.'

'It'll be fine. I'm sure you and your husband have taught him good manners. Do you have other children?' Gösta sat down at the table. The kitchen looked a bit worn, but it was bright and cheerful.

'No, just Adam. But we're not . . . I mean, we divorced when Adam was only a year old, and my ex-husband isn't interested in being part of his life. He has a new wife and kids, and apparently he doesn't have enough love to go around. The few times Adam went over there to visit, he felt like he was in the way.'

She was standing with her back to Gösta as she measured coffee from a tin, but now she turned around and shrugged apologetically.

'Sorry for dumping all of that on you. Sometimes the bitterness just spills out. But we're doing fine, Adam and I. And if his father can't see that Adam is an amazing little boy, that's his loss.'

'No need to apologize,' said Gösta. 'It sounds like you have good reason to feel disappointed.'

What bloody fools some men are, he thought. How could anyone just cast a child aside and devote himself to a new bunch of kids? He watched as Katarina set two cups on the table. She had a pleasant sense of calm about her. He thought she must be about thirty-five or so, and he remembered from the police report that she was an elementary school teacher. He had a feeling that she was both good at her job and well-liked.

'I didn't think I'd hear back from the police,' she said now as she sat down after pouring the coffee and setting out a packet of biscuits. 'But I don't mean to complain. When Victoria disappeared, I realized that was what you needed to focus all your time on.'

She held out the packet of biscuits to Gösta, and he took three. Oatmeal biscuits. His absolute favourite, aside from the Ballerina variety.

'It's true that the case has taken up most of our time. But I still should have looked at your report earlier. I'm sorry you've had to wait so long.'

'Well, you're here now,' she said, helping herself to a biscuit.

Gösta smiled gratefully. 'Why don't you tell me what you remember and why you decided to contact the police.'

'Well . . .' She hesitated, frowning. 'The first thing I noticed were the footprints in the garden. My lawn turns into a sea of mud whenever it rains, and it rained a lot early in the autumn. On several mornings I noticed footprints in the mud. They were big, so I was fairly certain the shoes must have belonged to a man.'

'And then you saw someone standing out there?'

Katarina frowned again.

'Yes. I think it was a couple of weeks after I saw the footprints the first time. For a while I wondered if it could have been Mathias, Adam's father, but that didn't seem likely. Why would he sneak over here when he barely stays in touch? Besides, the person was smoking cigarettes and Mathias doesn't smoke. I don't know if I mentioned that I found cigarette butts.'

'You didn't happen to save the butts, did you?' asked Gösta, even though he realized it was a long shot.

Katarina grimaced.

'I think I managed to throw out most of them. I didn't want Adam to find them. Of course I may have missed one or two, but . . .' She pointed towards the yard, and Gösta saw what she meant. Through the window he could see a thick layer of snow covering the lawn.

Gösta sighed. 'Did you get a good look at this person?'

'No, I'm afraid not. I mostly saw the glow of his cigarette. We had already gone to bed, but Adam woke up and was thirsty, so I came down here to the kitchen in the dark to get him a glass of water. And that's when I saw the glow of a cigarette in the garden. Someone was standing out there smoking, but I didn't really see the person. Just a silhouette.'

'But you think it was a man, not a woman?'

'Yes. If it was the same person who left the footprints. And now that I think about it, he seemed very tall.'

'Did you do anything? Did you reveal in any way that you'd seen him, for instance?'

'No. The only thing I did was ring the police. It made me a little uneasy, even though I didn't feel directly threatened. But then Victoria disappeared, and it was hard to think about anything else. And I haven't seen anything out of the ordinary since then.'

'Hmm . . .' said Gösta. He cursed himself for not looking at the report and making the connection earlier. But there was no use in crying over spilt milk. He needed to make the best of things now. He stood up.

'Do you happen to have a snow shovel? I'd like to go out and see if I can find any of those cigarette butts.'

'Sure. It's in the garage. You're welcome to use it. And you could clear the driveway while you're at it.'

Gösta put on his shoes and jacket and went out to the garage. It was nice and tidy, and he found the shovel leaning against the wall just inside the door.

Out in the garden he paused to think. It would be stupid to sweat unnecessarily. He needed to choose the right place to begin. Katarina had opened the terrace door facing the garden, so he asked her, 'Where did you find most of the cigarette butts?'

'Over there on your left, close to the house.'

He nodded and trudged through the snow to the spot she had pointed out. The snow was heavy, and he felt a twinge in his back as he lifted away the first shovelful.

'Are you sure you don't want me to do that?' asked Katarina, sounding concerned.

'No, I'm fine. It's good for this old body of mine to get some exercise every now and then.'

He noticed the boys peering at him from the window and waved to them before going back to shovelling. He rested now and then, but after a while he had cleared about a square metre of ground. He squatted down to study the area, but the only thing he saw was frozen mud with a few blades of grass. Then his eyes narrowed. Something yellow was sticking up at the edge of the square he'd cleared. Cautiously he brushed away the snow on top of it. A cigarette butt. He pulled it loose and then stood up, his back aching. He looked at the butt. Then he raised his eyes and saw what he was convinced the mysterious stranger had also seen as he stood and smoked. Because standing here in Katarina's garden he had a good view of Victoria's house. And of her bedroom window upstairs.

UDDEVALLA 1971

When Laila discovered that she was once again pregnant, she had mixed emotions. Maybe she wasn't suited to be a mother, maybe she wasn't capable of feeling the love for a child that was expected of her.

But all her worries proved unfounded. Everything was so different with Peter. So wonderfully different. She couldn't take her eyes off her son, couldn't get enough of breathing in his scent, caressing his soft skin with her fingertips. When she held him in her arms, as she was doing now, he would look up at her with such trust in his eyes that her heart overflowed. So this was what it was like to love a child. She never could have imagined it possible to have such strong feelings for another person. Even her love for Vladek paled in comparison with what she felt when she looked at her newborn son.

Yet the moment she glanced at her daughter, her stomach would knot. She saw the look in the girl's eyes, the darkness that stirred in her thoughts. Her jealousy towards her brother manifested itself in constant pinching and slapping, and fear kept Laila awake at night. Sometimes she would sit next to Peter's cot, keeping watch over him as she fixed her gaze on his peaceful face.

Vladek began slipping further away from her, as she did from him. They were being torn apart by forces they never could have foreseen. In her dreams she would sometimes run after him, trying to go faster and faster, but the harder she ran, the greater the gap between them. Finally all she could see was his back, way in the distance.

Words had also deserted them. All those conversations in the evenings at the dinner table, the little signs of love that had brightened their days. Everything had been swallowed up by a silence broken only by the sound of a child crying.

She kept on looking at Peter, filled with a protective instinct that pushed away all else. Vladek could no longer be her everything. Not now that Peter was here.

The big barn was quiet and cold. A little snow had blown through the crevices in the walls, mixing together with the dust and dirt. The hayloft had been empty for years, and the ladder leading up to it had been terribly rickety for as long as Molly could remember. Aside from their horse van, only old and forgotten vehicles were stored in the barn. A rusty combine-harvester, an unusable Grålle tractor, but mostly lots of cars.

In the distance Molly heard the sound of voices from the stable on the hill, but today she didn't want to go riding. It seemed so pointless since she wasn't going to compete tomorrow. Some of the other girls would no doubt be overjoyed to have a chance to ride Scirocco.

Slowly she wandered among the old cars. They were left over from her paternal grandfather's former business. When she was growing up she'd heard him constantly talking about it, boasting about all the finds he'd made all over Sweden. For a pittance he'd bought up cars that were considered scrap metal and then restored them and sold them for significantly higher sums. But after he fell ill, the barn had been transformed into a car junkyard. The space was filled with partially restored vehicles, and no one could be bothered to get rid of them.

She ran her hand over an old Volkswagen Beetle rusting away over in the corner. It wouldn't be long before she could start taking driving lessons. Maybe she could persuade Jonas to fix up this car for her.

She tried the handle, and the door opened. The car needed a lot of work inside too. The interior was rusty and dirty, and stuffing was coming out of the seats, but she could tell the car had the potential to be really great. She got into the driver's seat and cautiously placed her hands on the steering wheel. She would love having this little Beetle for her own. The other girls would be green with envy.

She pictured herself driving around Fjällbacka, magnanimously offering her friends rides. It would be a few years yet before she could drive on her own, but she decided to talk to Jonas about it soon. She would get him to fix up the car for her, whether he wanted to or not. She knew he could do it. Her grandfather had told her that Jonas used to help him restore the cars, and he'd shown a lot of talent for the work. It was the only time she'd ever heard her grandfather say anything nice about Jonas. Otherwise he mostly complained.

'So this is where you're hiding?'

She gave a start at the sound of Jonas's voice right next to the car window.

'Do you like it?' He grinned, and with some embarrassment she opened the door. She wasn't happy about being caught sitting in the car and pretending to drive.

'It's great,' she said. 'I was thinking of driving it once I have a licence.'

'It's not exactly in drivable shape.'

'No, but . . .'

'But you thought I might fix it up for you? Hmm . . . Well, why not? We've got plenty of time. I should be able to do it if I work on it every once in a while.'

'Really?' she said, her eyes shining, and she threw her arms around her father's neck.

'Yes, really,' he said, giving her a hug. Then he gently pushed her away and put his hands on her shoulders. 'But you have to agree to stop sulking. I know how important the competition was to you. We already talked about that. But it won't be long until the next one.'

'I know. You're right.'

Molly could feel her mood lifting. She started walking among the cars again. There were several others that might also be cool to drive, but she still liked the Beetle the best.

'Why don't you fix up these cars? Or else sell them for scrap?' She was standing next to a big black Buick.

'Your grandfather doesn't want me to. So they'll just stay here until they fall apart, or until Grandpa is gone.'

'Well, I think it's a shame.' She went over to a green camper van that looked like the Scooby Doo minibus. Jonas pulled her away.

'Come on. I don't like you to be in here. There's a lot of broken glass and rust. And not long ago I saw some rats.'

'Rats!' exclaimed Molly, taking a quick step back and looking about.

Jonas laughed. 'Come on. Let's go in and have a snack. It's cold out here. And I promise that our house is rat-free.'

He put his arm around her, and they headed for the door. Molly shivered. Her father was right. It was freezing cold in here, and she would die if she saw a rat. But she was still overjoyed about the car. She couldn't wait to tell the other stable girls all about it.

Tyra was secretly pleased that Liv had been reprimanded today. She was even more spoiled than Molly, if that was possible, and the look on Liv's face when Ida was given permission to ride Scirocco was priceless. She had sulked for the rest of the riding lesson, and Blackie could clearly sense it. He refused to settle down, which had made Liv even more cross.

Tyra was sweating under her heavy clothing. It was so hard to plod through all the snow and her legs ached. She longed for springtime when she'd be able to bicycle back and forth to the stable. Life would be so much simpler then.

The sledding hill was crowded with children. She had gone sledding over there many times, and she remembered the giddy feeling when she'd whooshed down the steep slope. Nowadays it didn't seem nearly as high or steep as it had when she was a child, but it was still more exciting than Doktorn hill. That one was only for the very young. She recalled going skiing near Doktorn hill, which had led to her first and only skiing holiday. To the surprise of the ski instructor, she had claimed to have learned to ski on Doktorn hill. Then she had set off down the ski slope, which turned out to be quite a bit higher and steeper, and that was putting it mildly. But she had managed fine, and her mother always told the story with such pride, amazed at how bold her little girl had been.

Tyra didn't know what had happened to that bold spirit of hers. It still existed when she interacted with the horses, but the rest of the time she felt like a coward. Ever since the car accident that had killed her father, Tyra had expected disaster to be lurking around every corner. She knew that everything could seem perfectly normal, only to be changed for ever in a matter of seconds.

With Victoria she had felt braver. It was as if she became somebody else, someone better, whenever they were together. They had always met at Victoria's home, never at hers. She said it was too noisy because of her little brothers, but the truth was that she was ashamed of her stepfather Lasse, at first because he had so often been drunk, and later because of his religious babbling. She was also ashamed of her mother for allowing herself to be cowed, tiptoeing about the house like a frightened mouse. They were not like Victoria's darling parents who were so completely normal.

Tyra kicked at the snow. Sweat was running down her back. It was a long walk, but earlier in the day she'd made up her mind to do this, and she had no intention of turning back now. There were things she should have asked Victoria about, answers she should have demanded. She felt heartsick at the thought that she would never know what happened. She had done everything for Victoria, and that's what she intended to keep doing.

The nondescript corridor inside the Institute for Sociology at Göteborg University was practically deserted. Having stopped to ask for directions they had been told they would find the criminologist here. Now they stood outside the door to his office. The nameplate said: Gerhard Struwer. Patrik knocked softly.

'Come in!' said a voice, so they opened the door and went in.

Patrik wasn't sure what he'd been expecting, but the man looked as if he'd stepped out of an advert for a Dressmann clothing shop.

'Welcome.' Gerhard stood up and shook hands with both Patrik and Martin. Then he turned to Erica, who had stayed in the background. 'Oh my, what an honour it is to meet Erica Falck.'

Gerhard sounded a bit too enthusiastic for Patrik's taste. But the way this day was going, it didn't surprise him that Struwer turned out to be a ladies' man. Good thing Erica wasn't susceptible to guys like him.

'The honour is all mine. I've seen the insightful analyses you've presented on TV,' replied Erica.

Patrik stared at her. Why was she speaking in such a flirtatious manner?

'Gerhard appears regularly on the programme *Missing*,' Erica explained to her husband with a smile. 'I especially liked your portrait of Juha Valjakkala,' she said to Struwer. 'You certainly put your finger on something that no one else had seen, and I think that—'

Patrik cleared his throat. This was not going the way he had planned. He studied Gerhard, noting that the man not only had perfect teeth, he had precisely the right amount of grey at his temples. And nicely polished shoes. Who the hell kept their shoes polished in the middle of winter? Patrik cast a gloomy look at his own winter boots, which looked like they needed to be sent through the car wash if they were ever going to get clean again.

'We have a few questions we'd like to ask you,' he said, sitting down on one of the visitor's chairs. He forced himself to keep a neutral expression. He refused to give Erica the satisfaction of seeing that he was jealous. Because he wasn't. He just thought it was unnecessary to waste valuable time on chit-chat about matters that had nothing to do with why they were here.

'Certainly. I've read with interest the material that you sent over.' Gerhard sat down behind his desk. 'Both regarding Victoria and regarding the other girls. Naturally I won't be able to do a proper analysis on such short notice and with so little background information, but there are a few things that strike me about the case.' He crossed his legs and steepled his hands, assuming a posture that Patrik found extremely irritating.

'Shall I take notes?' said Martin, giving Patrik a poke in the side.

He flinched, then nodded.

'Yes, by all means,' he said. Martin got out a notepad and pen and waited for Gerhard to continue.

'I think we're dealing with a very organized and rational individual. He or she – though for the sake of simplicity, let's just say "he" – has been too successful at erasing all traces to be considered either psychotic or demented.'

'How can you call it rational for someone to kidnap another person? Or to subject someone to what Victoria endured?' Patrik could hear that his tone was a bit sharp.

'When I use the word "rational", I'm referring to an individual who is capable of advance planning, foreseeing the consequences of what he's going to do, and acting accordingly. Someone who can quickly alter his plans if conditions change.'

'That seems crystal clear to me,' said Erica.

Patrik gritted his teeth and let Struwer go on.

'Presumably the perpetrator is also relatively mature. A teenager or someone in their twenties wouldn't have the necessary self-control or ability to plan so carefully. But in view of the physical strength required to control his victims, it has to be someone who is still strong and in good shape.'

'Or we could be talking about more than one perpetrator,' Martin interjected.

Gerhard nodded. 'Yes, we can't rule out the possibility that several individuals are involved. There have even been cases where an entire group has colluded in committing heinous crimes. Often some sort of religious motive is involved, as with Charles Manson and his cult of followers.'

'What do you think about the time sequence? The first three girls disappeared at regular intervals, with about six months in between. But then it was only five months later that Minna went missing. And Victoria disappeared about three months after that,' said Erica. Patrik had to admit that this was an excellent point.

'If we look at serial murderers in the United States, such as Ted Bundy, John Wayne Gacy, and Jeffrey Dahmer – and I'm sure you've heard these names numerous times – they often needed time to build up their energy, a sort of inner pressure. Criminals usually begin by imagining the crime, then they follow the victim that they've chosen, keeping watch for a while before they strike. Or it could be a matter of coincidence. The murderer fantasizes about a certain type of victim and then he happens to run into someone who fits the profile.'

'This may be a stupid question, but are there any female serial killers?' asked Martin. 'I've only heard of men.'

'It's more common for men to commit serial murders, but there have been some women too. Aileen Wuornos, for example. And there are others.'

Struwer again pressed his fingertips together.

'But getting back to the time aspect, it could be that the perpetrator keeps the victim prisoner for a lengthy period of time. After the victim has fulfilled her purpose, so to speak, or simply dies from exhaustion and injuries, then sooner or later he has to find a new victim to satisfy his needs. The pressure grows and grows until the perpetrator has to find some means of release. And that's when he strikes. In interviews many serial killers have said that it's no longer a matter of free will; they feel forced to take action.'

'Do you think that's the sort of behaviour we're dealing with in this case?' asked Patrik. Despite himself, he was fascinated.

'The time sequence seems to indicate something along those lines. And maybe his need has grown increasingly urgent. The perpetrator can no longer wait as long before seeking out a new victim. If you are in fact looking for a serial killer, that is. From what I understand, you haven't found any other bodies, and Victoria Hallberg was still alive when she reappeared.'

'That's right. Although it seems unlikely the perp intended to let her live. Don't you think it seems more plausible that she somehow managed to escape?'

'I agree. But even if we're only dealing with kidnappings, the perpetrator may follow the same behaviour pattern. It could also be someone who kills out of sexual desire. A psychopathic perpetrator who murders for enjoyment. And for sexual gratification. The autopsy on Victoria showed that she had not been subjected to sexual assault, but this kind of case often has a sexual motive. So far we don't know enough to determine if that's the situation here.'

'Did you know that research shows that half a per cent of the population can be labelled as psychopaths?' Erica said eagerly.

'Yeah, I know,' said Martin. 'I seem to remember reading about that in *Café*. Something about upper-level bosses.'

'I'm not sure we should trust the scientific findings reported in a publication like *Café*. But in principle, you're right, Erica.' Gerhard smiled at her, flashing his white teeth. 'A percentage of the general population meets the criteria for psychopathy. We tend to associate the term psychopath with murderers, or at least with criminals, but that's far from the truth. Outwardly, most of them appear to lead completely ordinary, well-functioning lives. They learn how to behave in order to fit in with society, and they may even be high achievers. But inside they may never be like other people. They lack the ability to feel empathy and understand anyone else's feelings. Their whole world and all their thoughts revolve around themselves. Whether psychopaths can become integrated into their community depends on how well they can imitate the feelings that are expected of them in various contexts. But they will never be totally successful. There's always something that doesn't ring true about them, and they have a difficult time establishing long-lasting and close relationships. Frequently they exploit people for their own purposes, and when they can no longer get away with it, they move on to the next victim, without feeling regret, remorse, or guilt.

'So, getting back to your comment, Martin: there is research showing that the number of psychopaths in the top echelons of business is higher than among the general population. Many of the traits I just described can be of benefit in certain positions of power, when ruthlessness and lack of empathy have their uses.'

'Are you saying that sometimes you can't tell if someone is a psychopath?' asked Martin.

'Yes. At least, not immediately. Psychopaths can be quite charming. But if someone, over a period of time, has a relationship with a psychopath, sooner or later it will become clear that things are not as they should be.'

Patrik had begun to fidget. His chair was uncomfortable, and he could feel his back starting to ache. He cast a glance at Martin, who was busily taking notes. Then he turned to Struwer.

'Why do you think these particular girls were chosen?'

'It's probably a question of the perpetrator's sexual preference. Innocent young girls who've yet to have any sexual experience. A young girl is also easier to control and frighten than an adult. I'd guess it's a combination of those two factors.'

'Do you think it's significant that they're similar in appearance? They all have, or had, brown hair and blue eyes. Is that something the perp is intentionally looking for?'

'It's possible. In fact, I'd say it's probable that the

resemblance is significant. The victims may remind the perpetrator of someone, and so his actions have to do with that person. Ted Bundy was an example of this. Most of his victims looked alike and reminded him of a former girlfriend who had rejected him. He took his revenge on her through his victims.'

Martin had been listening attentively. Now he leaned forward to say, 'What do you think was the purpose behind the injuries that Victoria suffered? Why would the perpetrator do something like that?'

'As I said, it's probable that the victims resemble someone who is important to the perpetrator. And in view of the type of injuries, I would say the purpose was to give him a feeling of control. By robbing the victim of all her primary senses, he totally controls her.'

'If that's the case, wouldn't it have been enough to keep her prisoner?' asked Martin.

'For most perpetrators who want to control their victims, I would say yes. But this individual has gone one step further. Just picture it: Victoria was robbed of her ability to see, hear, and taste. She was trapped in a dark, silent room and unable to communicate. Basically the perpetrator created a living doll.'

Patrik shuddered. What this man was saying was so bizarre and repulsive that it seemed like something straight out of a horror film. But it was real. However, interesting as Struwer's theories were, he'd yet to hear anything that seemed likely to take their investigation forward.

'Based on what we've been talking about here,' he said, 'do you have any idea how we should go about finding this person?'

Struwer paused as if formulating his response.

'I may be sticking my neck out here, but I would say the victim from Göteborg, Minna Wahlberg, is especially interesting. She has a different background from the other girls, and she's also the only one with whom the perpetrator was careless enough to be seen.'

'We don't know for sure that it was the perp driving the white car,' Patrik pointed out.

'No, that's true. But if we assume it was him, then it's interesting that she would willingly get into the car. We don't know how the other girls were taken, but the fact that Minna got into the car indicates that the driver was either someone who seemed harmless, or else she recognized him and was not afraid of him.'

'Are you saying that Minna may have known the perpetrator? That he has some link to her or to the town?'

What Struwer said matched what Patrik had also been thinking. Minna was different from the others.

'He doesn't necessarily have to have been acquainted with her personally, but she may have known who he is. The fact that he was seen picking her up, but he wasn't seen in any of the other instances, may mean that he was on familiar turf and felt a bit more secure.'

'If that's the case, shouldn't he have been even more careful? There was a greater risk that he would be recognized,' Erica objected. Patrik gave her an appreciative look.

'Logically speaking, that may be true,' Struwer replied. 'But we humans are usually not entirely logical, and patterns and habits are hard to break. He would feel more relaxed in his own environment, and that means there's a greater risk of making a mistake. And he did make a mistake.'

'I agree that Minna seems to stand out from the others,' said Patrik. 'We just had a talk with her mother, but we didn't find out anything new.' Out of the corner of his eye he saw Erica nodding in agreement.

'Well, if I were you, I'd keep following this aspect of the case. Focus on the differences – that's the general rule of thumb when we do profiles of criminals. Why was the pattern broken? What makes a specific victim so special that the perpetrator changes his behaviour?'

'So we should look at any deviations rather than at common denominators?' said Patrik, realizing that Struwer was right.

'Yes. That's my recommendation. Even though your main goal is to solve Victoria's disappearance, Minna's case may help you do that.' Gerhard paused. 'By the way, have all of you got together?'

'What do you mean?' asked Patrik.

'All the police districts – have you sat down together and gone over the information you have so far?'

'We keep in contact and share materials.'

'That's good, but I think it would be beneficial for all of you to meet in person. Sometimes a new lead can be triggered by something that's not written down, something that's between the lines in the investigative material. I'm sure you have personal experience of a gut feeling that points you in a certain direction. In many investigations it's that indefinable something which eventually leads to the capture of the perpetrator. And there's nothing strange about that. Our subconscious plays a much bigger role than many people think. It's often said that we use a very small portion of our brain's capacity, and I think that's true. So get together with the other investigative teams and listen to each other.'

Patrik nodded. 'All right. We should have done that already. We just haven't got around to it.'

'I'd say it'll be worth the effort,' replied Gerhard.

For a moment no one spoke. They had no more questions as they sat and pondered what Struwer had told them. Patrik had some doubt that it would move the investigation forward, but he was ready to consider anything and everything. Better to do that than to realize in hindsight that Struwer had been right, but they hadn't taken his remarks seriously.

'Well, thank you for your time,' said Patrik, standing up.

'The pleasure was all mine.' Gerhard fixed his blue eyes on Erica, and Patrik took a deep breath. He had an urge to put together a profile of Struwer. It shouldn't be too hard. The world was full of guys like him.

Terese always found it a bit odd to come to the stable. The farm was so familiar to her, because she and Jonas had been together for two years. But back then they were terribly young, or at least that was how it felt to her now, and so much had happened since then. Yet it was still strange to be here, especially because Marta was the reason they had split up.

One day, out of the blue, Jonas had started talking about how he'd met someone else and she was his soul mate. That was exactly how he'd put it. Terese had thought his choice of words seemed a bit pretentious. Later, when she met her own soul mate, she had understood what he meant. Because that was precisely how she felt when Henrik, Tyra's father, stepped forward to ask her to dance at a celebration on Ingrid Bergman Square. It was clear at once that the two of them belonged together. But then everything had changed in an instant. All their plans, all their dreams were shattered on a dark night when his car hydroplaned on the road, and he was killed. Then she and Tyra were left on their own.

It had never felt the same with Lasse. Their relationship was merely a way of escaping the loneliness and once again sharing her daily life with someone else. And it had turned out to be a complete disaster. She didn't know which was worse: all those years when he was drinking and they were constantly worrying about what he might do next; or his new sobriety, which she had initially welcomed, but it had led to other problems.

She didn't believe for an instant in Lasse's newly discovered religious faith, but she understood all too well what he found so enticing about the church and its congregation. It had given him a chance to leave behind all the bad decisions he'd ever made, as well as his old faults, without having to take any responsibility. As soon as he became a member of the church and was forgiven by God – and that happened unreasonably fast in her opinion – he had split himself in two parts. He ascribed everything that she and the children had endured to the old Lasse, who had lived a sinful and selfish life. The new Lasse, on the other hand, was a good and righteous person who couldn't possibly be blamed for anything the old Lasse had done. If she ever mentioned all the times he had hurt them, he reacted with suppressed anger at her 'harping on old wounds'. He told her how disappointed he was that she kept focusing on negative things instead of turning to God, as he had, to become a person who spread 'light and love'.

Terese snorted. Lasse had no clue what light and love were. He had never even apologized for the way he had treated his family. According to his logic, she was a petty person because she wasn't as forgiving as God, and every night she continued to turn her back on Lasse as they lay in bed.

Frustrated, she gripped the steering wheel hard as she turned into the stable yard. The situation was becoming unbearable. She could hardly stand the sight of him any more or the sound of him mumbling Bible verses, a sound that had become a constant backdrop in their flat. But she had to take care of practical matters first. They had two children together, and she was so exhausted that she didn't know whether she even had the energy at the moment to cope with a divorce.

'Okay, kids, stay here and behave yourselves while I go in and fetch Tyra.' She turned around and cast a stern glance at the two little boys sitting in the back seat. They giggled, and she knew that a battle would undoubtedly break out as soon as she got out of the car. 'I'll be right back,' she warned them. More giggles. She sighed, although she couldn't help smiling as she closed the car door behind her.

Shivering in the cold she went inside the stable, which hadn't existed when she frequented the farm. Marta and Jonas had built it together.

'Hello?' She looked around for Tyra but didn't see her with the other girls.

'Is Tyra here?'

Marta came out of one of the stalls.

'No, she left about an hour ago.'

'Oh.' Terese frowned. This morning she had promised that for once she would come and fetch Tyra. It seemed strange her daughter had forgotten about it, because she had been so happy that she wouldn't have to trudge home through the snow.

'Tyra is a very talented rider,' said Marta, coming over to Terese.

As always, Terese was struck by how beautiful Marta was. When she saw her for the first time, Terese had immediately realized she would never be able to compete. She felt big and clumsy next to Marta, who was slender and petite.

'That's nice,' she said, looking at the ground.

'She has such a natural way with horses. She ought to compete. I think she'd do well. Have you ever considered that?'

'Oh, er, I don't . . .' Terese stumbled over her words and felt even more uncomfortable. They couldn't afford it, but how could she say that? 'We've had other things to think about, with the boys and all. And Lasse is looking for work . . . But I'll give it some thought. It's nice to hear that you think she's talented. She's . . . well, I'm very proud of her.'

'And you should be,' said Marta, studying her. 'From what I understand, she's extremely upset about what happened to Victoria. We all are.'

'Yes, it's been hard for her. It will take time for her to get over it.'

Terese tried to think of some way to put an end to the conversation. She had no desire to stand here and chat. And she was starting to feel anxious. Where had Tyra gone?

'The boys are waiting out in the car, so I'd better get back to them before they kill each other.'

'Of course. And don't worry about Tyra. She probably just forgot that you were going to fetch her. You know how teenagers are.'

Marta went back to the stall, and Terese hurried across the yard towards the car. She wanted to get home. Hopefully Tyra was already there.

Anna sat at the kitchen table talking to Dan's back. Through his T-shirt she could see his muscles tensing, but he didn't say a word as he continued to wash the dishes.

'What should we do? We can't go on like this.' The mere thought of separation made her panic-stricken, but they needed to talk about the future. Even before the events of the past summer, their life together had been troubled. For a brief period she had livened up but for the wrong reasons, and now their marriage was nothing but chaos, a mass of broken dreams. And it was all her fault. There was no way she could dump part of the blame on Dan or make him shoulder any of the responsibility.

'You know how deeply I regret what I did, and I wish

so much that I could go back and make it not happen, but I can't. So if you want me to move out, I will. Emma and Adrian and I can find a flat for ourselves. I'm sure there's one available in the block of flats nearby that we could lease on short notice. Because we can't live like this. It's just not going to work. It's tearing us apart. Both of us, and the kids too. Can't you see that? They don't dare make any noise, in fact they hardly dare talk because they're afraid of saying something wrong and making the situation worse than it already is. I can't stand it any more. I'd rather move out. Please, Dan, say something!' And with that Anna began to sob. It felt like somebody else was crying, like she was listening to somebody else talking. As if she were hovering overhead, looking down at the fragments of what had once been her life, watching her husband who was her great love, and yet she had hurt him so badly.

Slowly Dan turned around. He leaned against the worktop and stared at his feet. She felt a stab in her heart when she noticed the deep furrows on his face, which was pale with hopelessness. She had fundamentally changed him, and she couldn't forgive herself for that. He had believed in the goodness of others, assuming that everyone was as honest as he was. She had shown him otherwise, shaking his faith in her and in the world.

'I don't know, Anna. I don't know what I want. The months just keep slipping by, and we take care of all the practical things while we tiptoe around each other.'

'But we need to try to solve this problem. Or else split up. I can't stand living in this limbo any more. And the children deserve better. We need to decide.'

She could feel her nose running as the tears continued to stream down her cheeks. She wiped her face on the sleeve of her shirt. She didn't feel like getting up to find a tissue, and the kitchen roll was on the worktop behind

Dan. She needed to keep a safe distance from him in order to have this conversation. Getting close enough to breathe in his scent and feel the warmth of his body would make everything fall apart. They hadn't even slept in the same room since the summer. He slept on a mattress in the den while she slept in their double bed. She had offered to change places with him, realizing she was the one who ought to be sleeping on the uncomfortable thin mattress and wake up with an aching back. But he merely shook his head at the idea, and every night he lay down to sleep on the mattress.

'I want to try.' She was whispering now. 'But only if you do. Only if you think there's even a small possibility. Otherwise the kids and I might as well move out. I can ring the Tanum estate agent this afternoon and see what's available. We don't need a big place to start with. We've lived in cramped quarters before. We'll be fine.'

Dan grimaced. Then he covered his face with his hands and his shoulders began to shake. Ever since summer he had worn a mask of bitter disappointment and anger, but now the tears poured out, falling from his chin and soaking his grey T-shirt. Anna couldn't just sit there. She went over to put her arms around him. She noticed that he flinched, but he didn't pull away. She felt the warmth of his body and the way he was trembling as he sobbed even harder. She pulled him closer, as if trying to keep him from falling to pieces.

When the tears finally stopped, he reached out and put his arms around her.

Lasse felt rage smouldering inside of him as he turned left past the mill and headed towards Kville. Why couldn't Terese ever come with him? Was it too much to ask that they should spend some time together, that she should show some interest in what had totally changed his life and made him a new person? Both he and the church had so much to teach her, but she chose to live in darkness instead of allowing God's love to shine upon her, as it shone upon him.

He stomped on the accelerator. He had wasted so much time pleading with her that he was going to be late for the leadership meeting. He'd also been forced to explain to her why he didn't want her to go to that stable, or be anywhere near Jonas. She had sinned with Jonas, she'd had sex with him even though they weren't married, and it made no difference that it had happened years ago. God wanted human beings to live a pure and true life, without any wicked deeds from the past sullying their soul. For his part, he had confessed and purged all such things from his life, cleansing his own soul.

It hadn't always been easy. Sin was all around him. There were so many shameless women offering themselves and not respecting God's will and commandments, women who tried to lead all men astray. Such sinners deserved to be punished, and he was convinced he was meant to carry out this task. God had spoken to him, and no one should doubt that he had become a new person.

At the church they saw and understood this. They showered him with love, affirming that God had forgiven him and that he was now a blank slate. He thought about how close he had come to falling back into old habits. But God had miraculously saved him from the weakness of the flesh and made him a strong and brave disciple. Yet Terese refused to see that he had changed.

He was still feeling annoyed when he arrived. Then he was filled with peace, as always, when he stepped through the doors of the modern church building which had been financed by generous members. Despite the church's remote location, the congregation was surprisingly large, thanks to the leader, Jan-Fred, who had taken over ten years ago after an internal struggle for control. Back then it was called the Kville Pentecostal Church, but he had re-christened it the Christian Faith, or simply the Faith, as it was commonly known.

'Hi, Lasse. Great to see you.' Jan-Fred's wife Leonora came to greet him. She was a gorgeous blonde in her forties who co-chaired the leadership group along with her husband.

'It's always wonderful to be here,' he said, kissing her on the cheek. He breathed in the scent of her shampoo, and with it a whiff of sin. But it lasted only a moment, and he knew that with God's help he would eventually succeed in driving out all the old demons. He had conquered his weakness for alcohol, but his weakness for women had turned out to be a much bigger trial.

'Jan-Fred and I were talking about you this morning.' Leonora linked her arm in his and ushered him towards one of the conference rooms where the leadership course was being held.

'Really?' he said, eager to hear what she would say next.

'We were talking about what amazing work you've done. We're all so proud of you. You are a true and worthy disciple, and we see great potential in you.'

'I'm merely doing what God has enjoined me to do. Everything is done in His service. He was the one who gave me the strength and courage to see my sins and cleanse them away.'

She patted his arm. 'Yes, God is good to us, weak and sinful as we are. His patience and love are infinite.'

They had reached the room, and he saw that the others had already taken their seats.

'What about your family? They weren't able to come today either?' Leonora gave him a sympathetic look. Lasse grimaced and shook his head.

'The family is important to God. What God has joined shall not be torn asunder. A wife should share her husband's life, and his faith in God. But you'll see – sooner or later she'll discover what a beautiful soul God has found in you. And she'll see that He has made you whole.'

'I'm sure she will. She just needs a little time,' Lasse murmured. He noticed the metallic taste of anger in his mouth, but he forced himself to push aside any negative thoughts. Instead, he silently repeated his mantra: light and love. That was what he was: light and love. He just needed to make Terese understand.

'Do we have to?' Marta was putting on clean clothes after taking a shower to wash off the stink of the stable. 'Couldn't we just stay home and do what other people do on a Friday night? Sit in front of the TV and eat tacos?'

'We have no choice, and you know it,' said Jonas.

'But why do we always have to eat dinner with them on Friday? Have you ever stopped to think about it? Why can't we have Sunday dinner together instead, like other people who visit their parents and parents-in-law?' She buttoned her blouse and combed her hair as she stood in front of the full-length mirror in their bedroom.

'How many times have we had this conversation? You know that on the weekends we're gone so often attending competitions, so Friday night is the only time that works. Why do you keep asking questions when you already know the answers?'

Marta heard the shrill tone creep into Jonas's voice. That always happened whenever he was annoyed. Of course she already knew the answers. She just didn't understand why they always had to think of Helga and Einar.

'But none of us finds it pleasant. I think we'd all feel relieved if we put an end to these dinners. It's just that no one dares say anything,' she went on as she sat down to pull on an extra pair of tights. It was always so cold in Einar and Helga's house. Jonas's father was stingy and always tried to save on electricity. She put on a jumper over her blouse. Otherwise she'd freeze to death before dessert was served.

'Molly doesn't like having dinner there either. How long do you think we can force her to go before she rebels?'

'No teenager enjoys family dinners. But she's just going to have to come with us. That's not asking too much, is it?'

Marta paused to study him in the mirror. He was even more handsome than when they first met. Back then he was shy and lanky, with acne marring his face. But she had seen something else beneath his insecure demeanour, something that she recognized. And with time, and her help, his insecurity had vanished. Now he was a self-confident, strong, and muscular man. And after all these years he could still make her tremble with longing.

Everything they shared kept their desire alive, and now she felt it awaken as it had so many times before. Quickly she removed her tights and knickers but kept on her blouse and jumper. She went over to him and unbuttoned the jeans he had just put on. Without a word he let her take them off, and she saw that he was already aroused. Firmly she pressed him down on to the bed and swiftly mounted him. He came, fast and hard, his back arched. She wiped several drops of sweat from his brow and slipped off him. Their eyes met in the mirror as she turned her back to put her knickers and tights back on.

Fifteen minutes later they were standing in the front hall of Helga and Einar's home. Molly stood behind them, grumbling to herself. Just as they had predicted, she had protested loudly about spending yet another Friday night with her grandparents. Her friends had evidently planned something much more fun for the evening, and her life would be ruined if she didn't get to join them. But Jonas had refused to budge, and Marta had stayed out of it entirely.

'Welcome,' said Helga. Enticing aromas came from the kitchen, and Marta noticed her stomach growling. That was the only good thing about having Friday dinner with her parents-in-law: Helga's fabulous food.

'We're having roast pork.' Helga stood on tiptoe to kiss her son on the cheek. Marta gave her an awkward hug.

'Would you go and get your father?' said Helga to Jonas.

'Sure,' said Jonas and headed upstairs.

Marta could hear the murmur of voices above, and then the sound of something heavy being moved towards the stairs. They had been given funding to build a wheelchair ramp, but it required a certain strength to manoeuvre Einar. By this time the sound of the wheelchair coming down the ramp was familiar to all of them. Marta could hardly remember how Einar had looked before his legs were amputated. In the past she'd always thought of him as a big, angry bull. Now he looked more like a fat toad sliding down the stairs.

'Everybody's here, as usual,' he said, squinting his eyes. 'Come and give your grandfather a kiss.'

Molly reluctantly went over to kiss him on the cheek.

'Okay, time to eat or the food will get cold,' said Helga, motioning for them to come into the kitchen where dinner was served.

Jonas pushed his father's wheelchair over to the table, and then they all sat down without saying a word.

'So, no jump racing tomorrow, is that right?' said Einar after a while.

Marta noticed a nasty glint in his eyes and knew he

had mentioned the topic out of sheer spite. Molly sighed loudly, and Jonas gave his father a warning look.

'After everything that's happened, we didn't think it would be right for her to go,' he said, reaching for the bowl of potatoes.'

'No, I can see you'd think that.' Einar glared at his son, who served his father some potatoes before helping himself.

'So how's it going? Have the police made any progress?' asked Helga. She served everyone slices of pork from a big platter before she took her place at the table.

'Gösta came to see me today, and he asked about the break-in,' said Jonas.

Marta stared at him. 'Why didn't you tell me about that?'

Jonas shrugged. 'It was no big deal. But they found traces of ketamine when they did the autopsy on Victoria, and Gösta wanted to know what sort of things were stolen from the clinic.'

'Good thing you reported it to the police.' Marta lowered her gaze. She hated not being in full control of everything that went on. The fact that Jonas hadn't told her about Gösta's visit filled her with silent rage. They would have to talk about this later when they were alone.

'Too bad about the girl,' said Einar, sticking a big piece of pork in his mouth. Gravy trickled down his chin. 'She was pretty, what little I saw of her. You keep me imprisoned upstairs, and I have nothing to look at. This old lady is the only person I get to see nowadays.' He laughed, pointing to Helga.

'Do we have to talk about Victoria?' Molly was poking at her food, and Marta tried to remember when she'd last seen her daughter eat a proper meal. But that was probably all due to the usual teenage worries about weight. No doubt it would pass.

'Molly found the old Volkswagen Beetle out in the barn,' said Jonas, wanting to change the subject. 'She'd like to have it. I was thinking of fixing it up so it'll be ready when she gets her driver's licence.' He winked at Molly, who was pushing the green beans around on her plate.

'Should she be allowed out there? She might hurt herself,' said Einar, shoving another bite into his mouth. The trail of gravy was still visible on his chin.

'You should really clean up that barn.' Helga got up to refill the platter. 'Get rid of all that old junk and rubbish.'

'I want it to stay the way it is,' said Einar. 'That place has lots of memories for me. Good memories. And you can hear for yourself, Helga, that Jonas is going to create new memories.'

'But why would Molly want an old Beetle like that?' Helga placed the platter back on the table and sat down again.

'It's going to be great. Super cool! Nobody else will have a car like that.' Molly's eyes shone.

'I agree. It could be great,' said Jonas, helping himself to a third portion. Marta knew that he loved his mother's cooking, and maybe that was the main reason they had to drag themselves over here every Friday.

'So do you remember how to do it? How to work on cars?' asked Einar.

Marta could almost picture the memories tumbling around in his head. Memories from a time when he'd been a bull and not a toad.

'I'm sure it's still all in my fingertips. I worked on enough cars with you that I think I can remember how to do it.' Jonas exchanged a glance with his father.

'Right. I suppose there's something to be said for handing down knowledge and interests from father to son.' Einar raised his wine glass. 'Let's drink a toast to

Persson senior and son, and to our shared interests. And congratulations, little lady. You're about to get yourself a new car.'

Molly raised her glass of Coke to join in the toast. She was beaming with joy at the thought of the car.

'Just be careful,' said Helga. 'Accidents can happen so easily. You should be glad you've had such good fortune so far, but don't tempt fate.'

'Why do you always have to be such a prophet of doom.' Einar's cheeks were flushed from the wine. He turned to look at the others. 'It's always been like this. I have all the ideas and visions, while my dear wife just moans and groans and sees nothing but problems. I don't think you've ever dared live life to the fullest, even for an instant. Have you, Helga? Have you ever lived? Or have you always been so bloody scared that you've merely steeled yourself and tried to drag the rest of us down with your fears?'

He was slurring his words, and Marta suspected that he'd already had a few drinks before coming downstairs. That too was par for the course at Friday dinner with her parents-in-law.

'I've done the best I could. And it hasn't always been easy,' said Helga. She got up and began to clear the table. Marta saw that her hands were shaking. Helga had always been the nervous type.

'You've had nothing but good fortune. You got a much better husband than you deserved. And I should get a medal for putting up with you all these years. I don't know what I was thinking. There were plenty of girls chasing me, but I suppose I thought you had nice big hips that would be good for birthing children. And then you barely managed to do it even once. *Skål!*' Einar again raised his glass in a toast.

Marta studied her nails. She wasn't really bothered by

his speech. She'd witnessed this drama too many times before. Even Helga usually paid no attention to Einar's drunken tirades, but tonight something was different. Suddenly she picked up a saucepan and flung it with all her might into the sink, making the water splash over the side. Then Helga slowly turned around. She kept her voice low, almost a whisper. But as they sat there in shocked silence, they couldn't help hearing the words she spoke.

'I. Can't. Stand. This. Any. More.'

'Hello?' Patrik stepped into the front hall. He was still in a bad mood after the trip to Göteborg, and nothing on the drive home had been able to divert his thoughts. The fact that Erica had mentioned his mother might have brought along a male friend didn't make the situation any better.

'Hello!' Kristina called cheerfully from the kitchen. Patrik glanced around suspiciously. For a moment he thought he must have entered the wrong house. Everything looked so neat and clean.

'Whoa,' said Erica, her eyes wide as she too stood in the doorway. She didn't sound entirely happy with the transformation.

'Did we hire a cleaning service?' asked Patrik. He hadn't realized the hall floor could look so clean, without a trace of dirt or clutter. It practically gleamed, and all the shoes were nicely lined up in the shoe rack, which was usually never used. Normally the shoes were tossed in a big pile on the floor.

'No. Just the firm of Hedström and Zetterlund,' said Kristina in the same cheerful voice as she appeared from the kitchen.

'Zetterlund?' said Patrik, though he already suspected who it might be.

'Hi! My name's Gunnar.' A man emerged from the living room, holding out his hand. As Patrik studied him, he noticed out of the corner of his eye that Erica was giving him an amused look. He shook hands with the man, who seemed a bit too enthusiastic, pumping his hand up and down.

'What a pleasant home you have, and such amazing children! That little lady of yours isn't easily fooled. She has a good head on her shoulders. And I can see that you have your hands full with those two little rascals, but they're so charming that they probably get away with anything. Am I right?' He continued to shake hands with Patrik, who managed a strained smile.

'Yes, they're great,' he said, attempting to pull his hand away. After another few seconds Gunnar finally released his grip.

'I assumed you'd be hungry, so I've made dinner,' said Kristina, going back into the kitchen. 'I've also done a couple of loads of laundry, and I asked Gunnar to bring along his toolbox. He has fixed a few things you didn't have time for, Patrik.'

Only now did Patrik notice that the bathroom door, which had been hanging crooked on its hinges for a while – getting on for two years in fact – was now properly screwed into place. He wondered what other things in his house Mr Fix-it had worked on. He had to admit he felt a bit annoyed. He had planned on fixing the door. It was on his To-do list. He just hadn't got around to it yet.

'It was no trouble,' said Gunnar. 'I used to own a construction company, so it took me no time at all. The trick is to deal with things at once so they don't start piling up.'

Patrik gave him another strained smile. 'Hmm . . . Thanks. I really appreciate it.'

'I know it's not easy for young people to find time for everything. What with taking care of the children, going to work, and all the daily chores, as well as maintaining the house. And there's always a lot to do with older homes. But this is a fine house, it certainly is. In those days, they knew how to build things right. Not like the houses today that are thrown together in a couple of weeks, and then people wonder why they have mould and water damage. The old building techniques have been forgotten.' Gunnar shook his head, and Patrik seized the opportunity to retreat to the kitchen where Kristina was standing by the cooker, having an intense conversation with Erica. Feeling a hint of spiteful glee, Patrik noticed that his beloved wife was also looking a bit strained as she tried to smile.

'I know that you and Patrik have a lot on your minds,' said Kristina. 'It's not easy to combine a career with raising children, and your generation has managed to persuade yourselves that you can do it all. But the most important thing for a woman – and don't take this the wrong way, Erica, I'm telling you this with the best of intentions – is to prioritize your children and your home. You may laugh at those of us who were housewives, but it was very satisfying to let the children stay home instead of shoving them off to some day-care centre. And they grew up in a clean and orderly setting. I'm not a believer in the idea that it's okay to ignore the dirt in the corners. I'm sure that's why children today have so many strange allergies, because people don't clean their homes any more. And you can't underestimate the importance of giving children home-cooked, nutritious meals. And when your husband comes home – and Patrik has a very responsible job – it's only right that he should come home to a clean and peaceful place and be served a proper meal. Not those awful ready-meals loaded with additives and preservatives that I found in your freezer. And I must say . . .'

Patrik listened with interest, wondering how his mother

even managed to take a breath as she rattled off this speech. He saw Erica gritting her teeth, and his glee changed to sympathy.

'We just do things a little differently, Mamma,' he interrupted her. 'And that doesn't mean it's worse. You did an amazing job with our family, but Erica and I have chosen to share the responsibility for our children and home, and her career is just as important as mine. Although I admit that sometimes I get lazy and let her take on a bigger burden, but I'm trying to be better about that. So if there's anyone you want to criticize, it should be me, because Erica works really hard to make everything function. And we're doing just fine. There may be a little dirt in the corners, and occasionally the laundry basket overflows, and yes, we do eat frozen fish sticks, blood pudding, and Scans meatballs, but nobody has died from that yet.' He went over and kissed Erica on the cheek. 'But we're incredibly grateful for your help, and for serving us home-cooked meals once in a while. That's something we appreciate even more after eating frozen foods.'

He gave his mother a kiss on the cheek too. The last thing he wanted was to make her unhappy. They wouldn't be able to get by without her help, and he loved his mother. But this was their home, his and Erica's, and it was important for Kristina to understand that.

'Well, it wasn't my intention to criticize. I just wanted to give you some good advice that might help,' she said, and she didn't seem particularly upset.

'So tell us about your boyfriend,' said Patrik, amused to see his mother blush. At the same time he found it a little strange. Or rather, to be honest, very strange.

'Well, you see . . .' Kristina began. Patrik took a deep breath and steeled himself. His mother had a boyfriend. He glanced over at Erica, who silently blew him a kiss.

* * *

Terese could hardly sit still. The boys were making such a row that she almost jumped up to yell at them, but she restrained herself. It wasn't their fault that she was going mad with worry.

Where the hell could Tyra be? As so often before, her worry was mixed with anger, and fear was making it hard for her to breathe. How could Tyra do this after what had happened to Victoria? Every parent in Fjällbacka had been a nervous wreck after Victoria disappeared. What if the perpetrator was still in the area? What if their child was in danger?

Her worry and anger were made worse because of the guilt she felt. Maybe it wasn't so strange that Tyra had forgotten her mother was going to pick her up today. She usually had to come home on her own, and several times before when Terese had promised to fetch her, something had come up to prevent her from doing so.

Should she ring the police? When Terese came home and Tyra wasn't there, she had tried to convince herself that her daughter was on her way, that maybe she'd stopped to visit a friend. She'd even prepared herself for the sullen comments that Tyra often made upon stepping into the front hall after a long, cold walk from the stable. Terese had been looking forward to pampering her daughter a bit, serving her O'Boy chocolate drink and sandwiches with Gouda cheese and lots of butter.

But Tyra hadn't turned up. She hadn't opened the front door and stomped the snow off her boots, muttering to herself as she took off her jacket. As Terese sat at the kitchen table, she realized how Victoria's parents must have felt on that day when their daughter didn't come home. She had met them on only a few occasions, which was actually rather strange. The two girls had been inseparable since they were little kids, but when Terese thought about it, she realized she hadn't met Victoria that often either. The girls had always gone to Victoria's house. For the first time, she wondered why, but then she painfully had to acknowledge the reason. She hadn't created the home she had dreamed of for her children, the secure setting that they needed. Tears welled up in her eyes. If only Tyra would come home, she would do everything in her power to change things.

She glanced at her mobile, as if a text from Tyra might magically appear on the display. As soon as she left the stable, Terese had phoned her daughter, but there was no answer. When she tried again after coming home, she heard the ring tone in Tyra's room. Like so many times before, Tyra had forgotten to take her mobile.

Suddenly a sound out in the hall startled her. But maybe it was just wishful thinking. It was almost impossible to hear anything over the shrieking and shouting of the boys. But then she heard a key turning in the lock. She leapt up and dashed to the front hall, throwing open the door. The next second she was holding her daughter in her arms and crying the tears that she'd held back for the past few hours.

'My sweet, sweet girl,' she whispered against her daughter's hair. She'd ask questions later. Right now the only thing of importance was that Tyra was here, safe at home.

UDDEVALLA 1972

The girl watched her wherever she went, making Laila feel like a prisoner in her own home. Vladek was as bewildered as she was, but the difference was that he physically vented his frustration.

Her finger still hurt. It had begun to heal, but the bone ached where it had grown back together. She'd gone to the doctor so many times over the past six months, and lately he'd started to get suspicious and ask her questions. Inwardly she had cried with longing to lay her head down on the doctor's desk and tearfully tell him everything. But the thought of Vladek made her hold back. The problem had to be solved within the family – that was how he saw it. And he would never forgive her if she didn't keep quiet.

She had drawn away from her own family. She knew that both her sister and her mother wondered why. In the beginning they had come to Uddevalla to visit her once in a while, but not any more. They merely phoned occasionally, asking her discreetly how things were going. They had given up, and she wished she could too. But that wasn't possible, so she kept them at arm's length, giving only brief answers to their questions and trying to keep her tone light, her comments unremarkable. She couldn't tell them anything.

Vladek's family was in touch even less often, but that was how it had been from the start. They were always travelling and had no permanent address, so how could they stay in contact? And it didn't really matter. It would have been just as impossible to explain things to them as to her own family. She and Vladek couldn't even explain the situation to themselves.

This was a burden the two of them had to bear alone.

Lasse whistled softly as he walked down the road. His sense of satisfaction from yesterday's church meeting was still with him. Feeling that he belonged was almost like a sober intoxication, and it was so liberating to leave behind all his past travails and realize that the answer to all his questions could be found in the pages of the Bible.

That was also the reason he knew he was doing God's will. Why else would God have given him the opportunity, putting him in the right place at the right time, precisely when a sinner needed to be punished? On that very day he had prayed to God for help to find a way out of his increasingly difficult situation. He had thought the answer to his prayer would come in the form of a job, but instead another path had opened before him. And the person in question was a sinner of the worst kind, a sinner who deserved justice of biblical proportions.

Terese had started asking Lasse about their finances. He was the one who paid the bills, but she was wondering how they could possibly live on the income from her job at the Konsum supermarket, since he wasn't making any money. He had muttered something about tax exemptions, but he could see she was sceptical. Well, it would all work out. She'd get her answer soon enough.

Right now he was on his way to the beach in Sälvik. He'd chosen this particular meeting place because it was usually deserted at this time of year. In the summertime the shore was swarming with people because it was close to the camping area in Fjällbacka, but now the place was empty and the closest house was a good distance away. It was the perfect spot to meet, and he had suggested it every time.

The ground was slippery, so he walked cautiously as he headed towards the beach. There was a thick blanket of snow, and he could see that the water was frozen a long way out from shore. At the end of the dock, near the bathing ladder, a hole had been cut in the ice for anyone crazy enough to insist on jumping in during the winter. Personally, he was a firm believer that the Swedish climate was not suitable for swimming at any time of the year, not even in the summer.

He was the first to arrive. The cold was seeping under his clothes, and he regretted not putting on heavier clothing. But he had told Terese that he was going to another meeting at the church, and he hadn't wanted to arouse her suspicion by bundling up in too many layers.

Impatiently he walked along the dock. Not a sound came from under his feet, since the water was frozen solid. He glanced at his watch and frowned in annoyance. Then he went out to the far end and leaned against the railing to look down. Those mad winter bathers must have been here very recently because no new ice had formed over the hole. He shivered. The water had to be freezing cold.

When he heard footsteps approaching, he turned around.

'You're late.' He pointed at his watch. 'Give me the money so we can get out of here. I don't want to be seen, and I'm about to freeze to death.'

He held out his hand, anticipation flooding through his body. God was good to find this solution for him. He despised the sinner who stood before him so much that his cheeks burned.

But suddenly Lasse's feeling of contempt turned to surprise. And then fear.

Thoughts of her book left her no peace. When Patrik explained that he had to go to work, Erica was at first annoyed, since she'd planned to pay another visit to the prison. But then she came to her senses. Of course he had to go to the station even though it was Saturday. The investigation of Victoria's disappearance had entered a new, intense stage, and she realized that Patrik would never give up until the case was solved.

Thank goodness Anna had been able to come over and babysit. Now Erica was once again sitting in the visitor's room at the prison. She had been uncertain how to start the conversation, but the silence didn't seem to bother Laila, who was pensively staring out of the window.

'I went over to the house a few days ago,' Erica said at last. She studied Laila to see how she would react, but her icy blue eyes gave no sign of a response. 'I should have done it much earlier, but I think that subconsciously I was reluctant to go there.'

'It's just a house.' Laila shrugged. Her whole body radiated indifference, and Erica wanted to lean forward and shake her. Laila had lived in that house and allowed her child to be locked up and chained like an animal in the dark cellar. How could she be indifferent to such cruelty, no matter what horrors Vladek had subjected her to or how much he had crushed her spirit?

'How often did he beat you?' Erica asked, trying to remain calm.

Laila frowned. 'Who?'

'Vladek,' said Erica, wondering whether Laila was playing dumb. She had seen the medical reports from Uddevalla and read about her injuries.

'It's so easy to judge someone,' said Laila, staring down at the table. 'But Vladek was not an evil man.'

'How can you say that after what he did to you and Louise?'

Even though she knew about the psychology of victims, Erica couldn't understand how Laila could persist in defending Vladek. She had killed him, after all, either in self-defence or as revenge for the violence that she and her child had suffered.

'Did you help him put the chains on Louise? Did he force you to do it? Is that why you won't talk? Is that why you feel guilty?' Erica was pressuring Laila in a way she hadn't done before. Maybe it was because of her talk yesterday with Nettan, and seeing that woman's despair about her missing daughter. Maybe that's what made her angry now. It wasn't normal for a parent to be so indifferent about the unimaginable suffering her child had endured.

Erica couldn't help herself. She opened the bag she always brought along and took out the folder with the photographs.

'Have a look at these pictures. Have you forgotten what the place looked like when the police arrived? Take a look!' Erica slid a photo across the table towards Laila, who reluctantly fixed her eyes on the image. Erica pushed another photo over to her. 'And this one. Here's what the cellar looks like today. See the chain and the bowls for food and water? Just like for an animal! But it was a little girl who was kept there. Your daughter. And you let Vladek keep her imprisoned in a dark basement. I understand why you killed him. I would have too if someone treated my child like that. So why do you keep defending him?'

Erica stopped to catch her breath. Her heart was pounding hard, and she realized that the guard outside was peering at her through the window in the door. She lowered her voice.

'Forgive me, Laila. I . . . I didn't mean to hurt you. But there was something about that house that really upset me.'

'I've heard they call it the House of Horrors,' said Laila, pushing the photographs back across the table towards Erica. 'That's a fitting name for the place. It definitely was a house of horrors. But not in the way you think.' Then she got up and knocked on the door to signal she wanted to leave.

Erica cursed herself as she remained sitting at the table. Laila probably wouldn't want to talk to her again. Then she wouldn't be able to finish writing her book.

But what did Laila mean by her last remark? Hadn't things happened the way everyone believed? Muttering to herself, Erica gathered up the photos and put them back in the folder.

She felt someone place their hand on her shoulder, interrupting her angry thoughts.

It was the guard who had been posted outside the door. 'Come with me,' the guard said. 'There's something I want to show you.'

'What is it?' asked Erica, getting up.

'You'll see. It's in Laila's room.'

'But isn't she in her room?'

'No. She went out into the yard. She usually takes a walk when she gets upset. She'll be out there for a while, but let's hurry in case I'm wrong.'

Erica glanced at the name badge on the guard's shirt. Tina. Then she followed her, thinking that this was the first opportunity she would have to see the room where Laila spent most of her time.

At the far end of the corridor Tina opened a door, and Erica went in. She had no clue how a prisoner's room would look, and she'd probably seen too many American TV programmes, since she was expecting a cell with a bare mattress. What she saw instead was a pleasant room with everything nice and tidy. A neatly made bed, a nightstand with an alarm clock and a little pink ceramic elephant sleeping sweetly, a table with a TV. There was a small window, set close to the ceiling, but it let in a good deal of light, and it was framed by yellow curtains.

'Laila doesn't think we know about this.' Tina went over to the bed and knelt down.

'Are you allowed to do this?' asked Erica, glancing towards the door. She didn't know which made her more nervous: the thought of Laila turning up, or the prospect of some supervisor claiming that the prisoner's rights had been violated.

'We're allowed to look at everything inside this room,' said Tina, reaching her hand under the bed.

'Yes, but I'm not a staff member here,' said Erica, trying to restrain her curiosity.

Tina pulled out a small box, stood up, and held it out to Erica. 'Do you want to see it or not?'

'Of course I do.'

'Okay. I'll keep watch. I already know what's inside.' Tina went over to the door, opened it slightly and peered out into the corridor.

After casting a nervous glance at Tina, Erica sat down on the bed and set the little box on her lap. If Laila came in now, any small amount of trust she might have established would be instantly gone. But how could she resist looking inside the box? Tina seemed to think she would find it interesting.

Holding her breath Erica opened the lid. She didn't know what she was expecting, but the contents certainly surprised her. One by one she took out the newspaper clippings while thoughts raced through her head. Why had Laila saved all these reports about the missing girls? Why was she so interested in them? Erica quickly looked through the articles, concluding that Laila must have cut out nearly everything that had been written about the disappearances in the local press and evening papers.

'She may be back any minute now,' said Tina, keeping her eyes on the corridor. 'But don't you think it's strange? She grabs the newspapers as soon as they arrive, and then she asks if she can keep them after everyone else has read them. I didn't know why until I saw what's in the box.'

'Thank you,' said Erica, carefully putting the clippings back inside. 'Where should I put it?'

'Next to the leg of the bed, in the far corner,' said Tina, still keeping an eye out for Laila.

Erica knelt down and carefully pushed the box back into place. She didn't know how to make use of what she'd just learned. Maybe it didn't mean anything. Maybe Laila was just interested in cases of missing girls. People could get obsessed with the strangest things. Yet she didn't really believe that was true when it came to Laila. There had to be some connection between Laila's life and these girls that she could never have met. And Erica was determined to find out what it was.

'There are a few things we need to discuss,' said Patrik.

Everyone nodded. Annika was ready with her notepad and pen, and Ernst was lying under the table waiting for any crumbs that might land on the floor. Everything was the same as always. Only the tense atmosphere in the kitchen made it clear that this was not an ordinary morning coffee break.

'As you know, Martin and I went to Göteborg yesterday. We met with Minna Wahlberg's mother Anette. We also had a talk with Gerhard Struwer, who gave us his views on the case, based on the materials we'd sent him.'

'Nothing but humbug,' muttered Mellberg, as if on cue. 'A waste of valuable resources.'

Patrik ignored him and went on.

'Martin has typed up his notes from yesterday, and you'll all get a copy.'

Annika picked up the stack of papers lying on the table and began handing them out to her colleagues.

'I'd like to focus on the most important points, and then you can read through the full report later, just in case I may have missed something.'

Trying to be as brief as possible, Patrik then gave a recap of both conversations.

'Based on what Struwer said, there are two things I'd like to talk about. First, he underscored that Minna is different from the other girls, both in terms of her background and the way in which she disappeared. The question is whether there's a reason for this. I think Struwer was right when he said that we should take a closer look at her disappearance. That's also one reason I wanted to meet with Minna's mother. Maybe the perpetrator had some personal connection to the girl, and if so, that might move us closer to solving Victoria's case. Of course we'll need to cooperate with the Göteborg police on this matter.'

'Exactly,' said Mellberg. 'These kinds of things can be rather sensitive, and—'

'Don't worry. We're not going to step on anyone's toes,' Patrik quickly added. He was amazed that Mellberg always had to insist on saying everything at least twice. 'And I'm hoping we'll have the opportunity to meet with them in person. Struwer also advised us to gather representatives from all the relevant police districts in order to go over the cases together. That won't be easy to arrange, but I think we should try to set up the meeting.'

'That's going to cost a fortune, with travel expenses and lodging for everybody. Management will never agree to it,' said Mellberg as he slipped a piece of cinnamon bun to Ernst.

Patrik restrained himself from sighing out loud. Working with Mellberg was often like pulling teeth. Nothing was ever easy or painless.

'We'll solve that problem when the time comes. These cases are such a high priority that resources should be readily available on a national level.'

'I think it's a good idea to get everyone together. Why don't we suggest meeting in Göteborg?' said Martin, leaning forward.

'That's an excellent suggestion,' replied Patrik. 'Annika, could you make the arrangements? I know it's the weekend and it might be hard to get hold of everyone, but I'd like to schedule the meeting as soon as possible.'

'Sure.' Annika jotted down a note to herself, adding a big exclamation mark.

'I hear you also met your wife in Göteborg yesterday,' Gösta said.

Patrik rolled his eyes. 'Why is it so difficult to keep anything secret in this place?'

'What? Was Erica in Göteborg? What was she doing there? Is she sticking her nose into police business again?' Mellberg was so indignant that his comb-over slipped down over his ear. 'You need to learn to control that woman. It's not right for her to go running around and getting involved in our work.'

'I've talked to her, and it won't happen again,' said Patrik calmly, but he could feel his annoyance from yesterday still simmering. He couldn't understand why Erica never took into consideration the possible repercussions of her meddling. She might even be obstructing the investigation.

Mellberg glared at him. 'She doesn't usually listen to you.'

'I know that, but I promise it won't happen again.' Patrik could hear how weak his words sounded, so he hurried to change the subject. 'Gösta, would you mind going over again what you told me on the phone yesterday?'

'Which part?' asked Gösta.

'About both visits. But the second one is especially interesting.'

Gösta nodded. Slowly and methodically he told them about his visit to Jonas and their talk about the ketamine that had been stolen shortly before Victoria went missing. Then he told his colleagues about the connection between Victoria and Katarina's report to the police. Finally, he described finding the cigarette butt in her garden.

'Good job,' said Martin. 'So there's a clear view of Victoria's bedroom from that woman's property?'

Gösta was feeling quite proud of himself. It was rare for him to receive praise for taking the initiative. 'Yes, you can see right in her window, and I think that's what the person did as he stood there smoking. I found the cigarette butt exactly where Katarina saw the man standing.'

'And the butt has been sent to the lab for analysis?' Patrik added.

Gösta nodded. 'Of course. Torbjörn has it now, and if there's any DNA on it, we'll be able to look for a match with a potential suspect.'

'We shouldn't jump to conclusions, but it could well have been the perp standing out there, keeping watch. Probably trying to find out about Victoria's routines, so later on he could kidnap her.' With a pleased expression, Mellberg clasped his hands over his stomach. 'Why don't we do what they did in that village in England? Test all the inhabitants in Fjällbacka and then compare the results with the DNA on the cigarette butt. And just like that, we'll have the guy. Brilliantly simple.'

'First of all, we don't know whether the perpetrator is a man or a woman,' said Patrik, making an effort to be patient. 'Second, we can't be sure the perpetrator is from around here, given that girls have disappeared from other areas. At the moment it seems likely that there's a connection with Göteborg, at least in Minna Wahlberg's case.'

'You're always so negative,' said Mellberg, unhappy to have his brilliant plan shot down.

'Maybe I'm just being realistic,' Patrik retorted, though he instantly regretted his remark. Letting Mellberg get under his skin was counter-productive. 'I heard that Paula was over here yesterday,' he said instead, and Mellberg nodded.

'That's right. I was talking to her about the case. When she heard that Victoria's tongue had been cut out, it reminded her of some previous report. The problem is, she couldn't remember which one, or when. She says nursing the baby has turned her brain to mush.'

Mellberg twirled his finger at his temple, but when Annika snorted, he quickly put down his hand. If there was one person that Mellberg didn't want to aggravate, it was the station's secretary. And possibly Rita as well.

'Paula spent a couple of hours in the archives,' said Gösta. 'But I don't think she found what she was looking for.'

'No. She's going to come back today.' Mellberg smiled at Annika, who was still glaring at him.

'I hope she realizes it's on her own time,' said Patrik.

'Sure, she knows that. To be honest, I think she needs to get away from home for a while,' Mellberg added, revealing a rare moment of insight.

Martin smiled. 'She must be climbing the walls at home if she prefers hanging out in the archives.'

The smile made his whole face light up, and Patrik realized how seldom he saw that happen these days. He really needed to keep a close eye on Martin. It couldn't be easy for him right now, as he grieved for Pia, tended to his duties as a single father, and also took part in such an onerous investigation.

Patrik smiled at his colleague. 'Well, for her sake, let's hope she finds out something. For our sake, too.'

Gösta raised his hand.

'Yes?' said Patrik.

'I keep thinking about that break-in at Jonas's clinic. Maybe it would be worth asking the stable girls about it. One of them might have seen something.'

'Good idea. You might try asking around after the memorial service this afternoon, but tread carefully. They're all bound to be very upset.'

'Okay. I'll take Martin along. It'll go faster if there are two of us.'

Patrik cast a glance at Martin. 'Hmm . . . I don't think it's necessary to—'

'It's fine. I'll go,' Martin said.

Patrik hesitated for a moment before saying, 'All right.' Then he turned to Gösta. 'And keep in touch with Torbjörn about the DNA results, okay?'

Gösta nodded.

'Good. We need to start knocking on doors in Katarina's neighbourhood to find out if anyone saw somebody sneaking around. And we have to check with Victoria's family, in case they noticed anyone watching them.'

Gösta ran his hand through his grey hair, making it stand straight up.

'I'm sure they would have told us by now if they'd seen anything like that. I think we did ask them if they'd noticed anyone hanging about their house, but I'll take a look at the interview transcript.'

'Have another talk with them in any case. I'll go out there and talk to the neighbours. And Bertil, could you stand by here at the station and help Annika make arrangements for the big meeting?'

'Of course. Who else could do it? They'll all be wanting to meet with the chief of police here, since I'm heading the investigation.'

'Okay, then. Let's be careful out there,' said Patrik, though his word choice made him instantly feel a bit foolish, as if they were all playing roles in an episode of *Hill Street Blues*. But it was worth it when he saw Martin smiling.

'Next week there's another jump-racing competition. Forget about the one you're missing and look forward to that instead.' Jonas stroked Molly's hair. He never ceased to be amazed by how much she resembled her mother.

'You sound like Dr Phil,' muttered Molly, her face buried in a pillow. Her joy over the promised car had quickly passed, and now she was again brooding over not being allowed to compete.

'You're going to regret it if you don't train properly. It won't even be worth competing then. And you'll be the one who's most disappointed if you don't win. Not me or your mother.'

'Marta could care less,' Molly grumbled.

Jonas pulled back his hand.

'Are you saying that all the kilometres we've driven and all the hours we've put in don't count? Your mother . . . Marta has invested a ton of money and time in preparing you for competitions, and you're being incredibly ungrateful when you say things like that.' He could hear how sharp his voice sounded, but it was time for his daughter to grow up.

Molly slowly sat up. She looked surprised that he had spoken to her in that tone, and she seemed about to protest. But then she lowered her eyes.

'Sorry,' she said quietly.

'Excuse me, but what did you say?'

'I'm sorry!' She was on the verge of tears as Jonas put his arms around her. He knew that he had always spoiled her, for better or worse. But right now she had reacted as she should. She needed to learn that life sometimes demanded that she give in.

'It's okay, sweetie, it's okay. Why don't we go over to the stable? You need to train if you're going to beat Linda Bergvall. She shouldn't think that she's guaranteed to win.'

'All right,' said Molly, wiping her tears on her sleeve.

'Come on. I don't have to work today, so I was thinking I could help you train. Mamma's already over there with Scirocco.'

Molly swung her legs over the side of the bed, and he saw the competitive instinct gleaming in her eyes. They were so alike in that regard. Both of them hated to lose.

When they got to the riding school, Marta was waiting for them, and Scirocco was already saddled. She made a point of looking at her watch.

'So the young lady decided to make an appearance after all. You were supposed to be here half an hour ago.'

Jonas gave his wife a warning look. One wrong word and Molly would run straight back to bed and start sulking again. He could see that Marta was debating with herself. She detested having to bow to her daughter's whims. And even though it was her own choice, Marta also detested the fact that she didn't share in the close relationship that he had with Molly. But she too liked to win, even if she did so through a daughter she had never wanted or understood.

'I've got him ready for you,' she said, handing the horse over to Molly.

With ease Molly swung herself up into the saddle and took the reins. Using her thighs and heels, she put Scirocco through his paces, and he willingly obeyed. As soon as Molly was on horseback, the truculent teenager disappeared. Up there she was a strong young woman, confident, calm, and sure of herself. Jonas loved to see the transformation.

He took a ringside seat to watch Marta work. Skilfully she instructed her daughter. She knew exactly how to make both the rider and the horse do their best. Molly had a natural gift for all aspects of horseback riding, but it was Marta who refined her talent. She was amazing as she stood there in the riding hall and with curt directives got the horse and rider to fly over the hurdles. It was going to be a great competition. The three of them were a wonderful team: Marta, Molly, and Jonas. Slowly he felt the familiar anticipation and tension beginning to build inside his body.

Erica was in her study, going through the long list of things she needed to get done. Anna had said that she and the kids could stay all day, if necessary, and Erica had swiftly seized upon the offer. There were so many people she ought to talk to, and so much material she should read, and she wished that she'd made more progress. Then maybe she'd understand why Laila had collected all those newspaper articles. For a moment she had considered going to Laila and asking her directly, but she realized that would be fruitless. Instead she had left the prison and driven home to do more research on her own.

'Maaammaaa! The twins are fighting!' Maja's voice made her jump. According to Anna, the children had behaved perfectly while Erica was gone, but now it sounded as if they were about to kill each other down in the living room.

She ran downstairs and rushed into the room. There stood Maja, glaring at her little brothers as they tussled on the sofa.

'They're bothering me, Mamma, and I want to watch TV. They keep taking the remote control and changing the channel.'

'Stop that,' cried Erica, sounding a bit more cross than she'd intended. 'If that's how it is, then neither of you gets to watch TV.'

She went over to the sofa and grabbed the remote. The boys stared up at her in surprise and then both started crying. She silently counted to ten, but she could feel her anger surging as sweat ran down her sides. She had never imagined it would take so much patience to be a parent. And she was ashamed that she'd once punished Maja for something she hadn't done.

Anna was in the kitchen with Emma and Adrian, but now she came into the living room. When she saw Erica's expression, she couldn't hide a wry smile.

'Looks like it'd be good for you to get out of the house more often. Isn't there someplace else you need to go, now that I'm already here?'

Erica was about to say she was grateful just to have peace and quiet to work when a thought occurred to her. There was in fact something else she needed to do. One item on her list, in particular, had sparked her interest.

'Mamma has to go out and work for a while,' she said to the kids. 'But Anna is here. And if you're nice, I think she'll fix you a snack.'

The boys instantly stopped crying. The word 'snack' seemed to have a magical effect on them.

Erica gave her sister a warm hug. She went into the kitchen to make a phone call to make sure the person she wanted to see would be home. Fifteen minutes later she was on her way. By that time the children were all sitting at the kitchen table drinking juice and eating buns and biscuits. No doubt consuming way too much sugar, but she'd worry about that later.

It wasn't difficult to locate the small terraced house just outside of Uddevalla where Wilhelm Mosander lived. He had sounded intrigued when she phoned, and he opened the door even before she rang the bell.

'Come in,' said the elderly man. She carefully kicked the snow off her boots and went inside.

She had never met Mosander before, but she knew quite a lot about him. In his day he was a legendary journalist at *Bohusläningen*, and he was most famous for his reports about the murder of Vladek Kowalski.

'I take it you're writing a new book,' he said as he led her into the kitchen. Erica saw that the room was small but clean and well-kept. There was no sign of a woman's presence, so she guessed that Wilhelm must be a bachelor.

As if he'd read her mind, he said, 'My wife died ten years ago so I sold our big monstrosity of a house and moved here. It's much easier to take care of, but it can seem a little spartan since I don't know much about curtains and things like that.'

'It's very cosy.' Erica sat down at the table, and Mosander served the obligatory coffee. 'And yes, I'm writing a book. It's about the House of Horrors.'

'What else do you think I might be able to tell you? I assume that you've already read most of the articles I wrote.'

'Yes, Kjell Ringholm at *Bohusläningen* helped me find all the newspaper articles. And of course I've gathered a lot of facts about the course of events and the trial. But what I need now is to talk to someone who was there. I'd like to hear your impressions. I'm thinking that you probably made observations and noticed things that you couldn't write about. Maybe you even have your own theories about the case. According to what I've heard, you've never been able to let the matter go.'

Erica sipped her coffee as she studied Wilhelm.

'Well, there's certainly a lot to write about.' Wilhelm's eyes glinted as he returned her gaze. 'I've never come across a case, either before or since, as interesting as that one. Anyone who knew about it couldn't help being affected.'

'I know. It's one of the most horrifying cases I've ever encountered. And I'd really like to find out exactly what happened that day.'

'That makes two of us,' said Wilhelm. 'Even though Laila confessed to the murder, I could never shake off the feeling that something didn't fit. I don't have any theory of my own, but I think the truth was more complicated than anyone realized.'

'Precisely,' said Erica eagerly. 'The problem is that Laila refuses to talk about it.'

'But she agreed to see you?' Wilhelm leaned forward. 'I never thought she'd do that.'

'Yes, we've met a few times now. I tried to make contact for a long time, sending letters and making phone calls, and I'd just about given up when she suddenly said yes.'

'Well, I'll be damned. She's kept silent all these years, and then she agrees to meet with you?' He shook his head, looking as if he could hardly believe his ears. 'I tried to get an interview with her so many times in the past, but without success.'

'She's not telling me anything though. So far I've got nothing of interest out of her.' Erica could hear how discouraged she sounded.

'So tell me, how is she? How is she doing?'

Erica felt the conversation was going off at a tangent,

but she resisted the urge to steer it back on track by resorting to the questions she'd come there to ask. A little give and take was necessary.

'She's very composed. Very calm. Yet she seems anxious about something.'

'Does she strike you as feeling guilty? About the murder? About what was done to her daughter?'

Erica paused to consider. 'Yes and no. She doesn't seem exactly remorseful, but she does take responsibility for what happened. It's hard to explain. Getting her to say anything about it is so difficult, I've had to read between the lines, so to speak. And it's possible that I'm misinterpreting because of my own reaction to what she did.'

'Yes, it was horrific.' Wilhelm nodded. 'Have you been inside the house?'

'Yes, just the other day. It's practically derelict now, after standing empty for so long. But it felt like something was still there, in the walls . . . And in the cellar.' Erica shuddered at the memory.

'I know what you mean. It's a mystery how anyone could treat a child the way Vladek did. Or that Laila could let it happen. Personally, I think in that sense she's just as guilty as he was, even though she was terrified of what he might do. She could have made other choices, and you'd think her maternal instinct would have been stronger than it was.'

'They didn't treat their son in the same way. Why do you think Peter got off so much easier?'

'I never could make any sense of that. I'm sure you read the article in which I interviewed several psychologists about it.'

'Yes. In their opinion Vladek's hatred for women meant that he was abusive only to the females in the family. But that doesn't seem entirely true. According to the medical records, Peter also suffered injuries. He once had his arm pulled out of the socket, and he also suffered a deep stab wound.'

'That's right, but it's nothing compared to what Louise endured.'

'Do you have any idea what happened to Peter? I haven't been able to track him down. Not yet, anyway.'

'No. I never did either. If you do find him, please let me know.'

'But aren't you retired now?' asked Erica, though she realized that was a stupid question. The Kowalski case had long ago ceased to be merely a news story for Wilhelm. Maybe it had always been something more. She could see in his eyes that over the years it had become an obsession for him. He didn't bother to answer her question, but continued to talk about Peter.

'It's a bit of a mystery. As you no doubt know, he was sent to live with his maternal grandmother after the murder, and he seemed to be doing well. But when he was fifteen his grandmother was murdered when someone broke into their house. Peter was away at a football camp on Gotland when it happened, and after that he seems to have disappeared into thin air.'

'Do you think he might have killed himself?' Erica speculated out loud. 'Maybe he did it in such a way that his body was never found.'

'Maybe. Who knows? And there was another tragedy in that family.'

'Are you thinking about Louise's death?'

'Yes. She drowned while she was living with a foster family. She wasn't placed with her grandmother but with a foster family. It was thought they could provide her with better support after the trauma she'd been through.'

'It was an unexplained accident, wasn't it?' Erica tried to recall the details she'd read.

'Yes. Both Louise and the couple's other foster daughter,

who was the same age, were apparently caught in the undertow and their bodies were never found. A tragic end to a tragic life.'

'So the only relative still alive is Laila's sister, who lives in Spain, right?'

'Yes, but they didn't have much contact with each other, even before the murder. I tried to talk to her a few times, but she didn't want anything to do with Laila. And Vladek left his own family and his old life behind when he decided to stay in Sweden with Laila.'

'Such a strange combination of love and . . . evil,' said Erica, unable to find a better word to describe what she meant.

Wilhelm suddenly looked very tired. 'What I saw in that living room and in that cellar was the closest to evil I've ever come.'

'You were at the crime scene?'

He nodded. 'Back then it was a little easier to get into places where I didn't belong. I had good contacts on the police force, and they allowed me to go in and have a look. There was blood everywhere in the living room. And apparently Laila was sitting there in the middle of it when the police arrived. She didn't offer the slightest resistance, just went with them quietly.'

'And Louise was chained up when they found her?' said Erica.

'Yes. She was down in the cellar, emaciated and wretched.'

Erica swallowed hard as she imagined the scene.

'Did you ever meet the children?'

'No. Peter was so young when it happened. All the journalists were smart enough to leave the children in peace. Both the grandmother and the foster family shielded them from publicity.'

'Why do you think Laila confessed so quickly?'

'I don't suppose she had any other option. As I said, when the police arrived she was sitting next to Vladek's body and holding the knife in her hand. And she was the one who notified the police. On the phone she had already said: "I've killed my husband." And by the way, that was all anyone ever got out of her. She repeated her statement during the trial, but apart from that no one was able to get her to break her silence.'

'So why do you think she agreed to talk to me?' asked Erica.

'Hmm . . . That does seem odd.' Wilhelm gave her a searching look. 'She was forced to meet with the police and the psychologists, but meeting with you is completely voluntary on her part.'

'Maybe she just wants company. Maybe she's tired of seeing the same faces everyday,' said Erica, even though she wasn't convinced by her own explanation.

'Not Laila. There must be some other reason. Has she said anything that especially caught your interest or surprised you? Has there been any clue that something has happened or changed?' He leaned forward even more, sitting on the edge of his chair.

'There is one thing . . .' Erica hesitated. Then she took a deep breath and told him about the articles that Laila had hidden in her room. She knew it was a long shot. The clippings probably had nothing to do with her meetings with Laila. But Wilhelm listened intently, and she saw a keen intelligence in his eyes.

'Have you thought about the date?' he said then.

'What date?'

'The date when Laila finally agreed to meet with you.'

Erica frantically searched her memory. It was about four months ago, but she couldn't recall the exact date. Then she remembered. It was the day after Kristina's birthday. She mentioned the date to Wilhelm, who gave her a crooked smile as he leaned down and picked up from the floor a thick stack of old copies of *Bohusläningen*. He began looking through them, then paused and with a pleased expression handed Erica a newspaper open to an inside page. She cursed her stupidity. Of course. That had to be the connection. The question was, what did it mean?

The air inside the barn was stifling, and an icy vapour issued from her lips as she breathed. Helga drew her coat closer around her. She knew that Jonas and Marta viewed the Friday dinners as an obligation. That was obvious from their long-suffering expressions. But the dinners were the anchor of Helga's existence, the only time when she could see all of them as members of a real family.

Yesterday it had been more difficult than usual to keep up the illusion. Because that was precisely what it was: an illusion, a dream. She'd had so many dreams. When she met Einar he had taken over and filled her whole world with his broad shoulders, his blond hair, and a smile that she'd interpreted as warm, though she later learned it meant something else entirely.

She stopped next to the car that Molly had talked about. She knew exactly which one it was, and if she had been Molly's age, she would have chosen it too. Helga looked about at the other cars in the barn. All of them abandoned and falling apart from rust.

She could remember where every single car had come from, every trip that Einar had made to buy suitable vehicles to restore. Each car had required many hours of work before it could be sold. The business hadn't brought in a huge income, but it had been enough for them to live comfortably. She'd never had to worry about money. That was one part of the bargain Einar had managed to keep: he had provided for her and Jonas financially.

Slowly she moved away from Molly's car, as she was now calling it, and went over to an old black Volvo that had big rust patches and broken windows. It would have been a wonderful vehicle if Einar had fixed it up. If she closed her eyes, she could picture his face whenever he brought home a new car. She could tell at once if the trip had been successful. Sometimes he was gone only a day, but sometimes he would head to distant regions of Sweden and be away for a week. When he drove into the yard with a feverish look in his eyes and flushed cheeks, she knew that he'd found what he'd wanted. For several days, sometimes even several weeks afterwards, he would be totally immersed in his work. That was when she could devote herself to Jonas and her housework. For a while she could escape his outbursts, the cold hatred in his eyes, and the pain. Those were her happiest days.

She put her hand on the car and shivered at the icy touch of the metal. The light inside the barn had slowly shifted as she wandered about. The sun was now shining through the gaps in the walls and reflecting off the black paint. Helga pulled back her hand. This car would never have a new life. It was a dead object, something that belonged to the past. And she intended to see that it stayed that way.

Erica leaned back in the visitor's chair. She had driven directly from Wilhelm's house to the prison. She needed to speak to Laila again. Fortunately, Laila seemed to have calmed down since the morning and agreed to meet with her. Maybe she hadn't been as upset as Erica thought.

They'd been sitting in silence for a while now, a hint of concern in Laila's eyes as she studied Erica.

'Why did you want to see me again today?'

Erica was debating with herself. She wasn't sure what to say, but she could tell that Laila would close up like a clam if she mentioned the newspaper clippings and revealed her suspicions about a connection.

'I couldn't stop thinking about what you said earlier,' she replied at last. 'You said it was a house of horrors, but not in the way everybody thought. What did you mean by that?'

Laila turned to look out of the window.

'Why would I want to talk about that? It's not something I want to remember.'

'I can understand that. But seeing as you've agreed to meet with me, I have a feeling you do want to talk about it. And maybe it would be a relief to share it with someone.'

'Talking is overrated. People go to therapists and psychologists and discuss things over and over with friends. They have to analyse every little detail. But certain things are best left alone.'

'Are you talking about yourself now, or about what happened?' said Erica gently.

Laila turned back from the window and looked at her with those strange icy blue eyes of hers.

'Maybe both,' she said. Her cropped hair looked even shorter than usual. She must have just had it cut.

Erica decided to change tack.

'We haven't talked much about the rest of your family. Could we do that now?' she asked in an attempt to find a crack in the wall of silence that Laila had built around herself.

Laila shrugged. 'I suppose so.'

'Your father died when you were very young, but were you close to your mother?'

'Yes. Mamma was my best friend.' A smile appeared on Laila's face, making her look several years younger.

'What about your older sister?'

Laila paused before replying. 'She's lived in Spain for

many years,' she then said. 'We've never had much contact, and she cut off all ties with me when . . . it happened.'

'Does she have a family?'

'Yes. She's married to a Spaniard, and they have a son and a daughter.'

'Your mother stepped in to take care of Peter. Why Peter but not Louise?'

Laila uttered a harsh laugh. 'Mamma could never have handled the Girl. But things were different with Peter. He and Mamma were very close.'

'The Girl?' Erica gave Laila an enquiring look.

'Yes. That's what we called her,' Laila said quietly. 'It was Vladek who started it, and the name stuck.'

Poor child, thought Erica. She tried to restrain her anger and focus on the questions she wanted to ask.

'So why couldn't Louise, or the Girl, live with your mother?'

Laila stared at her defiantly. 'Because she was a very demanding child. That's all I'm going to say about the matter.'

Erica was forced to accept that she wasn't going to get any further, so she changed tack again.

'What do you think happened to Peter after your mother . . . died?'

A touch of sadness appeared on Laila's face. 'I don't know. He just disappeared. I think . . .' She swallowed hard and seemed to have difficulty finding the right words. 'I think maybe he just couldn't go on any more. He was never that strong. He was such a sensitive boy.'

'Are you saying that you think he may have committed suicide?' Erica tried to formulate the question as cautiously as possible.

At first Laila didn't react, but then she nodded, her eyes lowered.

'But he was never found?' Erica persisted.

'No.'

'You must be incredibly strong to have endured so many losses in your life.'

'People can survive more than they think. If they have to,' said Laila. 'I'm not a particularly religious person, but it's said that God never puts a greater burden on your shoulders than He knows you can bear. And He must know that I can handle a lot.'

'There's going to be a memorial service in Fjällbacka church today,' said Erica, watching Laila closely. It was risky for her to turn the conversation to Victoria.

'Oh, really?' Laila gave her an inquisitive look, but Erica could tell she already knew about the service.

'It's for the girl who disappeared and then died. I'm sure you've heard about it. Her name was Victoria Hallberg. It must be so hard for her parents right now. And for the parents of the other girls who are still missing.'

'I suppose so.' Laila seemed to be struggling to keep her composure.

'Just imagine, their daughters have disappeared. And now that they know what happened to Victoria, they must be going through hell thinking that their girls may have been subjected to the same treatment.'

'I only know what I've read in the newspapers,' said Laila, swallowing hard. 'But it must be awful.'

Erica nodded. 'Have you been following the case?'

Laila gave her an evasive look. 'Well, we read the papers every day here. So I've followed the case just like everybody else.'

'Of course,' said Erica, thinking about the box containing the carefully cut out articles hidden under the bed in Laila's room.

'You know, I'm really tired. I don't feel like talking any more. You'll have to come back some other day.' Laila abruptly stood up.

For a moment Erica considered confronting Laila, telling her that she knew about the clippings and was convinced that Laila had a personal connection to the case, though she wasn't sure what it was. But she stopped herself. Laila's face was stony, and her hands were gripping the back of the chair so hard that her knuckles were white. Whatever it was she wanted to say, she clearly couldn't make herself do it.

Impulsively Erica stood up and stepped forward to pat Laila's cheek. It was the first time she'd ever touched her, and her skin was surprisingly soft.

'We'll talk more later,' Erica said gently. As she headed for the door, she could feel Laila's eyes steadily watching her.

Tyra could hear her mother humming out in the kitchen. She was always much happier when Lasse wasn't home. And she wasn't upset any more about yesterday. She had accepted Tyra's explanation that she'd simply forgotten her mother was coming and had gone home with a friend. It was better not to tell her anything. There would just be trouble if she heard the truth. Tyra wandered into the kitchen.

'What are you baking?'

Her mother stood at the kitchen table, her hands covered with flour. There were even specks of flour on her face. Neatness had never been her strong suit, and whenever she made dinner Lasse would always complain that the kitchen looked like a battlefield.

'Cinnamon buns. I thought we could have a little snack this afternoon after the memorial service. Plus I wanted to refill the freezer.'

'Is Lasse in Kville?'

'Yes, as usual.' Terese reached up to push back a lock of hair, making her face even whiter with flour.

'Pretty soon you're going to look like the Joker,' said Tyra, and she felt a warm fluttering in her stomach at the sight of her mother smiling. That happened so rarely these days. She mostly looked tired and unhappy. But the feeling vanished as quickly as it had come. Tyra's grief for Victoria was always present, extinguishing any cheerful feelings that might arise. And the thought of the memorial service made her stomach turn over. She didn't want to say goodbye.

She watched her mother in silence for a moment.

'So what was Jonas like as a boyfriend?' she wondered out loud.

'Why do you ask?'

'I don't know. I was just thinking about the two of you together.'

'I have to admit that he wasn't an easy person to understand. Always a bit closed off and withdrawn. And kind of a chicken-heart too. I remember having to fight to get him to even put his hand under my shirt.'

'Mamma!' Tyra covered her ears with her hands and glared at Terese. That wasn't the sort of thing she wanted to hear from her mother. She preferred to think of Terese as a Barbie doll, completely sexless.

'But it's true. He really was a chicken. His father was so domineering, and sometimes it seemed like Jonas and his mother were both afraid of the man.'

Terese rolled out the dough on the kitchen table and smeared on butter so it covered the entire surface.

'Do you think he was abusive towards them?'

'Who? Einar? Hmm . . . I never saw anything like that. I mostly heard him griping and grumbling. He's probably one of those guys whose bark is worse than his bite. I really didn't see him that often. He was either out on one of his buying trips, or else he was working on the cars in the barn.'

'How did Jonas and Marta meet?' Tyra pinched off a piece of dough and stuffed it in her mouth.

Terese stopped what she was doing and paused a few seconds before answering.

'You know, I've never actually heard how they met. One day she was just there. And it all happened so fast. I was young and naive, and I thought Jonas and I would be together for ever. But suddenly he broke up with me. And I've never been one to make a fuss, so I just went my own way. I was sad for a while, of course, but I got over it.' She began sprinkling cinnamon on the buttered dough, then rolled it up.

'Has there ever been any talk about Jonas and Marta since then? Any gossip?'

'You know what I think about gossip, Tyra,' said Terese sternly as she cut the rolled dough into thick slices. 'But to answer your question: no, I've never heard anything other than that they're very happy. And then I met your father. Jonas and I just weren't meant to be together. We were so young. You'll see, you're probably going to have a teenage love of your own.'

'Oh, stop it,' said Tyra, feeling herself blush. She hated it when her mother talked to her about boys and things like that. Terese didn't have a clue.

Now Terese gave her a searching glance. 'But why are you asking me all these questions about Jonas? And about Marta?'

'No special reason. I was just wondering.' Tyra shrugged and tried to look nonchalant. Then she swiftly changed the subject. 'Molly is going to get one of the cars out in the barn when she learns to drive. A Volkswagen Beetle. Jonas promised to fix it up for her.'

She couldn't keep a trace of envy from creeping into her voice, and she saw that her mother noticed.

'I'm sorry I can't give you everything I'd like to. We . . .

I . . . Well, life doesn't always turn out the way you'd thought it would.' Terese took a deep breath and scattered sugar over the buns, which she'd placed on a baking sheet.

'I know. It doesn't matter,' Tyra hastened to say.

She didn't mean to be ungrateful. She knew that her mother was doing the best she could. And she was ashamed even to be thinking about a car right now. Victoria would never have a car.

'How's it going with Lasse's job-hunting?' she asked.

Terese snorted. 'God doesn't seem to be in any hurry to deliver a job for him.'

'Maybe God has other things to think about than finding a job for Lasse.'

Terese finished what she was doing and looked at her daughter.

'Tyra . . .' She seemed to be searching for the right words. 'Do you think we could manage on our own? Without Lasse, I mean?'

For a moment there was utter silence in the kitchen. The only sound in the flat was the noise the boys were making in the next room.

Then Tyra said quietly, 'It would be fine. I think we'd manage just fine.'

She stepped forward and kissed her mother's floury cheek. Then she went to her bedroom to change her clothes. All the girls from the stable would be at Victoria's memorial service. They seemed to think of it as something exciting. She'd heard them eagerly whispering to each other, even discussing what they should wear. What idiots. Superficial, brainless idiots. None of them had known Victoria the way she had. Or at least not the way she thought she'd known her. With great reluctance Tyra took her favourite dress out of the wardrobe. It was time to say goodbye.

* * *

It had been a delightful break for her to babysit for the twins and Maja. Anna hadn't been lying when she told Erica that they had behaved perfectly all day, as children so often do. It was only with their parents that they displayed their worst behaviour. No doubt it had helped that she'd brought Emma and Adrian along. The two of them were idolized by their young cousins, since they were 'big kids', after all.

She smiled to herself as she wiped off the worktop. It felt strange to be smiling; she hadn't done it in so long. Yesterday, when she and Dan had talked here in the kitchen, she had felt a spark of hope return. She knew it might quickly fade, because afterwards Dan had again withdrawn into silence. But maybe they had taken a small step closer to each other.

She had been serious when she told him she was ready to move out if that was what he wanted. A couple of times she had even gone on the web to look for a suitable flat for herself and the children. But that wasn't what she wanted. She loved Dan.

In spite of everything, over the past few months they had taken several small steps towards bridging the chasm between them. On one anxious occasion, after they'd both had a few too many glasses of wine, he'd reached out to touch her body, and she had clung to him as if she were drowning. They had made love, but afterwards he'd looked so tormented that all she wanted to do was run away. They hadn't touched each other since. Except for the hug yesterday.

Anna looked out of the kitchen window. The kids were playing in the snow. Even though her children were too old for such games, they both still thought it was fun to build snowmen and have snowball fights. She wiped her hands on a dish towel and cautiously pressed her palms to her stomach. She tried to remember what it had felt like when she was pregnant with Dan's child. She couldn't blame her grief for what she'd done. That was not the sort of thing to blame on an innocent child. But sometimes her sorrow was mixed with guilt, and she couldn't help thinking that everything would have been different if their little son had lived. Then he would be playing out there in the snow with his older siblings, bundled up and looking like a little Michelin man, the way kids always looked in the winter when they were toddlers.

Anna knew that sometimes Erica worried that the twins reminded her of the son she had lost. And in the beginning they had. She had been jealous and harboured bad thoughts about how unfair it was, the way things had turned out. But that feeling had passed. Sometimes life was unfair, and there was no logic to it, no reasonable explanation for why she and Dan had lost their beloved baby. Now she could only hope that they'd find a way back to sharing a life together.

A snowball struck the windowpane, and she saw Adrian's alarmed expression as he reached up his mittened hand to cover his mouth. At the sight of him, she made up her mind. Quickly she ran out to the hall, threw on her winter coat, and then tore open the front door. Doing her best imitation of a scary monster, she growled, 'Hey, you two, time for a snowball fight!'

The children stared at her in surprise. Then they shouted their joy to the winter sky.

Gösta and Martin were sitting in the last pew of the church. Gösta had decided to attend Victoria's memorial service the minute he heard it was going to be held. Her terrible fate had stirred up anxiety and fear in Fjällbacka, and now her family and friends had gathered for her funeral. They needed to talk about Victoria, to share memories and work through all the emotions prompted by the news of how terribly she had suffered. It was only reasonable that he and Martin should be there, representing the police station.

It was hard for Gösta to push aside his own memories as he sat there on the hard pew. He had been here before for two other funerals: first his son's, and many years later, his wife's. Gösta twisted his wedding band on his finger. He had never felt right about taking it off. Maj-Britt had been the great love of his life, his beloved companion, and he'd never even thought about replacing her.

Life's paths were indeed inscrutable, he thought. Sometimes he wondered whether there might actually be some higher power guiding and steering human beings. In the past he'd never believed in anything like that. Back then he would have called himself an atheist, but the older he got, the more he felt Maj-Britt's presence. It was as if she were still at his side. And it was almost a miracle that after so many years Ebba had resumed such a natural place in his life and heart.

He looked around the church. It was beautiful. Built of the granite the Bohuslän area was known for, it had lovely tall windows that let in a flood of light. A blue-painted pulpit was on the left, and the altar was up front behind the carved altar rail. For once the church was packed to bursting point, and the congregation included close family members, distant relatives, and many of Victoria's peers. Some of them were probably classmates, but Gösta recognized quite a few girls from the stable. They sat together in two of the middle rows, and many of them were audibly sobbing.

Gösta cast a surreptitious glance at Martin and realized that maybe he shouldn't have suggested that his colleague come along. It wasn't long ago that Pia had been laid to rest in her coffin, and he saw from the pallor of Martin's face that he was thinking the same thing.

'I can handle this on my own, if you like,' Gösta whispered to him. 'You don't need to stay.'

'I'm fine,' replied Martin with a strained smile, but he kept his eyes fixed straight ahead throughout the entire service.

It was a moving ceremony, and as the last hymns faded, Gösta hoped it had provided some solace to the family. With noticeable effort, Victoria's parents got up from their seats in the front pew. Helena leaned on Markus for support as they walked along the centre aisle towards the door of the church, then everyone else slowly followed.

Outside family and friends gathered in small groups. It was a bitterly cold day, but beautiful, with sunlight glinting off the snow. Subdued and freezing, their eyes red from crying, everyone stood there talking about how much Victoria would be missed and what unimaginable suffering she must have endured. Gösta could see the fear in the young girls' faces. Were they next? Was the person who had kidnapped Victoria still in the area? He decided to give it a while before talking to them. He would wait until the group had dispersed and they began heading for home.

With blank expressions Markus and Helena moved among the mourners to exchange a few words with everyone. Ricky stayed a short distance away, wanting to keep to himself. Some of Victoria's friends went over to him, but they seemed to get only one-syllable responses and eventually they left him in peace.

Suddenly Ricky looked up and met Gösta's eye. He hesitated for a moment but then came over to the two officers.

'I need to talk to you,' he said in a low voice to Gösta. 'Someplace where no one can hear us.'

'Of course,' said Gösta. 'Is it okay if my colleague Martin comes too?'

Ricky nodded and led the way to the far corner of the cemetery.

'There's something I have to tell you,' he began, kicking at the ground with his shoe. The powdery snow whirled up around them and then settled back down like glitter. 'It's something I should have told you long ago.'

Gösta and Martin exchanged glances.

'Victoria and I never had any secrets from each other. Never ever. It's hard to explain, because we always stuck together, but all of a sudden I had a feeling she was keeping something from me. She was pulling away, and that made me worried. I tried to talk to her, but she was avoiding me more and more. Then . . . then I worked out what it was all about.'

'And what was it?' asked Gösta.

'Victoria and Jonas.' Ricky swallowed hard. He had tears in his eyes, and it looked as if it was causing him physical pain to say the words.

'What do you mean, Victoria and Jonas?'

'They were together,' said Ricky.

'Are you sure?'

'No, not a hundred per cent. But all the signs were there. And yesterday I met Victoria's best friend Tyra, and she told me she suspected something too.'

'Okay, but if that's true, then why do you think she didn't tell you about Jonas?'

'I don't know. Or rather, yes, I do. I think she was embarrassed. She knew I would think it was wrong, but she shouldn't have been ashamed for my sake. Nothing she did would ever have changed how I thought of her.'

'How long do you think the relationship had been going on?' asked Martin.

Ricky shook his head. He wasn't wearing a hat, and his ears were red from the cold.

'I don't know. But it was sometime before summer that I started feeling like she was a little . . . different.'

'In what way was she different?' Gösta wiggled his toes inside his shoes. They were starting to go numb from the cold.

Ricky paused to think. 'There was something secretive about her that I'd never noticed before. Sometimes she'd be gone for a couple of hours, and if I asked her where she'd been, she'd tell me it was none of my business. She'd never done that before. And she seemed both happy and . . . I don't know how to describe it, but happy and depressed at the same time. Her mood could change in an instant, shifting up and down. Maybe because she was a teenager, but I think there was some other reason too.' When he said that, he sounded so sensible that Gösta had to remind himself Ricky was only eighteen.

'So you suspected she was having a relationship with someone?' queried Martin.

'Yes, I did. But it never occurred to me it might be Jonas. Good Lord, he's . . . ancient! Plus he's married.'

Gösta felt a smile tugging at his lips. If Jonas, who was in his forties, was considered ancient, then he must be practically a fossil in Ricky's eyes.

Ricky wiped away a tear that had spilled down his cheek.

'I was so angry when I found out about it. He's almost a . . . paedophile.'

Gösta shook his head. 'In principle I agree with you, but the legal age is fifteen. How it should be regarded from a moral point of view is another story.' He mulled over what Ricky had just told them. 'So how did you find out they were having a relationship?'

'Like I said, I had a feeling that Victoria was with someone, and she didn't think my parents and I would approve.' Ricky hesitated. 'But I didn't know who it was, and she refused to tell me when I asked. That was so unlike her, because we always shared everything. Then one day I went over to the riding school to fetch her, and I saw them having a quarrel. I couldn't hear what they were saying, but I understood at once. I ran over and yelled to her that finally I understood everything and I thought it was disgusting. But she yelled back that I didn't understand a thing, and I was an idiot. Then she rushed off. Jonas just stood there, looking like a fool, and I was so furious that I really let him have it.'

'Did anyone hear you?'

'No, I don't think so. The older girls had gone out riding with the younger ones, and Marta was giving Molly a lesson out in the paddock.'

'Did Jonas admit to anything?' Gösta could feel anger surging inside of him too.

'No, not a thing. He just tried to calm me down, and he kept on saying that it wasn't true, that he'd never touched Victoria, that I was simply imagining things. What bullshit! Then his mobile rang and he said he had to leave. But I'm sure it was just an excuse because he didn't want to talk to me any more.'

'So you didn't believe him?' Gösta's toes were now completely frozen. Out of the corner of his eye he saw Markus looking their way, no doubt wondering why they were talking to his son.

'Of course not!' Ricky spat out the words. 'He was totally calm, but I could tell from the way they'd been arguing that it was about something personal. And Victoria's reaction confirmed it.'

'Why didn't you tell us about this before?' asked Martin.

'I don't know. Everything was so chaotic. Victoria never came home that night, and when we realized that she'd disappeared on her way home from the stable, we phoned the police. The worst thing was that I knew it was my fault! If I hadn't yelled at her and started quarrelling with Jonas, if I'd driven her home as planned, she wouldn't have been picked up by some fucking psychopath. Besides, I didn't want my parents to find out about her relationship with Jonas. They were already so worried, and I didn't want them to be subjected to a bunch of scandalous articles. Especially since I'd convinced myself that Victoria would eventually come back home. And since I hadn't told you about this right from the start, it got harder to do it later on. I've had such a guilty conscience and . . .' Tears poured out, and Gösta instinctively stepped forward to put his arm around Ricky.

'Hush. It's okay. And it's not your fault. Don't think it is. Nobody is blaming you. You wanted to protect your family, and we understand that. It's not your fault.' After a moment the tension seeped out of the boy's body, and he stopped crying.

Ricky looked up at Gösta.

'Somebody else knew about this,' he said quietly.

'Who?'

'I don't know. But I found some strange letters in Victoria's room. A bunch of drivel about God and sinners and burning in hell.'

'Do you still have the letters?' asked Gösta, holding his breath.

Ricky shook his head.

'No, I threw them out. I . . . I thought they were so awful, and I was afraid my parents would find them. They would have been really upset. So I threw the letters in the rubbish. Was that a stupid thing to do?'

Gösta patted his shoulder. 'What's done is done. But where in her room did you find them? And can you try to recall the exact wording?'

'I went through all her things after she disappeared. Before you came over to search her room. I thought I might find something about Jonas. The letters were in the back of one of the desk drawers. I don't remember everything they said. Just a few lines that sounded like Bible quotes. With words like "sinners" and "harlots" and things like that.'

'And you assumed they were referring to Victoria's relationship with Jonas?' asked Martin.

'Yes. That seemed the most likely. Someone who knew about it and wanted to . . . scare her.'

'And you have no idea who might have sent those letters?'

'No, I'm afraid not.'

'Okay. Thank you for telling us about this. That was the right thing to do,' said Gösta. 'You'd better go and join your parents now. They're probably wondering what we've been talking about all this time.'

Ricky didn't reply. He merely bowed his head and with heavy steps headed back towards the church.

By the time Patrik came home, it had already been dark for hours. As soon as he stepped in the door, he noticed a delicious aroma coming from the kitchen. It smelled as if Erica had made something extra special for Saturday dinner. He was guessing it was her pork casserole with blue cheese and potato wedges, which was one of his favourite dishes. He hurried into the kitchen.

'I hope you're hungry,' said Erica, putting her arms around her husband.

They hugged each other for a few moments, and then he went over to the cooker and lifted the lid of the turquoise Le Creuset pot, which she only used on special occasions. He'd guessed right. Slices of pork were simmering in a wonderful cream sauce, and in the oven the potatoes were turning a crispy golden brown. He saw also that she'd made a salad in a big bowl, a special blend of spinach, tomatoes, parmesan cheese, and pine nuts, mixed with the herb dressing he loved.

'I'm absolutely starving,' Patrik said, and it was true. His stomach was growling loudly, and he realized that he hadn't eaten anything all day. 'What about the kids?'

He nodded towards the table, which was set for two, with their best china and candles. A bottle of Amarone had already been opened. He realized this was going to be a great Saturday night after several exhausting days at work.

'They've already eaten. They're in the living room watching *Cars*. I thought for once you and I could have dinner together in peace and quiet. Unless you insist they sit at the table with us,' said Erica, giving him a wink.

'No, no. Let's keep the kids as far away from the kitchen as possible. Threats, bribes, I don't care what it takes. Tonight I want to have dinner with my beautiful wife.'

He leaned forward to kiss her on the lips.

'I'll just go in and say hi to them. Then I'll be right back. You can put me to work, if there's anything you need help with.'

'Everything's under control,' said Erica. 'Go in and give them all a kiss, and then the two of us will sit down and eat.'

Smiling, Patrik went into the living room. The lights were turned off, but in the glow from the TV he saw that the kids were mesmerized by Flash McQueen racing around the track.

'Look how fast he is,' said Noel. He was hugging his special blanket, as he always did when they sat on the sofa.

'But not as fast as Pappa!' shouted Patrik, throwing himself on the sofa and tickling the kids until they howled.

'Stopppp! Stopppp!' they all cried, even though their body language and expressions pleaded 'More, more!'

He kept on tussling with them a little longer. Their energy never seemed to run out. He felt their warm breath on his cheek as their laughter and shouts rose to the ceiling. At that instant he forgot about everything else. The only thing that existed was this moment with his children. Then he heard the sound of someone clearing her throat.

'Sweetheart, the food is ready.'

Patrik stopped at once. 'Okay, kids. Pappa has to go and have dinner with Mamma. Snuggle down on the sofa again. We'll come to put you to bed later.'

After tucking the blankets around them, he followed Erica back to the kitchen where the food was now on the table, and the wine was poured.

'Wow, everything looks great.' He began filling his plate. Then he raised his glass towards Erica.

'*Skål,* my dear.'

'*Skål,*' she said, and they both took several sips in silence. He closed his eyes to savour the taste.

They chatted for a while, and Patrik gave her a brief report on the day's developments. He told her that none of the neighbours had noticed anyone watching the Hallberg house. He also said that after the memorial service Gösta and Martin had talked to some of the stable girls, but none of them had anything to say about the break-in at Jonas's clinic. On the other hand, his colleagues had learned something far more interesting.

'You have to promise not to say anything to anybody about this,' Patrik said. 'Not even Anna.'

'Sure. I promise.'

'Okay. Well, according to Victoria's brother Ricky, she was having an affair with Jonas Persson.'

'You're joking,' said Erica.

'I know. It sounds strange. He and Marta have always seemed like the perfect couple. Apparently he denies the whole thing, but if it's true, then we have to wonder if it had anything to do with her disappearance.'

'Maybe Ricky misinterpreted the situation. It could be she was having an affair with someone else, someone she was going to see when she disappeared. Or maybe it was that person who kidnapped her.'

Patrik didn't speak as he pondered what she'd just said. Could Erica be right?

After a moment he saw that she had something else on her mind.

'I've been wanting to discuss something with you,' she said. 'It's a long shot and still very hazy, and maybe I'm way off base here, but I want to hear your opinion, anyway.'

'Okay. I'm listening,' said Patrik, putting down his knife and fork. The urgency in Erica's voice made him curious.

She began by telling him about the work she'd done on her book, about her conversations with Laila, about her visit to the house, and about her research so far. As she talked, Patrik realized that he'd paid little attention to her latest project. His only excuse was that Victoria's disappearance had demanded so much of him that he'd had no energy or time for anything else.

When Erica began telling him about the box containing the newspaper clippings, he was intrigued but still didn't think it was especially significant. It wasn't unusual for people to get fixated on certain cases and collect related materials. But then Erica recounted the other visit she'd made that day, to Wilhelm Mosander.

'Wilhelm took a great interest in the case back when he was covering it for *Bohusläningen*, and over the years he has tried to get in touch with Laila. He's not the only one, and I know it was a big deal when she suddenly agreed to see me. But it wasn't just a coincidence.' Erica paused to take a sip of her wine.

'What do you mean it wasn't a coincidence?' asked Patrik.

His wife fixed her gaze on him.

'Laila agreed to meet with me on the same day that the first report about Victoria's disappearance was published in the papers.'

At that second Patrik's mobile rang. With the instinct of an experienced police officer, he knew the phone call was not going to be good news.

Einar was sitting alone in the dark. A few lights illuminated the yard and the buildings outside his window. A short distance away he could hear some of the horses neighing in their stalls. They were uneasy tonight. Einar smiled. He had always felt most alive when things were not in harmony. He'd inherited that trait from his father.

Sometimes he actually missed him. His father was a strange man, but they had understood each other, just as he and Jonas did. Helga, on the other hand, would never be a part of what they shared. She was too stupid and naive.

He had always thought that women were silly creatures, but he had to admit that Marta was different. Over the years he'd even come to admire her. She was nothing like that frightened mouse named Terese who had started shaking if he so much as looked at her. He had detested her, but for a time there had been talk of an engagement between her and Jonas. Helga had always loved Terese, of course. She was exactly the sort of girl she would have taken under her wing. Helga had probably pictured herself having some nice girl to talk with, sharing household tips and wiping the snot off the faces of a bunch of snivelling grandchildren.

Thank God nothing ever came of it. One day Terese was gone, and in her place Jonas had brought home Marta. He had explained that she was going to live with them, that they were going to stay together for ever, and Einar had believed him. He and Marta had exchanged a glance and immediately understood each other. With a curt nod Einar had given them his blessing. For several nights Helga had wept quietly into her pillow, though she realized it would do no good to say anything. The decision had already been made.

He had never talked to Helga about their differing views of Marta. They didn't discuss those sorts of things. For a brief period, when he was courting Helga before their wedding, he had made a genuine effort and chatted about life, since he knew that was expected of him. But that ended as soon as their wedding night was over and he'd taken her by force, which was what he'd been looking forward to doing. After that there was no reason to continue with the ridiculous playacting.

As he sat in the wheelchair he could feel his stomach getting damp. He looked down. The colostomy bag, which he'd loosened a while ago, was now leaking badly. With a pleased expression he filled his lungs with air and bellowed:

'Helgaaa!'

UDDEVALLA 1973

Laila had never believed in the existence of evil, but she did now. Every day she saw it in the girl's eyes, staring back at her. Laila was scared and bone tired. How could she sleep with evil in the house? How could she rest even for a second? It was in the walls, present in every little nook and cranny.

She was the one who had let it in. She had even created it. She had nourished it, fed it, allowing it to grow until it could no longer be controlled.

She looked down at her hands. The scratches ran like red bolts of lightning over the back of her hands, and the little finger of her right hand pointed in a peculiar direction. She would have to go see the doctor and once again face the suspicious looks and listen to the questions she couldn't answer. Because how could she tell anyone the truth? How could she share the fear she felt? There were no words for it. And nothing would do any good.

She couldn't say anything. She had to keep lying, even though she could see from their expressions that they didn't believe her.

Her finger throbbed and ached. It was going to be difficult to take care of Peter and tend to her chores, but by now she'd learned how strong she was. How much she could bear, how much fear and terror she could live with, how close she could be to evil without recoiling. Somehow she would manage.

Terese had phoned everyone she could think of: the few relatives that Lasse had, though most of them were far away; his old drinking buddies; some of his newer friends; several former co-workers; and members of the church that he'd mentioned.

She was feeling guilty. Yesterday she'd stood in the kitchen, baking cinnamon buns and feeling something akin to joy because she'd decided to leave him. She hadn't started to worry until close to seven thirty in the evening when he hadn't come home for dinner and wasn't answering his phone. Usually Lasse came and went as he pleased, and lately he'd been at the church if he wasn't at home. But not this time. They hadn't seen him at church all day, which made her even more anxious. He had nowhere else to go.

The car was also missing. She'd borrowed her neighbour's car to drive around and look for him half the night, even though the police had told her they'd look into the matter in the morning. Lasse was a grown man, after all, and he might have just decided to go off on his own for a while. But she couldn't simply sit at home and worry. While Tyra stayed with the boys, Terese drove all over Fjällbacka and then out to Kville, where the church was located. Nowhere did she see their red Volvo estate car. She was grateful the police had at least taken her seriously when she reported Lasse missing. Maybe they'd heard the panic in her voice. Even during the periods when Lasse's drinking was at its worst, he had always come home at night. And he hadn't had a drink in ages.

Naturally the police officer who came to the house to talk with her had asked whether Lasse might have started drinking again. This was a small town, and he knew about her husband's past. She had explained in no uncertain terms that Lasse didn't drink any more. But when she thought about it, she realized that he'd been acting differently over the last few months. And it wasn't just his fanatical religious ranting; there was something else. Every once in a while she'd caught him smiling to himself, as if he were thinking about some big secret, something he didn't want to tell her.

Terese didn't know how to explain something so vague to the police. She could hear how crazy it would sound. Yet she was suddenly convinced that Lasse did have some sort of secret. And as Terese sat in the kitchen with the morning light slowly driving away the dark, what scared her most was that this secret might have got Lasse in terrible trouble.

Marta rode Valiant along the forest path, startling a flock of birds that flew up as she rode past. Valiant reacted nervously by setting off at a trot. She knew he wanted to run, but she reined him in and they continued at a slow pace on this quiet morning. Even though the temperature had dropped, she wasn't cold. She was warmed by the horse's body, and she also knew how to dress properly, wearing several layers. With the right clothing she could stay out riding for hours, even in winter.

Molly's training had gone well yesterday. Her daughter

was developing into an excellent rider, and Marta was actually quite proud of her. Usually it was Jonas who bragged about Molly, but when it came to horseback riding it was clear where the girl got her talent. It was a skill she shared with her mother.

Marta urged Valiant forward, enjoying the sensation when he started moving faster. She never felt as free as when she was riding a horse. It was as if she were always playing a role, and only in her interaction with a horse did she become her true self.

Victoria's death had changed everything. She noticed it in the mood at the stable, and at home. Even at Einar and Helga's house. The girls were subdued and scared. Some of them had come straight to the stable after the memorial service yesterday. She and Jonas had given a couple of them a lift in their car. The girls had sat in the back seat, not saying a word. No trace of their usual laughter and noise. And strangely enough the rivalry between the stable girls now seemed even fiercer than before. They squabbled over the horses, competed for Marta's attention, and glared with envy at Molly, since they knew she held a position that could never be threatened.

It was a fascinating dynamic. Sometimes she couldn't resist stoking the fire. She would let one girl ride a favourite horse more often than she should have been allowed. She would give a girl extra attention during several lessons while she ignored someone else. It worked every time, instantly heightening the intrigues and spreading discontent. She saw the envious looks and the cliques that formed. She found it all very amusing. It was so easy to play off the girls' insecurity, so easy to predict their reactions.

She'd always had a talent for such things, and maybe that was why she'd found it so difficult when her daughter was small. Young children were unpredictable. She couldn't make her daughter go along with her wishes in the same way. Instead she'd been forced to comply with Molly's needs. It was the child who decided when she would sleep and eat, and sometimes she would suddenly start crying for no reason. If Marta was honest with herself, she no longer found it as wearisome to be a mother. As Molly got older, it had become easier to deal with her, to foresee how she would act and respond. And once Marta discovered Molly's talent for horseback riding, she'd begun to feel closer to her daughter. As if they actually belonged together, and Molly wasn't just some strange creature who had come from her body.

Valiant now took off at a gallop, clearly glad to be racing along. Marta knew the route so well that she let him run as fast as he liked. Occasionally she had to duck under a branch, and snow fell on her from the trees as they thundered past. The snow also whirled up from the horse's hooves, so it was like racing through clouds. She was breathing hard, feeling her whole body working. People who didn't ride horses thought it was just a matter of sitting passively in the saddle. They didn't understand that every muscle was active. After a good ride, her whole body ached so wonderfully.

Jonas had rushed off to take care of an emergency early this morning. He was always on call, 24/7, and just before five his phone had rung: a cow had fallen ill on one of the nearby farms. In minutes Jonas was dressed and in his car. Having been woken by his mobile, Marta lay in bed, watching him get dressed in the dark. After all these years together, the situation was so familiar and yet it was never entirely pleasant. Living together hadn't always been easy. They'd had their quarrels, and there were times when she wanted to scream and punch him from sheer frustration. But the certainty that they belonged together had never faded.

Only once had she been afraid. She usually refused to admit it, didn't even want to think about it, but when she was out riding, when freedom took over her body and she was able to relax, the thoughts would surface. They had almost lost everything: each other, their life together, the loyalty and intimacy that they'd known from the first time they met.

There was a measure of insanity to their love. It was scorched at the edges by the fire that constantly burned, and they knew how to keep it going. They had explored their love in every way imaginable, testing the boundaries to see if it would hold. And it had. Only once had their love been close to breaking, but at the last second everything had settled down and returned to the way it ought to be. The danger was over, and she had chosen to give it as little thought as possible. That was best.

Marta urged Valiant to go even faster, and almost soundlessly they flew through the woods. Heading towards nothing, towards everything.

Patrik sat down at the kitchen table and gratefully accepted the cup of coffee that Erica handed to him. Their romantic dinner last night had been cut short when Terese Hansson phoned to say she was worried about her husband Lasse. Patrik had gone over to talk with her, and when he came back home Erica had cleared everything away. This morning no trace remained of their dinner. She had cleaned the kitchen so it sparkled, no doubt out of sheer spite since Kristina and Gunnar were supposed to come over in the afternoon for Sunday coffee.

He glanced at the painting propped against the wall. It had been there for a year because he'd never got around to hanging it up. If he didn't watch out, Mr Fix-it would show up with a hammer when he came to visit. Patrik knew he was being childish, but he wasn't exactly happy about another man fixing things in his home. That was something he ought to do himself – or at least pay somebody to do it, he hurried to add since he was fully aware that his handyman skills were limited.

'Forget about the painting,' said Erica with a smile when she saw what he was looking at. 'I'll put it away before they get here if you don't want Gunnar to hang it up.'

For a moment Patrik considered accepting her offer, but then he felt foolish.

'No, leave it there. I've had plenty of time to deal with it, but I just never have. The same is true for a lot of other things I should have done. I've only got myself to blame, and I should be grateful for his help.'

'You're not the only one who could hang up that painting and fix other things. I know how to use a hammer too. But we've had other priorities, such as taking care of our work, and spending time with the kids and each other. What does it matter if that painting is still sitting on the floor?' She sat down on his lap and put her arms around him. He closed his eyes and breathed in her scent; he never grew tired of it. Of course daily life had taken its toll on the passionate desire they'd felt in the beginning, but in his opinion it had been replaced by something even better. A calm and steady but enduring love. And there were still times when he felt as aroused by his wife as when they'd first met. Just not as often as in the past, which was probably nature's way of making sure that human beings got things done instead of spending all their days in bed.

'I had some plans for yesterday,' said Erica, nibbling on his lip. Even though Patrik was dead tired after working so hard the past few days and then tossing and turning last night, he could feel his body responding.

'Hmm . . . I did too,' he replied.

'What are you doing?' said a voice from the doorway, and they both jumped self-consciously. With young children in the house, it was almost impossible to kiss and make out in peace.

'We were just kissing a little,' said Erica, getting up.

'Blech. That's disgusting,' said Maja, and then she ran back to the living room.

Erica poured herself a cup of coffee. 'She won't be saying that ten years from now.'

'I don't even want to think about that.' Patrik shuddered. If it had been within his power, he would have stopped time so Maja never became a teenager.

'What are the police going to do now?' asked Erica, leaning against the worktop. Patrik drank some more of his coffee before answering. The caffeine was having only a marginal impact on the fatigue he felt.

'I just talked to Terese, and Lasse still hasn't turned up. She was out driving around and looking for him half the night. Now we need to help her.'

'Any theory about what might have happened to him?'

'No, not really. But Terese said Lasse has been acting strangely over the past few months. There's been something different about him, though she couldn't quite put her finger on it.'

'So she doesn't have a clue? Most people can sense if their spouse is up to something. Maybe a mistress? Or a gambling habit?'

He shook his head. 'No, but we'll be talking to some of his friends today. I've also asked Malte at the bank to print out an account statement so we can see if Lasse has made any withdrawals lately, or purchased anything that might explain where he's gone. Malte was going to run over to the bank, so he should have the information for us soon.' Patrik glanced at his watch. It was almost nine, and the morning light was finally appearing on the horizon. He hated winter with its eternal nights.

'That's one of the advantages of living in a small town. The bank manager can just "run over" and take care of things.'

'I know. It makes our job a lot easier. And I hope it will give us a lead. According to Terese, Lasse is the one who handles the family's finances.'

'I suppose you'll also check to see if he has paid for something with a credit card or made a withdrawal from a cashpoint machine, right? Maybe he was just fed up and decided to leave. Caught the next plane to Ibiza, or some place like that. You should check with the airlines. It wouldn't be the first time that an unemployed father of young kids fled the daily drudgery.'

'I've had the same thought myself, even though I'm not unemployed,' said Patrik with a grin. He was rewarded with a light swat on the shoulder.

'Don't you dare! Don't even think about going off to Magaluf and drinking shots with some sweet young thing.'

'I'd probably fall asleep after one drink. And then I'd phone her parents to tell them to come and get their daughter.'

Erica laughed. 'You have a point there. But you should still check with the airlines. You never know. Not everyone is as tired and ethical as you are.'

'I've already asked Gösta to do that. And Malte is going to look at credit card charges and cashpoint withdrawals too. Plus we're going to check on Lasse's mobile usage as soon as we can. So I've got the situation under control. Thanks.' He gave her a wink. 'What are your plans for today?'

'Kristina and Gunnar are coming over later this afternoon. And if you don't mind, I was thinking of asking them to babysit for a while so I could get some work done.

I feel like I need to keep going right now or I'll never understand why Laila is so interested in those missing girls. If I find a connection, maybe she'll open up about what happened that day when Vladek was murdered. I've always had a feeling she wanted to tell me something, but she just hasn't known how to do it. Or hasn't dared.'

The morning light was now coming through the windows and flooding the whole kitchen. It made Erica's blond hair shine, and Patrik realized again how much he loved his wife. Especially at moments like this when she was beaming with enthusiasm and passion for her work.

'By the way, the fact that the family car is missing might mean that Lasse has left the area,' said Erica, abruptly changing the subject.

'That may be true. Terese went out looking for him, but there are lots of places he could have left the car. On a trail in the woods, for example. Or if he parked it in a garage somewhere, it will be hard to find. I'm hoping we'll get some help from the public. That might make it easier to locate the car, if it's still here.'

'What kind of car is it?'

Patrik downed the last of his coffee and stood up. 'A red Volvo estate car.'

'You mean like that one out there?' said Erica, pointing towards the big car park down by the water near their house.

Patrik turned to look where she was pointing. His mouth fell open. There it was. Lasse's car.

Gösta ended the call. Malte had phoned to say that he was faxing over the bank documents, so Gösta got up to fetch them. He still thought it was amazing that someone could put a piece of paper in a machine and only minutes later what seemed to be the same paper magically appeared in another machine someplace else.

He yawned. It would have been nice to sleep later or even to have a free Sunday, but that wasn't going to happen, not the way things were going right now. He watched the papers slowly spill out of the fax machine. When all of them seemed to have arrived, he gathered them up and went into the kitchen. It was a more pleasant place to read than in his office.

'Would you like some help?' asked Annika, who was already sitting at the table.

'Sure. That would be great.' He divided the papers into two piles and gave one to her.

'What did Malte say about any credit card charges?'

'He said Lasse hasn't used the card since the day before yesterday, and there haven't been any cashpoint withdrawals either.'

'Okay. I sent a query to the airlines. But it seems so unlikely that he'd go abroad without paying for the ticket with a credit card, unless he decided to use cash.'

Gösta began leafing through the documents he'd placed on the table. 'Well, we can take a look at his bank account, to see if he made any large cash withdrawals recently.'

'It seems unlikely they'd have enough in their account for any big withdrawals,' said Annika.

'I know. Lasse is unemployed, and I can't imagine that Terese makes much. It's my guess that money's tight in that household. But wait a minute . . .' he said in surprise as he studied the figures on the statement in front of him.

'What is it?' Annika leaned forward to see what Gösta was looking at. He turned the page around and pointed at the amount at the bottom.

'My word!' she said in amazement.

'They've got fifty thousand Swedish kronor in their account. How the hell could they have so much money?' He quickly scanned the rest of the bank statement. 'There are a lot of deposits. And it looks like they were cash deposits. Five thousand at a time, once a month.'

'Lasse must have been the one who made the deposits, since he handles the family's finances.'

'That seems right. But we'll have to ask Terese.'

'Where do you think he got the money? Gambling?'

Gösta drummed his fingers on the table. 'I've never heard any gossip about him gambling, so I don't think so. We can check his computer, in case he's been gambling online. But if he was, there should have been deposits from the gaming company. Maybe these were payments for some sort of shady jobs he did, and he didn't want Terese to know.'

'Doesn't that sound a bit far-fetched?' Annika frowned.

'Not really, given the fact that he's now disappeared. Plus Terese said that he seems to have been hiding something from her over the past few months.'

'Well, it's not going to be easy to find out what those jobs were. We can't trace where the cash came from.'

'No, we can't. Unless we turn up a possible employer. Then we can inspect that person's bank account to see whether comparable sums were withdrawn.'

Gösta carefully examined each bank transaction again, with his reading glasses perched on the tip of his nose. He didn't find anything else suspicious. Aside from the cash deposits, it looked as if the family had been having a hard time making ends meet, and he noted that they seemed to have a lot of expenses.

'It's worrisome that there's so much money in the account, and yet he disappeared without taking any of it,' said Annika.

'That's what I was thinking too. It doesn't bode well.'

Gösta's mobile rang, and he grabbed it from the table. He saw on the display that the call was from Patrik.

'Hi. What? Where? Okay, we'll be right there.'

He ended the conversation and got up as he put his mobile in his pocket.

'Lasse's car is parked at Sälvik. And they've found blood at the bathing beach.'

Annika nodded. She didn't seem surprised.

Tyra stood in the kitchen doorway and looked at her mother. Her heart ached to see Terese's anxious expression. She'd been sitting there at the kitchen table as if paralysed ever since returning from her nighttime search.

'Mamma,' said Tyra, but there was no response. 'Mamma?'

Terese glanced up. 'What is it, sweetheart?'

Tyra went over and sat down at the table, taking her mother's hand. Her skin felt cold.

'Are the boys okay?' asked Terese.

'They're fine. They're playing at Arvid's house. But, Mamma . . .'

'Sorry. What did you want to tell me?' Terese rubbed her face. It looked as if she could hardly keep her eyes open.

'There's something I want to show you. Come with me.'

'All right.' Terese got up and followed Tyra into the living room.

'I found this a while ago, but I didn't know whether . . . I didn't know if I should say anything.'

'What is it?' Terese looked at her daughter. 'Is it something to do with Lasse? If so, you need to tell me this instant.'

Tyra reluctantly nodded.

'Lasse has two Bibles, but he reads only one of them. I wondered why, because the second one is right here. So I looked inside.' She took the Bible from the shelf and opened it. 'Look.'

Someone had carved a hole in the pages to make a hiding place.

'What on earth . . .?' said Terese.

'I discovered it a few months ago, and I've looked inside off and on. Sometimes there was money, and always the same amount. Five thousand kronor.'

'But I don't understand. Where would Lasse get that kind of money? And why would he hide it?'

Tyra shook her head. She could feel a knot forming in her stomach.

'I don't know, but I should have told you about it. What if something has happened to him because of the money? Then it will be all my fault, because if I'd told you before, maybe . . .' She couldn't hold back her tears.

Terese put her arms around her daughter.

'This is not your fault, and I can understand why you didn't tell me. I've had a feeling that Lasse was hiding something, so this must be it. Nobody could have predicted that anything would happen, and we don't know yet that it has. Maybe he fell off the wagon and got drunk, and he's passed out somewhere. I'm sure the police will find him soon.'

'I can tell you don't believe that,' sobbed Tyra against her mother's shoulder.

'Hush now. We don't know anything, and it would be foolish to try and guess what happened. I'll phone the police and tell them about the money. Maybe that will be of some help to them. And no one is going to blame you. You were just being loyal to Lasse because you didn't want to make trouble for him. And I think that was a nice thing for you to do. Okay?'

Terese stepped back and pressed the palms of her hands against Tyra's flushed cheeks, kissed her daughter on the forehead and then went off to ring the police. Tyra stayed where she was for a few moments, wiping away her tears. She was just about to join her mother in the kitchen when she heard her scream.

* * *

Mellberg was standing at the end of the dock, staring down at the hole in the ice.

'So, it looks like we've found him.'

'We can't be sure yet,' Patrik insisted. He was standing a short distance away, waiting for the crime scene technicians to arrive. But he'd been unable to hold Mellberg back.

'Lasse's car is parked over there. And you can see the blood here. It's clear as daylight that he was killed and then dumped in the hole in the ice. We won't see hide nor hair of him again until his body floats up in the spring.'

Patrik gritted his teeth when he saw Mellberg take a few more steps along the dock. 'Torbjörn is on his way. It would probably be best if we try not to disturb anything,' he pleaded.

'No need to tell me that. I know how to deal with a crime scene,' said Mellberg. 'You were hardly even born when I handled my first investigation, and you really ought to show a little respect for your elders because—'

He took a step back. When he noticed that he'd stepped into thin air, his pompous expression changed instantly. With a crash he fell into the hole, taking down with him a huge chunk of ice.

'Bloody hell!' shouted Patrik, rushing forward.

He almost panicked when he saw there was no life preserver or any other equipment within reach. Against his better judgement he considered lying down on his stomach on the ice in an attempt to pull Mellberg out. But just as he was about to throw himself on to the ice, Mellberg seized hold of the bathing ladder and hauled himself up.

'Damn, it's cold!' Panting hard, he sat down on the snow-covered planks. Patrik gloomily surveyed the havoc all around. Torbjörn would have to work miracles to make any sense of this crime scene after what Mellberg had done to it.

'Come on, Bertil, you need to get someplace warm. I'll take you over to my house,' he said, pulling Mellberg to his feet. Out of the corner of his eye he saw Gösta and Martin making their way down to the bathing area. He shoved Mellberg ahead of him.

'What the . . .?' Gösta stared in astonishment at his boss, whose hair and clothes were soaking wet. Mellberg huffed and puffed as he hurried past, heading up the steep path towards the car park and Patrik's house.

'Don't ask,' Patrik told his colleagues with a sigh. 'Just stay here and wait for Torbjörn and his team. And warn them that the crime scene is not in the best of shape. They'll be lucky to find anything at all.'

Jonas hesitantly pressed the doorbell. He had never been to Terese's flat before, and he'd had to look up the address on the Internet.

'Hi, Jonas.' Tyra peered at him with surprise when she opened the door. Then she stepped aside to let him come in.

'Is your mother home?'

She nodded and pointed. Jonas looked around. It was a pleasant and tidy place without anything fussy about it, just the way he'd thought it would look. He went into the kitchen.

'Hi, Terese.' She too gave him an astonished look. 'I just wanted to come over and see how you and Tyra are doing. I know it's been a long time since we last met, but the stable girls told me about Lasse. They said he's missing.'

'Not any more.' Terese's eyes were swollen from crying and she spoke in a monotone, her voice cracking.

'So they found him?'

'No, just the car. But he's probably dead.'

'What? What are you saying? Do you want me to phone someone to come over here to be with you? A pastor, or a friend?' He knew that her parents had passed away several years ago, and she had no siblings.

'Thanks, but Tyra is here. The boys are staying with good friends. I haven't told them anything yet.'

'Okay.' He seemed at a loss as he stood there in the kitchen. 'Would you like me to leave? Maybe you'd rather be alone.'

'No, stay.' Terese nodded towards the coffee machine. 'There's coffee. And milk in the fridge. I seem to remember that you take milk in your coffee.'

Jonas smiled. 'You've got a good memory.' He poured himself a cup and refilled hers. Then he sat down across from her.

'Do the police know what happened?'

'No. They didn't want to say much on the phone. Only that they have reason to believe Lasse is dead.'

'Do they usually notify families of a death over the phone?'

'I rang Patrik Hedström about . . . a different matter. And I could hear from his voice that something had happened, so he felt he had to tell me. But someone from the police department is supposed to come over here in a while.'

'How did Tyra take the news?'

Terese hesitated before answering.

'She and Lasse were never very close,' she said. 'During the years when he was drinking he was always so out of it. When he stopped drinking he found religion. And that often seemed just as alienating.'

'Do you think what's happened to him could be related to these new interests of his? Or to something in his past?'

She gave him a quizzical look. 'What do you mean?'

'Well, maybe there was some trouble within the church that got out of hand. Or maybe he went back to hanging out with his old drinking buddies and got mixed up in something illegal. Do you think somebody wanted to harm him?'

'No. And I have a hard time believing he would start drinking again. You can say what you like about that church, but it has kept him sober. And he never had a bad word to say about anybody in the congregation. They gave him love and forgiveness. Those are his words, not mine.' She couldn't hold back a sob. 'I didn't forgive him. In fact, I'd made up my mind to leave him. But now that he's gone, I miss him.' Tears spilled down her cheeks, and Jonas handed her a paper napkin from the holder on the table. She wiped her face.

'Are you okay, Mamma?' Tyra was standing in the doorway, looking at her anxiously.

Terese smiled through her tears. 'I'm okay. Don't worry.'

'Maybe it was stupid of me to come here,' said Jonas. 'I just thought I might be of some help.'

'It was nice of you to think of us. I'm glad you came,' said Terese.

At that moment the doorbell rang, startling both of them. It was a shrill sound, and the bell rang again before Tyra managed to open the door. On hearing footsteps approaching, Jonas turned and encountered yet another surprised look.

'Hi, Gösta,' he hastened to greet the officer. 'I was just leaving.' He got up and looked at Terese. 'Let me know if there's anything I can do. Don't hesitate to call.'

She gave him a grateful look. 'Thanks.'

As he left the kitchen, Jonas felt a hand on his arm. In a low voice so Terese wouldn't hear, Gösta said, 'There's something I want to talk to you about. I'll drop by as soon as I'm done here.'

Jonas nodded. He felt his mouth go dry. He didn't like the tone of Gösta's voice.

Erica couldn't stop thinking about Peter, the son that Laila's mother had taken in. The boy who later vanished. Why had the grandmother agreed to care for him but not his sister? And had he left voluntarily after his grandmother died?

There were far too many questions surrounding Peter, and it was time for her to try to answer at least some of them. Erica leafed through her notebook until she came to the pages with contact information for all the individuals involved. She always tried to be methodical and keep them all in one place. The problem was that sometimes she had a hard time deciphering her own handwriting.

From downstairs she heard the children laughing merrily as they played with Gunnar. They had quickly grown fond of their grandmother's pal, as Maja called him. They were having a great time, so with a clear conscience Erica could continue working a little longer.

She turned to look out of the window. She'd seen Mellberg drive up in his car and then come to a screeching halt. He jumped out and jogged down to the bathing beach. But no matter how much she craned her neck, she couldn't see that far, and she'd been given strict orders to stay away. So she would just have to wait patiently until Patrik came home and told her what they'd found.

Again she glanced at her notebook. She'd jotted down a phone number in Spain next to the name of Laila's sister. She reached for the phone as she squinted at what she'd written. Was the last digit a seven or a one? She sighed, thinking that if nothing else, she'd just have to try both. She decided to start with the seven, and punched in the phone number.

She heard a muted ring tone. It always sounded different when she rang a number outside of Sweden, and she wondered why that was.

'¡Hola!' said a man's voice.

'Hello. I would like to speak to Agneta. Is she home?' said Erica in English. She'd studied French in school, not Spanish, so she had almost zero knowledge of the language.

'May I ask who is calling?' said the man in flawless English.

'My name is Erica Falck.' She hesitated. 'I'm calling about her sister.'

A long silence followed. Then the voice spoke again, this time in Swedish, though with a slight accent.

'My name is Stefan. I'm Agneta's son. I don't think my mother wants to talk about Laila. They haven't been in touch for a long time.'

'I know. Laila told me that. But it still might be important for me to talk to your mother. Tell her it has to do with Peter.'

Silence again. She could feel resistance streaming towards her through the phone.

'Don't you ever wonder how your relatives in Sweden are doing?' Erica couldn't help asking.

'What relatives?' replied Stefan. 'Laila is the only one left, and I've never even met her. Mamma moved to Spain before I was born, so we've never had any contact with her side of the family. And I think that's what my mother wants.'

'Could you ask her? Please?' Erica could hear the pleading tone in her voice.

'Okay. But don't count on her saying yes.'

Stefan put down the phone and carried on a murmured conversation with someone. Erica thought he spoke excellent Swedish. His accent was barely noticeable, just a hint of a lisp, which she knew came from Spanish.

'You can talk to her for a few minutes. Here she is.'

Erica was startled to hear Stefan's voice again. She'd been far away, thinking about linguistic differences.

'Hello?' said a woman's voice.

Erica quickly pulled herself together and introduced herself. She said that she was writing a book about her sister's case, and she would be extremely grateful if she could ask a few questions.

'I don't know what I could tell you. Laila and I broke off all contact years ago, and I know nothing about her or her family. I couldn't help you even if I wanted to.'

'Laila told me the same thing, but I have a few questions about Peter, and I was hoping you could answer them.'

'What is it you want to know?' said Agneta, sounding resigned.

'I've been wondering why your mother didn't take in both Peter and Louise. It seems like it would have been only natural for the grandmother to take care of both children instead of splitting them up. Louise ended up in a foster home.'

'Louise needed . . . special care. And that wasn't something my mother could do.'

'But what sort of special care? Was it because she'd been so traumatized? And didn't any of you ever suspect that Vladek was abusing his family? Your mother lived here in Fjällbacka. Didn't she notice that something wasn't right?' The questions poured out of Erica, and at first she heard only silence on the phone.

'I really don't want to talk about this. It happened so long ago. It was a dark time, and I'd prefer to forget all about it.' Agneta's voice sounded faint and hesitant. 'My mother did everything she could to protect Peter. That's all I can say.'

'What about Louise? Why didn't she try to protect her?'

'Vladek took care of Louise.'

'Was it because she was a girl that she suffered the most? Was that why they always referred to her as simply the Girl? Did Vladek hate women, but not men, and so he treated his son better? Laila also suffered injuries.' She continued to ask questions because she was afraid that at any second Agneta would end the conversation.

'It was . . . complicated. I can't answer your questions. And I have nothing more to say.'

It sounded as if Agneta was about to hang up, so Erica hurried to change tack.

'I realize it must be painful to talk about this, but what do you think happened after your mother died? According to the police report, her death was due to a burglary gone wrong. I've read the report and talked to the officer who was in charge of the investigation. But I wonder if that's really what happened. It seems quite a coincidence for two murders to occur in one family, even with many years in between.'

'Things like that do happen. It was a burglary, just as the police decided. A thief, or possibly several thieves, broke into the house during the night. My mother woke up, and the thieves panicked and killed her.'

'With a poker?'

'Yes, they must have been in a hurry, and that was the only weapon they could find.'

'There were no fingerprints. None whatsoever. They must have been exceedingly careful thieves. It seems a bit odd that they'd planned the break-in so well but then panicked when someone inside the house woke up.'

'The police didn't think it was odd. They did a thorough investigation. They even theorized that Peter might have had something to do with it, but he was completely cleared of any involvement.'

'And then he disappeared. What do you think happened to him?'

'Who knows? Maybe he's living on an island somewhere in the Caribbean. It's a nice thought, but I'm afraid I don't believe it. I think the trauma of his childhood, and the fact that another person close to him was murdered, ended up being too much for him.'

'So you think . . . you think he committed suicide?'

'Yes, I do,' said Agneta. 'Unfortunately. But I hope I'm wrong. Now I'm afraid I have no more time to talk with you. Stefan and his wife are about to leave, and I'm going to babysit for their boys.'

'Just one more question,' Erica begged. 'What sort of relationship did you have with your sister? Were you close when the two of you were growing up?' She wanted to end with a more neutral question so that Agneta wouldn't refuse to speak to her if she phoned again.

'No, we weren't,' said Agneta after a long pause. 'We were incredibly different and had very little in common. And I've chosen not to get mixed up in Laila's life and the choices she made. None of the Swedes in our social circle here know that she's my sister, and I don't want you to tell anyone that we've talked. Not even Laila.'

'I promise not to say anything,' replied Erica. 'Just one last question. Laila has been collecting newspaper clippings about the girls who have disappeared during the past two years in Sweden. One of them went missing from here in Fjällbacka. She turned up again last week, but then she was struck by a car and died. She had suffered terrible injuries during the time she was held captive. Do you know why Laila would be so interested in these cases?' When Erica stopped speaking she heard only the sound of Agneta breathing.

'No,' she said curtly and turned away to shout something in Spanish. 'I need to take care of my grandsons now. And as I told you: I have no wish to be linked to any of this.'

Erica again assured Agneta that she wouldn't mention their talk to anyone, and then the conversation was over.

Just as she was about to type up her notes, she heard a loud commotion from downstairs in the front hall. Quickly she got up from her desk and dashed out of the room to peer over the railing.

'What on earth?' she said, and then ran downstairs. There stood Patrik pulling the wet clothes off a grumbling Bertil Mellberg. His lips were blue, and he was shaking with cold.

Martin stepped inside the station and stomped the snow off his boots. As he passed the reception area, Annika glanced up at him, peering over the rims of the glasses she wore for using the computer.

'How'd it go?'

'About the same as usual whenever Mellberg gets involved.'

Seeing the inquisitive look on Annika's face, he told her about Mellberg's latest exploits.

'Good Lord.' Annika shook her head. 'That man never ceases to amaze me. What did Torbjörn say?'

'He said that unfortunately it's going to be hard to secure footprints or anything else after Mellberg tramped around so much. But he took samples of the blood, and it should be possible to see if it matches Lasse's blood type. They can also compare it to his sons' DNA, so we should know whether it's his blood or not.'

'That's good, at least. Do you think he's dead?' asked Annika cautiously.

'There was a lot of blood on the dock and on the ice next to the hole cut for the bathers, but no blood traces leading away from the site. So if it's Lasse's blood, the chances are that he's dead.'

'How sad.' Annika's eyes filled with tears. She'd always

been soft-hearted, and ever since she and her husband Lennart had adopted a little girl from China, she'd become even more sensitive to all the injustices in life.

'Yes, it is. We hadn't imagined it would turn out like this. We thought we'd probably find him drunk somewhere.'

'What a sorry fate. His poor family.' Annika took a moment to regain her composure. 'By the way, I managed to get hold of all the investigators working on the missing girl cases, and the meeting is scheduled for tomorrow morning at ten o'clock in Göteborg. I've already told Patrik, and Mellberg's going with him. What about you and Gösta? Do you want to go?'

Martin had started to sweat in the heat inside the station. He took off his jacket and ran his fingers through his red hair, which was already feeling damp.

'I wish I could go. I know Gösta would like to be there too. But we'll stay here. We can't leave the station unmanned. Especially now that we have another murder investigation on our hands.'

'That's probably smart. And speaking of smart: Paula is down there in the archives again. Would you mind checking on her?'

'Sure. I'll do it now,' said Martin, though he first made a detour to his office to take off his coat.

Down in the cellar the door to the archives stood open. Even so, he knocked before entering, because he could see that Paula was deeply immersed in her work. She was skimming through the contents of the boxes set in front of her as she sat on the floor.

'So you haven't given up yet?' he said, walking over to her.

She glanced up as she set yet another folder aside.

'I probably won't find it, but at least I've had some time to myself. Who would have thought it could be so much work taking care of a baby? It wasn't like this with Leo.'

She unfolded her legs and then started to stand up. Martin held out his hand to help. 'Well, from what I've heard,' he said, 'Lisa is a little different. Is she home with Johanna now?'

Paula shook her head. 'Johanna took Leo out sledding, so Lisa is home with her grandmother.' She took several deep breaths and stretched out her back. 'So, how's it going otherwise? I heard that you found Lasse's car and that there was blood nearby.'

Martin gave her the same report he'd given Annika, telling her about the blood, the hole in the ice, and also about Mellberg's involuntary bath.

'You're kidding! How clumsy can that man be?' Paula stared at her colleague. 'Is he okay?' she then added, and Martin was touched that Paula was still able to worry about Mellberg. He knew that Bertil had a close relationship with Paula and Johanna's son, and there was something about the old guy that made people like him, even though at times he could be difficult.

'Yes, he's fine. He's over at Patrik's house getting thawed out.'

'Something always happens when Bertil gets involved.' Paula laughed. 'So, I was just thinking about taking a break. My back gets stiff from sitting on the floor hunched over all these file boxes. Want to keep me company?'

They went upstairs and were on their way to the kitchen when Martin stopped abruptly. 'I've just got to check on something in my office.'

'Okay, I'll go with you,' said Paula, following him.

He began rummaging through the papers on his desk as she went over to look at the books on the shelves, at the same time keeping a surreptitious eye on what Martin was doing. His desk was incredibly cluttered, as usual.

'Do you miss being at work?' he asked her.

'You can say that again.' She tilted her head to read the

titles on the spines of the books. 'Have you read all of these? Psychology books, crime scene techniques . . . My God, you even have copies of . . .' She didn't finish her sentence as she studied the series of books neatly lined up on the shelf.

'What an idiot I am. It wasn't in the archived files that I read about the severed tongue. It was in one of these.' She pointed to the books, and Martin turned around in surprise to see what she was talking about. Could that be possible? he thought.

Gösta drove into the yard in front of the stable. It was always difficult to speak to family members. In this instance, he hadn't had any definite information about Lasse's death to tell his wife. But there were clear indications that something had happened to him, and it seemed highly likely that he was no longer alive. Terese would be forced to deal with this uncertainty for a while.

He had been surprised to find Jonas at her flat. Why was he there? He'd looked nervous when Gösta said he wanted to have a talk with him. That was fine. If Jonas was feeling off balance for some reason, it would be easier to get him to reveal the truth. At least, that had been Gösta's experience in the past.

'Knock, knock,' he said out loud as he tapped on the front door of Jonas and Marta's house. He was hoping to speak to Jonas alone, so if Marta or their daughter was at home, he planned to suggest that they go over to the veterinary clinic.

Jonas opened the door. His face had a grey tinge to it that Gösta hadn't noticed before.

'Are you home alone? There's something I need to discuss with you in private.'

Jonas paused for a few seconds before answering, leaving Gösta waiting on the doorstep. With an air of resignation he then stepped aside, as if he already knew what Gösta was going to say. And maybe he did know. He must have realized that it was only a matter of time before the affair would reach the ears of the police.

'Come in,' said Jonas. 'I'm the only one here.'

Gösta looked around. The house seemed to have been furnished without much care or thought, and it was not particularly inviting. He'd never visited the Persson family before, so he hadn't known what to expect, but he'd assumed that beautiful people would live in beautiful surroundings.

'It's awful what happened to Lasse,' said Jonas. He motioned towards a sofa in the living room.

Gösta sat down. 'Yes. It's never pleasant to deliver that sort of news. By the way, why were you visiting Terese?'

'We dated for a while, back when we were young. Since then we've pretty much lost contact, but when I heard that Lasse had disappeared, I went over to find out if there was anything I could do. Her daughter spends a lot of time here at the stable, and she's been very upset about what happened to Victoria. I wanted to show them that I care, since they're going through such a hard time.'

'I see,' said Gösta. For a moment neither of them spoke. He saw that Jonas was tensely waiting to hear what he would say.

'I wanted to ask you about Victoria. About your relationship with her,' said Gösta at last.

'Oh,' said Jonas. 'Well, there's not much to say. She was one of Marta's students. One of the group of girls always hanging about the stable.' He plucked an invisible piece of lint from his jeans.

'From what I understand, that's not the whole truth,' said Gösta, keeping his eyes fixed on Jonas.

'What do you mean?'

'Do you smoke?'

Jonas frowned. 'No, I don't smoke. Why do you ask?'

'Okay. Never mind. Let's go back to Victoria. From what I've heard, the two of you were having a . . . well, an intimate relationship.'

'Who told you that? I hardly ever talked to her. If I happened to be in the stable, I might exchange a few words with her, just as I do with all the other girls.'

'We've talked to her brother Ricky, and he claims that you and Victoria were having an affair. On the day she disappeared, he saw you and his sister quarrelling outside the stable. What were you arguing about?'

Jonas shook his head. 'I don't even recall talking to her that day. But if I did, it definitely wasn't an argument. Sometimes I may have a few sharp words for the girls if they don't tend to their chores in the stable. That's probably all it was. They don't always like being reprimanded. They're teenagers, you know.'

'I thought you just said that you rarely had any contact with the girls at the stable,' said Gösta calmly, leaning back on the sofa.

'Well, obviously I do have some contact with them. I'm a part-owner of the riding school, even though Marta actually runs it. Occasionally I lend a hand with practical matters, and if I notice something isn't being done properly, I speak up.'

Gösta paused before going on. Could Ricky have exaggerated what he saw? But even if they weren't having a row, Jonas still should have remembered speaking to Victoria.

'Argument or not, according to Ricky, he ended up yelling at you. He saw the two of you from some distance away, and then he ran over shouting. He kept on yelling at you after Victoria ran off. You really don't remember any of this?'

'No. He must be mistaken.'

Gösta realized he wasn't going to get anywhere by

insisting, so he decided to move on, even though he didn't find Jonas's answer convincing. Why would Ricky lie about confronting Jonas?

'Victoria had also received threatening letters hinting at the same thing, that she was having an affair with someone,' Gösta said.

'Letters?' said Jonas, looking as if thoughts were whirling through his head.

'Yes. Anonymous letters that were sent to her home.'

Jonas looked genuinely surprised. But that didn't necessarily mean anything. Gösta had been fooled in the past by a person's innocent expression.

'I don't know anything about anonymous letters. And I really didn't have a relationship with Victoria. First of all, I'm married – happily married. And second, she was only a child. Ricky is mistaken.'

'Well, let me thank you for your time,' said Gösta, getting up. 'I'm sure you realize that we have to take this sort of information seriously, and we'll be looking into it some more and interviewing other people.'

'You're not going to go around asking about something like that, are you?' said Jonas as he too stood up. 'You know what people are like here. The mere fact that you ask the question is enough to make them believe it's true. Don't you realize what sorts of rumours will start to spread and what that would mean for the riding school? This whole thing is a misunderstanding. A lie. Good Lord, Victoria was the same age as my daughter. What do you take me for?' His face, normally so open and pleasant, was now contorted with anger.

'We'll be discreet. I promise,' said Gösta.

Jonas ran his hand through his hair. 'Discreet? This is madness!'

Gösta went to the hall, and when he opened the door he found Marta standing on the porch. He gave a start.

'Hi,' she said. 'What are you doing here?'

'Er, uh . . . I was just checking on a few things with Jonas.'

'Gösta had some more questions about the break-in,' called Jonas from the living room.

Gösta nodded. 'Yes, that's right. There were a few things I forgot to ask the other day.'

'I heard about Lasse,' said Marta. 'How's Terese doing? According to Jonas, she seemed quite calm.'

'Well . . .' Gösta didn't know how to respond.

'What's happened? Jonas said the police had found Lasse's car.'

'I'm afraid I can't talk about an ongoing investigation,' said Gösta, pushing past her. 'And now I need to get back to the station.'

He held on to the railing as he went down the front steps. At his age, there was always the risk that he might not get up again if he stumbled and fell.

'Let us know if there's anything we can do!' shouted Marta as he headed for his car.

He waved in reply. Before he got into the driver's seat, he glanced back at the house, where Marta and Jonas were now visible as shadows in the living room window. In his heart, Gösta was certain that Jonas had lied about the argument and maybe even about the relationship. There was something off about what he'd said, but it wasn't going to be easy to find out the truth.

UDDEVALLA 1973

Vladek's behaviour was becoming more and more erratic. His workshop had gone bankrupt, and he paced the house like an animal in a cage. He talked a lot about his former life, about the circus and his family. He could talk about these things for hours, and all of them would sit and listen.

Sometimes Laila would close her eyes and try to imagine everything he was describing. The sounds, the smells, the colours, all the people he mentioned with such love and longing. It was painful to hear him say how much he missed them and to hear the underlying desperation in his voice.

Yet those moments also gave her an occasional breathing space. For some reason everything would quiet down and the chaos would stop. They all sat there as if in a trance, listening to Vladek, allowing themselves to be spellbound by his voice and his stories. His tales gave her an opportunity to rest.

Everything he described sounded as if it came from the world of fantasy and fairy tales. He talked about people who could walk a tightrope high above the ground, circus princesses who could do handstands on the back of a horse, clowns who made everyone laugh when they sprayed water at each other, zebras and elephants that performed tricks no one would have believed they were capable of doing.

And most of all, Vladek talked about the lions. The dangerous and powerful lions that had obeyed his every command. He had trained them as cubs, and they did everything he asked of them in the circus ring. The audience watched with bated breath, waiting for the wild beasts to launch themselves at him and tear him to pieces.

Hour after hour Vladek would talk about the people and the animals in the circus, about his family members who for generations had passed down the magic and the delight. But the minute he stopped talking, he would be yanked back to the reality that he wanted more than anything to forget.

The worst part was the uncertainty. It was like having a hungry lion wandering around, waiting to pounce on its prey. The outbursts and attacks were always unexpected, each time coming from a different direction than she had imagined. And her sense of exhaustion meant that she was less and less on guard.

'My God, what a spectacle that must have been,' said Anna with a laugh when she heard about Mellberg, who had eventually thawed out enough to go back to the station with Patrik. She was peering with interest at Gunnar, whom Erica had described in detail over the phone. Anna had taken an instant liking to the man when he greeted them in the front hall and took the time to say hello to the children first. Adrian was now enthusiastically helping him to hang up a painting in the kitchen.

'But how are they doing?' she asked in a more serious tone of voice. 'This whole situation with Lasse is so awful. Do the police know what might have happened?'

'It was only a short time ago that they found him. Or rather, not him, but his car and what looks like a murder scene. The divers are on their way over here. But it's doubtful they'll be able to find his body. It might have been washed out to sea.'

'I've seen Tyra occasionally when I've dropped off the girls at the stable. Such a sweet girl. Terese seems nice too. I've only said hello to her a few times. I feel so sorry for both of them.'

Anna glanced at the plate of cinnamon buns that

Kristina had set on the kitchen table, but she wasn't tempted to have any.

'Are you getting enough to eat?' asked Erica, giving her a stern look. During their childhood she had been more of a mother than a big sister for Anna, and she still had a hard time relinquishing that role. But Anna had stopped fighting it. Without Erica's care and concern she would never have made it through all the difficult times in her life. Her beloved older sister was always willing to help, whatever the situation. And lately it was only at Erica's house that Anna was able to find a way to relax and forget her feelings of guilt.

'You look pale,' Erica went on, and Anna forced herself to smile.

'I'm okay. I've been feeling a bit under the weather lately, that's all. I know it's probably psychosomatic, but I just don't have much of an appetite.'

Kristina was standing at the worktop, cleaning up even though Erica had told her several times to leave it be and sit down. Now she turned around to study Anna's face.

'Erica's right. You do look pale. You need to eat and take better care of yourself. In times of crisis it's especially important to eat and sleep well. Do you have any sleeping tablets? If not, I can give you some of mine. It goes without saying that if you don't get enough sleep, you can't do anything else properly.'

'Thanks, I appreciate the offer, but I'm not having any trouble sleeping.'

That was a lie. Most nights Anna tossed and turned in bed, staring at the ceiling and trying to push away the encroaching memories. But she didn't want to get stuck in the quagmire of taking pills. She didn't want to resort to chemical means to assuage the anxiety that she had brought upon herself. Maybe there was also a certain amount of masochism in this decision, a desire to atone for her sins.

'I don't know if I believe you, but I'm not going to nag,' said Erica, even though Anna knew that was precisely what her sister would proceed to do. To placate her, she reached for a bun. Erica also took one.

'Eat up. You need an extra layer of fat in the wintertime,' said Anna.

'Very funny,' said Erica, pretending to throw the bun at her sister.

'Good Lord, you two are hopeless.' Kristina sighed and turned away, having decided to clean the fridge. Erica was about to stop her but then realized it was a battle she couldn't win.

'So how's it going with your book?' asked Anna, trying to swallow a bite of cinnamon bun that just seemed to swell the more she chewed.

'I'm not sure. There are so many strange aspects, and I hardly know where to begin.'

'Why don't you tell me about it?' replied Anna, taking a sip of coffee. Then she listened wide-eyed as Erica recounted what she'd learned over the past few days.

'It seems like Laila's story is somehow connected to the missing girls. Why else would she save all those newspaper clippings? And why did she decide to meet with me on the same day that the papers reported on Victoria's disappearance?'

'So you don't think that was a coincidence?' asked Anna, though she knew what the answer would be.

'No. I'm convinced there's some sort of connection. Laila knows something that she doesn't want to tell anyone. Or maybe she does, but for some reason she can't. That was probably why she agreed to see me, so she'd have someone to confide in. But so far I haven't been able to make her feel comfortable enough to tell me what it's about.' Erica looked frustrated as she ran her hand through her hair.

'Ugh. It's a miracle that some of the things in here haven't crawled out on their own,' said Kristina with her head stuck inside the fridge. Erica gave Anna a look that said she refused to be provoked. She chose to ignore the ongoing efforts of her mother-in-law.

'Maybe you need to find out more information,' suggested Anna. She had given up eating any more of the cinnamon bun as she finished her coffee.

'I know, but as long as Laila keeps silent, that's almost impossible. Everyone else involved is gone now. Louise is dead, and so is Laila's mother. Peter disappeared and is most likely dead too. Laila's sister doesn't seem to know anything. There's really nobody left for me to talk to, since everything happened inside those four walls of their home.'

'How did Louise die?'

'She drowned. She and another girl were both living with the same foster family, and one day they went swimming and never came home. Their clothes were found on a rock, but their bodies were never found.'

'Have you talked to the foster parents?' asked Kristina from behind the fridge door. Erica gave a start.

'No. I didn't even think of that. They had nothing to do with what happened to the Kowalski family.'

'But maybe Louise confided in them, or maybe she talked to the other foster children.'

'Hmm . . .' said Erica. She was feeling a little foolish because her mother-in-law had pointed out something that was so obvious.

'I think Kristina's suggestion is great,' Anna said hastily. 'Where does the family live?'

'In Hamburgsund. I suppose I really ought to drive over there.'

'Gunnar and I can stay with the children. Why don't you go now?' said Kristina.

Anna added her support. 'I'll stick around here for a while too. The kids are having so much fun together, and there's no reason why I have to rush home.'

'Are you sure?' said Erica, already on her feet. 'But it's probably best if I phone them first, to find out if it's okay for me to drop by.'

'Go on,' said Anna, waving her hand. 'I'm sure I'll find something to keep me busy here. This place is such a mess.'

Erica gave her the finger in response.

Patrik stood in front of the whiteboard in the kitchen. There were far too many loose ends, and he felt compelled to make a list of everything that needed to be done. He wanted to be prepared when he arrived at the meeting in Göteborg tomorrow. And while he was away, his colleagues needed to continue investigating Lasse's probable death. Feeling stressed, he reminded himself to relax his shoulders and take a few deep breaths. He'd had a health scare a couple of years back when his body rebelled and he fell apart. That had been a wake-up call for him. Sooner or later his energy might drain away even though he loved his job.

'We're now dealing with two investigations,' he said. 'Let's start with Lasse.' He wrote Lasse's name in big letters on the board and drew a line underneath.

'I've talked to Torbjörn, and he's done the best he could,' said Martin.

'Right. Well, we'll have to see what he's able to find out.' Patrik had a hard time restraining his anger when he thought about the way Mellberg had destroyed the crime scene. Thank goodness he'd gone home now, so at least he wouldn't be able to sabotage the investigation any further today.

'We have Terese's permission to take a blood sample

from their older son. As soon as that's done, it will be compared with the blood taken from the dock,' Martin added.

'Good. We can't say for sure that it's Lasse's blood we found, but for now I suggest we assume that Lasse fought for his life out there on the dock.'

'I agree,' said Gösta.

Patrik looked at his other colleagues and they nodded.

'I asked Torbjörn to go over Lasse's car as well,' said Martin. 'In case Lasse and the murderer arrived there together. The techs also secured a number of tyre tracks in the car park. We might need them to make a match if we're able to prove that someone had driven over there.'

'Good idea,' said Patrik. 'We haven't yet got reports on Lasse's mobile usage, but we've had more luck with the bank. Isn't that right, Gösta?'

Gösta cleared his throat.

'Yes. Annika and I have gone over Lasse's bank statements, and he was making regular deposits of five thousand Swedish kronor each time. When I went to see Terese, she told me that her daughter Tyra had found a secret hiding place where Lasse had stowed away five thousand kronor in cash on several occasions. My guess is that he kept the money hidden until he had a chance to go to the bank.'

'Did Terese have any idea where the money came from?' asked Martin.

'No. And I believe her.'

'She sensed that Lasse wasn't telling her about something, so maybe that's what it was,' said Patrik. 'We need to find out where the money came from and what the payments were for.'

'Since the amount was always the same, could we be talking about blackmail?' asked Paula from her position standing in the doorway. Annika had asked her to join them at the table, but she'd said she needed to be able to dash out and answer her mobile if Rita phoned about Lisa.

'What are you thinking?' said Gösta.

'Well, if the money was from gambling, for instance, the amounts would be different each time. The same would be true if he was being paid for odd jobs, since he'd probably get an hourly wage, which wouldn't have generated the same amount every time. But if we're talking about blackmail, it would be reasonable for him to receive a specific amount at regular intervals.'

'I think Paula is right,' said Gösta. 'Maybe Lasse was blackmailing someone who finally got tired of it all.'

'In that case, the question is: what was the reason for the blackmail? His family doesn't seem to know anything, so we need to expand our search and talk to Lasse's circle of friends. We have to find out if anybody knows anything . . .' Patrik paused before adding, 'Let's talk to everyone who lives in the surrounding area, and that mostly means my neighbours. Knock on the doors of all the houses on the road to Sälvik. Find out if anyone saw a car driving towards the beach. There's not a lot of traffic this time of year, but there are plenty of nosy people watching from behind the curtains.'

He wrote down the tasks on the whiteboard. He'd hand out the assignments later. Right now he just wanted to put together a list of everything that needed to get done.

'Okay, now let's consider Victoria's case. Tomorrow is the big meeting in Göteborg with all the police departments involved. Thanks, Annika, for making the arrangements.'

'No problem. It wasn't difficult. Everyone was very positive about the idea, and they seemed surprised that they hadn't thought of having this kind of meeting earlier.'

'Better late than never. So what are the latest developments?'

'The most interesting,' said Gösta, 'is probably the fact that Victoria's brother claims she was having an affair with Jonas Persson.'

'Have we found anyone else who could confirm Ricky's suspicions?' asked Martin. 'And what does Jonas have to say?'

'No, not yet. And Jonas denies it, of course. But I don't think he's telling the truth. I thought I'd have a talk with some of the girls at the stable. It would be hard to keep that sort of relationship secret.'

'Did you talk to his wife too?' asked Patrik.

'I'd prefer not to say anything to Marta until we know more. I don't want to cause any trouble if it turns out not to be true.'

'All right. That's fine. But sooner or later we're going to have to talk to her too.'

Paula cleared her throat. 'Sorry, but I don't understand why this would have anything to do with the case. We're looking for someone who kidnapped girls in other parts of Sweden too. Not just here in Fjällbacka.'

'True,' said Patrik. 'But if Jonas hadn't had an alibi for the time when Victoria disappeared, why couldn't he be the perpetrator, just as well as anybody else? Maybe it will turn out that Jonas wasn't the one she was having an affair with. Maybe it was someone else, and that person also kidnapped her. Basically we need to work out how Victoria came in contact with the kidnapper. And what was it in her life that made her vulnerable? It could be anything. We know now that someone was watching her family's house. If it was the perpetrator, he may have had her under surveillance for quite a while, which means he could have done the same thing with the other girls. Anything in Victoria's personal life could be significant in terms of why she was chosen.'

'She had also received anonymous letters that were far

from pleasant,' said Gösta, turning to Paula. 'Ricky found them, but unfortunately he threw them out. He was worried his parents might see them.'

'Okay, I get it now,' she said. 'That sounds reasonable.'

'Have we had word from the lab about the cigarette butt?' asked Martin.

'Nothing yet,' said Patrik. 'And it won't be of any interest until we have something to compare it to. What else?' he said, looking around at his colleagues. It seemed like there were more and more question marks.

He fixed his gaze on Paula, suddenly remembering that she and Martin had said they'd found something to report. He could see that Martin was eager to speak, so he nodded at him.

'Well,' said Martin, 'Paula and I have both felt there was something familiar about Victoria's injuries, especially the fact that her tongue had been cut out.'

'So that's why you've been spending all that time in the archives,' said Patrik. His curiosity increased when he saw Paula's cheeks flush bright red.

'Yes,' she told him. 'Except I was on the wrong track. What I was looking for was not in the archives, but I knew I'd seen it somewhere.' She came forward to stand next to Patrik so everyone could see her.

'And you thought it was in a report from an old case?' said Patrik, hoping that she'd quickly get to the point.

'Exactly. But I was in Martin's office, looking at his books, when it suddenly came to me. I remembered reading about the case in *Nordic Crime Chronicles*.'

Patrik felt his pulse quicken. 'Go on,' he said.

'Twenty-seven years ago, on a Saturday evening in May, a young and newly married woman named Ingela Eriksson disappeared from her home in Hultsfred. She was only nineteen, and her husband immediately came under suspicion because he'd previously been charged with beating up both Ingela and his former girlfriends. There was an intensive police investigation, and her disappearance got a lot of coverage in the media since at that time the evening papers happened to be publishing a lot of articles about domestic violence. Then Ingela was found dead in a wooded area behind her home, and that was the nail in the coffin for her husband. The ME determined that she'd been dead for some time, but her body was intact enough to conclude that she'd been subjected to horrific torture. Her husband was found guilty of homicide, but he continued to maintain his innocence until he died in prison five years later. He was killed by a fellow prisoner in a fight over a gambling debt.'

'So what's the connection?' asked Patrik, though he had an idea what she was going to say.

Paula opened the book she was holding and pointed to the passage describing Ingela's injuries. Patrik silently read what it said on the page. Her injuries were exactly the same as Victoria's, down to the smallest detail.

'What does it say?' Gösta took the book from Paula and swiftly read the passage. 'Bloody hell.'

'You can say that again,' Patrik remarked. 'It seems we're dealing with a perpetrator who has been active much longer than we first thought.'

'Or he's a copycat killer,' said Martin.

After that no one said a word.

Helga glanced at Jonas, who was sitting at the kitchen table. Upstairs she could hear Einar grunting and moving about in bed.

'What did the police want?'

'Gösta just wanted to ask me about something,' said Jonas, rubbing his face.

She could feel the knot forming in her stomach. Her

uneasiness had slowly grown over the past few months, and her anxiety was now so great that she was practically suffocating.

'What about?' she insisted, sitting down across from him.

'Nothing special. Just something about the break-in.'

She felt hurt by the sharpness of his tone. He didn't usually snap at her like that. Even though they had an unspoken agreement not to discuss certain topics, he'd never used that tone of voice with her before. She looked down at her hands. They were gnarled and wrinkled, with brown spots on top. The hands of an old woman, like her mother's hands. When had they started looking like this? She'd never thought about it until now, as she sat here at the kitchen table while the world she had so carefully constructed was slowly collapsing around her. She couldn't let that happen.

'How's Molly?' she asked instead. She had a hard time hiding her disapproval. Jonas refused to allow the slightest criticism of his daughter, but sometimes Helga wanted to shake the spoiled girl, to make her understand how lucky she was, how privileged.

'She's okay now,' said Jonas, and his face lit up.

Helga felt a pang in her heart. She knew she had no right to be jealous of Molly, but she still wished she would see the same love in Jonas's eyes when he looked at her as when he looked at his daughter.

'We're going to the jump racing next Saturday.' He avoided meeting her eye.

'Do you have to?' she said, hearing the entreaty in her voice.

'Marta and I have agreed.'

'It's always Marta this and Marta that. I wish the two of you had never met. You should have stayed with Terese. She was such a nice girl. And then everything would have been different!'

Jonas gave her a stunned look. He'd never heard her raise her voice before, at least not since he was a child.

She knew she should have kept quiet. She should have carried on in the same way as always, the way that had made it possible for her to survive all these years, but it felt like some strange force had seized hold of her.

'She has destroyed your life! She weaselled her way into our family, and she's been like a parasite living off of you, off all of us, she's—'

Smack! The slap silenced her at once. In shock, Helga raised her hand to her cheek, which stung badly. Her eyes filled with tears, and not just because of the pain. She knew that she'd stepped over a line, and now there was no turning back.

Without looking at her, Jonas left the kitchen. When she heard the front door slam, Helga knew she could no longer afford to look on in silence. That time was past.

'Let's get with it, girls!' The annoyance that was audible in her voice spread through the riding school. All the girls were feeling tense, and that was exactly what Marta intended. Without a certain amount of fear, they'd never learn anything.

'What are you doing, Tindra?' She glared at the blond-haired girl who was struggling to get her horse to jump over one of the hurdles.

'Fanta is refusing to jump. She keeps balking.'

'You're the one in charge. Not the horse. Don't forget that.'

Marta wondered how many times she'd repeated those words. She shifted her gaze to Molly, who was in full control of Scirocco. Things were looking good for the competition. In spite of everything, the girls were well prepared.

At that moment Fanta refused for the third time, and Marta began to lose patience.

'I don't know what's wrong with all of you today. Either you start focusing, or this lesson is over.' She noticed with satisfaction the dismay on the girls' faces. They slowed, turned their horses towards the centre, and brought them to a halt in front of Marta.

One of the girls cleared her throat. 'We apologize. But we heard about Tyra's father . . . or rather, her stepfather.'

So that was the explanation for the group's nervous mood. She should have thought of that, but whenever she entered the stable, she forgot about the world outside. It was as if all thoughts, all memories were swept away. What remained was the smell and sound of the horses, and the respect they showed towards her. It was so much greater than the respect she ever got from people in general. And from the girls, in particular.

'What happened is awful. I can understand that you're feeling sorry for Tyra, but that sort of emotion has no place here. If you can't stop thinking about it, if you allow yourselves to be affected by anything other than what's taking place right here, then you might as well dismount and go home.'

'I have no trouble focusing. Did you see me take that high hurdle?' said Molly.

The other girls couldn't help rolling their eyes. Marta knew that her daughter lacked any sense for what should be said or even thought in certain situations. And that seemed strange. Personally, she had always been a master of the art. Words once spoken could never be taken back, a wrong impression could never be repaired. She didn't understand how Molly could be so tactless.

'So do you expect me to give you a medal, or something?' she said now.

Molly crumpled, and Marta saw that the other girls

couldn't hide their glee. This was exactly what she'd intended. Molly would never be a real winner if she didn't have a desire for revenge. That was something Jonas didn't understand. He treated Molly with kid gloves, spoiling her and ruining her chances of ever becoming a true survivor.

'Molly, I want you to trade horses with Tindra. Then we'll see if things go as well for you, or maybe it was all the horse's doing.'

Molly looked like she wanted to protest, but she stopped herself. No doubt the cancelled competition was still fresh in her mind, and she didn't want to miss a chance to compete in the next one. For now, in spite of everything, it was her parents who decided, and she was well aware of that.

'Marta?' She turned around when she heard Jonas calling from the stands. He waved for her to come over, and his expression told her it was urgent.

'Keep going, girls. I'll be right back,' she said over her shoulder as she climbed up to where her husband was standing.

'There's something we need to talk about.' He was rubbing the fingers of his right hand.

'Can't it wait? I'm in the middle of a lesson,' she said, even though she could tell what his answer would be.

'No,' he replied. 'We need to talk now.'

As they left the riding hall, she could hear the sound of the horses behind her.

Erica pulled into a parking spot in front of the café in Hamburgsund. It was a beautiful drive from Fjällbacka, and she had enjoyed the brief period of peace and quiet in the car. When she'd called to explain her visit, the Wallanders had hesitated at first. They conferred with each other as Erica waited on the phone, listening to their murmured conversation. In the end they had agreed to meet with her, but not at their home. They preferred to meet at a café in town.

She saw them as soon as she got out of her car and hastily approached their table. They stood up to greet her, looking a bit embarrassed. Tony, the man of the family, was tall and muscular with big tattoos on his forearms. He wore a checked shirt and blue work trousers. His wife Berit was much shorter, but her petite body looked sinewy and strong, and her face was weather-beaten.

'Oh, did you already get coffee for yourselves? I was planning to treat you,' said Erica, looking at the cups on the table. On a plate were two half-eaten almond pastries.

'We got here a little early,' said Tony. 'And we wouldn't think of letting you treat us.'

'But you must want coffee yourself. We'll wait while you get a cup,' said Berit.

Erica instinctively liked them. Down-to-earth: that was the first phrase that popped into her head to describe the couple. She went over to the counter to get coffee and a piece of pastry. Then she went back to the table to join them.

'Why did you prefer to meet here, if you don't mind me asking? I could have driven over to your house, and that would have saved you the trouble of coming into town,' she said. She took a bite of the pastry, which tasted delightfully fresh.

'Oh, we didn't think that would be appropriate,' said Berit, fixing her eyes on the table. 'Our house is so messy and cluttered. Not somewhere we'd invite someone like you.'

'But you really shouldn't feel that way,' said Erica. Now it was her turn to be embarrassed. She hated being treated differently, or as somebody more important, just because she occasionally appeared on TV or in the newspapers.

'What did you want to ask us? What do you want to know about Louise?' said Tony, offering her a way out of the awkward situation.

Erica gave him a grateful look and took a sip of the strong coffee before replying.

'Well, first of all, I was wondering how you happened to take Louise in as a foster child. Her brother was sent to live with their maternal grandmother.'

Berit and Tony exchanged a glance, as if to work out who should answer the question. Berit was the one who spoke.

'We never learned exactly why the grandmother didn't take both children. Maybe she thought she could handle only one. Louise was also in much worse shape than her brother. At any rate, the authorities told us that a seven-year-old girl was in urgent need of a new home after going through a traumatic situation. She came to us from the hospital, and later the social worker told us more about the circumstances.'

'How was Louise doing when she came to you?'

Tony clasped his hands on the table and leaned forward. He fixed his gaze on a spot behind Erica as he thought back to the year when Louise had come to live with them.

'She was terribly emaciated, with bruises and cuts all over her body. But they'd cleaned her up at the hospital and cut her hair, so she didn't look as wild as in the pictures they'd taken of her.'

'She was so sweet. Really sweet,' said Berit.

Tony nodded. 'Yes, there was no doubt about that. But she needed to put on weight and she needed to heal, in terms of both body and soul.'

'How did she behave?'

'She was very quiet. We hardly heard a word out of her for months. She just sat and watched us.'

'She didn't say anything?' Erica wondered if she should be taking notes, but she decided just to listen attentively and write it all down later. Sometimes she missed the nuances if she tried to take notes and listen at the same time.

'Well, yes, she did speak. But mostly one word at a time. Thanks. Thirsty. Tired. Things like that.'

'But she did talk to Tess,' Berit added.

'Tess? The other girl who lived with you?'

'Yes. Tess and Louise became good friends right from the start,' said Tony. 'We could hear them at night as they lay in bed and talked. So I assume it was just us she refused to talk to. Louise never did anything she didn't want to do.'

'What do you mean? Was she rebellious?'

'Hmm . . . No, she was actually very quiet.' Tony scratched his bald head. 'I don't really know how to describe it.' He turned to Berit for help.

'She never talked back, but if you asked her to do something she didn't want to do, she would simply walk away. And it made no difference if you yelled at her. The words rolled right off of her. Plus it was hard to be as strict as we maybe should have been because we knew Louise had gone through so much.'

'Our hearts bled for her,' said Tony, his expression darkening. 'How could anyone treat a child that way?'

'Did she get more talkative later on? Did she say anything about her parents and what happened?'

'Eventually she did start talking more,' said Berit. 'But I can't say she ever got to be talkative. And she rarely spoke about herself. She would answer questions, but she avoided looking anyone in the eye, and she never confided in us. She may have told Tess something about what she'd been through. That seems likely. It was as if those two were in their own world.'

'What sort of background did Tess have? Why was she sent to live with you?' Erica ate the last bite of her pastry.

'She was orphaned after a miserable childhood,' said Tony. 'Her father was never in the picture, as far as we know, and her mother was a drug addict who died from an overdose. Tess came to us right before Louise did. They were the same age and looked almost like sisters. We were so happy that they had each other. They helped out a lot with the animals, and we needed all the help we could get. We had a couple of bad years with sick animals and things going wrong on the farm. Two extra pairs of hands were worth gold, and both Berit and I believe that work is a good way to heal the soul.' He reached out to squeeze his wife's hand. They exchanged a quick smile.

It warmed Erica's heart to see how strong their love was even though they'd lived together for so long. That was what she wanted in her marriage with Patrik, and she thought there was a good chance their love would remain equally strong as the years passed.

'They played a lot together too,' Berit added.

'Oh, right. They were always playing circus,' said Tony, his eyes shining at the memory. 'That was their favourite game. Playing circus. Louise's father had once been part of a circus, and his stories must have sparked her imagination. They made a little circus ring out in the barn and did all sorts of tricks. Once I found a rope that they'd strung from the loft, and those crazy girls were planning to use it as a tightrope. They'd put hay underneath, but they could have hurt themselves badly, so we had to put a stop to that. Do you remember when the girls wanted to be tightrope artists?'

'Yes. Those two could certainly get into mischief sometimes. And the animals were very important to them. I remember when one of our cows was sick. They sat up all night with her until she died at dawn.'

'And they never caused you any problems?'

'No, not those two. We had other foster children who came and went. And we had a lot more trouble with some of them. But Tess and Louise looked out for each other. Sometimes I thought they distanced themselves from reality a little too much. We never felt that we really reached them. But they seemed to be doing fine. They even slept together. If I looked in on them at night, I'd find them lying in bed face to face with their arms around each other.' Berit smiled.

'Did Louise's grandmother ever come to visit her?'

'Once. I think Louise was about ten at the time.' She glanced at her husband, who nodded.

'How did it go? What happened?' asked Erica.

'It was . . .' Berit again glanced at Tony, who shrugged and then took over.

'Nothing special happened. They sat in our kitchen, and Louise didn't say a word. Her grandmother didn't say much either. Mostly they just stared at each other. I seem to remember that Tess hovered outside the kitchen door, sulking. Louise's grandmother wanted to visit with Louise alone, but I insisted on being present, and she reluctantly agreed. By that time Louise had been living with us for three years. We were responsible for her, and I had no idea how she would react when her grandmother suddenly turned up. Her visit could have summoned up bad memories for the girl, but that didn't seem to happen. Both of them just sat there. To be honest, I don't know why she came.'

'Peter didn't come with her?'

'Peter?' said Tony. 'You mean Louise's little brother? No, her grandmother came alone.'

'What about Laila? Did she ever try to get in touch with Louise?'

'No,' said Berit. 'We never heard a peep from her. I

had a hard time understanding it. How could she be so cold-hearted and not even wonder how her daughter was doing?'

'Did Louise ask about her mother?'

'No, never. As we said, she never talked about her old life, and we never pressured her to do so. We were in constant contact with a child psychologist who recommended that we should let her decide if and when she wanted to talk about things. But of course we did ask her a number of questions. We wanted to make sure she was doing all right.'

Erica nodded, wrapping her fingers around her coffee cup to warm them up. Every time the door to the café opened, an icy gust of wind swept over her.

'So what happened on the day they disappeared?' she asked cautiously.

'Are you cold? You can have my coat, if you like,' said Berit.

Her concern made Erica realize why this couple had opened their home to so many foster children over the years. They both seemed to be tremendously kind and thoughtful.

'No, thanks. I'm fine,' said Erica. 'But do you feel like you could tell me what happened that day?'

'It's so many years ago now, so it's okay,' said Tony, but Erica saw a dark shadow pass over their faces as they recalled that fateful summer day. She had read about what happened in the police report, but it was a whole different matter to hear about it from people who had actually been there.

'It was a Wednesday in July. Not that it's important what day of the week it was, but . . .' Tony's voice broke, and Berit gently placed her hand on his arm. He cleared his throat and went on.

'The girls said they wanted to go swimming. We weren't

the least bit worried, because they often went off on their own. Sometimes they'd be gone all day, yet they always came home towards evening when they started to get hungry. But not on that day. We waited and waited, but the girls didn't turn up. When it was close to eight o'clock, we realized that something must have happened, so we went out to look for them. When we didn't find them, we rang the police. Not until the next morning were their clothes discovered out on the rocks.'

'Did the police find their clothes, or did you?'

'The police had organized a search party, and one of the volunteers found the clothes.' Berit couldn't hold back a sob.

'They must have been pulled down by the strong undertow out there. Their bodies were never found. It was a terrible tragedy.' Tony looked down. The event had clearly affected them deeply.

'What happened after that?' Erica's heart ached at the thought of those two girls struggling in the water.

'The police investigated and concluded that it was an accident. We . . . well, for a long time we blamed ourselves. But the girls were both fifteen years old, and they were used to looking out for themselves. Over the years we've come to realize that it wasn't our fault. No one could have foreseen what happened. The two of them had lived long enough in confined circumstances, so we had allowed them to run free from the moment they came to stay with us.'

'And that was wise,' said Erica. She wondered whether the foster children who had lived with Berit and Tony knew how lucky they had been.

She stood up and held out her hand.

'Thank you for taking the time to meet with me. I really appreciate it, and I'm sorry for stirring up difficult memories for you.'

'You also brought back some nice memories,' said Berit, shaking Erica's hand warmly. 'We've had the good fortune to take care of many children over the years, and all of them have left an impression. But Tess and Louise were special, and we've never forgotten them.'

It was so quiet. As if the void left by Victoria's death had filled the whole house, as if it had filled all of them and was threatening to break them apart.

They made clumsy attempts to deal with their grief by trying to talk about Victoria, but in the midst of recounting a memory, the words would suddenly fade. How could life ever be the same?

Ricky knew it was only a matter of time before the police would pay them another visit. Gösta had already phoned to ask again whether they were certain they hadn't seen any suspicious person in the neighbourhood in the days before Victoria disappeared. Clearly the police had some indication that somebody had been watching their house during that time. Ricky realized that they would also ask his parents if they knew anything about Victoria's relationship with Jonas, or about the letters he'd found. That would actually be a relief for him. As he grieved for his sister, it had been a great burden to carry this secret alone, trying to keep his parents from learning about it.

'Could you pass the potatoes?' His father held out his hand without looking him in the eye. Ricky picked up the casserole dish and handed it to him.

That was the only sort of conversation they could manage now. Talking about ordinary, practical things.

'Would you like some carrots?' His mother handed Ricky the carrots. Her hand brushed against his as he took the dish, and she flinched as if she'd been burned. Their grief was so painful that they could hardly bear to touch each other.

He looked at his parents as they sat at the kitchen table across from him. His mother had cooked the dinner, but the food had been prepared without much thought, and it looked as lacklustre as it tasted. They ate in silence, each of them lost in thought. Soon the police would arrive and destroy the silence, and he knew that he should be the one to tell them first.

'There's something I need to tell you. About Victoria . . .'

His parents froze and stared at him, looking at him in a way they hadn't done in a long time. His heart began hammering in his chest, and his mouth went dry, but he forced himself to go on. He told them about Jonas and the argument he'd witnessed at the stable, about Victoria running off, about the letters he'd found, about the ugly words and curses.

They listened attentively, and then his mother lowered her gaze. But not before Ricky caught a strange look in her eye. It took a moment before he understood what it meant.

His mother already knew.

'So he didn't kill his wife? Or did he?' Rita frowned as she listened patiently to Paula.

'He was convicted of murder, but he never stopped claiming he was innocent. I haven't managed to locate anyone who worked on the case, but I've had some of the investigative materials faxed over to me, and I've read a number of newspaper articles. The evidence was purely circumstantial.'

Paula walked around the kitchen rocking Lisa in her arms as she talked. For now her daughter was quiet, but that would change at once if Paula stopped moving. She couldn't remember the last time she'd sat down to eat a whole meal.

Johanna cast a glance in her direction, and Paula

thought to herself that it really was her turn to carry Lisa around. There was no reason she should be considered more suited to the task simply because she'd given birth to the baby.

'Sit down,' Johanna reproached Leo, who stubbornly insisted on standing up in his high-chair between bites of food.

'Good Lord, if we all followed your example we'd be as thin as rails,' said Mellberg, giving Leo a wink.

Johanna sighed. 'Please don't encourage him, Bertil. It's hard enough trying to teach him some manners.'

'What difference does it make if the boy wants to get a little exercise between bites? We should all do that. Watch.' Mellberg took a bite, stood up, sat down, and then did it again. Leo roared with laughter.

'Can't you do something?' Johanna turned to Rita with a pleading expression on her face.

Paula could feel laughter bubbling inside of her. She knew that Johanna would be cross, but she couldn't hold it in any longer. She laughed so hard the tears ran down her cheeks, and she thought Lisa actually smiled too. Rita couldn't restrain herself either, and encouraged by the response of their audience, Leo and Mellberg began standing up and sitting down in unison.

'What sins did I commit in some past life that made me end up with this bunch of lunatics?' said Johanna with a sigh, but her lips twitched and she had to smile. 'Okay, do whatever you like. I've already given up any hope of this kid growing up to be a responsible adult.' Laughing, she leaned forward and kissed Leo on the cheek.

'I want to hear more about the murder,' said Rita when the raucous mood in the kitchen had subsided. 'If there's no proof, how could they convict him? In Sweden we don't put people in prison for crimes they haven't committed, do we?'

Paula smiled at her mother. Ever since they'd arrived from Chile in the seventies, Rita had put Sweden on such a high pedestal that the country didn't always live up to her expectations. She had also adopted all its traditions and celebrated Swedish holidays with a frenzy that even staunchly patriotic Swedes would have considered a bit much. On all the other days she made specialities from her native country, but on Midsummer and other holidays there was hardly ever anything but herring in the fridge.

'As I said, the evidence was circumstantial, so there were indications that he was guilty, but . . . How can I explain this?'

Mellberg cleared his throat. 'Circumstantial evidence is a legal term for something that is less than factual but that may still lead to a suspect being either released or charged with a crime.'

Paula stared at him. He was the last person she'd expected to answer that question, and to do it so well.

'Exactly. And in this case, we can say that the past behaviour of Ingela's husband had an influence on his conviction. Former girlfriends as well as Ingela's women friends all testified that he was often abusive. On several occasions he had beaten Ingela and even threatened to kill her. Since he had no alibi for the time of her disappearance, and since her body was found in the woods near their home, the case against him seemed clear.'

'But now the police want to change their view?' said Johanna as she wiped Leo's mouth.

'Maybe. It's hard to say. But the injuries are very specific in both cases. And over the years there have been voices raised to defend Ingela's husband, claiming that he was telling the truth. They've said that because the police were unwilling to investigate any other leads, a murderer was allowed to walk free.'

'Is it possible that someone heard about this murder case and decided to do the same thing?' asked Rita.

'That's precisely what Martin suggested during our meeting. It's been almost thirty years since Ingela was murdered, so it's more likely a copycat killer is at work, rather than the same person deciding to kill again.' After a quick glance at Lisa, who was sound asleep, Paula sat down at the table. She would eat her dinner while holding her daughter in her arms.

'At any rate, it's worth taking a closer look at the old case,' said Mellberg, helping himself to more food. 'I was thinking of reading through the investigative materials tonight so I can bring it up at the meeting in Göteborg tomorrow.'

Paula repressed a sigh. Of course Mellberg would take all the credit for her discovery.

Patrik came in and looked around wide-eyed.

'Did we have a cleaning crew here today? Oh, right, I forgot that Mamma and Mr Fix-it came over.' He kissed Erica on the cheek. 'Okay, let's hear the damage report. How many things did he repair?'

'You don't want to know,' she said and led the way to the kitchen where she was cooking dinner.

'That bad, huh?' With a sigh Patrik sat down at the table. The children rushed in and threw themselves at their father, wanting a hug. But the next instant they were gone because *Bolibompa* was on TV. 'When did that green dragon get to be more popular than me?' he said with a wry smile.

'A long time ago,' said Erica, leaning forward to kiss him on the lips. 'But you're still much more popular with me.'

'More than Brad Pitt?'

'Afraid not. You'll never beat out Brad Pitt.' She winked

and opened a cupboard to take out some glasses. Patrik got up to help her set the table.

'So how's it going? Have you made any progress?'

He shook his head. 'No, not yet. The technical reports take a while. The only thing we know is that someone has been paying Lasse five thousand kronor at regular intervals.'

'Blackmail?'

Patrik nodded. 'Yes, that's the theory so far. We're trying not to rule out anything, but the most likely explanation is that he was blackmailing someone who got tired of paying him. The question is, who? At the moment we have no idea.'

'Are you ready for the meeting tomorrow?' Erica was stirring something in a saucepan on the cooker top.

'Yes, I think all of us are prepared. But Paula came up with a new theory today. There may be a connection to an old case from twenty-seven years ago. The victim was Ingela Eriksson. She was murdered in Hultsfred.'

'The woman who was tortured and then killed by her husband?' Erica turned around to stare at Patrik. 'Why would that case be linked to your investigation?'

'Oh, right. For a minute I forgot that you know so much about the history of Swedish crime. So do you recall how she was tortured?'

'No. The only thing I remember is that he beat her and dumped her body in the woods near their home. So tell me what the connection is.' She couldn't hide the eagerness in her voice.

'Ingela Eriksson suffered the exact same injuries as Victoria.'

For a moment neither of them spoke.

'Are you kidding?' Erica then said.

'No, I'm afraid not.' Patrik sniffed at the air. 'What's for dinner?'

'Fish soup.' Erica began ladling soup into the bowls on the table, but Patrik could tell her thoughts were elsewhere. 'Either her husband was innocent and the same killer kidnapped the girls, or else you're dealing with a copycat murderer. Or of course it could just be a coincidence.'

'I don't believe in coincidence,' said Patrik.

Erica sat down at the table. 'Neither do I. Are you going to mention this at the meeting tomorrow?'

'Yes. I've brought home copies of the investigative materials. Even Mellberg said he was planning to read up on the case.'

'So it's the two of you who are going?' She cautiously tasted the soup.

'Yes. We need to leave very early in the morning. The meeting starts at ten o'clock.'

'I hope it turns out to be productive.' She studied his face for a moment. 'You look tired. I know it's important for you to solve this case, but you need to take care of yourself.'

'I am. I know what my limits are. Apropos looking tired, how was Anna today?'

Erica paused before replying.

'I honestly don't know. I don't feel like I'm connecting with her these days. She seems to be wallowing in guilt, and I don't know how to bring her back to reality.'

'Maybe that's not your job,' he said, but he knew his words would fall on deaf ears.

'I'm going to have a talk with Dan,' said Erica. Her tone of voice indicated that the discussion about Anna was now closed.

Patrik understood and didn't ask any more questions. Erica was clearly worried about her sister, and he was ready to listen if she wanted to talk about it. Until that time, she would keep her thoughts to herself.

'I think I need to see a crisis therapist.' She served both of them more soup.

'Really? Why? What did my mother say now?'

'For once it has nothing to do with Kristina. And I'm not sure crisis therapy is going to be enough. I may need to have my memory erased too after seeing Mellberg almost naked this morning.'

Patrik couldn't help himself. He let loose such a howl of laughter that he got fish soup up his nose.

'I don't think any of us will ever forget that sight. But we're supposed to share both the good times and the bad. Just try not to picture him when we're having sex.'

Erica gave her husband an astonished look.

UDDEVALLA 1974

The border began to blur between what was normal and what was not. Laila saw it happening but every once in a while she couldn't resist the temptation to bow to Vladek's will. She knew it wasn't right, but sometimes she just wanted to pretend for a while that they were living an ordinary life.

They continued to be spellbound by Vladek's stories, which blended the commonplace with the extraordinary, the horrifying with the amazing. They would often gather around the kitchen table with only a small lamp turned on in the room. Sitting in the dim light they would all be drawn into his tales. They could hear the sound of the audience applauding; they saw the tight-rope walkers swaying high overhead; they laughed at the clowns and their antics; and they were captivated by the circus princess who, with grace and strength, balanced on the back of the horse racing around the ring, adorned with plumes and spangles. But most of all they saw Vladek and the lions in the circus ring. The way he stood there, strong and proud, wielding power over the wild beasts. Not because of the whip in his hand, as the audience thought, but because the lions respected and loved him. They trusted him and so they obeyed.

His best trick, his grand finale, was when he seemed to defy death by putting his head inside the maw of one of the lions. At that moment a hush came over the audience. They could hardly believe what they were seeing. The trick with the dimming of the lights was also very effective. When the lights went out in the circus ring, the spectators grew uneasy as they imagined the wild animals somewhere in front of them, animals that could see in the dark and might be eyeing them as prey. Then all the audience members would fearfully grab the hand of the person seated next to them. Suddenly, out of the darkness, fiery rings would appear, with flames shooting out hypnotically. And the lions would ignore their fear of fire and gracefully jump through the hoops because they put such trust in the person who had tamed them and who was now asking them to perform this trick.

As Laila sat there listening, she longed for something that might dispel her own darkness. She yearned to trust in someone again.

The streets were deserted as Helga walked through Fjällbacka on this chilly morning. In the summer the small town hummed with life. The shops were open, the restaurants were packed, and out in the harbour scores of boats would be moored close together as crowds of people strolled past. Now in the winter it was utterly quiet. Everything had been shuttered for the season. Fjällbacka seemed to be in a state of hibernation, waiting for another summer. But Helga had always preferred the calmer times of year. That was when her home was also more peaceful. In the summers Einar used to come home drunk more often and in a worse frame of mind.

After he fell ill, things had changed, of course. His words became his only weapon, but they could no longer hurt her. No one could hurt her any more except for Jonas. He knew where she was most vulnerable and fragile. The absurd thing was that she continued to try and protect him. It made no difference that he was now a grown man, tall and strong. He still needed her, and she would defend him against all evil.

She passed Ingrid Bergman Square and went over to look at the frozen water. She loved the archipelago. Her father had been a fisherman, and she would often go out in the boat with him. But all that had ended when she married Einar. He was from inland, and he'd never grown accustomed to the capriciousness of the sea. He would mutter that if people were meant to go out on the water, they would have been born with gills. Jonas had never been keen on boating either, so she hadn't ventured out since she was seventeen, even though she lived in the most beautiful archipelago region in Sweden.

For the first time in years she felt a desperate longing to go out in a boat. But even if she'd had one, that would have been impossible. The ice was so thick, and the few boats that had not been pulled up on land were now frozen solid in the harbour. In that sense, they were much like her. This was how she'd felt all these years: so close to where she truly belonged and yet unable to free herself from her prison.

It was because of Jonas that she had survived. Her love for him had always been so strong that everything else paled in comparison. All his life she had prepared herself to step forward and block the path of the rapidly advancing train that was now about to crush him. She was ready and had no doubts whatsoever. Everything she did for Jonas she did gladly.

She stopped to look at the bronze bust of Ingrid Bergman. She and Jonas had come to the square when the unveiling ceremony took place. Roses had also been presented, cultivated in honour of the famous actress. Jonas had been so excited. Ingrid's children were supposed to be there, as well as the son's girlfriend, Caroline of Monaco. At that time Jonas was at an age when his world was filled with knights and dragons, princes and princesses. He probably would have preferred to see a knight, but a princess would have to do. It was touching to see him looking so eager as they got ready for the big event. He carefully put water on his hair and then combed it smooth. And he picked flowers from their garden, bluebells and bleeding-hearts, which he nearly squeezed to death in his sweaty hand before they even reached the square. Einar teased him mercilessly, of course, but for once Jonas had ignored his father. He was going to see a real princess.

Helga still remembered the look of surprised disappointment on her son's face when she pointed out Caroline. He had looked up at her with his lip quivering and said, 'But, Mamma, she looks like a perfectly ordinary person.'

In the afternoon, after they got home, she'd found all his fairy tale books in a big heap behind the house. Tossed out like rubbish. Jonas had never been good at handling disappointment.

Now Helga took a deep breath, turned around, and began walking back home. It was her responsibility to spare him from disappointments. Both big and small.

Detective Inspector Palle Viking, who had been appointed chairman of the meeting, cleared his throat.

'I want to welcome all of you here on behalf of the Göteborg police. Thank you for your cooperation with these investigations so far. I think we ought to have met earlier, but you all know how difficult and complicated collaboration across districts can be, so maybe it will turn out that this is actually the perfect time for us to meet.' He looked down and added, 'The fact that Victoria Hallberg reappeared, and in such a terrible state, is a tragedy of course. Yet it gives us an idea of what may have happened to the other girls, and this information could move our investigations forward.'

'Does he always talk like this?' whispered Mellberg.

Patrik nodded. 'He joined the police force relatively late in life, but he's had a meteoric career. I've heard he's extremely good at his job. Before becoming a police officer he did research in the field of philosophy.'

Mellberg's mouth fell open. 'No kidding? But Palle Viking must be a made-up name.'

'No, it's not. But it certainly matches his appearance.'

'Right. Good Lord. He looks like that guy . . . what's his name? The Swede who boxed against Rocky.'

'Now that you mention it . . .' Patrik smiled. Mellberg was right. Palle Viking was a dead ringer for Dolph Lundgren.

When Mellberg leaned forward to whisper something more, Patrik shushed him. 'I think we'd better listen.'

In the meantime, Palle was continuing with his introductory remarks. 'I thought we'd each take a turn to report on our respective investigations. We've already shared most of the information, but I've seen to it that you've all received folders with the most current reports from each team. You will also be given copies of the videotaped interviews we've done with family members. That was an excellent idea, by the way. Thanks for suggesting it, Tage.' He nodded to a short, stocky man with a big moustache who was responsible for investigating the disappearance of Sandra Andersson.

When Jennifer Backlin went missing six months after Sandra, the police already suspected there might be a connection between the two cases. Tage had advised the Falsterbo police to follow their example and videotape their interviews with family members. The idea was to allow the families to have peace and quiet to report any observations they'd made in connection with the disappearances. By going to the family's home, the investigators could also get a better idea of what the missing girl was like. Since then, all of the police departments had followed suit, and now they would get to see each other's videos.

On the wall hung a big map of Sweden marked with

the places where the girls had disappeared. Even though he'd done the same thing back at the station, Patrik squinted his eyes and tried again to see if there was any sort of pattern. But he couldn't see anything linking the sites, except that they were all either in the southwest or middle of Sweden. There were no pins marking locations in the east, and none north of Västerås.

'Shall we start with you, Tage?' Palle motioned to the detective from Strömsholm who stood up to go to the front of the room.

One by one the officers took the floor to report on all aspects of their investigations. Patrik was disappointed that no new insights or leads emerged. They were merely hearing a repeat of the same meagre information available in the investigative materials they'd already shared. He could tell he was not the only one who felt discouraged, and the mood in the room began to sink.

Mellberg was the last to speak, since Victoria was the last of the girls to disappear. Out of the corner of his eye Patrik saw that his boss was bursting with pride at having his moment in the spotlight. He sincerely hoped that Mellberg was up to the task and had at least done a minimum of homework.

'So, how's it going everybody!' said Mellberg, as usual incapable of judging the mood of a situation or dealing with it in an appropriate manner.

His greeting was met with a few murmured remarks. Good Lord, thought Patrik, this does not bode well. But much to his surprise, Mellberg gave a concise presentation of their investigation. He also reported on Gerhard Struwer's theories about the perpetrator. For a short time Mellberg even came across as a competent detective. Patrik held his breath as his boss approached the topic that would be new material for the other officers.

'We have a reputation for carrying out highly efficient

police work in Tanumshede,' Mellberg began, and Patrik had to suppress a snort. The others seated at the table were not as restrained, and one person actually sniggered.

'One of our officers has discovered a connection between Victoria Hallberg and a significantly older homicide case.' He paused and waited for a reaction, which he got. Everyone fell silent and gave him their full attention. 'Does anyone recall the murder of Ingela Eriksson? In Hultsfred?'

Several officers nodded, and the detective from Västerås said, 'Yes, she was found tortured to death in the woods behind her house. Her husband was convicted, even though he denied killing her.'

Mellberg nodded. 'He later died in prison. The case was built on circumstantial evidence, and there is reason to believe that the husband was in fact innocent. He claimed that he was home alone on the evening when his wife disappeared. She had told him she was going to visit a female friend, but the woman denied that was true. At any rate, he had no alibi and there was no witness to support his claim that his wife had been home earlier in the day. The husband stated that they'd received a visit from a man in response to an advert they'd posted, but the police were unable to locate this person. Since the husband was known to have abused women in the past, including his wife, the police immediately turned their attention to him. They don't seem to have been especially interested in investigating other avenues.'

'But how is that case related to the missing girls?' asked the Västerås officer. 'That must have been nearly thirty years ago.'

'Twenty-seven. Well, the thing is . . .' said Mellberg, again pausing for dramatic effect. 'The thing is that Ingela Eriksson had suffered the exact same injuries as Victoria.'

For a few moments no one spoke.

'Could it be a copycat?' Tage from Strömshold finally asked.

'That's one possibility.'

'Doesn't that seem more likely? It would be unusual for the same perpetrator to be at work. Because why would he let so many years go by before striking again?' Tage looked around at his colleagues. Several murmured their agreement.

'Right,' said Palle, turning in his seat so everyone could hear him. 'Though there may have been some reason why the perpetrator didn't commit any more crimes during those years. Maybe he was in prison, for example, or maybe he was living abroad. And there could have been other victims that we don't know about. Every year six thousand people disappear in Sweden, so there could be other missing girls that no one has connected to the case. We need to consider the possibility that it might be the same perpetrator. But,' and here he raised his finger, 'we shouldn't take for granted that there is a connection. Couldn't it be a coincidence?'

'The injuries are identical,' Mellberg objected. 'Down to the smallest detail. You can read about it in our report. We've brought copies for everyone.'

'Why don't we take a break so we can read the material?' Palle suggested.

Everyone stood up and took a copy from the pile on the table in front of Mellberg. They crowded around him to ask questions, and he beamed happily at all the attention.

Patrik raised one eyebrow. Mellberg hadn't taken credit for the discovery, which was surprising. Even Mellberg had his good moments. But it might not have hurt for him to remind himself why they were all gathered here. Four missing girls. And one of them was dead.

* * *

Marta was up early, as usual, since the chores in the stable couldn't wait. For his part, Jonas had risen even earlier to drive over to a nearby farm where a horse had come down with severe colic. Marta yawned. They'd stayed up late, which meant she'd had far too little sleep.

Her mobile buzzed. She took it out of her pocket and looked at the display. Helga was inviting her and Molly over for coffee. She must have looked out the window and seen that Molly had stayed home from school, and now she wanted to know why. The truth was that Molly had said she had a stomach ache, and for once Marta chose to believe her.

'Molly, your grandmother wants us to come over for coffee.'

'Do we have to?' Molly replied from one of the horse stalls.

'Yes, we do. Come on.'

'But I have a stomach ache,' Molly whined.

Marta sighed. 'If you can work out here with a stomach ache, then I'm sure you can manage to have coffee with your grandmother too. Come on. Let's get it over with. Jonas and Helga had an argument yesterday, and I'm sure he'll be happy if we try to make peace with her.'

'But I was planning to take Scirocco out for a ride.' Molly was starting to sulk as she came out of the stall.

'With a stomach ache?' said Marta, an angry glint in her eye. 'You'll still have time for that later. We'll have a quick visit with your grandmother, and then you can come back here and train in peace and quiet for the rest of the afternoon. I don't have any lessons until five o'clock today.'

'Okay,' muttered Molly.

As they crossed the yard, Marta clenched her fists in annoyance. Molly had always been handed everything on a platter. She had no idea what it was like to endure a wretched childhood and have to get by on her own. Sometimes Marta had the urge to show her what life was like for someone who wasn't as pampered as she was.

'We're here!' she called, going inside her mother-in-law's house without knocking.

'Come in and sit down. I've baked sponge cake, and there's tea for both of you.' Helga turned to greet them as they came into the kitchen. She looked like the archetypal grandmother, with a flour-covered apron around her waist and a cloud of grey hair framing her face.

'Tea?' said Molly, wrinkling her nose. 'I'd rather have coffee.'

'I'd prefer coffee too,' said Marta, sitting down.

'I'm afraid we're all out of coffee. I haven't had time to do any grocery shopping. Put in a spoonful of honey, and it'll taste fine.' She pointed to a tin on the table.

Marta reached for the honey and stirred a big spoonful into her tea.

'I hear you're going to compete at the weekend,' said Helga.

Molly sipped the hot tea. 'Yes, I didn't get to go last Saturday, so I'm not about to miss the next one.'

'Of course not.' Helga pushed the plate of sponge cake over to Marta and Molly. 'I'm sure you'll do great. Are both of your parents going with you?'

'Yes. They wouldn't miss it.'

'I don't know how you put up with all that driving around,' Helga said to Marta. 'But I suppose that's expected these days. Parents always have to be ready to put in an appearance.'

Marta gave her a suspicious look. Helga wasn't usually so positive.

'Yes, you're right. And the training sessions have gone well. I think we have a good chance of winning.'

Molly couldn't help smiling. It was so rare for her to receive praise from her mother.

'You're so talented. You both are,' said Helga with a smile. 'I once dreamed of learning to ride when I was a girl, but I never had the chance. And then I met Einar, of course.'

Her smile faded and her expression closed up. Marta studied her in silence as she stirred her tea. Einar was good at erasing a smile. She knew that from experience.

'How did you and Grandpa meet?' asked Molly. Marta was surprised at her sudden interest in someone other than herself.

'At a dance in Fjällbacka. Your grandfather was so handsome back then.'

'He was?' said Molly in surprise. She could hardly remember her grandfather from the time before he was confined to a wheelchair.

'Yes, he was. And your father looks so much like him. Wait here and I'll fetch a photo to show you.' Helga stood up and went into the living room. She came back with an album which she leafed through until she found the right photograph.

'Look. Here's your grandfather in his heyday.' There was an odd bitterness to Helga's voice.

'Oh, he's so cute! And he looks exactly like Pappa. Not that Pappa is cute. I mean, that's not something you notice about your own father.' Molly studied the photo. 'How old was Grandpa in this picture?'

Helga thought for a moment. 'He must have been about thirty-five.'

'What kind of car is that? Was it yours?' said Molly, pointing to the car that Einar was leaning against.

'No, that was one of the cars he bought and fixed up. An Amazon. He made it look so great. Say what you like about him, but he was a genius when it came to fixing up cars.' Again that bitter tone crept into Helga's voice. Marta gave her mother-in-law a surprised look as she took another sip of the sweetened tea.

'I wish I'd known Grandpa back then,' said Molly.

Helga nodded. 'I can understand that. But your mother knew him then, so you can ask her about him.'

'I guess I never thought about that before. He's always been the grumpy old man upstairs,' said Molly with the blunt candour of a teenager.

'The grumpy old man upstairs. That's an excellent description.' Helga laughed.

Marta smiled. Her mother-in-law seemed so unlike herself today. For a number of reasons that were more or less obvious, they had never cared much for each other. But today Helga didn't seem as superficial as usual, and Marta appreciated that, though it probably wouldn't last. She took a bite of sponge cake. She was glad this courtesy visit was almost over.

It was very quiet at home. The children were at the day-care centre and Patrik was in Göteborg, which meant that Erica would be able to work undisturbed. She'd brought her files downstairs from her study to spread them out on the floor in the living room. Papers were strewn all about. The latest addition was a copy of the homicide report in the Ingela Eriksson case. It had taken a good deal of persuasion, but eventually Patrik had agreed to give her a copy of one of the printouts he was taking along to Göteborg. She'd read it several times. The similarities with Victoria's injuries were uncanny.

Erica had already re-read all her notes from her meetings with Laila, as well as from the phone conversation with Laila's sister and her talks with Louise's foster parents and some of the prison staff. She'd spent many hours interviewing people in an effort to understand what had happened on the day Vladek Kowalski was murdered. Now she was also trying to find a connection between his murder and the five missing girls.

She surveyed the material in front of her, trying to grasp the big picture. What was it that Laila wanted to tell her? And what was holding her back? According to the staff, in all these years she'd had no contact with anyone outside of the prison. No visitors, no phone calls, no . . .

Erica sat up straight. She had forgotten to ask whether Laila had ever received any post. How could she have been so stupid? She picked up her mobile and tapped in the number of the prison, which she knew by heart.

'Hi, this is Erica Falck.'

The guard who answered said, 'Hi, Erica. This is Tina. Were you planning to come over for a visit?'

'No, I'm not visiting today. I just wanted to ask about something. Has Laila ever received any post in all these years? And has she ever sent any letters?'

'Yes, she has received a few postcards. And I think some letters too.'

'Really?' said Erica. That was not what she'd expected to hear. 'Do you know who sent them?'

'No, but maybe one of my colleagues does. The postcards were completely blank. And she refused to accept them.'

'What do you mean?'

'From what I heard, she didn't even want to touch them. She asked the guard to throw them away. But we saved them in case she changed her mind.'

'So you still have them?' Erica could hardly hide her excitement. 'Could I see them?'

After the guard promised to let her see the postcards, Erica ended the call, stunned at this turn of events. It had to mean something. But she couldn't for the life of her work out what it could be.

* * *

Gösta scratched his head. The station felt deserted. Annika was the only other person there. Patrik and Mellberg were in Göteborg, and Martin had gone over to Sälvik to knock on doors in the neighbourhood near the beach. The divers had not yet found Lasse's body, but that wasn't so strange given the difficult circumstances. He had spoken to some of Lasse's acquaintances, but none of them knew anything about the money. Now he was sitting here wondering whether he should drive to Kville to talk to the head of Lasse's church.

Gösta was just about to get up when his phone rang, and he picked it up at once. It was Pedersen.

'That was fast. What did you find out?'

He listened intently.

'Really?' Gösta then said. After asking a few more questions, he ended the call and sat in silence for several minutes. Thoughts whirled through his mind as he tried to make sense of what he'd just heard. Slowly a possible theory began to take shape.

He put on his jacket and hurried past Annika who was sitting at her desk in the reception area.

'I'm going over to Fjällbacka for a while.'

'What are you going to do there?' she called after him, but he was already going out the door. He'd explain later.

The drive from Tanumshede to Fjällbacka took only fifteen or twenty minutes, but it seemed endless. He wondered whether he should phone Patrik to tell him about Pedersen's report, but he decided it wasn't necessary to interrupt the meeting. It'd be best if he went ahead on his own, and then he might have something new to report when Patrik and Mellberg came home. Right now the important thing was to take the initiative. And he was fully capable of handling this alone.

When he reached Jonas and Marta's farm, he rang the

bell and after a few minutes a sleepy-looking Jonas opened the door.

'Did I wake you?' asked Gösta, glancing at his watch. It was one in the afternoon.

'I was out on an emergency call early this morning, so I was just catching up on my sleep. But come in. I'm awake now.' He made an attempt to smooth down his hair, which was standing on end.

Gösta followed him out to the kitchen and sat down at the table even though Jonas hadn't invited him to take a seat. He decided to get right to the point.

'How well do you know Lasse?'

'I'd say that I don't know him at all. I've said hello a few times when he came to fetch Tyra at the stable, but that's about it.'

'I have reason to believe that you're not telling the truth,' said Gösta.

Jonas was still standing, and a look of annoyance appeared on his face.

'I'm starting to get sick and tired of all this. What exactly do you want?'

'I think that Lasse knew about your relationship with Victoria. And he was blackmailing you.'

Jonas stared at him. 'You can't be serious.'

He looked genuinely surprised, and for a moment Gösta questioned the theory he'd come up with after speaking to Pedersen. But he shook off the doubt. This had to be how everything fit together, and it wouldn't be very difficult to prove.

'Don't you think it would be best if you told me the truth? We'll be looking at your mobile phone records and your bank account, which will tell us that the two of you have been in contact and that you've withdrawn cash to give to Lasse. You can spare us the trouble by telling me about it now.'

'Get out of here,' said Jonas, pointing toward the front door. 'I've heard enough.'

'We're going to find out anyway. It's all there in black and white,' Gösta went on. 'So what happened? Did he demand more money? Did you get tired of paying him and so you killed him?'

'I want you to leave.' Jonas's voice was ice-cold. He ushered Gösta to the door and practically pushed him out of the house.

'I know I'm right,' said Gösta as he stood on the front steps.

'You're wrong. First of all, I was not having an affair with Victoria, and secondly, Terese said that Lasse disappeared sometime between Saturday morning and Sunday morning, and I have an alibi for that whole period. So the next time I see you, I'll expect an apology. And I'll be happy to tell one of your colleagues what my alibi is. But I'm not talking to you.'

Jonas slammed the door shut, and Gösta again felt a twinge of doubt. What if he was wrong, even though all the puzzle pieces seemed to fit? There was one more visit he needed to make, and then he'd get started on exactly what he'd just told Jonas he would do. He would examine his bank account and mobile phone records, which would reveal the truth. Then Jonas could say whatever he liked about his supposed alibi.

It would soon be time. Laila had a feeling that any day now another postcard would turn up. A couple of years ago the cards had suddenly started arriving. By now she'd received a total of four. Several days after she got each postcard, a letter would arrive containing a newspaper clipping. All the cards were blank, but she had worked out what the message was meant to be.

The postcards scared her, and she'd asked the staff to

throw them out. But she had saved the newspaper clippings. Every time she took them out of the hiding place, she hoped to understand more, now that she was not the only target of the threats.

Feeling tired, she lay down on the bed. In a few minutes she would have to endure another pointless therapy session. She had slept badly last night, plagued by nightmares about Vladek and the Girl. It was hard to understand how things had turned out as they had. How did what was abnormal gradually end up seeming normal? They had slowly been changed until they could no longer even recognize themselves.

'It's time now, Laila.' Ulla was knocking on her open door. With an effort Laila got up. The fatigue she felt seemed to get worse every day. The nightmares, the waiting, all the memories of how her life had slowly but surely gone wrong. She had loved him so much. His background had been completely different from her own. She had never imagined that she'd ever meet someone like him, and yet they had been drawn to each other. It had seemed like the most natural thing in the world until the evil took over and destroyed everything.

'Are you coming, Laila?' said Ulla.

Laila forced her feet to move. She felt like she was walking through water. Fear had prevented her from speaking for such a long time. It had prevented her from doing anything at all. And she was still afraid. Terrified. But the fate of the missing girls had touched her deeply, and she could no longer keep silent. She was ashamed of her cowardice, the fact that she'd allowed the evil to prey on so many innocent lives. Meeting with Erica was at least a beginning. Maybe it would finally give her the courage to reveal the truth. She thought about something she'd once heard, about how the beating of a butterfly's wings could cause a storm somewhere else in the world. Maybe that was what would happen now.

'Laila?'

'I'm coming,' she said with a sigh.

Fear gripped her body, and she saw only horrors wherever she looked. On the floor she saw wriggling snakes with glittering eyes, on the walls spiders and cockroaches were swarming. She screamed, and the sound echoed like a dreadful choir. She struggled to flee the creatures, but something was holding her tight, and the more she fought, the more it hurt. From far away she heard someone calling her name, louder and louder, and she tried to move towards the urgent voice, but again she was held back, and the pain only increased her panic.

'Molly!' The voice pierced the sound of her own screams, and everything seemed to stand still. She heard her name repeated, now calmer and quieter, and she saw the vermin begin to dissolve and then disappear as if they'd never existed at all.

'You're hallucinating,' said Marta, and her voice now sounded very clear.

Molly squinted her eyes and tried to see where she was. Her head felt fuzzy and she was terribly confused. Where had the snakes and cockroaches gone? They were right here. She'd seen them with her own eyes.

'Listen to me. Nothing that you're seeing is real.'

'Okay,' she said, her mouth dry. Again she tried to move towards Marta's voice.

'I can't move,' she said. She kicked her legs, but couldn't get free. It was pitch-dark all around her, and she realized that Marta was right. Those creatures couldn't be real because she wouldn't have been able to see them in the dark. But it felt as if the walls were closing in on her, and she couldn't get enough oxygen into her lungs. She could hear her own breathing getting fast and shallow.

'Calm down, Molly,' said Marta in that stern tone of hers. The voice that always made the girls in the stable pay strict attention. And this time it worked too. Molly forced herself to breathe more calmly, and after a while her panic began to subside and her lungs filled with oxygen again.

'We need to stay calm. Otherwise we'll never make it through this.'

'But what is . . . Where are we?' Molly sat up and ran her hand down her leg. A metal ring was fastened around her ankle, and with more fumbling she discovered the crude links of a chain. In vain she tried to tug at it as she howled into the dark.

'I told you to calm down! You'll never get free doing that.'

Marta's tone was insistent and firm, but this time she couldn't hide her own panic, and Molly finally understood. She abruptly stopped screaming and whispered into the dark:

'The person who took Victoria has taken us too.'

She waited for Marta to reply, but her mother didn't say a word. And her silence scared Molly more than anything else.

The detectives had eaten lunch in the cafeteria at the police station, and when they gathered once again in the conference room, they were all feeling drowsy and a bit bloated. Patrik shook himself to wake up. He'd been getting very little sleep lately, and his body felt heavy with fatigue.

'So, let's get started again,' said Palle Viking, pointing at the map. 'The disappearances all occurred in a relatively limited geographic area, but no one has been able to see any connection between the various sites. As for the girls, there are several similarities in terms of appearance and background, but we haven't found any other common denominators, such as shared interests, or participation in the same internet forums, or anything like that. There are also some clear differences, especially when it comes to Minna Wahlberg, just as our Tanumshede colleague pointed out earlier this morning. Here in Göteborg we've made great efforts to locate anyone else who might have seen the white car, but as you all know, so far the results have been zero.'

'The question is why the perpetrator was so careless in that particular instance,' said Patrik, and everyone turned to look at him. 'He didn't leave a single scrap of evidence in any of the other kidnappings. And here I'm assuming that it was the driver of the white car who kidnapped Minna, though we don't know that for sure. But Gerhard Struwer – the profiler we told you about earlier – thinks we should focus on those occasions when the perp deviates from his normal pattern.'

'I agree. One theory we've discussed is that the murderer knew the girl personally. We've already interviewed a lot of people who knew Minna, but I think it would be worthwhile to keep digging.'

The others murmured their agreement.

'I've heard rumours that even your wife has had a chance to talk to Minna's mother,' said Palle with an amused smile.

The other officers sniggered, and Patrik could feel himself blushing.

'Yes, well, my colleague Martin Molin and I went to see Minna's mother, and my wife Erica also . . . happened to be there.' He could hear how apologetic he sounded.

Mellberg snorted. 'That is one nosy woman.'

'It's all in our report,' Patrik hurried to say, trying to

drown out Mellberg's comment. He nodded towards the papers they'd all received. 'Although there's no mention of Erica's visit.'

More sniggering, and he sighed. Patrik loved his wife, but sometimes she put him in very embarrassing situations.

'I'm sure your report of the conversation will be sufficient,' said Palle with a smile. Then he turned serious. 'But we've also heard that Erica has a good head on her shoulders, so it'd be wise to find out if she learned anything that the rest of us might have missed.'

'I've already talked to her about it, and I don't think she learned anything new.'

'Have another talk with her. We need to find out what makes Minna's case different.'

'Okay, I'll do that,' Patrik acquiesced.

They devoted the next few hours to discussing the cases from all possible angles. Theories were proposed, suggestions considered, and new investigative angles brainstormed and then divided among the various police districts. Crazy ideas were received with the same open-mindedness as more sensible suggestions. They were eager to find something that might move the investigations forward. They all shared a sense of powerlessness since they'd failed to find the missing girls. Everyone present was thinking about their meetings with family members who were all going through such sorrow, despair, anxiety, and horror because they didn't know what had happened. And then came the even greater horror when Victoria reappeared, and they realized that their daughters might have met the same awful fate.

By the end of the day the subdued but determined detectives dispersed to drive home and continue their investigations. The fate of five girls rested on their shoulders. One girl was dead. Four were still missing.

* * *

The prison was calm and quiet when Erica entered. She greeted the guards and after reporting her arrival and signing in, she was escorted to the staff room, where she sat down on a chair. While she waited, she berated herself again for being so careless. She didn't like making this sort of mistake.

'Hi, Erica.' Tina came in and closed the door behind her. In her hand she held several postcards with a rubber band around them. She placed them on the table in front of Erica. 'Here they are.'

'Is it okay if I have a look?'

Tina nodded, and Erica reached out to remove the rubber band from the cards. Then she hesitated, worrying about destroying fingerprints. But she quickly realized that the cards had already been handled by so many people that any fingerprints of interest had vanished long ago.

There were four postcards. Erica spread them out with the front picture showing. They were all scenes from Spain.

'When did the last one arrive?'

'Hmm . . . Let me think. Maybe three or four months ago.'

'And Laila has never said anything about them? Never mentioned who might have sent them?'

'Not a word. But she gets very upset when they turn up, and it takes her days to calm down.'

'She doesn't want to keep them?' Erica studied the postcards.

'No. She always tells us to throw them away.

'Didn't you think this was all rather strange?'

'Well, yes . . .' Tina hesitated. 'Maybe that's why we decided to save them.'

Erica let her eyes wander around the cold and impersonal room as she thought things over. The only attempt to make the room more pleasant was the addition of a withered yucca in a pot on the windowsill.

'We don't spend much time in here,' said Tina with a smile.

'I can see why,' said Erica, turning her attention back to the postcards. She flipped them over. Just as Tina had said, they were all blank except for Laila's name and the address of the prison, stamped in blue ink. The postmarks were from different places, but none of them had a connection with Laila, as far as Erica knew.

Why pictures from Spain? Was it Laila's sister who had sent the postcards? If so, why? That didn't seem likely, given that all the postmarks were Swedish. She wondered if she should ask Patrik to check on Agneta's visits to Sweden. Maybe the two sisters had kept in touch more often than Laila had claimed. But maybe this had nothing at all to do with Agneta.

'Would you like to ask Laila about them? I can see if she'd be willing to talk to you,' said Tina.

Erica paused before replying. She glanced at the withered yucca on the windowsill and then shook her head.

'Thanks, but first I need to spend some time thinking this over. Maybe I can work out what it's all about.'

'Good luck,' said Tina, and stood up.

Erica gave her a wry smile. Luck was exactly what she needed at this point.

'Could I take the postcards with me?' she asked.

Tina hesitated. 'Okay, but only if you promise to bring them back.'

'I promise,' said Erica and put them in her bag. Nothing was impossible. There had to be a connection somewhere, and she refused to give up until she found it.

Gösta wondered if he ought to wait for Patrik to return, but he had a feeling that time was of the essence. He decided to follow his instinct and proceed, based on what he knew.

Annika had phoned to say that she'd gone home early because her daughter was ill. Maybe he should go back to the station and hold down the fort. But Martin would probably be back soon, so he said to hell with it and drove to the neighbourhood known as Sumpan.

Ricky opened the door and silently let him in. Gösta had sent him a text message on the way over to make sure the family was at home. The tension was palpable as he went into the living room.

'Have you come up with something new?' asked Markus.

Gösta saw the gleam of hope in their eyes. It was no longer hope that Victoria would be found; instead, it was a desire for some sort of explanation and a sense of closure. Gösta felt bad that he was going to disappoint them.

'No. Or at least, nothing that we can confidently say has anything to do with Victoria's death. But there's a strange circumstance that has a connection to the other case we're investigating right now.'

'You mean Lasse?' said Helena.

Gösta nodded. 'Yes. We've discovered a link between Victoria and Lasse. And it has to do with something else I've discovered. I'm afraid it's a bit sensitive.'

He cleared his throat, not sure how to tell them. All three sat in silence, waiting. He could see the anguish in Ricky's expression, no doubt a result of his guilty conscience, which would probably haunt him for the rest of his life.

'We still haven't found Lasse's body, but there was blood on the ground near his car, and we sent it to the lab for analysis. The blood turned out to be Lasse's.'

'But what does that have to do with Victoria?' asked Markus.

'Well, as you know, we suspect that someone had been watching your house. We found a cigarette butt in your neighbour's garden, and it was sent to the lab,' said Gösta. He was now approaching the topic he wished he could avoid. 'On his own initiative, the lab tech compared the blood from the dock with the DNA on the cigarette, and they matched. In other words, it was Lasse who had been watching Victoria, and most likely he was also the one who sent her the unpleasant letters, which Ricky told us about.'

'He told us too,' said Helena, casting a glance at Ricky.

'I'm sorry I threw them out,' he muttered. 'But I didn't want you to see them.'

'Don't worry about it,' said Gösta. 'What's done is done. At any rate, we're now working on the assumption that Lasse was blackmailing someone who got tired of paying the money and killed him. And I have an idea who that person might be.'

'I'm sorry, but you've lost me,' said Helena. 'What does this have to do with Victoria?'

'Yes, why was he watching her?' asked Markus. 'And what did she have to do with him blackmailing someone? Please explain.'

Gösta sighed and took a deep breath. 'I think that Lasse was blackmailing Jonas Persson because he knew that Jonas was having an extramarital affair with a much younger girl. With Victoria.'

He felt his shoulders relax now that he'd finally said it. But he held his breath as he waited for Victoria's parents to react. Their response was not at all what he'd expected. Helena looked up and fixed her eyes on his. Then she smiled sadly.

'You've got it all wrong, Gösta,' she said.

Much to Dan's surprise, Anna had volunteered to drive the girls over to the stable for their riding lesson. She needed to get out of the house and get some fresh air.

Not even the proximity of the horses could keep her away. She shivered and pulled her jacket closer around her. On top of everything else, she was feeling more and more ill. She was starting to worry that it was no longer something psychosomatic. She might be coming down with the stomach flu that was raging at the kids' school. So far she'd warded off the worst of the nausea by eating ten white peppercorns, but she could tell that soon she'd be leaning over a bucket to throw up.

Several girls were standing outside the stable, shivering in the cold. Emma and Lisen ran over to them, and Anna followed.

'Hi. Why are you standing outside?'

'Marta hasn't arrived yet,' said a tall girl with dark hair. 'She's never late.'

'I'm sure she'll be here soon.'

'But Molly is supposed to be here to help out,' said the girl. The others nodded. She was apparently the leader of the group.

'Have you gone over to the house to knock on the door?' asked Anna, looking in that direction. She could see lights on inside, so someone must be home.

'No, we'd never do that.' The girl looked horrified.

'Then I'll go. Wait here.'

Anna hurried across the yard to Jonas and Marta's house. Running only made the nausea worse, and she leaned heavily on the railing as she climbed the steps. She had to ring the bell twice before Jonas opened the door. He was drying his hands on a dishcloth, and judging by the cooking smells wafting from inside, he was in the middle of making dinner.

'Hi,' he said, giving her an inquisitive look.

Anna cleared her throat.

'Hi. Is Marta here? And Molly?'

'No, they must be over at the stable.' Jonas glanced at

his watch. 'Marta has a lesson right now, and I think Molly was going to help out.'

Anna shook her head. 'They haven't turned up. Where do you think they could be?'

'I have no idea,' said Jonas. 'I haven't seen them since early this morning because I had to go out on an emergency call, and when I got back they weren't here. Then I took a nap before going over to the clinic. I just assumed that they spent the afternoon at the stable. Molly has an important competition coming up soon, so I thought they were doing some extra training. And the car is here.' He pointed at the blue Toyota parked in front of the house.

Anna nodded. 'What should we do? The girls are waiting, and . . .'

Jonas picked up his mobile from the chest of drawers in the front hall and tapped in a pre-programmed number.

'Huh. She's not answering. That's strange. She always has her mobile with her.' Jonas was starting to look worried. 'I'll check with my mother.'

He rang his mother, and Anna heard him explain the situation. At the same time he assured Helga that there was nothing to be concerned about, everything was fine. It took a moment before he was able to end the conversation.

'Mothers and phone calls,' he said with a slight grimace. 'It's easier to get pigs to fly than to get mothers off the phone.'

'Sure. Right,' said Anna, as if she knew what he was talking about. The truth was that her mother had hardly ever phoned.

'Apparently they dropped by to visit my mother this morning, but she hasn't seen them since. Molly stayed home from school today because of a stomach ache, but they were supposed to train this afternoon.'

He put on his jacket. 'I'll go with you to look for them,' he told Anna. 'They must be somewhere around here.'

They made a big circuit of the grounds, looking inside the old barn and the riding hall and ending up in the common room. But Marta and Molly were nowhere to be seen.

By now the girls had gone inside the stable, and they could be heard talking to the horses and to each other.

'I suppose we should wait a little longer,' said Anna. 'But then we'll just go home if they don't turn up. Maybe it was a miscommunication about the schedule.'

'Maybe so,' said Jonas, but he sounded doubtful. 'I'll take another look around. Don't give up yet.'

'Sure,' said Anna and went inside the stable, keeping a safe distance from the horses.

They were on their way home. Patrik had insisted on driving, claiming it would help him to unwind.

'Well, that was certainly intense,' he said. 'It was good to have a chance to go through everything, but I was hoping we'd get something more concrete out of the meeting. I was hoping for an "aha" sort of moment.'

'I'm sure it'll happen eventually,' said Mellberg, sounding unusually cheerful. Evidently he was still feeling a rush from all the attention he'd garnered after telling the others about Ingela Eriksson.

He'll be living off that moment for weeks, thought Patrik. But he realized that he too needed to stay positive. It wouldn't be a good idea to report to his colleagues in the morning and say they'd come to a dead end.

'Maybe you're right. Maybe the meeting will lead to something. Palle is going to put extra manpower into reviewing the Ingela Eriksson case, and if all of us focus on Minna Wahlberg's disappearance, we should be able to find out what makes it different from the other cases.'

He stepped harder on the accelerator. He was impatient to get home so he could digest what they'd heard and possibly discuss it with Erica. She often managed to see patterns in what looked like nothing but chaos to him. And no one was better at helping him when he needed to make sense of all the ideas whirling through his mind.

He was also considering asking her a favour, but he had no intention of telling Mellberg. His boss was the one who always grumbled the most about Erica's tendency to get involved in police investigations. Even though Patrik could also get angry with her on occasion, she did have an ability to view things from new angles. Palle had asked him to speak to Erica again, and she was already involved in the case since she had discovered a possible link between Laila and the missing girls. He had considered mentioning this at the meeting, but in the end decided not to. First he wanted to find out more. Otherwise there was a risk of distracting everyone's attention and derailing the investigation instead of moving it forward. So far Erica hadn't found anything to support her theory, but Patrik knew it was always worthwhile to listen to her whenever she had a gut feeling about something. She was seldom wrong, which could be extremely annoying at times but also a big help. That was why he wanted to ask his wife to watch the videotaped interviews. So far they had failed to find a common denominator among the girls, and maybe Erica would see something everyone else had missed.

'I was thinking we should all meet at eight o'clock tomorrow morning to discuss everything,' he said now. 'And I want to ask Paula to come in too, if she can.'

Mellberg didn't reply as Patrik focused on his driving. The road was getting a little too slippery for his taste.

'What do you think, Bertil?' he said when there was still no reaction from his boss. 'Could you find out if Paula could come over to the station tomorrow?'

The only reply was a loud snore. He glanced over at Mellberg and saw that he was sound asleep. Probably exhausted after working a whole day. He wasn't used to that.

FJÄLLBACKA 1975

The situation had become unbearable. There were too many questions from neighbours and the authorities, and they realized they couldn't keep living where they were. After Agneta moved to Spain, Laila's mother had been in touch more often. She was lonely, and when she mentioned to them that a house was for sale outside Fjällbacka for a good price, it was easy to make the decision. They would move back to Fjällbacka.

At the same time, Laila knew it was madness. It would be dangerous to develop closer ties with her mother. Yet she also felt a spark of hope. Maybe she would be able to help them. Maybe everything would be simpler if they were left in peace in their new house, which was in a remote location and far from any neighbours.

Her hope didn't last long. Vladek's temper grew worse, and they had row after row. There was nothing left of the relationship they'd once had.

Yesterday her mother had suddenly turned up at their house. Worry was written all over her face, and at first Laila had wanted to throw herself into her mother's arms and cry like a child. Then she had felt Vladek's hand on her shoulder and sensed his raw strength. The moment passed. Calmly and quietly she had said what had to be said, even though it hurt her mother terribly.

Her mother gave up. When Laila saw her head back to her

car, looking defeated and with slumped shoulders, she had wanted to scream after her. Shout that she loved her, that she needed her. But the words refused to come out.

Sometimes Laila wondered how she could have been stupid enough to think that moving might change things. The problem was theirs, and no one could help them. They were on their own. And she couldn't allow her mother to enter their private hell.

Occasionally she would move close to Vladek in bed and remember those first years when they'd slept in each other's arms every night, even when it was too warm under the covers. Now she barely slept at all. She would lie awake next to Vladek, listening to him snoring and breathing deeply. She saw him flinch in his sleep and noticed the way his eyes moved restlessly behind his eyelids.

It was snowing. As if hypnotized, Einar watched the flakes slowly drifting down. From downstairs he heard the usual sounds, which he'd heard day after day over the past years. Helga pottering about in the kitchen, the vacuum cleaner roaring, the clatter of plates being placed in the dishwasher. The endless cleaning which had consumed her whole life.

Good Lord, how he despised her. What a weak and wretched person she was. He had hated women all his life. First his mother, followed by all the others. His mother had loathed him from the very beginning. She had tried to clip his wings and prevent him from being himself. But she'd been laid to rest in the earth long ago.

His mother had died of a heart attack when he was twelve years old. He had watched her die, and that was one of his best memories. Like a treasure hidden away inside of him, it was a memory that he took out only on special occasions. Then he would recall every detail, as if a film were playing before his eyes: the way she had clutched at her chest, how her face had crumpled with pain and surprise, and how she'd slowly collapsed on the floor. He hadn't called for help. Instead, he had knelt down beside her so he could memorize every expression.

He fixed his eyes on her face as it froze, and then her skin grew more and more blue from lack of oxygen as her heart began to shut down.

In the past he'd felt sexually aroused whenever he thought about the pain she'd endured at that moment and the power he'd held over her life and death. Einar wished that he could feel the same way now, but his body refused him that pleasure. No memory that he conjured up could give him that amazing feeling of blood pumping into his groin. These days his only pleasure was tormenting Helga.

He took a deep breath. 'Helga! Helgaaa!'

The sounds downstairs stopped. She was probably sighing, and he enjoyed that image. Then he heard her footsteps on the stairs and Helga came into the room.

'The bag needs to be changed again.' He had purposely opened it so it would leak before he called her. He knew that she knew. It was all part of the game, because no matter what he did, she had no choice. He should never have married someone who assumed she had options, or someone with her own will. Women should not think they could decide for themselves. Men were superior in all respects, and a woman's only task was to give birth to children. But Helga had not been very good at that either.

'I know you're doing this deliberately,' said Helga, as if reading his mind.

He just looked at her without replying. It didn't matter what she thought because she still had to wipe up the mess.

'Who was that on the phone earlier?' he asked.

'It was Jonas. He was asking about Molly and Marta.' She unbuttoned his shirt, making no effort to be gentle.

'Oh? Why's that?' he said, fighting back an urge to slap her.

He missed being able to control her with a show of strength, using wordless threats to make her lower her gaze, comply and submit. But he would never allow her to control him. His body may have betrayed him, but mentally he was still stronger than she was.

'They weren't over in the stable. Some of the girls were waiting outside because they had a lesson, but Molly and Marta hadn't turned up.'

'Is it really that difficult to run a business properly?' said Einar, flinching when Helga pinched him. 'What the hell are you doing?'

'Sorry. I didn't mean to do that,' said Helga. Her voice lacked the submissive tone he was used to hearing, but he decided not to say anything. He was too tired today.

'So where are they?'

'How would I know?' snapped Helga as she went into the bathroom to fetch some water.

He gave a start. It really wasn't acceptable for her to speak to him that way.

'When did Jonas last see them?' Einar called, listening for her reply over the sound of water running into a basin.

'Early this morning. They were still asleep when he left on an emergency call out at the Leandersson farm. But when they stopped by here later in the morning, they didn't mention going anywhere. And the car is still parked in front of the house.'

'So they must be around here somewhere.' Einar watched Helga carefully as she came back from the bathroom carrying the basin of water and a rag. 'Marta needs to understand that she can't just skip lessons like this. She'll lose her students, and then what are they going to live on? I don't want to criticize Jonas's veterinary practice, but it's never going to make them rich.' He closed his eyes, enjoying the warm water on his skin and glad to be clean again.

'They'll manage,' said Helga, wringing out the rag.

'Well, they shouldn't think they can borrow money from us.'

His voice got louder at the thought of having to part with any of the money he had so laboriously saved, money that Helga knew nothing about. It had amounted to quite a sum over the years. He had been good at what he did, and he'd never had expensive tastes. The plan was for the money to benefit Jonas some day, but Einar was nervous that his son, in a fit of generosity, might give some of it to his mother. Jonas was like him, but he also had a weak side that he must have inherited from Helga. He wasn't aware of it, and that worried Einar.

'All clean now?' he asked as she put another shirt on him and buttoned it with fingers that bore the marks of all the housework she did.

'Yes. Until the next time you decide to amuse yourself by tearing open the bag.'

She stepped back to look at him, and he felt annoyance creeping over him. What was going on with her? It was as if she were examining an insect under a magnifying glass. Her eyes were coldly appraising as she stared at him. Worst of all, there was no sign of fear in her expression.

For the first time in many years Einar felt something he hated: uncertainty. He was at a disadvantage, and he knew that he had to re-establish his position of power over her immediately.

'Tell Jonas to come here,' he said as harshly as he could. But Helga did not reply. She just kept looking at him.

Molly was so cold that her teeth were chattering. Her eyes had grown accustomed to the dark, and she could make out Marta's shadowy shape. She wanted to crawl over to her mother to get warm, but something held her back. It was the same thing that always held her back.

She knew that Marta didn't love her. It was something she'd known for as long as she could remember, and in reality she hadn't ever missed her love. How could she miss something that she'd never had? Besides, she'd always had Jonas. He was the one who brushed the grit from her legs when she fell off her bicycle, and the one who chased away the monsters from under her bed as he tucked her in at night. He had helped her with her homework, explaining everything about the planets and the solar system. He had been all-knowing and all-powerful.

Molly had never understood how Jonas could be so obsessed with Marta. Sometimes she'd seen her parents exchange glances at the kitchen table and then she'd noticed the hunger in her father's eyes. What was it that he saw? What had he seen in her the first time they met? That time she'd heard about so often.

'I'm freezing,' she said now, turning to look at the motionless figure in the dark. Marta didn't reply, and Molly began to sob. 'What happened? Why are we here? Where are we?'

She couldn't stop the questions from spilling out. They had piled up inside her head, and uncertainty was mixed with fear. She gave another yank on the chain. A sore spot had formed on her ankle, and she winced with pain.

'Stop that. It won't do any good,' said Marta.

'But we can't just give up.' Out of sheer stubbornness, Molly tugged on the chain again, only to feel pain shoot up through her leg.

'Who says we're giving up?' said Marta quietly.

How could she be so calm? Her composure only served to scare Molly even more, and she felt panic seize hold of her.

'HELP!' she cried, and her scream bounced off the walls. 'We're in here! HELP!'

A deafening silence set in after her screams faded.

'Cut that out. It's not going to help,' said Marta in the same icy calm voice.

Molly wanted to hit and scratch her. She wanted to pull her hair and kick her. Anything to provoke a reaction other than that ghastly calm.

'Someone will come and help us,' said Marta at last. 'But we have to wait. Everything depends on not losing control. Just stay quiet, and it will all work out.'

Molly didn't understand what Marta meant. What she said sounded crazy. Who was going to find them here? But gradually her panic subsided. She knew Marta well enough to realize that if she said someone would help them, then that's what would happen. Molly scooted back against the wall and rested her head on her knees. She would do as Marta said.

'My God, I'm tired,' said Patrik, rubbing his face. Gösta had phoned just as he came in the door, probably wanting to hear how the meeting had gone. But after a moment of hesitation, Patrik had decided not to take the call, and he'd put his phone away. If there was an emergency, they would just have to come over to the house. He only had enough energy for one thing right now, and that was to discuss everything with Erica in peace and quiet.

'Why don't you just try to relax tonight?' said Erica.

Patrik smiled. He'd already seen from her expression that she had something to tell him.

'No, I need your help,' he said, going into the living room to say hello to the children. All three jumped up and ran over to throw their arms around him. That was one of the many wonderful things about having kids: after being away all day, he was welcomed home as if he'd been on a long trip, sailing around the world.

'Okay, that's fine,' said Erica, and he could hear how relieved she sounded. He wondered what she wanted to tell him, but first he needed to eat.

Half an hour later, his hunger assuaged, he was ready to listen to whatever it was his wife was so eager to discuss.

'Today I realized that I'd forgotten to look into something.' She sat down across from him. 'I'd asked the prison staff whether Laila had ever received visitors or phone calls, and she hadn't.'

'I remember you telling me about that.' Patrik looked at his wife in the glow from the candle on the kitchen table. She was so beautiful. Sometimes he seemed to forget that. Maybe it was because he'd become so used to looking at her that he didn't react. He ought to tell her more often, say nice things to her, even though he knew that she was happy with the small moments they shared in their daily life – evenings spent sitting on the sofa with her head resting on his shoulder, Friday dinners with good food and a glass of wine, lying in bed and talking before they fell asleep. All those things that he also loved about their life.

'Sorry, what were you saying?' He realized that he'd been lost in his own thoughts. Fatigue was making it hard for him to stay focused.

'Well, I totally forgot about another way that Laila might have stayed in contact with the outside world. It was so stupid of me, but luckily I remembered.'

'Get to the point, sweetheart,' he teased her.

'Okay. I'm talking about the post. I forgot to find out if she'd ever received any post or sent any letters.'

'Judging by your ill-concealed glee, you found out something. Am I right?'

Erica nodded eagerly. 'Yes. But I have no idea what it means. Wait here. I want to show you what I found.'

She got up and went into the front hall to fetch her bag. Then she carefully took out the postcards and placed them on the kitchen table in front of Patrik.

As she sat down, she said, 'These cards were sent to Laila, but she refused to accept them. In fact, she told the staff to throw them away. It's lucky that they didn't. As you can see, they all have pictures from Spain.'

'Who sent them?'

'I have no clue. They were postmarked in various towns in Sweden, but I can't find any connection between the places.'

'What does Laila say about them?' He picked up one postcard, turned it over and looked at the address stamped in blue.

'I haven't talked to her yet. I wanted to try and find the connection first.'

'Any theories?'

'No. I've been thinking about these postcards ever since I got them. But aside from Spain, there doesn't seem to be any common denominator.'

'Doesn't Laila have a sister who lives in Spain?'

Erica nodded and picked up another of the postcards. It showed a matador holding a red cape in front of a ferocious bull.

'Yes, she does. But it seems that they haven't had any contact in all these years, and besides, the cards were sent from Sweden, not Spain.'

Patrik frowned as he tried to think of any other possible links. 'Have you looked on a map to see where these towns are located?'

'No, but I was thinking of doing that. Come with me, and we'll mark them on the map in my study.'

She strode out of the kitchen carrying the postcards in her hand. He got up more slowly and followed.

Upstairs Erica turned over the first of the postcards to

look at the postmark and then at the map. When she found the town she was looking for, she put an 'X' next to the name. She did the same with the other three cards. Patrik watched in silence, leaning against the doorframe with his arms folded. From downstairs he could hear Emil's father in an Astrid Lindgren film shouting as he chased his son towards the woodshed.

'Okay, have a look,' said Erica, stepping back to study the map. She had marked the hometowns of all the missing girls with red ink. She used blue ink to indicate the towns on the postmarks. 'I still don't see anything.'

Patrik came into the room and stood next to her. 'No, I don't see any pattern either.'

'And nothing came out during the meeting today that might help?' asked Erica without taking her eyes off the map.

'No, nothing,' he said, shrugging with resignation. 'But since you're already so involved, I thought I'd tell you what we discussed. Maybe you'll notice something that we missed. Come on, let's go back to the kitchen and talk.'

He left the room and slowly headed downstairs, as he continued to talk to her over his shoulder.

'As I mentioned, I wanted to ask for your help. All the districts have videotaped their interviews with the families of the girls, and we now have copies of all the videos. Before we only had the written reports to go on. I'd like you to watch the interviews with me and tell me anything that comes to mind.'

Erica was right behind him on the stairs, and she put her hand on his shoulder.

'Of course I'll watch them. We can do that as soon as the kids go to bed. But first I want to hear what everybody said today at the meeting.'

They sat down at the kitchen table again, and for a

moment Patrik wondered whether he should suggest that they raid the freezer to see what sort of ice cream they could find.

'One of my colleagues in Göteborg wanted me to ask you again about your talk with Minna's mother. We all have a feeling that her case is different, and even the smallest detail you can remember might help.'

'Okay. But I told you about our conversation right after I talked to her, and by now it's no longer fresh in my mind.'

'That's all right. Just tell me what you remember,' said Patrik, silently cheering when he saw Erica go to the freezer and take out a container of Ben & Jerry's ice cream. Sometimes he thought it was true that people who lived together for a long time learned to read each other's minds.

'You're having ice cream?' Maja had come into the kitchen and stood there glaring at her parents. 'That's not fair!'

Patrik watched as she took a deep breath, and he knew what was coming next.

'Anton! Noel! Mamma and Pappa are having ice cream, and they're not giving us any.'

He sighed and got up. He took out a family-size container of ice cream and got three bowls from the cupboard. Then he began serving up the ice cream. Parents had to choose their battles.

He had just filled the third bowl and was looking forward to helping himself to a big portion of chocolate fudge brownie when the doorbell rang. And it kept on ringing.

'What now?' He cast a glance at Erica and then went to open the door. There stood Martin, looking tense.

'Why the hell don't you answer your phone? We've been looking all over for you!'

'What's happened?' said Patrik, feeling his stomach knot.

Martin gavc him a worried look.

'Jonas Persson rang the station. Molly and Marta have disappeared.'

Behind him Patrik heard Erica gasp.

Jonas was sitting on the living-room sofa, feeling his anxiety grow. He didn't know what the police were doing here. Shouldn't they be out somewhere, searching? Incompetent fools.

As if he could read his thoughts, Patrik Hedström came over to place his hand on Jonas's shoulder.

'We're going to search the surrounding area now, but we'll wait to go into the woods until daylight. What we need you to do is make a list of all of Marta and Molly's friends. And maybe you could start phoning some of them.'

'I've already called everyone I could think of.'

'Make the list anyway. There may be names you'd forgotten. And I'm going to have a word with your mother too, in case she recalls anything more about what they were planning to do this afternoon. Does Marta keep a daily calendar or diary? Does Molly? Anything could be useful at this point.'

'Marta uses the diary on her mobile, which she probably took with her, even though she's not answering. She never goes anywhere without it. Molly's mobile is still in her room. And I have no idea if she keeps any sort of diary.' He shook his head. What did he really know about Molly's life? What did he know about his daughter?

'Okay,' said Patrik, again patting him on the shoulder. Jonas was surprised how comforting that was. His touch seemed to make him feel calmer.

'Could I go with you to talk to my mother?' He stood

up to indicate that it wasn't a request. 'She gets easily nervous, and this has upset her.'

'Sure, that's fine,' said Patrik, and headed for the door.

Jonas followed and they walked in silence across the yard to Helga and Einar's house. There he strode ahead of Patrik to climb the front steps and pull open the door.

'It's just me, Mamma. And a police officer who wants to ask you a few questions.'

Helga came into the hall. 'Police officer? What do the police want? Has something happened?'

'Nothing to worry about,' Patrik replied quickly. 'We're just here because Marta and Molly haven't turned up, and Jonas hasn't been able to get hold of them. But these sorts of situations usually end up being nothing but a misunderstanding. They're probably visiting a friend and just forgot to tell anyone.'

Helga nodded and looked a bit calmer.

'That's probably all it is. I don't really see why it's necessary to bother the police with this right now. I'm sure they have plenty of other things to do.'

She led the way to the kitchen and went back to emptying the dishwasher.

'Sit down, Mamma,' said Jonas.

By now his anxiety was at fever pitch. He couldn't understand what was going on. Where could they be? In his mind he'd gone over the conversations he'd had with Marta during the past few days. Nothing gave him any reason to believe that something was wrong. Yet he was filled with fear – the same fear he'd felt ever since their first meeting. The fear and conviction that one day she would leave him. And that scared him more than anything else. Whatever was perfect was bound to be ruined. The balance had to be destroyed. That was the philosophy he had made his own. How could he have believed that he would remain untouched? Or that the same rules didn't apply to him?

'How long were they here?' Patrik was quietly asking his questions, and Jonas closed his eyes to listen as his mother answered. He could hear from her tone of voice that she didn't like being put in this situation. He knew she thought they should have handled things without bringing in the police. In their family, they always took care of everything on their own.

'They didn't mention any plans, just said they would be training with the horses later on.' Helga looked up at the ceiling as she talked. Jonas recognized this long-time habit of hers. All these familiar gestures, repeated over and over in an endless cycle. He had accepted that he was part of this cycle, and Marta had too. But without her, he couldn't and wouldn't be able to participate. It would no longer have any meaning.

'So they didn't say they were going to visit anyone? Or mention any errands they needed to run?' Patrik went on.

Helga shook her head. 'No, and in that case they would have taken the car. Marta was always rather lazy, that way.'

'Was?' said Jonas, and he heard his voice rise to a falsetto. 'Don't you mean "is", not "was"?'

Patrik looked at him in surprise. Jonas propped his elbows on the table and rested his head in his hands.

'Sorry. I've been up since four this morning and haven't had much sleep. It's just not like Marta to miss a lesson, and definitely not like her to go off without telling me.'

'I'm sure they'll come home soon. And Marta will be cross when she hears that we've made such a fuss,' said Helga, trying to console him. But there was a slight undertone, and Jonas wondered if Patrik had heard it.

Jonas wished he could believe her, but all his senses

told him something was wrong. What would he do if they were gone? He would never be able to explain to anyone how he and Marta were like one and the same person. Since the first moment, they had breathed in unison. Molly was his flesh and blood, but without Marta, he was nothing.

'Excuse me, I've got to go to the loo,' Jonas said, standing up.

'I'm sure your mother is right,' Patrik called after him.

He didn't reply. He didn't really need the loo. He just wanted a few minutes alone to compose himself so they wouldn't see that everything was about to fall apart.

He could hear his father grumbling and groaning upstairs. He was probably making extra noise because he could hear voices in the kitchen. But Jonas had no intention of going upstairs to see him. Right now Einar was the last person in the world he wanted to see.

Whenever he came near his father, he would feel a scorching heat, as if from a blazing fire. It had always been like that. Helga had tried to be the cooling force between them, but she'd never succeeded. Now only a quiet smouldering remained inside of Einar, and Jonas didn't know how long he'd be able to help his father keep it alive. Or how long he was obligated to do so.

Jonas went into the bathroom and leaned his forehead against the mirror. It felt pleasantly cool. He could feel how flushed his cheeks were. When he closed his eyes, images flashed through his mind – so many memories from the life he had shared with Marta. He felt his nose running, and he leaned down to get some toilet paper, but there was none. Outside the door he could hear a murmur of voices from the kitchen, as well as the noise Einar was making upstairs. Jonas squatted down and opened the cupboard under the sink, which was where Helga kept the extra rolls of toilet paper.

He peered inside the cupboard. There was something hidden next to the toilet paper. At first he didn't understand what he was seeing. The next instant he understood everything.

Erica had offered to help search, but Patrik had pointed out the obvious: someone needed to stay home with the kids. Reluctantly she'd agreed he was right, and she decided to spend the evening watching the videotaped interviews with family members. They were all in a box in the front hall, but from experience she knew she shouldn't start watching them until the children were asleep in their beds. So she pushed aside all thought of the videos and sat down on the sofa with the kids.

She sat through yet another DVD film about Emil, smiling at his antics as she snuggled close to the twins and Maja. This wasn't always easy since they all wanted to sit next to her, but she ended up pulling Anton on to her lap, with Noel and Maja on either side, leaning against her. She was filled with gratitude for everything she had in her life. She thought about Laila and wondered if she'd ever had similar feelings for her children. It seemed unlikely, in light of what she'd done.

As Emil poured blueberry soup over Mrs Petrell's head, she noticed that the children were dozing off. A few minutes later she heard the unmistakable sound of their quiet breathing as they slept. Carefully she untangled herself and got up. Then she carried them upstairs one by one and put them to bed. She paused for a few seconds in the boys' room, looking at their blond heads resting on their pillows. So secure, so content, so unaware of the evil that existed in the world. Then she tiptoed out and went downstairs to the front hall to fetch the videos. She sat down on the sofa again and studied the labels on the

DVDs. She decided to play them in order, starting with the first girl who disappeared.

She felt a rush of sympathy when she saw Sandra Andersson's family. Their faces were haggard as they tried to answer the police officers' questions. They were eager to help, but they were tormented by all the thoughts stirred up by the interview. Certain questions were repeated several times, and even though Erica knew why this was done, she could understand the family's frustration at not being able to answer.

She moved on to the second and third videos, trying to keep all her senses on high alert. But she began to feel discouraged when she failed to find anything, though she couldn't say what she was looking for. She realized that asking her for help was a long shot, and Patrik probably hadn't thought she'd actually find something. But she was still hoping for that moment of epiphany when she would see everything clearly and all the pieces would magically fall into place. It had happened to her before, and she knew it was always possible, but in this case she saw only grieving families with too many unanswered questions.

She turned off the DVD player. The suffering she'd witnessed in the eyes of the parents had started to get to her. Their pain was so apparent in their gestures and in their voices, which kept breaking with the effort to hold back their tears. Erica couldn't bear to watch any more of the interviews. She decided instead to give Anna a call.

Her sister sounded tired on the phone. Erica was surprised to hear that Anna had been present when it was discovered that Marta and Molly were missing. For her part, Erica could report that the police were now involved. Then they chatted for a while about their own lives which, in spite of everything, continued on. She didn't ask how Anna was doing. Tonight she just couldn't bear to hear her sister say that everything was fine, when that was so clearly a lie. She simply let Anna talk and pretended that nothing was wrong.

'So, what's up? Tell me why you called,' said Anna.

Erica wasn't sure how to reply. She had already mentioned the videos, but now she tried to sort out her feelings.

'It's just so strange to be sitting here watching these interviews. It's like sharing the grief of these families. I can tell how awful it must be for them to go through something like this. At the same time I can't help feeling relieved that my own children are safe in bed upstairs.'

'Yes, thank God for our children. Without them I don't know how I would have survived. If only . . .'

Anna didn't finish her sentence, but Erica knew what she was thinking. There should have been one more child.

'I have to go now,' said Anna. Erica had a sudden urge to ask whether Dan had mentioned that she'd phoned him earlier in the day. But she stopped herself. It might be best to let them handle things at their own pace.

They said goodbye and ended the phone call. Then Erica got up from the sofa and put the next DVD in the player. It was the interview with Minna's mother, and she recognized the flat she'd visited only a few days ago. She also recognized the resigned expression on Nettan's face. Like the other parents, she tried to answer the police officers' questions. She too wanted to help, but there the similarity ended. In appearance she was very different from the other family members. Her hair was dull and uncombed, and she was wearing the same nubby cardigan she'd had on when Erica visited. She chain-smoked through the whole interview, and Erica could hear the officers coughing occasionally from all the smoke.

They mostly asked the same questions she had asked, and that helped to refresh her memory before telling

Patrik again about her own interview with Nettan. The main difference was that she had been allowed to look through the photo album, and that had given her a more personal view of Minna and her mother. The police hadn't seemed to bother with that. Yet Erica had always been more interested in the people involved in or affected by a crime. What sort of personal lives had they led? What were their relationships with others? What did they remember? She loved to look through photo albums, to see the family celebrations and daily life through the human eye behind the camera lens. Someone had chosen to photograph each specific scene, and it was interesting to see how he or she had depicted a life.

In Nettan's case, it had been painfully clear that she placed great importance on the various men who had come and gone. It was easy to see that she'd been longing for a family, a husband for herself and a father for Minna. There were pictures of Minna sitting on some man's shoulders, of Nettan at the beach with some other man, and both of them with Nettan's latest boyfriend, standing in front of a car packed with hopes for a wonderful summer holiday. Those were important images for Erica to see, even if they didn't seem relevant to the police.

She removed the DVD and put in another. This was the interview with Victoria's parents and brother. But again she didn't notice anything in particular. She glanced at her watch. Eight o'clock. Patrik would probably be late getting home, if he came home at all. She suddenly felt more alert, so she decided to watch all the videos again and pay even closer attention.

A couple of hours later she was finished. And she was forced to admit that she hadn't discovered anything new. She decided to go to bed. There was no need to wait up for Patrik, since he hadn't phoned, and that meant he must be busy. She would have given anything to know what was happening, but after living so many years with a policeman, she'd learned that sometimes it was necessary to restrain her curiosity and simply wait. This was undoubtedly one of those occasions.

Tired and overwhelmed with too much input, she got into bed and pulled the covers up to her chin. Both she and Patrik liked to sleep in a cool room. The chill in the bedroom made it even more enjoyable to get under the warm duvet. Almost at once she began to drift off. In that no-man's-land between sleep and consciousness, images from the videos began whirling through her mind. They rushed past in no particular order, each one quickly replaced by another. Her body got heavier, and as she began to slide into sleep, the flood of images slowed, until her brain stopped on one picture. And all of a sudden she was wide awake.

Feverish activity had taken over the station. Patrik had planned to call a brief meeting to coordinate their efforts as they searched for Molly and Marta, but the work was already in full swing. Gösta, Martin, and Annika were phoning friends and acquaintances, ringing Molly's classmates, the stable girls, and everyone else on the list that Jonas had provided. Those names led to more names, but so far they hadn't found anyone who knew where Molly and Marta could be. By now it was getting so late that a reasonable explanation for their absence seemed less and less likely.

Patrik walked down the corridor to the kitchen. As he passed Gösta's office he caught a glimpse of his colleague jumping up from his chair.

'Hey, wait!'

Patrik stopped in mid-stride.

'What is it?'

Gösta's cheeks were flushed. 'Well, the thing is, something

happened when you were gone today. I didn't want to talk about it when we were at Jonas's house, but Pedersen phoned earlier. He said it was Lasse's blood on the dock.'

'Just as we thought.'

'Yes, but that's not all.'

'Okay. What else did he find out?' asked Patrik impatiently.

'On impulse Pedersen compared the blood with the DNA on the cigarette butt that we sent to the lab for analysis. The one we found in the garden of Victoria's neighbour.'

'And?'

'They matched,' said Gösta, eager to see Patrik's reaction.

'Are you saying that Lasse was the person watching her house?' He stared at Gösta as he tried to make sense of everything. 'He was the one spying on Victoria?'

'Yes. And he was probably also the one who sent those threatening letters. But unfortunately we'll never know for sure, since Ricky threw them out.'

'So Lasse may have been blackmailing someone because he knew that person was having an affair with Victoria,' said Patrik, thinking out loud. 'Someone who wanted to keep the relationship secret. Even if it meant paying blackmail.'

Gösta nodded. 'Exactly what I was thinking.'

'Do you think it was Jonas?' said Patrik.

'That was my thought, but it turns out that Ricky was wrong.'

Patrik listened to Gösta's explanation, and suddenly everything he'd thought was turned upside down.

'We need to tell the others about this. Go find Martin and I'll get Annika.'

A few minutes later they were all seated in the kitchen. It was pitch dark outside, and snow was falling. Martin had made a fresh pot of coffee.

'Where the hell is Mellberg?' asked Patrik.

'He was here for a while, but then he went home for dinner. He probably fell asleep on the sofa,' said Annika.

'Okay. We'll get by without him.' Adrenaline was making him jittery. Even though it was annoying that Mellberg always managed to sneak off, Patrik knew they'd get more work done in his absence.

'So what's happened?' asked Martin.

'We've received some new information that might be of great importance to our search for Molly and Marta.' Patrik could hear how bombastic he sounded, but that sometimes occurred when the situation was as serious as it was now. 'Could you tell everyone what you found out, Gösta?'

Gösta cleared his throat and explained how they'd discovered that Lasse was the one spying on Victoria.

'He must have found out that Victoria was having an affair with someone. And since he clearly regarded the relationship as morally objectionable, he started sending threatening letters to her. At the same time he began blackmailing the other person.'

'Do you think he was the one who kidnapped Victoria?' asked Martin.

'That's one possible theory, but Lasse doesn't seem like the type of criminal that Struwer described. And I have a hard time believing that he'd be capable of carrying out that sort of crime,' said Patrik.

'But who was Lasse blackmailing?' asked Annika. 'It had to be Jonas, right? Since he was the one having an affair with Victoria.'

'That was my conclusion, of course. But . . .' Gösta paused for effect, and Patrik could tell that he was enjoying having everyone's full attention.

'But it wasn't him,' Patrik interjected. He nodded to Gösta to go on.

'Ricky thought, just as we did, that Jonas was having a relationship with his sister. But his mother knew something about Victoria that no else knew. It wasn't boys that she fell in love with.'

'What?' said Martin, sitting up straighter. 'How come nobody knew about this? We didn't hear a word about it when we talked to her friends and classmates. Why did her mother know about her sexual preference when no one else did?'

'I suppose Helena, as her mother, suspected the truth. Then she happened to see something when Victoria brought a friend home. She later mentioned it to her daughter, so that Victoria would know she could be open about such things with her family. But Victoria panicked and begged her not to tell Ricky or her father.'

'Obviously it would be a sensitive issue for her,' said Annika. 'At her age it can't be easy, especially in a small town like this.'

'Right. Sure. But I'm guessing she got so upset because at that time she had just started a relationship with someone, and she didn't think her parents would want her to be with that person.' Gösta reached for his coffee cup.

'So who was it?' asked Annika.

Martin frowned. 'Was it Marta? That would explain the argument between Jonas and Victoria. Maybe it was about Marta.'

Gösta nodded. 'And that means Jonas probably knew about it.'

'So we're assuming that Lasse was blackmailing Marta? She got tired of paying the money, and she killed him? Or was Jonas so angry when he found out that he took matters into his own hands? Or is there some other possible scenario that we've missed?' Martin pensively scratched the back of his head.

'No. I think it has to be either the first or second option,' said Patrik, looking at Gösta, who nodded agreement.

'Then we need to talk to Jonas again,' said Martin. 'Is it possible that Marta and Molly were not kidnapped by the same perpetrator as the other girls? Could Marta have taken Molly with her and fled so she wouldn't be arrested for murder? Maybe Jonas knows where they are and this is all a sham.'

'In that case, he's an awfully good actor, and—' Patrik stopped when he heard footsteps out in the corridor. He was surprised to see his wife come into the room.

'Hi,' said Erica. 'The front door was open, so I came in.'

Patrik stared at her. 'What are you doing here? And where are the children?'

'I phoned Anna and asked her to come over.'

'But why?' said Patrik before he remembered that he'd asked her for a favour. Had she found something? He gave her an enquiring look, and she nodded.

'I've found a common denominator for the missing girls. And I also think I know why Minna is different from the others.'

Bedtime was the hour that Laila hated most. In the darkness of night her life would catch up with her, everything that she'd managed to suppress in the daytime. At night the evil could once again reach her. She knew it was out there. It was just as real as the walls of her room and the much too hard mattress of her bed.

Laila stared up at the ceiling. It was pitch-dark in the room. Just before she fell asleep, she sometimes felt herself hovering in the air, with the blackness threatening to swallow her whole.

It was so strange to think that Vladek was dead. That was something she still had trouble comprehending. She could hear the sounds from the day they met, the happy laughter, the carnival music, the sounds of animals that she'd never heard before. And the smells were just as strong now as back then: popcorn, sawdust, grass, and sweat. But strongest of all was her memory of his voice. He had filled her heart even before she saw him. When her eyes met his, it was with a certainty in her gaze, and the next second she saw the same look on his face.

She tried to recall whether she'd ever had any sort of premonition of the misfortune that would result from their meeting, but she couldn't think of anything. They came from such different worlds and had led completely different lives, so naturally they'd had difficulties to overcome. But neither of them had ever had any notion of the disaster awaiting them. Not even Krystyna the fortune teller. Was she blind on that day? This woman who otherwise saw everything? Or had she seen but decided she was mistaken because she could tell how great their love was for each other?

Back then nothing had seemed impossible. Nothing had seemed strange or wrong. Everything was centred around creating a future together, and life had duped them into believing that they would succeed. Maybe that was why later on the shock was so great, and why they dealt with it in such an indefensible manner. She had known from the start that it wasn't right, but her survival instinct had taken precedence over her good sense. Now it was too late for regrets. All she could do was lie here in the dark and ponder their mistakes.

Jonas was surprised by how calm he felt. He took time to make all the proper preparations. There were so many years of memories to choose from, and he wanted to make the right choice, because when he'd gone there would be no one to return to. And he didn't think there was any hurry. Uncertainty had fuelled his anxiety, but now that he knew where Marta was, he could make his plans with an icy precision that helped him to keep his mind sharp and clear.

He squinted into the dim light as he crouched down. One of the light bulbs had burned out, and he hadn't got around to replacing it. That sort of neglect bothered him. It was important always to be prepared, to have everything in order, and to avoid mistakes.

When he stood up he hit his head on the ceiling where it slanted downward. He swore loudly, and for a moment he permitted himself to draw the smell into his nostrils. They had so many memories in here, but the memories were not bound to a specific place and could be relived over and over. He touched the suitcase. If marvellous moments had size and shape, then this suitcase would be so heavy it would be impossible to lift. Instead it was light as a feather in his hand, and that surprised him.

Cautiously he climbed up the ladder. He didn't want to drop the suitcase. It contained not only his life, but a life shared in perfect harmony.

Up until now he had been walking in someone else's footsteps. He had continued something that had already been started and hadn't yet put his own mark on it. Now it was time for him to step forward and leave the past behind. That didn't scare him. On the contrary. All of a sudden he saw everything so clearly. The whole time he'd had the power to change it all, to break with the old and instead build something that was better and his own.

The thought made him dizzy, and outside he closed his eyes and breathed in the cold night air. The ground seemed to be shaking and he held out his arms to keep his balance. He stood like that for a few minutes before he lowered his arms again and slowly opened his eyes.

On impulse he went over to the stable. He pushed open the heavy door, turned on the light, and carefully set the suitcase with its precious contents on the floor next to the wall. Then he opened all the stalls and shooed the horses out. One by one the surprised horses walked out the stable door. They paused in the yard, sniffing at the air and neighing before they headed off, swishing their tails in the night air. He smiled as he saw them disappear into the dark. They would enjoy a brief period of freedom before being captured. He was on his way to a new kind of freedom, and he had no intention of ever being captured.

It was so blessedly peaceful to sit here in her parents' old house, where Erica and Patrik now lived, with only the sleeping children upstairs to keep her company. Here no guilt was hiding in the walls. Only memories from her childhood, and thanks to Erica and their father Tore, they were happy memories. Anna was no longer bitter or angry about her mother's strange indifference to her daughters. Not after finding out why. And ever since then, Anna had felt only sympathy for Elsy, who had experienced something that had made her afraid to love her own children. She believed her mother had loved them, but she just hadn't known how to show it. She hoped that Elsy was looking down on them from heaven and knew that her daughters understood and had forgiven her. She hoped Elsy knew that they loved her.

She got up from the living-room sofa and began cleaning up a bit. Things were surprisingly neat and tidy for a change, and she smiled at the thought of Kristina and Mr Fix-it. Mothers-in-law were a breed all their own. Dan's mother was the polar opposite of Kristina. She was almost too considerate, always apologizing for getting in the way whenever she came to visit. The question was, which kind was better. But it was probably the same thing with mothers-in-law as with children: you just had to take whatever you got. You could choose your husband, but not your mother-in-law.

And she had chosen Dan with all her heart. Then she had betrayed him. The thought of what she'd done made her feel sick again. She rushed for the toilet. It felt like her whole stomach turned inside out as she threw up her dinner.

Anna rinsed out her mouth. Beads of sweat appeared on her forehead and she splashed water on her face, taking a look at herself in the mirror. She almost took a step back when she saw the naked despair in her eyes. Was this what Dan saw every day? Was this why he couldn't bring himself to look at her any more?

The doorbell rang, startling her. Who would be coming over to see Erica and Patrik so late at night? Quickly she dried her face and went to the hall to open the door. There stood Dan.

'What are you doing here?' she asked in surprise before a feeling of dread sunk its claws into her. 'The children? Did something happen to the children?'

Dan shook his head. 'No, everything's fine. I wanted to talk to you, and I didn't think it could wait, so I asked Belinda to come over and babysit for a while.' Dan's older daughter no longer lived at home with them, but sometimes she'd come over, much to the delight of her younger siblings. 'But I have to go back soon.'

'Okay.' Anna looked at him, and he didn't look away. 'Can I come in? I'm freezing to death out here.'

'Oh, sure, come on in,' she said politely, as if speaking to a stranger, and stepped aside.

So this was the end. He didn't want to talk about it at home, with the children around and in the place that still held such good memories for them. Even though she'd started to long for all the anxiety and sorrow of their situation to come to an end, whatever that might mean, she now felt herself wanting to scream in protest. She didn't want to lose the most precious thing she'd ever had. He was the great love of her life.

With heavy steps she led the way into the living room, sat down, and waited. She immediately began thinking about practical matters. Erica and Patrik would probably let her and the children stay in their guestroom until she found a new flat. Tomorrow she'd pack up the essentials. Now that the decision had been made, they might as well move at once. No doubt Dan would be relieved by that. He must be as tired of living with her and all her guilty feelings as she was.

She felt her heart sink when Dan came into the room. Wearily he ran his hand through his hair, and as so often before, she was struck by how handsome he was. It wouldn't be hard for him to find someone else. Plenty of girls in Fjällbacka would have their eye on him . . . She forced such thoughts out of her mind. It was too painful to think of Dan in someone else's arms. That was too much for her.

'Anna . . .' said Dan, sitting down next to her.

She saw that he was struggling to find the right words, and for the thousandth time she wanted to shout: I'm sorry, I'm sorry, I'm sorry! But she knew it was too late. She looked down at her lap and said quietly, 'I understand. You don't have to say anything. I'll ask Patrik and Erica if we can stay here for a while. We can move out tomorrow and just take the essentials. I can get the rest of our things later.'

Dan gave her a dismayed look. 'Do you want to leave me?'

Anna frowned. 'No. But I thought that's why you came here. To say that you're leaving me. Isn't that what you want?' She could hardly breathe as she waited to hear his answer. There was a roaring in her ears and her heart was trembling with newly sparked hope.

So many emotions flitted across Dan's face that she couldn't decipher them.

'Dearest Anna, I've tried to imagine leaving you, but I can't. Today Erica phoned me . . . and, well, she made me understand that I needed to do something if I didn't want to lose you. I can't promise this will be easy or that everything will suddenly be fine, but I can't imagine life without you. And I want us to have a good life. We both seem to have lost our way for a while, but now we're here, we have each other, and I want us to stay together.'

He took her hand and pressed it to his cheek. She felt the stubble under her palm and wondered how many times she had stroked his face.

'You're shaking,' said Dan, squeezing her hand tighter. 'Is this what you want too? Do you want us to stay together?'

'Yes,' said Anna. 'Yes, Dan. That's what I want.'

FJÄLLBACKA 1975

The knives scared her more than anything else. Sharp and shiny, they would suddenly appear in places where they didn't belong. At first she had merely picked them up and put them back in the kitchen drawer, hoping that her exhausted and beleaguered mind was just playing tricks on her. But then they'd turn up again. Next to the bed, in the chest of drawers with her underwear, on the coffee table in the living room. Lying there like some sort of macabre still-life, and she didn't understand what it meant. She didn't want to understand.

One evening while sitting at the kitchen table, she felt a knife stab into her arm. The blow came out of nowhere, and she was surprised by the pain. Bright red, the blood gushed out of the wound. Mesmerized, she watched it for a moment before jumping up to dash to the worktop and grab a dishtowel to stanch the blood.

It took time for the wound to heal. It got infected, and when she cleaned it, the pain was so bad that she had to bite her lip to keep from screaming. The gash needed to be stitched, but she simply taped it together as best she could. They had decided to avoid going to the doctor here in Fjällbacka.

But she knew there would be more such wounds. A few days might pass peacefully, but then all hell would break loose, and an anger and a hatred that defied description would surface. She felt paralysed and powerless. Where did such evil come from? She suspected she would never find an answer to that question. And to be truthful, there probably was no answer.

The kitchen was utterly quiet. Everyone was looking expectantly at Erica, who remained standing even though both Gösta and Martin had offered her their chair. There was so much nervous energy inside her that she knew she wouldn't be able to sit still.

'Patrik asked me to have a look at these interviews.' She pointed to the box of DVDs that she'd placed on the floor.

'Yes, I did. Erica is good at seeing things that other people may have missed,' said Patrik apologetically, but no one seemed to have any objections.

'At first I didn't see anything worth noting, but the second time I watched them . . .'

'Yes?' said Gösta, his eyes fixed on her face.

'I realized that the common denominator had nothing to do with the girls themselves. It had to do with their siblings.'

'What do you mean?' said Martin. 'It's true that all of them except for Minna and Victoria had younger sisters, but what does that have to do with the kidnappings?'

'I'm not sure exactly. But all the sisters were videotaped in their own bedrooms, and they all had posters on the walls, plus those kinds of ribbons that are won in horseback-riding competitions. They're all avid riders. And Victoria was too, even though she didn't compete.'

For a moment everyone was silent. The only sound was the chugging of the coffeemaker, and Erica could see that everyone was trying to put together the puzzle pieces.

'But what about Minna?' Gösta then said. 'She didn't have any younger siblings. And she wasn't interested in horseback riding.'

'Right. Exactly,' said Erica. 'And that's why I don't believe Minna was one of the perpetrator's victims. It's not even certain that she was kidnapped, or that she's dead.'

'Then where is she?' asked Martin.

'I don't know. But I was thinking of ringing her mother tomorrow morning. I have a theory.'

'Okay, but what conclusion can we draw from the fact that the missing girls had younger sisters involved in horseback riding?' said Gösta, looking confused. 'Aside from Victoria, none of the girls disappeared in the vicinity of any stable or jump-racing competition.'

'But maybe the perpetrator was drawn to those sorts of settings and on some occasion had seen the girls in the stands because they happened to be watching their sisters ride. I thought we should check the date of their disappearances to see if any competitions were being held in the area at the time.'

'If that was the case, wouldn't one of the families have mentioned it?' said Annika, pushing up her glasses, which had slid down her nose. 'Wouldn't they have said that they were attending a competition on the day their daughter went missing?'

'They probably didn't connect it to the disappearance. Everyone's focus was on the girls and their circle of friends, their interests and activities, and so on. No one was thinking about the younger sisters.'

'Bloody hell,' said Patrik.

Erica looked at him. 'What is it?'

'Jonas. Time after time he has turned up in the investigation in different connections: the ketamine, the row with Victoria, their purported relationship, Marta's infidelity, and the blackmailing. And the whole time he has been chauffeuring his daughter around to various jump-racing competitions. Do you think he's the one who could have done it?'

'He has an airtight alibi for the time of Victoria's disappearance,' Gösta pointed out.

Patrik sighed. 'I know. But we need to take a closer look at him now that so many things are pointing in his direction. Annika, could you try and find out whether there were any horseback-riding competitions on the days in question? And whether Molly Persson was on the participant list?'

'Sure,' said Annika. 'I'll see what I can find out.'

'So maybe there wasn't a break-in at the veterinary clinic, after all,' said Gösta.

'Right. Jonas might have reported it to the police in order to steer suspicion away from himself if Victoria was found. But aside from the issue of his alibi, there are still a lot of other questions. How was he able to kidnap the girls if both Molly and Marta were in the car? Where did he hold the girls captive? And where are they now?'

'Maybe the same place as Molly and Marta,' said Martin. 'Maybe they found out what he's been doing, and . . .'

Patrik nodded. 'That's possible. We need to search their house again, and the rest of the farm too. Considering where Victoria turned up, she might have been held somewhere on the property. So let's go out there again.'

'Don't we need to wait for a search warrant?' asked Gösta.

'We should, but there's no time. Marta and Molly may be in serious danger.'

Patrik went over to Erica and stared at her for a

moment. Then he leaned down and gave her a big kiss, without worrying about the others in the room.

'Good job, sweetheart.'

Helga looked out of the window on the passenger side, her expression blank. The snow was falling heavily, and it was starting to look like the sort of blizzards they used to have in the past.

'What are we doing?' she asked.

Jonas didn't say anything, but she hadn't really expected him to reply.

'How did I go wrong?' she said, turning to look at him. 'I had such high hopes for you.'

The snowy conditions forced him to keep his eyes on the road, so he spoke without looking at her.

'You didn't do anything wrong.'

His words should have pleased her, or at least made her feel calmer. But instead she felt even more concerned. What should she have done if she'd known?

'There's nothing you could have done,' he said, as if reading her mind. 'I'm not like you. I'm not like anyone else. I'm . . . special.'

His tone of voice betrayed no emotion, and she shivered.

'I loved you. I hope you realize that. And I still love you.'

'I know,' he said calmly as he leaned forward to peer through the windscreen at the whirling snow. The wipers were doing their best, but they couldn't keep up with the amount of snow coming down. He was driving so slowly that it felt like the car was only inching forward.

'Are you happy?' She wondered where the question came from, but it was meant with all sincerity. Had he been happy?

'Up until now my life has probably been better than most people's,' he said with a smile.

His smile gave her goose bumps. But no doubt that

was true. He'd certainly had a better life than she'd had, at any rate. She had spent her days cowering and in terror of the truth she didn't want to see.

'Maybe we're the ones who are right, and you're the one who's wrong. Have you ever thought of that?' he added.

She didn't really understand what he meant. She had to think about it for a moment, and when she realized what he was saying, she was filled with sorrow.

'No, Jonas. I don't think I'm the one who's wrong.'

'Why not? You've now demonstrated that we're not so different.'

She grimaced at the thought, resisting the truth that might lie behind his words.

'The most basic instinct in the world is for a mother to protect her child. There's nothing more natural than that. Everything else is . . . unnatural.'

'Is it?' For the first time he turned to look at her. 'I don't agree.'

'Could you just tell me what we're going to do once we arrive?' Helga tried to see as far ahead as she could on the road. But the darkness and the heavy snowfall made it impossible.

'You'll see when we get there,' he said. Outside the car the snow continued to fall.

Erica was in a bad mood when she got home. Her joy at having aided the investigation by providing some new information had been replaced by dissatisfaction because she wasn't allowed to accompany the police out to the farm. She'd tried every possible argument to persuade Patrik, but he had stubbornly refused, so there was nothing for her to do but drive home. Now she would probably lie awake all night, wondering what was going on.

Anna came into the hall from the living room to greet her.

'Hi,' said Erica. 'How'd it go with the kids?' Then she stared at her sister in surprise. 'You look so happy. Did something happen?'

'Yes, Dan came over. Thank you so much for talking to him.' She put on her jacket and stuck her feet into her boots. 'I think everything's going to be fine now, but I'll tell you all about it tomorrow.' She kissed Erica on the cheek and then headed out into the snowstorm.

'Drive carefully! It's really slippery out there!' Erica called after her and then closed the door before too much snow blew inside.

She smiled to herself. What if things were finally going to settle down for her sister? Thinking about Dan and Anna, she went into the bedroom to get a cardigan. Then she looked in on the children. They were all sound asleep, so she went to her study. She stood in front of the map for a long time, just staring at it. She knew she ought to go to bed, but the blue Xs were still baffling her. She could swear that they were somehow connected to everything else, but she couldn't work out what the link could be. Why had Laila saved those newspaper clippings about the missing girls? What was her connection to all of this? And how did it happen that Ingela Eriksson and Victoria had exactly the same injuries? There were so many loose ends, but she had a feeling the answer was right in front of her, if only she could see it.

Frustrated, Erica turned on her computer and sat down at her desk. The only thing she could do right now was to go through all the material she'd collected. She knew she wouldn't be able to fall asleep, so she might as well do something useful.

She read page after page of her notes. She was grateful that she was in the habit of typing them into the computer. Otherwise later on she'd never be able to decipher her own scribblings.

Laila. At the centre of everything was Laila. She was like a sphinx, silent and inscrutable. She held the answers, but she merely sat in silence, staring at life and her surroundings. Could she be protecting someone? If so, who and why? And why did Laila refuse to speak about what happened on that fateful day?

Erica began reading methodically through all the transcripts of her conversations with Laila. In the beginning she was even less willing to speak than she was now. Erica had only scanty notes from those first meetings, and she remembered how strange it had felt to sit there with someone who hardly said a word.

It was only when she had asked Laila about her children that she started to talk. She had avoided saying much about her poor daughter, so the conversation was mostly about Peter. As Erica continued to read, she recalled the mood in the room and Laila's face when she spoke of her son. Her expression was brighter than usual, but also full of longing and sorrow. Her love for him was unmistakable. She described his soft cheeks, his laughter, his quiet manner, the way he lisped when he began to talk, the blond lock of hair that kept falling into his eyes, the . . .

Erica abruptly stopped reading and went back to the last passage. She read it again, then closed her eyes to think. And suddenly everything fell into place. She'd found one of the important puzzle pieces that had been missing. It was a long shot, but plausible enough for a likely scenario to emerge. She had an urge to phone Patrik, but she decided to wait. She wasn't positive. And there was only way to find out if she was right. Only Laila could confirm what she suspected.

Patrik could feel the tension in the air as he got out of the car in the yard in front of Jonas and Marta's house. Were they really about to find answers to all their questions?

For some reason that frightened him. If the truth was as gruesome as he thought, this wasn't going to be easy, either for him and his colleagues or for the families of the missing girls. Yet during his years on the police force he had learned that knowing was always better than not knowing.

'We'll fetch Jonas first.' He had to shout to be heard over the howling wind. 'Gösta, you take him back to the station and interview him while Martin and I search the house.'

With their shoulders hunched against the cold, they went up the steps to the front door and rang the bell, but no one came to open the door. The car was gone, and it was unlikely that Jonas had gone to bed, now that Marta and Molly were missing. So after ringing the bell again, Patrik cautiously pushed down on the handle. The door wasn't locked.

'We're going in,' he said, and the others followed.

No lights were on inside, and there wasn't a sound. They quickly concluded that no one was home.

'I suggest we search all the farm buildings as fast as we can to make sure Molly and Marta aren't anywhere else on the property. Then we'll come back here and do a more thorough search of the house. Torbjörn is on standby in case we need his team.'

'Okay.' Gösta looked into the living room. 'I wonder where Jonas is?'

'Maybe he went out to search for his wife and daughter,' said Patrik. 'Or else he knows exactly where they are.'

They went back outside, and Patrik held on to the railing so he wouldn't slip on the stairs, which were covered with a thick layer of new-fallen snow. He paused to survey the grounds. After a moment he decided to wait to go over to Helga and Einar's house. They might get worried and confused, and it was better to search the other buildings first in peace and quiet.

'We'll start with the stable, then Jonas's clinic,' he said.

'Look over there. It's open,' said Martin, heading towards the long stable building.

The door was swinging back and forth in the wind. Cautiously they went inside the stable, which was eerily quiet. Martin walked along the centre aisle, looking into the horse stalls.

'It's totally empty.'

Patrik felt a hard knot starting to form in his stomach. Something was very wrong. What if they'd had the perpetrator under their very noses? What if he'd been in their district the whole time, and now they'd discovered everything too late?

'By the way, have you phoned Palle?' asked Gösta.

Patrik nodded. 'Yes, he's been informed. They're ready to send reinforcements if we need them.'

'Good,' said Gösta, opening the door to the riding arena. 'It's empty in here too.'

In the meantime Martin had checked the common room and feed room, and now he came back to the stable.

'Okay, let's go over to the clinic,' said Patrik. He stepped outside into the cold, with Gösta and Martin close behind. The snow felt like tiny needles striking their cheeks as they dashed back to the house.

Gösta tried the clinic door. 'It's locked.'

He cast an enquiring glance at Patrik, who nodded. With ill-concealed glee, Gösta backed up a few steps, then launched himself forward to kick at the door. He repeated the manoeuvre several times, and finally the door flew open. Considering the type of substances stored in the clinic, the place was far from burglar proof, and Patrik couldn't hold back a smile. It wasn't every day that he got to see Gösta practising Kung-fu.

It was a small place, and the search didn't take long. Jonas wasn't there. Everything was neat and tidy, except for the medicine cabinet, which stood open. Some of the shelves inside were bare.

Gösta studied the contents. 'He seems to have taken a lot with him.'

'Damn it,' said Patrik. It was extremely worrisome to think that Jonas had fled with ketamine and other substances that were now missing from the cabinet. 'Do you think he might have drugged his wife and daughter and then kidnapped them?'

'What a sick devil that guy is.' Gösta shook his head. 'How could he seem so normal? That's almost the worst thing of all. The fact that he was so . . . pleasant.'

'Psychopaths can fool anyone,' said Patrik. He went back out into the night after casting one last look at the clinic.

Martin was shivering as he followed. 'Where should we look next? His parents' house or the barn?'

'The barn,' said Patrik.

They ran as fast as they dared across the slippery yard.

'We should have brought torches with us,' said Patrik when they went inside the barn. It was so dark they could hardly make out the cars that were parked inside.

'Sure. Or we could just turn on a light,' said Martin, pulling a string on the wall.

A faint, ghostly light illuminated the big space. Here and there snow was coming in through gaps in the wall, yet it seemed slightly warmer in the barn because they were at least out of the biting wind.

Martin shuddered. 'It looks like some sort of car graveyard.'

'No, not at all. These are amazing cars. With a little love and attention they'd be worth a lot of money,' said Gösta, running his hand over the bonnet of a Buick.

He began walking among the cars as he took a look around. Patrik and Martin did the same, and a few minutes later they concluded that there was nothing to find in here either. Patrik was feeling discouraged. Maybe they needed to put out an All Points Warning for Jonas. Clearly he wasn't here, unless he happened to be hiding in his parents' house. But Patrik didn't think so. He assumed that only Helga and Einar were asleep over there.

'We're going to have to wake up his parents,' said Patrik, pulling the string to turn off the light.

'How much should we tell them?' asked Martin.

Patrik paused to consider. It was a relevant question. How should he tell the parents that their son was probably a psychopath who had kidnapped and tortured young girls? That wasn't something they'd taught him to deal with at the police academy.

'We'll play it by ear,' he said at last. 'They know we're looking for Marta and Molly, and now Jonas is missing too.'

Once again they crossed the windswept yard. Patrik knocked loudly on the front door. When nothing happened, he tried again. A light switched on upstairs, possibly in the bedroom. But no one came to open the door.

'Shall we go in?' asked Martin.

Patrik tried the door. It was open. Sometimes it made things easier for the police that people who lived out in the country seldom locked their doors. He stepped into the front hall.

'Hello?' he shouted.

'Who the hell is that?' an angry voice yelled from upstairs. They quickly assessed the situation. Einar must be home alone, and that was why no one had opened the door.

'Police officers. We're coming up.' Patrik signalled for Gösta to follow him as he said in a low voice to Martin, 'Take a look around while we talk to Einar.'

'I wonder where Helga is,' said Martin.

Patrik shook his head. He was wondering the same thing. Where was Helga?

'We'll have to ask Einar,' he said and hurried upstairs.

'What do you think you're doing, waking people up in the middle of the night like this!' snarled Einar. He was partly sitting up in bed, wide awake. His hair was tousled, and he wore only a white undershirt and underpants.

Patrik ignored his question. 'Where's Helga?'

'She's asleep over there.' Einar pointed at a closed door across the hall.

Gösta went to open the door and peered inside. Then he shook his head. 'Nobody's there, and the bed hasn't been slept in.'

'What? Where the hell is she? Helgaaa!' bellowed Einar, his face turning red.

Patrik stared at him. 'So you don't know where she is?'

'No. If I did, I would have told you. Why is she out running around?' A trickle of saliva ran out of his mouth and on to his chest.

'Maybe she went out to look for Marta and Molly,' Patrik suggested.

Einar snorted. 'I can't believe what a fuss everybody's making. I'm sure they'll turn up on their own. It wouldn't surprise me if Marta got upset about something Jonas did or didn't do, and she decided to leave for a while and take Molly with her, just to punish him. That's the sort of childish things women always do.' His words dripped with scorn, and Patrik had to restrain himself from speaking his mind.

'So you don't know where Helga is?' he repeated patiently. 'Or where Molly and Marta are?'

'No! I told you I don't know!' shouted Einar, punching the covers with his fist.

'What about Jonas?'

'Is he missing too? No, I don't know where he is either.' Einar rolled his eyes, but Patrik noticed that he cast a quick glance out of the window.

A feeling of great calm came over him, as if he'd

suddenly landed in the eye of the storm. He turned to Gösta.

'I think we need to do another search of the barn.'

A mouldy and clammy smell filled her nostrils. Molly felt as if she were going to suffocate in the stifling air, and she swallowed hard to rid her mouth of the musty taste. It wasn't easy to stay calm the way Marta wanted.

Once again Molly asked, 'Why are we here?' as she stared into the darkness.

And again she got no answer.

'Don't waste your energy,' Marta finally said.

'But we're being held prisoner! Somebody has locked us up in here, and it must be the same person who took Victoria. I heard what happened to her. I don't understand why you're not scared.'

She could hear how weak her voice sounded, and she began to sob as she rested her head on her knees. She felt the chain tighten, and she moved closer to the wall so the shackle wouldn't cut into her ankle.

'It wouldn't do any good,' said Marta. That was the same thing she'd repeated for the past few hours.

'But what are we going to do?' Molly yanked on the chain. 'We're going to starve to death and then rot in here!'

'Don't be so dramatic. We'll get help.'

'How can you know that? We're still here and nobody has come to help us.'

'I'm convinced that things will work out. And I'm not a spoiled brat who's used to having everything served to her on a platter,' snapped Marta.

Molly started crying again. Even though she knew that Marta didn't love her, it was hard to understand how she could be so unaffected in such a horrible situation.

'Maybe that was a bit harsh,' said Marta in a gentler tone of voice. 'But there's no point in screaming and crying. It's better if we save our energy while we wait for someone to come and help us.'

Molly fell silent, feeling placated. That was as close to an apology as Marta was capable of.

For a while neither of them spoke, but then Molly gathered her courage. 'Why have you never loved me?' she asked quietly. She had wanted to ask that question for such a long time, but she'd never dared. Now, in the shelter of darkness, it suddenly didn't seem as frightening to say the words.

'I was never suited to be a mother.'

'Then why did you have a child?'

'Because that's what your father wanted. He wanted to see himself in a child.'

'So did he wish you'd had a boy instead?' Molly was amazed at her own boldness. All these questions that she'd held inside like tiny, tightly wrapped packages were now being opened. And she spoke without feeling hurt, as if the answers had nothing to do with her. She just wanted to know.

'I supposed he did before you arrived. But after you were born, he was just as happy to have a daughter.'

'That's great to hear,' said Molly sarcastically, though she didn't mean to complain.

'I did the best I could, but I was never meant to have a child.'

It was strange that their first honest conversation was taking place when it might be too late. But there was no reason to keep anything hidden any longer, and maybe that was what was needed so they could stop pretending.

'How can you be so sure that we'll be rescued?' Molly was freezing as she sat on the cold floor, and the wind was starting to seep inside. She was filled with panic at the thought that she might have to pee right where she was sitting.

'I just am,' said Marta. As if in reply to her confident words, they suddenly heard a door open.

Molly pressed her back against the wall. 'What if it's him? What if he's coming to hurt us?'

'Take it easy,' said Marta. And for the first time since Molly woke up here in the dark, she felt Marta's hand on her arm.

Martin and Gösta stood as if paralysed at one end of the room. They didn't know how to deal with the incomprehensible evil staring them in the face.

'My God,' said Gösta. Martin had no idea how many times he'd said that, but he had to agree. My God.

Neither of them had really believed Patrik when he came out of Einar's room and said there was something in the barn. But they'd helped him to search the place again, making a more thorough job of it this time. And when he found the trap door in the floor under one of the cars, all their objections vanished. Eager to find Molly and Marta, Patrik had yanked open the trap door and dashed down the narrow ladder into the dim light below. Patrik had a hard time seeing anything, but he was able to determine that no one was there. So they decided to call in Torbjörn and his team. In the meantime, they'd wait up above in the barn.

Now that the tech experts had arrived, spotlights lit up the entire space like a stage set. After the team had secured prints from the ladder and sections of the floor, Patrik went down, with Gösta and Martin following.

Martin heard Gösta gasp for breath when he entered the room, and he was still in shock at the sight before them. The cold walls and the hard-packed dirt floor, the filthy mattress covered with dark patches that were most likely dried blood. In the middle of the room a metal pole had been stuck in the ground and a couple of rough ropes were fastened to it, also spattered with blood. The air was heavy, making it hard to breathe, and the stench of something rotting filled the space.

Torbjörn's voice roused him from his horrified thoughts.

'Something stood over there. Mostly likely a camera tripod.'

'Are you saying that somebody filmed what went on in here?' Patrik craned his neck to see where Torbjörn was pointing.

'I think so. Have you found any films or videos?'

'No,' said Patrik, shaking his head. 'Maybe over there.'

He walked over to a dirty bookcase against the wall. Martin followed. The dust on one shelf had been cleared away in one spot, and next to it was an empty DVD case.

'He must have come down here to get them so he could take them along,' said Martin. 'The question is, where did he go?'

'Yes. And did he take Molly and Marta with him?'

Martin could feel the nauseating atmosphere taking a toll on his strength.

'Where the hell could they be?'

'I have no idea,' said Patrik. 'But we need to find him. And them.'

Martin saw Patrik's jaw clench as he tried to control his anger.

'Do you think that he . . .' He couldn't finish the sentence.

'I don't know. I don't know anything any more.'

The resigned tone of Patrik's voice almost made Martin lose hope, but he understood how he felt. They had made a real breakthrough in the investigation, but they hadn't succeeded when it came to the most important task: to find Molly and Marta. And after what they'd found down here, they were probably in the hands of a very sick man.

'Come and look at this!' called Torbjörn from up in the barn.

'We're coming!' Patrik called in reply.

All three of them climbed back up the ladder.

'You were right,' Torbjörn told Patrik as he hurriedly led the way to the far end of the barn where the horse transport van was parked. It was bigger and sturdier than many others Martin had seen on the roads. On closer inspection it seemed unnecessarily spacious for anyone, such as the Persson family, who needed to transport only one horse.

'Look. The van was reconfigured. That side wasn't used for a horse. Instead, the floor was raised to create an empty space underneath, big enough to hold a person if they weren't too big. You'd think someone would have noticed, but there was hay on top, and maybe the mother and daughter had other things to think about.'

'How the hell did . . .?' said Gösta, looking at Patrik in surprise.

'I was wondering how Jonas was able to bring the girls here. It would have been impossible in the car if Molly and Marta were with him. So the horse van was the only option.'

'Of course.' Martin felt stupid that he hadn't thought of that, but everything had happened so fast and he'd hardly been able to take it all in. Now he was seeing the details, and a clearer picture began to emerge.

'Secure all the evidence you can find to prove the girls were inside there,' said Patrik. 'We're going to need to be on our toes. Jonas must be one clever bastard to have managed all this without anybody noticing.'

'Yes, sir,' said Torbjörn, but with no trace of a smile.

None of them felt like joking. In fact, Martin felt close to tears, thinking about all the evil people in the world. How could they live so close, and yet do such horrific things under cover of their seemingly normal behaviour?

He squatted down to look inside the space. It was dark

outdoors, and the lights in the barn were dim, but the spotlights that Torbjörn had brought along made it possible for him to get a good look.

'Imagine waking up inside there.' He felt his chest tighten with claustrophobia.

'He probably kept them sedated the whole time. Partly for practical reasons, and partly so Molly and Marta wouldn't hear anything.'

'So he took his own daughter along when he kidnapped girls the same age?' said Gösta. He stood a short distance away, his arms folded. It was clear from his expression that he still couldn't believe what he was seeing.

'We need to find the films,' said Patrik.

'And Jonas,' Martin added. 'Do you think he suspected we were on his trail, and he left the country? If so, where are Molly and Marta? And Helga?'

Patrik shook his head. His face was grey with exhaustion as he stared at the small space inside the horse van.

'I don't know,' he said again.

'You finally came,' said Marta when the light went on and footsteps reached the bottom of the stairs.

'I got here as fast as I could.' Jonas knelt down to put his arms around her. As always, it felt as if they merged into one.

'Jonas!' cried Molly, but he didn't move. After a moment he let Marta go and turned to his daughter.

'Calm down. I'm going to get both of you out of here.'

Molly started sobbing hysterically, and Marta had an urge to slap her. Everything was fine now. They were going to be freed. That was what her daughter had been wailing about. Marta herself had never been worried. She knew that Jonas would find them.

'What is Grandma doing here?' Molly asked.

Marta exchanged a glance with Jonas. During the hours

they'd sat here in the dark, she'd worked it all out. The sweetened tea that Helga had offered them, and the way everything had suddenly gone black. She was impressed that her mother-in-law had been able to lug them into her car and then drag them down here. But women were stronger than men thought, and after living so many years on the farm, Helga had the strength that she'd needed.

'Grandma had to come with me. She has the keys. Isn't that right?' Jonas held out his hand towards his mother who was standing silently behind him.

'It was the only way,' Helga said. 'The police were after you, and I had to do something that would make you seem less suspicious.'

'So you were willing to sacrifice my wife and my daughter?' said Jonas.

After a slight pause, Helga put her hand in her pocket and took out two keys. Jonas tried to unlock Marta's shackle with one of the keys. It didn't work, but with a little click the other one did. She massaged her ankle.

'Shit. That really hurts,' she said, grimacing. She looked up at Helga and was pleased to see the fear in her eyes.

Jonas went over to Molly and squatted down. He had a hard time getting the key in the lock because Molly was holding on to him so tight, sobbing against his shoulder.

'She's not yours,' said Helga quietly.

Marta stared at her. She wanted to throw herself at the woman to shut her up, but she didn't move. She waited to see what would come next.

'What?' Jonas pulled away from Molly without taking off the shackle.

'Molly isn't your daughter.' Helga could no longer hide the fact that she was enjoying saying those words out loud.

'You're lying!' he said, standing up.

'Ask her. She'll tell you.' Helga pointed at Marta. 'You don't need to believe me. But ask her.'

Marta quickly weighed her options. Various strategies and lies raced through her mind, but it was futile. She could lie to anyone without so much as blinking and without arousing the slightest suspicion. But it was different with Jonas. She'd been forced to live with the lie for fifteen years, but at this moment she couldn't lie to him.

'It's not a hundred per cent certain,' she said, her gaze fixed on Helga. 'She could be Jonas's daughter.'

Helga snorted. 'I can count. She was conceived during the two weeks when Jonas was away taking a course.'

'What? When?' said Jonas, looking from his mother to Marta.

Molly had fallen silent and was staring at the grown-ups in bewilderment.

'How did you find out?' asked Marta, standing up. 'Nobody knew.'

'I saw you,' said Helga. 'I saw the two of you in the barn.'

'Did you see that I fought against him? Did you see that he raped me?'

'As if that makes any difference.' Helga turned to Jonas. 'Your father slept with your wife while you were away, and he is Molly's father.'

'Tell me she's lying, Marta,' said Jonas.

She felt a stab of annoyance that he was so upset. What did it matter? It had only been a question of time before Einar assaulted her. Even Jonas must have realized that, since he knew his father so well after everything that had happened. It was unfortunate that she got pregnant, but Jonas had never wondered. He had never counted up the weeks, even though he was a veterinarian. He had simply accepted Molly as his own.

'What Helga says is true. You were away, and your father could no longer resist the temptation. That shouldn't surprise you.'

She looked at Molly, who was listening in silence, her eyes wide and slowly filling with tears.

'Quit blubbering. You're old enough to hear the truth, even though it would have been better if no one ever found out. But what's done is done. So what are you planning to do now, Jonas? Are you going to punish me because your father raped me? I kept quiet because it was best for everyone.'

'You're sick,' said Helga, curling her hands into fists.

'You think *I'm* sick?' Marta felt laughter bubbling up inside of her. 'In that case I'd say that I've simply become like everyone around me. You're not exactly well yourself, considering what you've done.' She pointed to the shackle that still held Molly captive.

Jonas didn't speak as he looked at her. Molly grabbed hold of his leg.

'Please, please get me out of here. I'm so scared.'

Brusquely he stepped away so she had to let go. She sobbed loudly, holding out her hands.

'I don't understand what you're all talking about. I'm scared. Get me out of here.'

Jonas went over to stand close to Marta, and she looked into his eyes. Then she felt his hand caress her cheek. What they shared had not been broken. It was still there and always would be.

'It wasn't your fault,' he said. 'Nothing was your fault.'

He stood still for a moment with his hand on her cheek. She felt the strength radiating from him, the same wild and unbridled power that she'd instinctively known he possessed the very first time she saw him.

'We have a lot to do,' he said, looking deep into her eyes.

She nodded. 'Yes, we do.'

For the first time in ages Anna had slept soundly and without dreaming, although it was late by the time she finally fell asleep. She and Dan had talked for hours, deciding to let the wounds heal, even though they knew it would take time. They wanted to stay together.

She rolled on to her side and stretched out her arm. Dan lay next to her, and instead of turning away, he took her hand and placed it on his chest. Smiling, she felt his warmth spread through her body, from her toes and up to her stomach and . . . She leapt out of bed and ran for the bathroom, getting there just in time to empty the contents of her stomach into the toilet.

'Sweetheart, what is it?' said Dan, sounding worried as he came to stand in the doorway. In spite of her misery, Anna couldn't help tears of joy from welling up because he'd called her 'sweetheart'.

'I think it's some sort of stomach flu. I've had it for a while.' She stood up shakily and ran water into the sink to rinse her mouth. She could still taste the vomit, so she decided to brush her teeth.

Dan stood behind her, looking at her in the mirror. 'How long has this been going on?'

'I'm not sure. But I've felt sick to my stomach off and

on for a couple of weeks. It feels like it just won't stop,' she said with the toothbrush in her mouth. She felt Dan's hand on her shoulder.

'That doesn't sound like stomach flu. Have you considered another possibility?' Their eyes met, and Anna abruptly stopped brushing her teeth. She spat out the toothpaste and turned around to stare at him.

'When was your last period?' he asked.

Frantically she tried to remember. 'I guess it was a while ago. But I thought that was because of . . . all the stress. Do you think that . . .? We only did it once.'

'Once is enough, as you well know.' He smiled and put his hand on her cheek. 'Wouldn't it be great if it's true?'

'Yes,' she said as tears spilled from her eyes. 'Yes. That would really be great.'

'Shall I drive over to the chemist's shop and buy a pregnancy test?'

Anna mutely nodded. She didn't want to get her hopes up if it turned out she merely had the stomach flu.

'Okay. I'll go right now.' Dan kissed her on the cheek.

She sat down on the bed to wait. She touched her breasts. They were a bit tender and swollen, and her belly was a little swollen too. Was it possible that something had been able to grow inside the barren landscape that her body had become? If it was true, she promised never to take anything for granted. She didn't want to risk losing something so rare and precious again.

She was roused from her thoughts by Dan coming back into the bedroom, out of breath.

'Here,' he said, handing her a paper bag from the chemist.

With trembling fingers she opened the little package. Casting a panic-stricken glance at her husband, she went into the bathroom. She sat on the toilet and stuck the stick between her legs, trying to aim properly. Then she set the stick on the edge of the sink and washed her hands. They were still shaking, and she couldn't take her eyes off the tiny window on the stick, which would show her if their future was about to change, if they were going to welcome a new life or not.

She heard the door open. Dan came in, stood behind her, and put his arms around her. Together they stared at the stick. And waited.

Erica had slept restlessly, and only for a few hours. She would have liked to set off at once, but she knew that she wouldn't be able to see Laila until ten o'clock at the earliest, since she hadn't phoned in advance to make an appointment. Besides, she needed to take the children to the day-care centre.

She stretched out her arms as she lay in bed. Fatigue made her body feel stiff and sluggish. She put her hand on the empty place next to her. Patrik had still not come home, and she wondered what had happened out there on the farm. She wondered whether they had found Molly and Marta, and what Jonas had said. But she didn't want to bother Patrik by phoning him, even though she had something new to tell him. She hoped he would be pleased with her efforts. Sometimes he was annoyed if she got involved in his work, but that was only because he worried about her safety. This time he had specifically asked her for help. And there was no possibility that she'd get in any sort of trouble. She simply wanted to talk to Laila, and after that she'd give all the information to Patrik so he could use it in the investigation.

Wearing her nightgown and with her hair tousled, she tiptoed out of the bedroom and went downstairs. She loved having a little time to herself so she could drink a cup of coffee in peace and quiet before the children woke. She'd brought some of the printouts with her to the kitchen so she could read through them again. It was important to do her homework before the visit. But she didn't get very far before she heard shouts from upstairs. With a sigh she got up to see to her children, who were now wide awake.

After taking care of all the morning chores and dropping off the kids at the day-care centre, Erica still had some time left, so she decided to double-check a few things. She went into her study and again stood in front of the map. She stared at it for a long time without seeing any sort of pattern. Suddenly she squinted her eyes and smiled. Why hadn't she seen that earlier? It was so simple.

She reached for the phone and rang Annika at the station. Five minutes later, after having ended the conversation, she was even more convinced that she had guessed right.

The picture was getting clearer and clearer. And if Erica explained what she'd discovered yesterday, Laila wouldn't be able to keep silent any longer. This time she would have to tell the whole story.

Filled with new hope, Erica left the house and got into her car. Before she drove off she made sure she had the postcards with her. She would need them in order to get Laila to reveal the secrets she'd been holding on to for so many years.

When Erica reached the prison, she spoke to the guard on duty.

'I'd like to see Laila Kowalski. I didn't call in advance to say I was coming, but could you ask her if she'd be willing to see me? Tell her I want to talk about the postcards.'

Erica held her breath as she waited outside the gate. Soon it buzzed to let her in, and with a pounding heart she walked towards the main building. Adrenaline was racing through her blood, making her breathing too fast and shallow. She stopped to take a few deep breaths to calm down. It was no longer just a matter of an old homicide case; now it was about five missing girls.

'What do you want?' said Laila the minute Erica entered the visitor's room. She was standing with her back turned, looking out of the window.

'I've seen the postcards,' said Erica, sitting down. She took them out of her bag and placed them on the table.

Laila didn't move. The sun shone on her hair, which was cropped so close that in places her scalp was clearly visible.

'They shouldn't have saved them. I expressly told them to throw those cards out.' She sounded more resigned than angry, and Erica also thought she heard a hint of relief in her voice.

'Well, they weren't thrown out. And I think you know who sent them. And why.'

'I had a feeling that sooner or later you'd work it out. I suppose that in my heart I was hoping you would.' Laila turned around and sank on to the chair across from Erica. She kept her eyes lowered, staring at her clasped hands resting on the table.

'You didn't dare say anything because the postcards represented a veiled threat. A message that only you would understand. Am I right?'

'Yes. And who would ever believe me?' Laila shrugged and her hands trembled. 'I was forced to protect the only thing I have left. The only thing that is still important to me.'

She raised her head and stared at Erica with her icy blue eyes.

'You know what I mean, don't you?' she added.

'That Peter is alive and you think he might be in danger? That he's the one you've been protecting? Yes, that's what I guessed. And I think you and your sister have been in much closer contact than you've wanted to let on. I think the discord between the two of you was a smokescreen to hide the fact that she took Peter in when your mother died.'

'How did you find out?' asked Laila.

Erica smiled. 'During one of our conversations you mentioned that Peter lisped, and when I rang your sister, a man answered. He said he was her son. He lisped too. At first I thought it was because he had a slight Spanish accent. It took a while before I made the connection, and it was still a long shot.'

'How did he sound?'

Erica felt heartsick when she realized that Laila hadn't seen or spoken to her son in all these years. Impulsively she placed her hand on top of Laila's.

'He sounded very pleasant, very nice. I could hear his children in the background.'

Laila nodded but didn't remove her hand. Her eyes filled with tears, and Erica could see she was struggling not to cry.

'What happened? Why did he have to flee?'

'He came home and found my mother – his grandmother – dead. He knew who did it, and he realized that his own life was in danger. So he contacted my sister, who helped him get to Spain. She took care of him as if he were her own son.'

'But how did he manage without the proper ID and that sort of thing?' asked Erica.

'Agneta's husband is a high-powered politician. He was somehow able to ensure that Peter got new papers, and that he was acknowledged as their son.'

'Did you work out the connection between the postmarks on the cards?' asked Erica.

Laila looked at her in surprise and pulled her hand away. 'No, it never occurred to me to look at them. I know only that I got a postcard every time someone disappeared, because a few days later a letter would arrive with newspaper clippings.'

'Really? Where were the letters sent from?' Erica couldn't hide her surprise. She hadn't known anything about this.

'I have no clue. There was no return address, and I threw out the envelopes. But the address was stamped, not handwritten, just like on the postcards. And of course I was terrified. I knew that Peter's whereabouts had been discovered, and he might be the next victim. I thought that was the only way to interpret the pictures on the postcards.'

'I understand. But what about the newspaper clippings? How did you interpret them?' Erica gave her an inquisitive look.

'As I said, there was only one option. The Girl was alive and wanted to get revenge by taking Peter away from me. The newspaper clippings were her way of telling me what she was capable of doing.'

'How long have you known that she was alive?' asked Erica. She spoke the words quietly, but even so they seemed to echo in the room.

In those icy blue eyes staring at her, Erica saw all the secrets, sorrow, loss, and anger that had accumulated over the years.

'Ever since she murdered my mother,' said Laila.

'But why did she do that?' Erica was not taking notes as she listened. The important thing right now was not to gather material for her book. She wasn't even sure whether she'd ever finish writing it.

'Who knows?' Laila shrugged. 'Revenge? Because she wanted to? Because she took pleasure in killing her? I never understood what went on in her mind. She was a stranger, a creature who didn't function like the rest of us.'

'When did you notice that things weren't right with her?'

'Early on. Almost right from the beginning. Mothers can tell when things aren't as they should be. But I'd never . . .' She turned away, but Erica caught a glimpse of the pain in her eyes.

'Why . . .?' Erica wasn't sure what to say. These were difficult questions to ask, and no matter what the answers, she knew it would be hard for her to understand.

'We made a mistake. I know that. But we had no idea how to deal with the situation. And Vladek came from a world with different customs and ideas.' She gave Erica a pleading look. 'He was a good person, but he was confronted with something he couldn't handle. And I did nothing to stop him. Everything just got worse and worse. Our ignorance and fear took over, and I admit that in the end I hated her. I hated my own child.' Laila stifled a sob.

'How did you feel when you realized she was still alive?' asked Erica cautiously.

'I mourned when I heard that she'd died. Believe me, I really did, even though I might have been grieving for the daughter I never had.' She met Erica's eyes and took a deep breath. 'But I mourned even more when I realized that in spite of everything she was still alive, and that she had killed my mother. The only thing I prayed for was that she wouldn't take Peter away from me too.'

'Do you know where she is?'

Laila shook her head. 'No. For me, she's just an evil shadow moving about out there.' Then her eyes narrowed. 'Do you know?'

'I'm not sure, but I have my suspicions.'

Erica placed the postcards on the table with the picture side down. 'Take a look at this. These cards were all postmarked at places between the town where a girl disappeared and Fjällbacka. I noticed it when I marked all the locations on a map of Sweden.'

Laila looked at the postcards and nodded.

'Okay. But what does it mean?'

Erica realized that she'd started at the wrong end. 'Well, the police recently discovered that each time a girl was kidnapped, a jump-racing competition was being held in the town where she disappeared. Since Victoria disappeared on her way home from Jonas and Marta's stable, they have always been a focus of the investigation. Now it turns out that riding competitions are the common denominator. And now that I've also discovered a link between the postmarks, I've started to wonder whether . . .'

'What?' said Laila tonelessly.

'I'll tell you, but before I do, I want to hear what happened on the day Vladek died.'

A long silence followed. But then Laila began to tell her story.

FJÄLLBACKA 1975

It was a day like all the others, just as dark and filled with hopelessness. Laila had spent another sleepless night, with the minutes slowly plodding towards morning.

The Girl had spent the night in the cellar. Laila no longer felt sad about putting her down there. She had abandoned all thought of trying to protect her. She had given up any notion that it was a mother's duty to do everything for her child. Instead, she felt only relief that she no longer had to be afraid. Peter was the one that Laila needed to protect.

She had stopped worrying about her own injuries. The Girl could do whatever she liked to her. But the darkness in her daughter's eyes when she succeeded in causing pain was far too frightening to ignore, and several times the Girl had injured Peter when she unexpectedly exploded in rage. He hadn't known how to defend himself, and on one occasion she had pulled his arm out of the socket. Whimpering and terrified, he had hugged his arm to his body, and they'd been forced to take him to the hospital. On the following day Laila had found knives under his bed.

It was then that Vladek had finally crossed the boundary. Suddenly the chain and shackles appeared in the cellar. She hadn't heard him working down there, hadn't realized that he'd found a way for them to sleep securely at night and have some peace during the day. He said it was the only solution. It wasn't good enough to lock the Girl in her bedroom, and she needed to understand that what she did was wrong. They couldn't handle her fury, those unpredictable outbursts, and the bigger and stronger she got, the worse the injuries she'd be able to inflict. Even though Laila knew it was madness, she hadn't felt able to object.

The Girl had protested at first. She screamed and hit her father, scratching his face as he stoically carried her down to the cellar and put on the shackles fastened to the chain. Vladek had treated his wounds with antiseptic cream and bandaged them as best he could. To his customers he'd said that the cat had scratched him. No one questioned his explanation.

Finally the Girl had resigned herself to the situation and stopped resisting. Listlessly she submitted to being chained. If they had to leave her there for a long time, they would put food and water in bowls, as if feeding an animal. And that was how they had to treat her as long as she continued to enjoy causing pain and was fascinated by blood and screams. When she wasn't in the cellar or in her bedroom, she had to be constantly watched. And most often it was Vladek who did that. Even though the Girl was small, she was already very strong and quick, and he didn't trust that Laila would be able to control her. Nor did she. So Vladek would watch the Girl while she took care of Peter.

On that morning everything went wrong. Vladek had also found it hard to sleep in the night. The moon had been full, and hour after hour he had lain awake beside Laila, staring up at the ceiling. When they finally got up, he was feeling cross and exhausted. It turned out there was no milk left, and since Peter refused to eat anything but oatmeal and milk for breakfast, Laila put him in the car and drove over to the Konsum supermarket.

Half an hour later they were back home. Carrying Peter in her arms, Laila got out of the car and hurried to the house. He was hungry, and he'd already had to wait too long for his breakfast.

As soon as she stepped into the front hall, she knew that something was wrong. There was an eerie silence in the house, and Vladek didn't answer when she called his name. She put Peter down and held her finger to her lips to tell him to keep quiet. He gave her a worried look but obeyed.

Cautiously Laila went into the kitchen. It was empty, but she saw the remains of breakfast on the table. One cup for Vladek and one for the Girl.

Then she heard a voice in the living room. A shrill girl's voice monotonously rattling off one sentence after another. Laila tried to decipher the words. Horses, lions, fire – words from all the enchanting stories about the circus that Vladek had told them.

Slowly Laila moved towards the sound. She had a bad feeling inside, and she was reluctant to take the last few steps. She didn't want to see what she suspected she would find, but there was no turning back.

'Vladek?' she whispered, but she knew it was in vain.

She went over to the sofa, and then she couldn't hold back the scream. It rose up from her stomach, from her heart and her lungs, and it filled the whole room.

The Girl was smiling, looking almost proud. She didn't react to the sound except to tilt her head to look at Laila, seeming to savour her mother's pain. She was happy. For the first time Laila saw happiness in her daughter's eyes.

'What have you done?' She could hardly form the words as she staggered forward and tenderly pressed her hands to Vladek's cheeks. His eyes were open wide, staring sightlessly at the ceiling. And she remembered that day at the circus when their eyes met and they both knew that from then on, their lives were about to change. If they had known what would happen later, they probably would have gone separate ways and continued to live the lives that were expected of them. That would have been best. Then the two of them would not have created this monster.

'This is what I've done,' said the Girl.

Laila raised her eyes to look at her daughter as she perched on the arm of the sofa. Her nightgown was covered in blood, and her long dark hair was tangled, hanging loose down her back. She looked like a troll child. The anger she must have felt when she repeatedly stabbed her father had already faded, and she seemed calm and amenable. Even content.

Laila turned back to look at Vladek, the man she loved. She saw stab wounds in his chest and a deep gash in his throat, as if he were wearing a red scarf.

'He fell asleep.' The Girl drew her legs up to her body and rested her head on her knees.

'Why did you do that?' asked Laila, but the Girl merely shrugged.

A sound behind them made Laila turn around. Peter had come into the living room. His eyes were filled with terror as he stared at Vladek and then at the Girl.

His sister looked at him. Then she said, 'You have to save me.'

Laila felt a chill race down her spine. The Girl was speaking to her, not to Peter. She looked at the slender girl and tried to remind herself that she was only a child. But she knew what the Girl was capable of doing. In truth, she had always known. That was why she understood the menace behind the words. She would have to do exactly that: save her.

Laila stood up. 'Come with me. Let's wash off the blood. Then I'm going to have to chain you up, like Pappa used to do.'

The Girl smiled. Then she nodded and followed after her mother.

Mellberg was beaming as he came into the station kitchen.

'Why does everybody look so tired?'

Patrik glared at him. 'We've been working all night.'

He blinked his eyes, which felt gritty with fatigue. He could barely keep them open any more after a whole night with no sleep. Briefly he recounted what they'd found at the farm. Mellberg sat down on one of the hard kitchen chairs.

'It sounds like you've solved the case. Wrapped up everything nice and tidy.'

'Not quite. This isn't the resolution we were hoping for.' Patrik fidgeted with his coffee cup. 'So much is still up in the air. Marta and Molly are missing, Helga seems to have disappeared, and God only knows where Jonas has gone. Even though we're almost certain Jonas was the one who kidnapped four of the girls who disappeared over the past two years, he was only a child when Ingela was murdered. And then we have the murder of Lasse Hansson. If Victoria was having an affair with Marta, was it Marta who killed him? And if so, how did she do it? Or did she tell Jonas about the blackmail, and then he took matters into his own hands?'

Mellberg kept trying to say something, but Patrik refused to let him speak. Now the chief cleared his throat and said with a pleased expression, 'I think I've found a link between the Ingela Eriksson case and Victoria's disappearance, something besides their injuries. And Jonas is not the guilty party. Or rather, he might be partially guilty.'

'What do you mean?' Patrik sat up straight, suddenly wide awake. Was it possible that Mellberg had actually managed to discover something relevant?

'Last night I read through all the investigative materials again. Do you recall Ingela Eriksson's husband saying that on the day she vanished they'd had a visit from someone in reply to an advert?'

'I think so,' said Patrik, wanting to lean forward and drag the words out of Mellberg.

'Well, it was an advert for a car. The man was interested in buying an old car so he could restore it. You know who I'm thinking about, don't you?'

In his mind Patrik pictured the barn where they'd spent several hours last night.

'Einar?' he said in disbelief.

He felt the gears slowly begin to turn as a theory started to take shape. A horrifying theory, but not entirely improbable. He stood up.

'I'm going to tell the others. We need to drive out to the farm ASAP.' He was no longer the least bit tired.

Erica drove along the road that hadn't yet been ploughed after the night time snowfall. She was undoubtedly going too fast, but she was having a hard time focusing on her driving. All she could think about was what Laila had told her. And the fact that Louise was alive.

She had tried to ring Patrik to tell him what she'd found out, but he wasn't answering his phone. Frustrated, she tried to sort through her impressions, but one thought kept taking precedence over all the others. Molly was in danger if she was with Louise, or Marta as she called herself now. Erica wondered how she'd happened to choose that name and how she had met Jonas. What were the odds that two such dysfunctional people would cross paths? There were several historical examples of fateful duos: Myra Hindley and Ian Brady, Fred and Rosemary West, Karla Homolka and Paul Bernardo. But that didn't make the whole situation any less terrifying.

It occurred to Erica that Patrik and his colleagues might have already found Molly and Marta, but she thought it was unlikely. If they had, he would have phoned to give her at least a brief report. She was certain of that. But where could they be?

She passed the north entrance to Fjällbacka via Mörhult and braked as she entered the sharp curve where the road headed down towards the row of newly built boathouses. It would be asking for trouble to drive this section at full speed. Again and again her thoughts returned to Laila's account of that horrifying day and what took place in that house in its remote location. It had been a House of Horrors even before people began calling it that, before anyone knew the truth.

Erica stomped on the brakes. Her car skidded and her heart pounded as she fought to keep control. Then she slapped her hand on the steering wheel. How could she be so stupid? She accelerated past the Richter Hotel and the restaurant in the old tinned goods factory. She had to restrain herself from racing like a madwoman through Fjällbacka's narrow streets. Only when she reached the other side of town did she dare to increase her speed, but only as fast as the icy conditions would permit.

Keeping her eyes fixed on the road, she again tried to ring Patrik. No answer. She tried both Gösta and Martin, but without success. They were probably busy with something, and she wished she knew what it was. After a moment of hesitation, she again tapped in Patrik's number and then left a message on his voicemail, telling him as briefly as she could what she'd found out and where she was headed. He would probably be cross, but she had no choice. If she was right but failed to do anything, the consequences might be disastrous. And she would be very careful. She'd learned a few things over the years, after all. She had her children to think of, so she wasn't about to take any risks.

She parked a short distance away so the car engine wouldn't be heard and then sneaked over to the house. It looked completely abandoned, but there were fresh tyre tracks in the snow, so someone must have been here recently. As quietly as she could, she opened the front door, all her senses on alert. At first she heard nothing, but then she became aware of a faint sound. It seemed to be coming from below, and it sounded like someone was calling for help.

All thoughts of proceeding cautiously instantly vanished. She dashed towards the cellar door and tore it open.

'Hello? Who's there?' Erica heard the panic in what sounded like an elderly woman's voice. Frantically she tried to recall where the light switch was located.

'It's Erica Falck,' she called. 'Who's down there?'

'It's me,' she heard, and assumed it had to be Molly. 'Me and my grandmother.'

'Stay calm. I'm just trying to find a light switch,' Erica told her, silently cursing until she finally found it. As she touched the switch, she prayed that the electricity was still working. Then she automatically squinted her eyes in the glare. Down below she could see two figures huddled next to the wall, both of them holding up their hands to shade their eyes.

'Good Lord,' said Erica, racing down the steep stairs. She went straight over to Molly, who sobbed as she clung to her. Erica let the girl cry on her shoulder for a moment before she gently pulled away.

'What's going on here? Where are your parents?'

'I don't know. Everything is so strange,' Molly said, her teeth chattering.

Erica looked at the shackles fastened to the rough chain. She felt the same horror she'd felt the first time she was in this basement. It was the same chain from so many years ago, the chain used to fetter Louise. Erica turned to the elderly woman and gave her a kind look. Her face was dirty, making all the wrinkles look even deeper.

'Do you know if there are any keys so I can get you loose?'

'My key is over there.' Helga pointed to a bench standing next to the opposite wall. 'If you unchain me, I can help you look for Molly's key. It's not the same as mine, and I didn't see what happened to it.'

Erica was impressed that the old woman was so calm. She got up to get the key. Behind her Molly was sobbing uncontrollably, muttering things she couldn't understand. With the key in her hand, Erica came back to kneel beside Helga.

'What happened? Where are Jonas and Marta? Are they the ones who chained you up? Good Lord, how could anyone do that to their own child?'

She chattered nervously as she fumbled with the lock. But then she stopped herself from saying anything more. She was talking about Molly's mother and father. No matter what they'd done, they were still her parents.

'Don't worry. The police will catch them,' she said quietly. 'What your son has done to you and Molly is terrible, but I promise you he'll be caught and put in prison. I know enough to guarantee that he and his wife will never be released.'

The lock opened, and Erica stood up to brush off her knees. Then she reached out her hand to help the elderly woman to her feet.

'Let's try to find the other key,' she said.

Molly's grandmother looked at her with an expression

that she couldn't read. Suddenly Erica felt uneasiness churn in her stomach. After a moment of eerie silence, Helga tilted her head to one side and said calmly:

'Jonas is my son. I'm afraid I can't allow you to destroy his life.'

With unexpected swiftness, she bent down to pick up a shovel that lay on the floor. She raised it overhead, and the last thing Erica heard was Molly's shrill scream echoing off the walls. Then everything went black.

It was a strange feeling to return to the farm after all the hours they'd spent there last night in the glare of the spotlights, which had revealed things that no human being should have to see. A quiet calm had descended over the property. The horses had all been caught, but instead of coming back here, they were being cared for by neighbours on nearby farms. Since the owners were missing, the police had had no other choice.

'In light of what we now know, maybe we should have stationed someone here to keep watch,' said Gösta as they crossed the deserted yard.

'My view exactly,' said Mellberg.

Patrik nodded. In hindsight it was always easy to see the obvious, and Gösta was right. Fresh tyre tracks led to Einar and Helga's house and then away. But there were no tyre tracks or footprints outside Jonas and Marta's house. Maybe they'd thought someone was still there, watching their house. Patrik felt his uneasiness growing. The theory unfolding before them was so inconceivable that it was impossible to know what might happen next.

Martin opened the front door and went in.

They didn't say a word as they cautiously took a look around. The whole house had an empty air to it, telling Patrik that everyone who could had left. That would be their next problem: trying to locate the four people who had disappeared, some of them voluntarily, some of them not. Hopefully they were all still alive, but he had his doubts.

'Okay. Martin and I will go upstairs,' he said. 'Bertil, you and Gösta stay here, just in case somebody turns up.'

With every step he took, Patrik became more convinced that something was terribly wrong. His whole psyche seemed to be warning him of what they would encounter upstairs. But his feet kept going.

'Shhh,' he said, holding out his arm to stop Martin from moving past him. 'Better to be safe than sorry.'

He got out his service weapon and took off the safety. Martin did the same. With guns raised, they crept the rest of the way up the stairs. The first rooms along the hall were empty, so they headed for the bedroom at the far end.

'Oh, my God.' Patrik lowered his gun. His brain registered what he was seeing, but he still couldn't take it in.

'Bloody hell,' said Martin from behind him. Then he backed away, and Patrik could hear him throwing up in the hall.

'We won't go in,' said Patrik. He had stopped on the threshold and was now surveying the macabre scene in front of him. Einar was partially reclining in bed. The stumps of his legs lay on top of the covers, and his arms lay limply at his sides. A syringe lay next to his left arm, and Patrik guessed that it contained ketamine. His eye sockets were empty and bloody. It looked as if the procedure had been done in haste, since the acid had spilled out and etched furrows on his cheeks and chest. Blood had run out of his ears, and his mouth was a sticky red grimace.

To the left of the bed, the TV was on, and only now did Patrik notice what was on the screen. Mutely he pointed at the images, hearing Martin swallow hard behind him.

'What the hell is that?' he whispered.

'I think we've found some of the videos that were missing from the barn.'

HAMBURGSUND 1981

She was sick and tired of all their questions. Berit and Tony were always asking her how she felt and if she was sad. She didn't know how to answer, didn't know what they wanted to hear. So she kept quiet.

And she stayed calm. In spite of all the hours she'd spent in the cellar when she was forced to eat from a bowl like a dog, she had always known that her mother and father would protect her. But Berit and Tony would not. They might send her away if she didn't behave, and she wanted to stay here. Not because she was happy with the Wallanders on their farm, but because she wanted to be with Tess.

They had taken to each other from the very first moment. They were so alike. And she had learned so much from Tess. For six years now she had lived on the farm, and sometimes it had been hard to control her rage. She longed to see pain in someone else's eyes, and she missed the sense of power that she'd had, but with Tess's help she'd learned how to rein in her impulses and hide beneath a shell of normality.

Whenever their longing grew too great, they would turn to the animals. But they always made sure that the injuries they inflicted looked as if they'd been caused by something else. Berit and Tony never suspected. They simply bemoaned their bad luck. And they never realized that she and Tess had kept watch over the sick cow because they enjoyed seeing the animal's torment as the light in her eyes was slowly extinguished. Their foster parents were so stupid and naive.

Tess was much better than she was at fitting in and not drawing attention. At night she would whisper about fire, about the all-encompassing euphoria of watching something burn. She said she could hold that desire in her hand and crush it so hard that there would be no risk of ever being caught if she let it out.

The nights were what she liked most. Ever since the beginning, she and Tess had slept in the same bed. At first for the feeling of warmth and security, but gradually something else had crept in. A trembling took over their bodies as their skin touched under the covers. Cautiously they had started to explore each other, running their fingertips over unfamiliar shapes until they knew every millimetre of each other's bodies.

She didn't know how to describe the feeling. Was it love? She had never loved anyone, or hated anyone either. Her mother probably thought she did, but it wasn't true. She didn't feel hatred, just an indifference towards things that other people seemed to think were important in life. But Tess knew how to hate. Sometimes she would see the hatred blazing in her eyes and hear the contempt in her voice when she talked about people who had treated them badly. Tess asked a lot of questions. About her father and mother and little brother. And about her grandmother. After her grandmother came to visit, Tess talked about her for weeks, wondering whether she was someone who deserved to be punished. She couldn't understand Tess's anger. She didn't hate anyone in her family, she simply had no feelings for them whatsoever. They had ceased to exist the moment she came to stay with Tony and Berit. They were her past. Tess was her future.

There was only one thing she wanted to remember about her old life: the stories her father had told about the circus. All the names, all the towns and countries, all the animals and tricks, the way the circus had smelled and sounded, all the colours that had made it into a magical fireworks show. Tess loved to listen to the stories. She wanted to hear them again every evening, and she would always ask questions about the people in the circus, about how they lived, what they said, and then she would listen breathlessly to the answers.

The more they got to know each other's bodies, the more she wanted to tell Tess. She wanted to make her happy, and her father's stories were something she could offer.

Her entire existence now revolved around Tess, and she realized more and more that she had behaved like an animal. Tess explained how everything functioned in daily life. They should never appear weak or allow themselves to be governed by what was inside of them. They had to learn to wait until the right moment; they had to teach themselves self-control. It was difficult, but she kept on practising, and her reward was being able to crawl into Tess's arms every night and feel her warmth spread through her own body, feel her fingers on her skin, her breath in her hair.

Tess was everything. Tess was the whole world.

They stood in the cold of the yard, breathing in as much fresh air as they could. Torbjörn was inside the house. Patrik had phoned him as he kept his eyes fixed on the TV screen. Then he'd forced himself to remain in the doorway and watch the video.

'How long do you think he was doing it?' asked Martin now.

'We'll have to go through all the videos and match them up with any reported disappearances. But it looks like they go way back in time. Maybe we'll be able to tell based on Jonas's age in the videos.'

'My God. To think he forced his own son to watch and then filmed the whole thing. Do you think he made his son participate too?'

'It didn't look like it, but maybe there's more on the other videos. If nothing else, Jonas seems to have repeated the crimes later on.'

'And with Marta's help,' said Martin, shaking his head in disbelief. 'What sick people they are.'

'I never even imagined that she was involved in all this,' said Patrik. 'But if it's true, I'm even more worried about Molly. Would they harm their own child?'

'I have no idea,' said Martin. 'You know what? I always

thought I knew a lot about my fellow human beings, but this proves that I know absolutely nothing. Under normal circumstances, I would say they'd never hurt her, but I don't think we can expect these people to behave in accordance with any rules whatsoever.'

Patrik knew that they were both picturing the same images in their minds. Those grainy films, with all sorts of breaks and flickers, transferred to DVDs but recorded with old equipment. Einar was tall and strong, even handsome. He was in the room under the barn, which was almost impossible to find unless someone was actually looking for it, and no one had thought of doing that for all these years. What he'd done to those girls, whose names the police didn't yet know, was beyond description, as were his eyes when he looked into the camera. The girls screamed as he calmly instructed his son on the best angles to film. Sometimes Einar would take the camera and turn it towards Jonas. Back then he was a gangly teenager, though Patrik surmised that they would see him grow older in later videos. And on one occasion they saw a young Marta.

But what had made Jonas carry on his father's odious deeds? When had that happened? And how had Marta been dragged into the world of horror that the father and son had created? If they were never found, the police might never obtain a clear picture of what went on. He wondered what Helga had known about all this. And where was she now?

He got out his mobile and glanced at the display. Three missed calls from Erica and a voice message. Filled with an awful sense of foreboding, he tapped the voicemail icon and listened. Then he swore so loudly that Martin jumped.

'Get Gösta. I think I know where they are. And Erica is already there.'

Patrik ran for his car. Martin followed as he shouted to Gösta, who had gone around to the back of the house to take a piss.

'What's going on?' Gösta came running towards them.

'Marta is Louise!' Patrik yelled over his shoulder.

'Who?'

Patrik yanked open the door on the driver's side. Martin and Gösta got in the car.

'Erica went to see Laila this morning. Marta is Louise, the little girl who was chained up in her parents' cellar. Everyone thought she died in a drowning accident, but she didn't. I don't know any more of the details, but if Erica says it's true, then it probably is. She thinks that Marta and Molly are in the house that belonged to Marta's parents. And she's gone over there to find out, so we need to get there fast!'

He turned the key in the ignition, stomped on the accelerator, and pulled out of the yard. Martin stared at Patrik in bewilderment, but he didn't care.

'You stupid, stupid woman,' Patrik snarled between clenched teeth. 'Sorry, sweetheart,' he then added. He didn't mean to swear at his beloved wife, but fear was making him furious.

'Watch out!' shouted Gösta as the car skidded.

Patrik forced himself to slow down even though he wanted to floor the accelerator. Terror was eating away at him like a wild animal.

'Shouldn't we tell Bertil where we're headed?' said Martin.

Patrik swore. He'd forgotten that Mellberg was back at the farm. He'd gone inside with Torbjörn to 'assist with the technical inspection'. Right now he was no doubt driving Torbjörn and his team mad.

'Right. Go ahead and ring him,' said Patrik without taking his eyes off the road.

Martin phoned Mellberg, and after a few remarks, he ended the conversation.

'He says he'll be right behind us.'

'I just hope he doesn't get in the way.'

They had turned on to the side road leading to the house, and Patrik clenched his teeth even harder when he saw the Volvo estate car up ahead. Erica must have parked it a short distance away so as not to be observed by anyone at the house, and that made him feel a bit calmer.

'We'll drive all the way up to the front door,' he said, and neither of his colleagues offered any objection.

He came to a halt in front of the ramshackle house and jumped out without waiting for Gösta and Martin. But when he reached the front door, he heard them come up behind him.

'Shhh,' he said, putting his finger to his lips.

Inside they found the door to the cellar closed, but something told Patrik that it had to be the logical place to start. He thought it was here that Louise would have gone. He opened the door, glad that it didn't make a sound. But as he set his foot on the first step, the board creaked loudly and he instantly heard a shrill scream from below.

'Help! HELP!'

He rushed down the stairs with Martin and Gösta following close behind. A single light bulb lit the room, and he stopped abruptly at what he saw. Molly was sitting on the floor, rocking back and forth with her knees drawn up. She was screaming shrilly, her eyes wide as she stared up at them. And next to her lay Erica, stretched out on her stomach, with blood trickling from her head.

Patrik dashed over and with a pounding heart put his hand on his wife's neck. Her skin was warm to the touch, and she was breathing. He was filled with relief. And he saw that the blood was coming from a cut over her eyebrow.

Then Erica opened her eyes and groaned. 'Helga . . .' she said.

Patrik turned to look at Molly. Martin and Gösta had helped the girl stand up, and now they were trying to release her from the shackle around her ankle. Patrik realized that Erica was also chained.

'Where's your grandmother?' he asked Molly.

'She left. But not long ago.'

Patrik frowned. They should have seen her on the road.

'She hit Erica,' Molly added, her lip quivering.

Patrik looked at the wound on his wife's face. The injury could have been much worse, and if she hadn't left him a voicemail to say where she was headed, he would never have thought to look for her here. Then Erica and Molly would have starved to death in this cellar.

He stood up and got out his mobile. The coverage wasn't too good down here, but it was enough to get through. He issued instructions, then ended the call and turned to Gösta and Martin. They had found the key to the shackle on Molly's ankle.

'I've asked Mellberg to keep an eye out for Helga and stop her if he sees her.'

'Why did she hit Erica?' asked Gösta as he gently patted Molly on the back.

'To protect Jonas,' Erica said, sitting up with a groan and putting a hand to her head. 'I'm bleeding,' she said, looking at her sticky fingers.

'It's not a deep cut,' Patrik said curtly. Now that his fears had subsided, he had an urge to yell at her for coming out here on her own.

'Did you find Jonas and Marta?' Erica got to her feet, still a bit wobbly, and then swore when she noticed her leg was shackled. 'What's this?'

'I assume you were meant to die down here,' said Patrik. He looked around for another key. For a moment he considered making her stay here a little longer. And there might be no choice, because he didn't see a key. She'd have to wait until they could saw off the chain.

'No, we haven't found them yet.' He didn't want to tell her what they'd discovered at the farm. Not while Molly was listening. Right now she was sobbing her heart out, with her face pressed against Gösta's chest.

'I have a feeling we're never going to see them again,' said Erica, but then she glanced at Molly and didn't say anything more.

Patrik's mobile rang. It was Mellberg. He listened for a moment, and while Mellberg was still talking, he whispered to the others:

'He's got Helga.'

Patrik had a hard time cutting off Mellberg's triumphant outpouring, but he eventually managed to end the conversation.

'Apparently he found her walking along the road. He's on his way back to the station with her.'

'We need to find Jonas and Marta. They're . . . they're not well,' said Erica in a low voice so Molly wouldn't hear.

'I know,' Patrik whispered, and then he couldn't help himself, he had to reach out and put his arms around Erica, holding her close. Good Lord, what would he have done if he'd lost her? If the children had lost her? Then he pushed her away and said sombrely, 'We've put out an APW. The police are watching all the airports and borders for them. Tomorrow the papers will have photos. They're not going to get away.'

'Good,' said Erica. She reached up to wrap her arms around Patrik's neck. 'But could you please get me out of here now?'

FJÄLLBACKA 1983

When she saw the posters announcing that Cirkus Gigantus was coming to Fjällbacka, she instantly made up her mind. Her pulse quickened. It was a sign. The circus had become a part of her. She knew how it smelled and sounded, and she felt as if she knew the people and the animals. They had played the game so many times. She was the circus princess who made the horses obey as the audience applauded and whistled.

She had wanted them to do it together, and they would have if things hadn't gone so horribly wrong. Now she came to the circus alone.

Vladek's family welcomed her with open arms, greeting her as his daughter. They said they were planning to visit him, but she explained that he'd died of a heart attack. Nobody thought it was odd. He wasn't the first person in his family to have a weak heart. She realized that she'd been lucky, but there was a risk that someone in Fjällbacka would start talking about Vladek and reveal what had really happened. For three long days she held her breath until the circus packed everything up and left Fjällbacka. Then she was safe.

She was only fifteen, so they also asked questions about her mother, wanting to know whether she was allowed to leave her mother behind. She bowed her head and even managed to shed a few tears. She said that Laila had died of cancer many years ago. Vladek's sister-in-law placed a bony hand on her cheek and wiped away the crocodile tears. After that they asked no more questions. They merely showed her where she could sleep and gave her food and clothes. She had never dreamed it would be so easy, but she quickly became one of the family. For them blood was thicker than water.

She waited two weeks before going to Vladek's brother to say that she wanted to learn to perform. She wanted to be part of the circus and follow in the footsteps of her ancestors. Everyone was overjoyed, just as she had anticipated. She suggested she might help out with the horses. She wanted to be like Paulina, the beautiful young woman who wore a glittery costume for every performance and did tricks on the back of a horse.

She was allowed to start as Paulina's assistant. She spent every waking hour with the horses as she watched the practice sessions. Paulina loathed her from the first moment they met. But she was not a member of the family, so after a talk with Vladek's brother, Paulina reluctantly began to train her. And she was a diligent pupil. She understood horses, and they understood her. It took her only a year to learn the basics, and after two years she was just as accomplished as Paulina. Then when the accident occurred, she took over.

No one saw it happen, but one morning Paulina was found dead among the horses. It was assumed that she'd fallen off and hit her head, or maybe one of the horses had kicked her. It was a disaster for the circus. But as luck would have it, she was able to put on one of Paulina's lovely costumes and carry on with the show as if nothing had happened. After that she was the one who performed Paulina's tricks every evening.

She spent three years travelling with the circus. Living in a world in which the strange and fantastical converged, no one noticed that she was different. It had been the perfect place for her. But now the circle was complete, and she would soon be back where she'd started. Tomorrow Cirkus Gigantus would arrive in Fjällbacka again, and it was time to tackle something that she'd put off for far too long. She had allowed herself to be someone else, to be a circus princess riding white horses with swaying plumes and glittery bridles. She had been living in a fantasy world, but now she had to return to reality.

'I'm going out to get the post,' said Patrik, stuffing his feet into his boots. During the past few days he and Erica had hardly seen each other. He and his colleagues had been busy from morning to night with all the interview sessions and follow-up work. But now Friday had finally arrived, and he had decided to take the morning off.

'Damn, it's cold out!' he said when he came back inside. 'We must have got a metre of snow overnight.'

'I know. It seems like it's never going to stop.' Erica gave him a weary smile as she sat down at the kitchen table.

He sat down across from her and began looking through the post. Erica rested her head on her hands and seemed lost in thought. He put down the post and studied her face.

'So how's it going? Be honest.'

'I don't know. Mostly I'm feeling a little uncertain about how to proceed with my book. Or whether to keep working on it at all. It's a whole different story now.'

'But don't you think Laila would want you to write it?'

'Yes. I think she sees the publication of the book as a sort of safety measure. She thinks that Marta won't dare do anything else if people read about who she really is and what she has done.'

'And there's no risk that the opposite might happen?'

Patrik cautiously ventured. He didn't want to tell Erica what to do, but it made him uneasy to see her writing a book about people who were as evil as Jonas and Marta. What if they decided to take revenge on her?

'No, I think Laila is right. And in my heart I know that I need to finish this book. You don't have to worry,' said Erica, looking him in the eye. 'Trust me.'

'It's those two I don't trust. We have no idea where they are.' He couldn't hide the concern he was feeling.

'But they probably won't dare come back here. There's nothing left for them here.'

'Except their daughter,' said Patrik.

'They don't care about Molly. Marta never has, and Jonas's interest in her seems to have vanished as soon as he found out that she's not his daughter.'

'The question is: where have they gone? It seems unbelievable that they could have left the country, considering that the police are on high alert.'

'I have no clue,' said Erica, looking through the post and slitting open one of the envelopes. 'But Laila is worried they'll go to Spain and try to find Peter.'

Patrik nodded. 'I realize that. But I'm convinced they're still in Sweden, and sooner or later we'll get them. And when we do, they're going to have a lot to answer for. We've already identified some of the girls in the videos. Some that Einar kidnapped and some that were victims of Jonas and Marta.'

'I can't understand how you were able to watch those videos.'

'It was horrifying.'

Some of the images appeared again in Patrik's mind. They would no doubt stay in his consciousness for ever, as a reminder of what evil people were capable of.

'Why do you think they decided to kidnap Victoria?' he said then. 'That must have been incredibly risky.'

Erica paused before replying. There was no obvious answer. Jonas and Marta were gone, and the videos showed what they'd done but provided no motive.

'I think Marta fell in love with Victoria, but when Jonas discovered the relationship, there was no question where her loyalties lay. Maybe she sacrificed Victoria to appease Jonas. Maybe it was her way of asking for his forgiveness.'

'We should have realized much sooner that Marta was involved,' said Patrik. 'She had to be the one who took Victoria captive.'

'But how could you have known that? It's impossible to comprehend the actions and motivations of these people. I tried to talk to Laila about the whole thing yesterday, but even she couldn't explain Marta's behaviour.'

'No, I realize that, but I still can't help blaming myself. And no matter what, I'm going to try to work out the reasons behind what they did. For example, why did Marta and Jonas choose to follow in Einar's footsteps? Why did they torture their victims in such a macabre way?' Patrik swallowed hard, overcome with nausea at the thought of those videos.

'I think that Jonas's madness took root during his childhood, when Einar forced him to film his assaults,' said Erica. 'And Marta – or Louise – was equally damaged by what she'd experienced as a child. If what Gerhard Struwer said is true, then it all had to do with control. Apparently Einar kept the girls imprisoned, except for Ingela Eriksson and maybe others we don't know about. By transforming them into passive dolls, he satisfied his own perverse needs. And then he passed on those needs to Jonas, who in turn initiated Marta. Maybe the passion in their relationship depended on the power they exerted over the girls.'

'My God, what a horrible thought.' Patrik felt another wave of nausea come over him.

'So what does Helga say?' asked Erica. 'Did she know about everything?'

'She refuses to talk. She says only that she's willing to accept her punishment, and she claims we'll never find Jonas. But I think she did know what was going on and simply chose to close her eyes. In some ways she was also a victim.'

'She must have been living in hell all these years. And even if she was aware of Jonas's true nature, he's her son and she loves him.'

Patrik sighed. 'So much guessing and speculating. It's so frustrating that we still don't have all the answers. We just have to keep wondering. But at least you're sure that Marta is Louise Kowalski, right?'

'Yes, I am. I can't explain it logically, but it seemed obvious when I realized that Marta and Jonas had kidnapped the girls in connection with horseback-riding competitions. Plus they had to be the ones who sent the postcards and newspaper clippings to Laila. Who but Louise would have a reason to hate Laila and threaten her? Besides, Marta's age coincides with Louise's. And Laila has confirmed my theory. She has long suspected that Louise was still alive. She was afraid that Louise wanted to kill both her and Peter.'

Patrik gave his wife a sombre look and said, 'I wish I had more of your intuition, but please stop acting so impulsively. At least this time you had the presence of mind to leave me a phone message and tell me where you'd gone.' He shuddered at the thought of what might have happened if he hadn't rescued Erica from the ice-cold cellar in the House of Horrors.

'But everything worked out fine in the end.' Erica took another envelope from the stack of post and slit it open with her finger. She took out a bill. 'I can't believe Helga was willing to sacrifice both Marta and Molly so that her son could go free.'

'Well, you know how strong a mother's love can be,' said Patrik.

'Speaking of that,' said Erica, her face lighting up. 'I talked to Nettan again, and it sounds like she and Minna are finding their way back to each other.'

Patrik smiled. 'It was lucky you happened to think about that car.'

'Uh-huh. I'm just sorry I didn't make the connection earlier, when I saw the car in the photo album.'

'The strange thing is that Nettan didn't make the connection herself. Both Palle and I had asked her about the white car.'

'I know. And when I asked her again, she got very cross. She said that of course she would have said something long ago if she knew of anyone who had a white car. But when I mentioned the photo of her former boyfriend Johan standing in front of a white car, she suddenly fell silent. Then she said Minna would never have voluntarily got into his car. She hated him more than anyone.'

'Parents often know so little about their teenage daughters,' said Patrik.

'How true. But who would have thought that Minna would fall in love with her mother's ex-boyfriend? Especially since they were always arguing. Or that she would get pregnant and then decide to run away with him because she was afraid Nettan would be angry with her.'

'Well, it's not the first thing anyone would think of.'

'At any rate, Nettan has promised to help Minna with the baby. They're both furious with that shithead Johan, who apparently got tired of Minna as soon as the pregnancy started to show. And I think Nettan was so relieved when they found Minna safe and sound in Johan's cabin that she's going to do everything in her power to make things right for her daughter.'

'At least something good has come from all this misery,' said Patrik.

'Yes. And soon Laila will be reunited with her son. After more than twenty years . . . The last time I talked to her, she said that Peter is going to come and visit her at the prison. And I'll get to meet him too.'

Erica's eyes shone with joy and anticipation. It made Patrik happy to see how pleased she was that she'd been able to help Laila. Personally, he longed to put this whole case behind him. He'd had enough of evil and darkness.

'It's going to be nice to have Dan and Anna over for dinner tonight,' he said, changing the subject.

'Yes. It's wonderful that they've been able to work things out at last. And Anna said they have good news to tell us. I hate it when she does that and then doesn't give me any details. But I couldn't get another word out of her. She said I'd just have to wait until tonight.'

Erica was looking through the post piled up on the table. Mostly bills, but at the bottom was a thick white envelope that looked very elegant.

'What could this be? It looks like a wedding invitation.' She got up to fetch a knife to open the envelope. Inside was a beautiful card with two gold rings on the front. 'Do we know anyone who's getting married?'

'Not that I know of,' said Patrik. 'Most of our friends have been married for ages.'

Erica opened the card. 'Uh-oh,' she said, and looked at Patrik.

'What?' He grabbed the card out of her hand. Then he read it aloud, his voice incredulous.

'We wish to invite you to be a guest at the wedding of Kristina Hedström and Gunnar Zetterlund.'

He glanced up at Erica and then looked back at the invitation.

'Is this a joke?' he said, turning the card over.

'I don't think so.' Erica started to giggle. 'It's so sweet!'

'But they're so . . . old,' said Patrik, trying not to think about his mother wearing a white gown and veil.

'Don't be silly,' said Erica, getting up to give him a kiss. 'It's going to be great. Our very own Mr Fix-it in the family. Wc won't have anythiug lefl lo repair in the house, and maybe he'll even build an extension so we'll have twice the amount of space.'

'What a dreadful thought,' Patrik said, but he couldn't help laughing. Erica was right. He wished nothing but joy for his mother, and it was wonderful that she'd found love in her old age. He just needed some time to get used to the idea.

'Sometimes you're so childish,' said Erica, ruffling his hair. 'It's lucky you're so nice.'

'You too,' he said and smiled.

He decided to try and put all thoughts of Victoria and the other girls behind him. There was nothing more he could do to help them. But here at home he had his wife and children, who needed him and gave him so much love. There was nothing about his life that he would change. Not a single thing.

They still had no idea where to go, but she wasn't worried. People like her and Jonas always found a way. For them there were no boundaries, no obstacles.

Her life had already started over twice. The last time in the abandoned house where she'd met Jonas. She was lying on the floor asleep when she opened her eyes and saw a boy looking at her. As soon as their eyes met, they knew they belonged together. She had seen the darkness in his soul, and he had seen the darkness in hers.

She had been drawn to Fjällbacka by an irresistible force. When she was travelling with the circus, all of Europe had been her home, but she had always known she would return. She had never felt anything so strongly, and when she finally came back, Jonas was there waiting for her.

He was her destiny, and in the murky light of the house, he had told her everything. About the room underneath the barn, and about what his father did to girls down there. Girls that no one ever missed. Girls who belonged nowhere and were of no worth.

They decided to follow in Einar's footsteps, but unlike him they chose girls who would be missed, girls who were loved. Creating a puppet, a helpless doll, from someone who was important to someone else had made their enjoyment even greater. That may have been their downfall, but they wouldn't have done it any other way.

She was not afraid of the unknown. It simply meant that they were forced to create new worlds somewhere else. As long as they had each other, it didn't matter. When she met Jonas, she had become Marta. His twin, his soul mate.

Jonas filled her heart. He was her whole life. And yet she still hadn't been able to resist Victoria. It was so strange. She had always understood the importance of self-control and had never allowed herself to be governed by her desires. But she wasn't stupid. She realized that she was attracted to Victoria because the girl reminded her of someone who had once been a part of her, someone who still was. Victoria had unconsciously summoned up old memories, and she hadn't been able to let her go. She wanted both Jonas and Victoria.

It had been a mistake to give in to the temptation to touch the skin of a young girl once again, a girl who reminded her of a love she had lost. After a while she realized the relationship was untenable, and besides, she'd begun to tire of the situation. There were actually more differences than similarities. So she surrendered Victoria to Jonas. He forgave her, and her love for him seemed even greater because of what they then shared.

It was unforgivable that they hadn't properly closed the trap door in the floor of the barn that night. They had grown careless, allowing Victoria to move about freely in the room. But they had never imagined she would be able to climb the ladder, get out of the barn, and then flee on foot through the woods. They had underestimated Victoria, and they'd taken a risk when they allowed her death to occur so close to home. It had cost them dearly, but neither of them saw this as the end. Instead, it was a new beginning. A new life. Her third.

Her first new life began on one of those summer days when the heat was so strong it almost felt like her blood was boiling inside her body. She and Louise had decided to go for a swim. And she was the one who suggested they go past the bathing beach and jump into the water from the rocks.

They counted to three and then jumped, holding hands. They thrilled at the speed of their fall and the wonderful cold of the water when they plunged in. But the next second it felt like a pair of strong arms seized hold of her and pulled her down into the deep. The water closed over her head, and she fought the undertow with all her might.

When her head breached the surface again, she began swimming towards land, but it was like trying to move through tar. She made only slight progress as she kept turning her head to look for Louise. Her lungs were straining too hard for her to manage a shout, and her brain was filled with only one thought: to survive, to make it to shore.

Suddenly the undertow let her go, and with every stroke she was moving forward. A few minutes later she reached the shore. Exhausted, she stretched out on her stomach, with her legs in the water and her cheek pressed against the sand. When she'd caught her breath, she sat up with great effort and looked about. She called to Louise, but there was no answer. She held her hand up to shade her eyes and studied the surface of the water. Then she sprang to her feet and clambered up on the rocks where they had jumped. She ran back and forth, searching, shouting, getting more and more desperate. Finally she sank down on to the rocks and sat there for a long time, waiting. She thought maybe she should run for help. But if she did, their plans would never be realized. Louise was gone, and it was better if she went on alone rather than give up altogether.

She left everything on the rocks. Their clothes and their other belongings. She had loaned Louise her favourite blue swimsuit. In a strange way she was glad that Louise was wearing that suit when she went down into the deep. As if it were a gift.

Then she walked away, leaving the sea behind. At a nearby house she stole some clothing that had been hung on a line to dry, and with great determination she then walked to the place where she knew she'd find her future. To be safe, she went through the woods, which meant she didn't reach Fjällbacka until night time. When she saw the circus in the distance – with its bright colours, cheerful sounds, and noisy spectators – the whole scene was strangely familiar. She had arrived home.

On that day she became Louise, the girl who had done what she herself had longed to do. The girl who had seen blood gush out of a person's body until the flame of life was extinguished. Filled with envy, she had listened to Louise's stories about the circus, and about Vladek's life as a lion tamer. It sounded so exotic compared with her own dreary background. She had wanted to be Louise, wanted to have her past.

She had developed a hatred for Peter and Laila. Louise had told her everything. About how her mother had taken the blame for the murder, how her grandmother had taken in the beloved son but refused to have anything to do with Louise. Even though Louise had never asked her to seek revenge, that was what she would do. Hatred had turned her blood cold, and she had done what she needed to do.

Then she had gone to Louise's home, her own home, and there she had met Jonas. She was Tess. She was Louise. She was Marta. She was Jonas's other half. And she wasn't yet done. Only the future would reveal who she would now become.

She smiled at him as they sat in the stolen car. They were free and brave. They were strong. They were lions who could not be tamed.

Several months had passed since Laila was allowed to see Peter for the first time in so many years. She still remembered the feeling when he came into the room. He was so handsome, so like his father, but with her slender build.

She was also grateful to see Agneta at last. They had always been close, but it had been necessary for them to part ways. And her sister had given her the greatest gift anyone could receive. She had taken her son under her wing and given him refuge and a family. He had been safe with them, at least during the years when Laila had kept everything secret.

Now she no longer needed to keep quiet. It was so liberating. It would take a while, but eventually her story would be told. The Girl's story too. Right now she didn't dare believe that Peter was safe, but the police were searching for the Girl, and presumably she was too smart to try to go anywhere near him.

Laila had wondered whether she would feel anything for her daughter, the child who in spite of everything was her own flesh and blood. But no, the Girl had been a stranger right from the beginning. She had not been part of Laila or Vladek. Not the way Peter was.

Maybe Laila would even be released from prison now,

if she could convince the authorities that her story was true. She didn't know whether she was hoping for that or not. She had spent such a large part of her life here, that it no longer made any difference. The most important thing was that she and Peter could resume contact again, and that he could come to visit her once in a while. Someday he might even bring along his wife and children. That was enough to make her life worth living.

A discreet knock on the door roused her from her happy thoughts.

'Come in,' she called, with a smile on her lips.

The door opened, and Tina came into the room. For a moment she didn't say a word.

'What is it?' Laila finally asked.

Tina was holding something in her hand, and when Laila saw what it was, her smile faded.

'There's a postcard for you,' said Tina.

Laila's hand shook uncontrollably as she took the card. There was no message, and the address was stamped in blue ink. She turned the card over. A matador stabbing a bull.

For several seconds Laila was silent. Then she opened her mouth and screamed.

ACKNOWLEDGEMENTS

First, let me say that I am solely responsible for any errors or deliberate alterations of the facts. For the sake of the story, I've taken certain liberties by changing the location and chronology of various actual events.

As usual, whenever I write a book there are so many people I want to thank, and I'm always afraid that I might forget someone. But I'd like to name a few who deserve special thanks. Everyone at my Swedish publisher Forum has done a great job with *The Ice Child*. I'd especially like to thank Karin Linge Nordh, who has worked with me ever since my second book. She is always a steadfast supporter even when emotions sometimes run high, since we're both such emotional people and are passionate about books and our work. Thank you, Karin, for being such a wonderful publisher and great friend. I also want to send a big thanks to Matilda Lund, who helped to make *The Ice Child* the book that it is. And thanks also to Sara Lindegren – you do such an awesome job marketing the books, but you also deserve a medal for bravery, or maybe you should have your head examined, because you've dared to entrust your child's religious education to me.

And I would never manage to write any books at all

if not for the help I receive in my daily life, from my mother Gunnel Läckberg, from 'Mamma Stiina' (Christina Melin), and from Sandra Wirström. Heartfelt thanks also to my three wonderful children Wille, Meja, and Charlie, who never hesitate to help out whenever their mother needs to write.

I also want to thank my amazing friends. I won't mention any names because there are so many of you, and I don't want to risk leaving anyone out. But you know who you are, and I am so grateful to all of you. And thank you to my agent Joakim Hansson and his colleagues at the Nordin Agency.

A big THANK YOU to Christina Saliba, who has not only been my supporter and a huge inspiration as a businesswoman, but who has become like a Lebanese sister to me. I especially want to thank you for making my fortieth birthday party so memorable. Thanks also to Maria Fabricius and the rest of the staff at MindMakers who have been working with me. You rock!

Last but definitely not least, I want to send special thanks to my beloved Simon. You came into my life when I was in the middle of writing this book, and you gave me faith, hope, and love. Thank you for supporting me in everything, and for your motto in life: 'Happy wife, happy life.' You make me happy.

Camilla Läckberg
Gamla Enskede
30 September 2014